CRESCENT CITY WOLF PACK

1

WEREWOLVES ONLY

CARRIE PULKINEN

Werewolves Only

Contact Information: www.CarriePulkinen.com

ISBN: 978-0-9998436-2-8

CHAPTER ONE

DETECTIVE MACEY CARPENTER DUCKED UNDER THE police tape blocking off an alley on St. Peter Street and smoothed her hair toward the tight bun she wore near the nape of her neck. Storm clouds gathered in the darkening sky, and the summer air hung thick and wet. It was a typical steamy August night in the French Quarter, but the heavy humidity did nothing to quell the chorus of offending odors dancing in the air. She wrinkled her nose.

Slipping her hands into a pair of blue latex gloves, she snapped them at the wrists. The slight sting helped to separate the gruesomeness she'd soon see from the ordinary life she'd return to later. Disconnecting the good from the bad in her mind kept the nightmares at bay.

She paced into the alley, and three men in blue nodded curtly as they passed. "Carpenter," the blond with a crew cut muttered.

She nodded back and inhaled a deep breath. Angling up her nose to catch the wind, she rifled through the array of scents it presented her. The overpowering aroma of the female victim's Chanel couldn't cover the metallic reek of blood. Lucky for the woman, most of the blood seemed to belong to the attacker.

Macey shook her head. Seven sexual assaults in three weeks' time. In each case, the victims described a different man. Different, yet similar enough that they had to be connected. But how? The assailant had disappeared every time but this one. What the hell was going on in this town?

She stepped into the courtyard and took in the landscape of the crime scene. Six nineteenth-century buildings backed onto a shared park. Willows lined the square, their sorrowful branches looming over the grief-stricken scene. A weathered stone fountain bubbled at the center of the wooded garden, and a thirty-foot magnolia tree towered in the corner, the perfume of its citrusy, white flowers mingling with the stale stench of death, creating a sickly-sweet fragrance that made her stomach turn.

"It's about time you got here, boss." Bryce Samuels winked and sauntered toward her.

Macey stopped and put her hands on her hips before shaking her head at her partner. "Traffic. What have we got?" After dropping her bag near a wall, she knelt to examine the alleged rapist's body. A series of jagged, foot-long gashes stretched from chest to pelvic bone, almost as if it had taken three slashes with the blade to lay the guy open. The pupils were dilated—the blood-red eyes frozen in a look of surprised terror.

"Victim's over there." Bryce gestured with his head to a stone bench near the common's entrance. A green-eyed redhead sat, wrapped in a stiff blanket, giving a statement to a uniform. "Same story as the others. Difference is, this time…there's evidence."

Macey followed his gaze to the body that lay before

her. "Unless it was a sloth, I don't see how a dog or a bear could've done this with only three nails. Look here." She traced her gloved hand along each rip in the flesh. "It doesn't make sense."

Bryce crossed his arms. "No, it doesn't. But this is the first time the attacker is actually still at the scene."

"I know." Macey pulled off her gloves and dropped them in a trash bag. "Let's talk to the victim."

"Shall we?" Bryce motioned with his hands, and Macey took the lead. The uniform had finished his questioning, and the woman sat alone, shivering in the sweltering August heat. Funny how shock could do that to a body.

Her dark green blanket slipped off one slumped shoulder, revealing a black T-shirt with a restaurant name embroidered on the breast. The woman inhaled a shaky breath as Macey approached, but she didn't lift her gaze from the cobblestone path.

Macey sat on the edge of the bench, the cool stone taming the Louisiana summer. Bryce leaned against the wall behind her.

"Hey there. I'm Detective Macey Carpenter, but you can call me Macey."

The redhead sniffled and wiped her eyes.

Macey folded her hands in her lap. "What's your name?"

"It's Amy. Couldn't you read that in your report?" Her sarcasm didn't mask the fear in her voice. She wiped her eyes again and stared straight ahead.

Macey's chest tightened. She'd dealt with her own personal grief, so she could imagine what this poor woman was going through. Although, Macey had spent more than her fair share of time in denial, and Amy seemed to have skipped that stage and plowed straight into anger. "I could have looked at the report, but I'd rather hear it from you. You know…since you were here and all. I want to help."

"Doesn't everyone?" Amy wrapped the blanket tighter around her shoulders, her bobbed hair swishing forward to cover her face as she stared at the ground. "Everyone says they want to help, but when you tell the truth, do they believe you?" She blinked at Macey. "Hell no, they don't. And why am I not in the hospital? I was raped, for Pete's sake. Just because some…*thing* saved me and killed the asshole, I have to be questioned first? What? You think I killed him? I didn't, but believe me, if I could've…I would've in a heartbeat. Men like that don't deserve to live."

Macey took a deep breath. She understood anger. Resentment. Desperation. Those feelings were nothing new to her, though she'd buried them long ago. And though they rarely reared their ugly heads anymore, she still hadn't mastered acceptance. "What *thing* saved you, Amy? Was it an animal?"

Amy scoffed. "Animal. Man. Alien. It doesn't matter. No one believes me anyway."

Macey placed her hand on Amy's. "I believe you. Trust me. I've been on the trail of this *thing* for weeks. You aren't the first victim to tell me this story, but you are the first to have evidence. Please…I need you to tell me everything."

Amy took a deep breath and looked her square in the eyes. Holding her gaze, Macey gave her all the trust and reassurance she could without words. Amy exhaled and slumped her shoulders. "Okay. I'll tell you."

As Luke Mason stepped through the door of O'Malley's Pub, a curtain of cool, crisp air blasted his sweat drenched skin. At ninety-eight degrees and one hundred percent humidity, the Vieux Carré felt more like a Dutch oven than a French Quarter. He closed his eyes and let the coolness soothe his aching limbs as he entered the building. The low ceiling and bare brick walls were typical of the nineteenth-century structures in the Quarter. Shaded lights hung from exposed beams, casting a smoky glow over the bar.

He sat on a stool and took a long, refreshing gulp of the Blue Moon beer that sat ready on the counter, waiting for him.

"Rough day at the office?" Chase, the bartender, cocked his head toward the scar across Luke's bicep. Luke looked at his arm and shrugged. The thin, raised scab had been a gash two hours ago.

"Piece of scaffolding jumped out and got me. No biggie." He downed the rest of his beer and asked for another.

"Well, if that's all." Chase set down the mug he was polishing and poured another Blue Moon. At six foot one, he stood several inches shorter than Luke, but his height didn't make him any less of a fighter. If Luke trusted anyone to have his back no matter what, it would be him. An intricate series of tattoos sleeved Chase's arms, and he sported piercings in his ears and eyebrow.

Luke's only tattoo occupied his right shoulder. A fleur-de-lis designed from a wolf head signified his allegiance to the pack. The star in the center symbolized his bloodline —a direct descendent of the first family. And he wasn't just a descendent; he was next in line for pack leader. He finished his beer and slid the empty glass to his friend.

"What are you gonna do about James?" Chase placed the glass in the sink.

Luke wiped his hand down his face. "Is he back there?"

Chase nodded. With his hands on the bar, Luke heaved himself from the stool and shuffled toward the back room. He chuckled at the sign on the door—*Employees and Werewolves Only*—written in marker on a piece of cardboard. It came about as a joke from the customers—that his father, with his long, salt-and-pepper beard and almost-furry arms, looked like a wolf-man. They didn't know how right they were.

The Crescent City Wolf Pack—at two hundred members strong and growing—was the sixth largest in the nation. Werewolves tended to congregate in towns with immense wooded areas. While New Orleans itself consisted of more city than forest, the vast swamp lands surrounding the area made for prime hunting grounds. And for tough wolves.

Hunting gators wasn't any easier than it looked on television. While a bite rarely killed a werewolf, it sure hurt like hell. But the thrill of the hunt was worth double the pain. What other choice did they have? Nutria? The beaver-sized swamp rats satisfied the hunger, but they did nothing for the rush. Deer were abundant—and fun to chase—but nothing beat the thrill of hunting gators. They made worthy opponents.

The door shut behind him with a *thud*. Bright fluorescent lights hummed from above, giving the stone corridor a greenish glow. He turned the corner and descended a short flight of brick steps to the office.

The blinds drawn over the window blocked his view of the scene inside. He tried the knob but found it locked. It must've been more serious than he'd thought. He fished in his pocket and pulled out a key to unlock the door. When Luke stepped inside, James sat slouched in a chair, shaking his head. Stephen, third in command and Luke's cousin, leaned against the oak desk, his arms crossed over his chest.

"What are you going to do about this?" Stephen spat, shifting his weight to his feet and gesturing to James. "The cops are going to be looking for him."

Luke raised an eyebrow and regarded his cousin. Everyone knew Stephen wanted to be pack leader—and he already had a mate—but his moral compass didn't quite point in the right direction.

"No one will know who—or what—to look for." Luke turned to James. "The woman never saw you in human form?"

"No." James shook his head and dragged his hands down his face. "I don't know what happened. He should've disintegrated like the others. There wasn't supposed to be blood. Demons don't bleed."

Stephen cut him off. "This obviously wasn't a demon."

James sighed as Luke took the chair next to him. "It was a demon, Luke. I smelled it. Its eyes were red, and…"

Luke put a palm on his shoulder, and James covered it with his own four-fingered hand. He'd lost his pinkie on a construction site when he worked for Luke. "It's okay, man. We'll figure it out."

"Figure it out?" Stephen paced the floor, his hands balled into fists. "What's there to figure out? He killed a human, and he needs to be dealt with. You should put him in the pit."

Luke narrowed his eyes. His cousin would happily throw people into the pack's specially designed prison for minor infractions without learning all the facts. "I'll take that into consideration. You can go now."

Stephen's jaw tightened with an audible *click*. "You'd better take care of this."

"I said you can go."

Stephen glared at James and stormed out the door, slamming it behind him.

Luke shook his head. "Ignore him. He's peeved because he has no power in enforcing."

"He will if he has his way."

"He won't." The good of the pack always came first. He'd learned that by watching his father lead.

James's face went serious. "I hope not. I'll go rogue before I'll serve a tyrant like that. I know he's your cousin and all…but, shit. He scares me. A lot of us."

"Nothing to worry about. He won't become alpha."

James furrowed his brow. "You've only got about a month before your old man retires. You can find a mate by then?"

"If I'm going to become alpha, I don't have a choice." He rose to his feet and stepped around his desk, settling into a large leather office chair that squeaked as it absorbed his weight. He'd have to get the WD-40 after it soon. Picking up a pen and a pad of paper, he squared his gaze on James. No more friendliness. It was time to play his role as enforcer.

"The monster attacking that woman smelled like a demon. He gave you every reason to believe he came straight from hell, but he wasn't a demon. At least, not full demon."

James twisted in his seat. Sweat beaded on his forehead. Luke's main job was to deal with rogues and other rule-breakers. Not a job he enjoyed, but he didn't have a choice. His father was pack leader, which made Luke second in command. He couldn't stand seeing his friend cower like this, but he had to keep his aura of power strong to keep the pack under control.

"Tell me what happened, James. From the beginning."

CHAPTER TWO

MACEY GAVE THE VICTIM A SAD SMILE AS THE EMT closed the ambulance door. *Poor woman. The nightmares she's going to have.* She shook her head and returned to the scene.

As she walked up the alley, a sultry breeze wafted the scent of burnt flesh to her nostrils. Surely Bryce hadn't dropped a cigarette on the body again. Though it had only happened once, five years prior, no one on the force would let him live it down.

"Bryce!" She quickened her step and found him talking with the coroner. "Why do I smell burning flesh?" She wiped a bead of sweat off her brow as she marched toward her partner.

"I know what you're getting at, but I haven't smoked in years, so don't you even start on me with that crap, blondie." He signed the coroner's tablet and turned to face her. "Anyway, I don't smell anything but death."

Macey bit her bottom lip and glanced around the alley. Two men with a stretcher loaded the body into a van as the rest of the uniforms packed up their stuff to head out. Nothing appeared to be burning, but she couldn't deny the distinct, sharp scent of cinder in the air.

She trailed her hand along a building as she paced toward the courtyard, allowing the stories of long ago to seep into her senses. That old carriage house had seen so much. If only it could talk to the rest of the world the way it spoke to her. If only it could tell her who the killer was...

"You coming? Donuts are on me tonight." Bryce jingled his car keys in his hand, pulling Macey out of her mini trance.

She looked at her partner. He wore his light brown hair cut short on the sides, shaggy on top, and his goofy smile made his eyes sparkle when he laughed. If she didn't think of him so fondly as an older brother, she might have been attracted to him. Good thing she wasn't. Being partners was close enough for her comfort. Macey preferred to keep everyone at arm's length, and Bryce had already worked his way up to her elbow.

"Nah. I think I'm going to hang around here a while. See if anything comes to me. You know?"

He knew more about Macey's "ability" than anyone else. She hated calling it an ability, but wasn't that what it was?

He wrapped his arm around her. "You do that, boss. But don't spend too much time alone out here."

"No worries."

Macey stepped out of the alley and into the courtyard. Undoing the second button on her once-crisp, cornflower shirt, she rolled her sleeves up to her elbows. A bead of sweat dripped between her breasts. *Damn this heat.*

She sat on the edge of the fountain and closed her eyes, letting the melody of cascading water clear her mind and open her soul. There had to be something there. Some clue she'd missed. The dead man's energy tumbled through the air, teasing her, twisting, swirling, dancing around the edges of her senses. So close, yet unattainable because she couldn't touch it.

Seven women. Four rapes, three attempted rapes. No words had been exchanged. A man with red eyes had grabbed them and assaulted them in an alley. For the first two, the story ended there. The perpetrators got away. But for the remaining five victims, the story took an unimaginable twist. A beast, they'd called it, or some kind of animal that moved so quickly they couldn't identify it, swooped in and allegedly killed the attackers.

So, why was this the first body they'd found? In the four previous cases, the investigators had discovered nothing more than a pile of ash left behind. If an animal killed the rapists, where had it taken the bodies?

And where had the ashes come from? The lab hadn't determined what they used to be, though they definitely weren't human remains.

But the dead guy this time looked like…a dead guy. Why was there a body and no ash? There had to be something else to all these incidents. The women must have been leaving some important detail out of their stories.

But what was it?

An icy breeze tickled the back of her neck, raising goose bumps on her skin. She shivered and reached behind her to peel the sweat-soaked shirt away from her back. *Probably a ghost. Maybe the attacker's ghost.* She'd heard of people who could talk to spirits. People who could manipulate energy and communicate with entities in other dimensions. She truly believed they could, though most called it bogus. People tended to only believe in things they could see.

Macey believed in spirits. When a person died, their energy had to go somewhere. Objects—buildings, furniture, trees, anything really—absorbed a lot of it. That kind of energy, she could see. Though, saying she "saw" it was a stretch. Images could appear in her mind, but not before her eyes.

She blew out a hard breath and rose from the fountain. Her ability had gotten her nowhere in this case. It took time for objects to absorb energy, and this string of crimes was happening far too rapidly.

Seven incidents within a three-week span. New Orleans was never considered the safest city in the world, but this…this was outrageous. She shook her head. She needed a vacation. A nice, long break somewhere cool. Maybe Alaska. Let Bryce handle this one. He excelled at old-fashioned police work, which this case obviously required.

Macey's ability seemed useless.

She trudged toward the alley, berating herself for even considering a vacation. She wouldn't abandon this case any more than she'd abandon—well, anything. If she'd learned one thing from her childhood, it was to stick by something or someone until the end. No matter what. She'd had first-hand experience with having her world ripped apart when the people she'd needed most left her alone, and she would never let it happen again.

A light breeze blew up the alley, making the sticky August heat minutely more bearable. Macey took a deep breath, welcoming the relief. The scent of cinder tickled her senses again. Thunder clapped in the distance, and an ominous black sky threatened to downpour at any second.

Her shoes squeaked on the cobblestone as she high-tailed it back to where the body had lain. The cleanup crew hadn't arrived to wash the pavement, so she had a chance. She closed her eyes and inhaled. The scent grew stronger.

She knelt, studying the cobblestone. This didn't look like blood. Rain began to fall in thick droplets around her, splashing into the semi-dried coagulation.

Crap. Not yet! Where were her gloves? She glanced across the alley to find her bag resting twenty feet away, where she'd left it.

Thunder cracked as the droplets fell quicker. Macey reached out and swept her fingers through the muck that was once blood. Closing her hand, she darted under an awning to examine the substance. She rubbed her thumb across the tips of her fingers and brought them to her nose.

A quick sniff determined what she'd stuck her hand in wasn't blood.

It was ash.

Sticking to the shadows, out of the detective's line of sight, Luke ran a hand through his hair as rain pelted him in the corner of the courtyard. The towering magnolia tree provided a shield from the downpour, but thick drops bounced off the waxy leaves and splattered around him. "You're sure no one saw you?"

"Just the woman," James said.

Luke looked at his friend. James was the quickest shifter and most skilled attacker in the pack. That's why he was the lead wolf on the demon hunting team. He'd never considered James careless enough to mistake a human for a demon. Something didn't add up.

"I trust you. The guy was most likely half demon, and it's hard to tell on those. We'll have to figure out where he came from—and who made him—if we're going to stop this fiasco before the cops find out too much. If it's the same person who's summoning these new demons, we can stop it all with one punch."

James shoved his hands in his pockets. "Let's hope it is."

"You too rattled to patrol tonight?"

He chuckled. "Nah. I'm good."

Luke rested his forearm on the tree above his head and shielded his eyes from the rain as James trotted away. This was the same female that showed up at every one of these incidents. He'd been watching her for the past three weeks. Detective Macey Carpenter. Everyone in the Quarter knew who she was, whether personally or not. She'd busted more criminals since she'd joined the force than anyone he'd ever heard of.

Macey had a tough, no bullshit reputation, and he'd seen her around enough to know it was true. When she walked into a room, she did it like she owned it—with strength and confidence. Maybe a little too much confidence. She was only human, after all. She didn't realize how fragile she was, and he was done with women like that. That's what he told himself as the familiar fluttering in his stomach—that happened every time he saw her—had him leaning away from the tree, the desire to erase the distance between them pulling him from the shadows.

He shook himself to break the trance. The truth was, he found himself oddly attracted to the petite fireball. She may have been tough, but her feminine side always showed through, no matter how much she tried to hide it. She always wore her golden hair slicked back into that damn bun, but he could imagine what it looked like falling down around her bare shoulders—

Nope. He had to stop right there. When he did mate, it had to be with another werewolf. There was no way around the antiquated law. He'd be alpha in a month, and he *had* to have a mate for that to happen. He didn't need to waste his time with a human. Especially one who had gotten dangerously close to discovering a secret she shouldn't know. So why was he hiding in the courtyard, watching her like a stalker?

He told himself it was his job. The pack did its best to keep peace in the supernatural community and to keep their existence a secret from the humans. Psychics and witches may have found a way to coexist…exposing *some* of their powers to the mundane…but there was no way in hell people would be as accepting of a predatory species like his. He had to stop Macey from learning anything about the demons…and especially the werewolves. Keeping tabs on the sexy detective proved a nice bonus, and it helped to quell the odd feeling of possessiveness brewing in his chest. His wolf had decided she was his to protect.

Macey bent down to tie her shoe, and her shirt gaped at the second button, revealing the lacey edge of a light pink bra. He took a deep breath to slow the sprint of his heart. *Not wasting my time with humans.*

Still, he did admire the way her black pants hugged her curves as she strutted through the rain and into the alley before disappearing around the corner.

With Macey out of sight, Luke stepped out of the shadows and made his way toward the alley. As he passed by the fountain, he paused to take a deep breath. The scent of rain mixed with the magnolias' sweet perfume smelled like summer in New Orleans. Like home. He smiled, relishing the downpour, even if it did add steam to the sauna of the Quarter.

The detective had found ash; that had been obvious from the curious look on her face as she'd swiped her fingers through the substance on the ground. A cop wouldn't have put her hand in a puddle of blood. Luckily, though, she wasn't able to save any as evidence.

And lucky for James, this confirmed Luke's belief that he hadn't killed a human. A heaviness lifted from his chest, and he tilted his head back, letting the rain fall onto his face. He wouldn't have to punish his friend.

He strode to the spot where the half-human body had lain, but the demon ash had already washed away. He surveyed the area for any other signs of the supernatural but found none. The rain had taken care of everything for him; a steady stream flowed between the worn stones, twisting and jutting right, then left, before cascading down a storm drain.

Now, he had to get to the morgue and decapitate the body before the damn demon came back to life.

The chances of reanimation were slim—or so legend stated—but it was best not to take chances. Besides, he had no idea what one looked like on the inside. Maybe it didn't have all the same human organs.

He had to get that body out of the morgue before the autopsy. And since the alpha was vacationing in Europe, Luke was the man to do it. His father had offered to come home when the outbreak started three weeks prior, but Luke assured him he could handle it. His parents had scheduled their two-month-long trip for right before his old man's retirement so Luke could work out the kinks in his new leadership role before it became official.

Of course, his dad had planned the retirement three and half years ago—when Luke had a fiancée and actually met all the qualifications to become alpha—and by law, it couldn't be changed. But if he could wipe out the demon infestation on his own, that would surely make his old man proud. This would prove to the pack that—mate or no mate—he was ready to be alpha.

He exited the alley onto St. Peter Street and turned right. His truck sat parked at the bar, and he needed to get to the morgue on Earhart. He fished in his pocket for some change and handed it to a bum huddled under an awning.

The man responded with a gnarled smile. "Bless you, sir."

Luke nodded and stepped past him. As he rounded the corner, he glanced up to see a pair of gleaming crimson eyes watching him. He inhaled sharply, and a low growl escaped his throat. Though the figure looked like a man, the creature ahead was all demon.

CHAPTER THREE

MACEY TAPPED HER PEN ON THE DESK AND STARED right past the case file she should have completed half an hour ago. What piece of this puzzle was she missing? She glanced at her right hand and ran her thumb across the pads of her first three fingers where the ash had been. She'd stopped by her house on the way to the station to wash up and change into dry clothes. And though the black residue had completely washed off on her trek through the rain, she could still sense the gritty substance on her skin.

A rap on her door brought her back to the present.

"Need some help with that paperwork, boss? We need to get it filed." Bryce leaned a shoulder against the door frame and took a bite of a Snickers bar.

Macey shook her head. "Do you ever eat real food?"

Bryce examined the candy, turning it over in his hands. "Looks real to me. I can feel it. I can see it." He held it up to his nose. "I can smell it." He took a bite and mumbled with the chocolate in his mouth. "And I can definitely taste it. Wanna bite?" He offered her the half-eaten bar.

She wrinkled her nose. "No thanks. All you eat is junk food."

Bryce swallowed the candy and snorted. "You're one to talk. I've seen how many beignets you can put away in one sitting."

She signed the last page of the file and stacked the papers without making eye contact with her partner. "That's different."

"How so?"

She looked into his eyes. "I eat healthy food too. You should think about taking some cooking lessons or something."

"Nah." He plopped into the chair across from her desk. "I need to find me a wife. Have a little lady in the kitchen making gumbo every night. That'd be nice. 'Course, she'd have to quit her job so she'd have time to iron my clothes and take care of all the babies we'd be making."

Macey bit her bottom lip. *Ten...nine...eight...* She knew he was messing with her. *Seven...six...five...* He was trying to get her riled up. Trying to get her to react. *Four, three-two-one.* Damn it, she was taking the bait.

She slapped her palms on her desk and lifted out of her seat. "You just keep on with that little fantasy, mister. And if you find a woman like that, you'd better keep her away from me, or I'll knock some sense into her myself." She dropped into her chair and crossed her arms over her chest. "Quit her job to take care of a man. Men can take care of themselves."

"What?" Bryce raised his hands. "C'mon, Mace. You know I'd take care of her too. I'd make her real happy...if you know what I mean." He raised his eyebrows in emphasis.

His goofy grin melted the tension in Macey's chest. Why did she let him get to her like that? "Oh, please. You know you couldn't make a girl any happier than BOB could."

"Bob? You mean I've got to compete with another man for my imaginary wife?"

She laughed. "No, dummy. B-O-B. Battery Operated Boyfriend?"

"Bob." He pressed his lips together and gazed at the ceiling. "Battery Oper—oh! I get it. Clever. And I'm offended."

"No, you're not. All done." She pushed the file across the desk. "Any word on the autopsy report?"

And just like that, they were back to business. That was the good thing about working with a bunch of men. She could switch gears in the middle of a conversation, and they didn't mind at all. And they didn't gossip...as much. So she constantly had to prove her worth as a female detective. She'd done fine so far.

Bryce picked up the file and flipped through the pages. "You know they won't get to it 'til the morning."

She groaned. "I know, but it's killing me." She lowered her voice and leaned forward. "After y'all left, I went back to the scene...where the body was. The blood was gone."

"That's good. Don't want to leave the city dirty. The cleanup crew is working fast these days."

"No, Bryce, listen. It hadn't been cleaned up yet. I didn't find any blood, but I did find ash. Ash...like at the other scenes."

He gave her a puzzled look. "Ash, huh? Did you turn it in to evidence?"

She let out a long sigh. "No. The bottom dropped out as soon as I found it. Washed it all away."

"Damn."

She slumped in her seat. "Tell me about it."

"Where do you think it came from? I'm sure there's a logical explanation somewhere out there."

Was there? She was beginning to wonder.

"Maybe all the attackers were carrying something," he said.

She raised an eyebrow. "Like what?"

"I dunno. Something burnt." He flashed a grin and winked.

Macey rolled her eyes. "You think? But that still doesn't explain why the blood was gone. It's strange." She rubbed her temple with two fingers, trying to ward off the impending headache that threatened to make her night even worse. "I'm wondering if it could be something… paranormal."

Bryce heaved himself up from his seat. "What? Like ghosts? Did you see something out there tonight?"

She shook her head. "No. Nothing's soaked in yet. I can't see anything, and you know I don't talk to ghosts. I…" She traced her finger along the faux wood pattern of her desk. He was going to think she'd gone insane. "I don't think the rapists are human." She bit her bottom lip and implored him with her gaze. It was the only explanation.

He stared at her and blinked. "Not huma—c'mon Mace. You know I believe in your ability or intuition…or whatever you call it, but that's as far as I'm willing to go. If they weren't human, they'd have to have been animals. And all the victims identified them as men."

"With red eyes."

"Contacts. Drugs. Or glare from the streetlights. *Something.*"

"You saw the body; they weren't contacts." Macey exhaled sharply and narrowed her eyes. She yanked open the desk drawer, grabbed her purse, and flung it over her shoulder. "*Something's* not right about this, and I'm going to find out what." She rose to her feet and strutted toward the door.

Bryce touched her elbow. "Where are you going?"

"To the morgue. I need to see the body."

───────────

When Luke made eye contact, the fiend grinned and tilted its head before it shimmied up a drain pipe and crouched on a rooftop overlooking an alley. With the black sky as a backdrop, it appeared as nothing more than a fuzzy mass —nothing a human eye would detect. Luke held its gaze, watching its crimson eyes as it crawled across the roof and disappeared into the alley below.

Shit. The morgue's gonna have to wait.

His beast wanted to take over. If he shifted, and stalked the demon in his wolf form, he'd have a better chance of making the kill. But the rain had let up, and locals and tourists alike were out, braving the steamy streets to make it to their destinations. There were too many people around. He'd have to chase his prey into the woods, where he could shift without being seen. He trotted up the sidewalk, and with his back to the wall, he peered into the passageway. The demon stood frozen, its back to the exit, as a growling wolf stared it down.

Goddammit!

Thick chocolate fur stood on end over the wolf's solid

body. It shifted its weight back onto muscular haunches, preparing to pounce. With his lips peeled back over ferocious fangs, Chase, in wolf form, snarled at his prey. Luke stepped into the alley, blocking the exit. Chase would hear about this. How would they explain the appearance of a giant wolf in the French Quarter?

The demon lunged left, its talons hooking onto a second-story windowsill. Before it could drag itself up, Chase snapped onto its leg and yanked it off the wall. The fiend skidded across the cobblestone and landed at Luke's feet. Without his own claws or something sharp to behead it, Luke's chances of killing the demon were nil, so he grabbed it by the neck and hauled it off the ground. "My friend wants to play with you." He shoved the fiend toward Chase, but it ducked and rolled, avoiding the werewolf's advance.

"Playtime's over." Luke picked up a metal trash can lid and hurled it at the demon, striking it in the back of the head. Chase sprang forward, teeth bared and claws extended. He swiped a massive paw across the demon's chest as his jaws snapped down on the fiend's face. Before Chase's paws hit the pavement, the demon fell into a pile of ash. He'd hit the sweet spot in one swipe.

All a werewolf had to do was puncture the demon's heart with a claw, and it was vanquished. Unfortunately, demons didn't really die. They went to their own hellish dimension, where they waited for some other idiotic human to conjure them back.

The sound of laughter and footsteps echoed down the alley. Luke snapped his head to the left to find a group of people sipping hurricanes twenty feet away. In their drunkenness, he could probably explain away their visions of a wolf in the French Quarter, but why take the chance? He turned to his friend. "Go."

Chase jumped behind a wall and ran toward a park. Luke casually walked down the passageway, stopping to kick his boot through the ash to spread out the evidence, and followed the wolf's path. Chase's shift at the bar didn't end for another three hours. He better not have been skirting his duties to play with the demons.

Once they were safely out of sight, human Chase stepped out from behind a sycamore and smoothed his T-shirt down his stomach. "Third one tonight. Thanks for your help."

Luke marched toward his friend, ready to give him a reaming, but Chase's statement caught him off guard. "Third one?"

"Yeah. James found one off Rampart shortly after he left you at the other scene. Tracked him two miles out of the city before he got him."

He shook his head. "Damn. All right. But you need to be more careful where you shift, man. You were *in* the Quarter."

Chase shrugged. "I know. But I saw you, and when it jumped off the roof, I knew we had it."

He had a point. Hell, Luke probably would've done the same thing. They'd vanquished the fiend, and that was the important thing. His cousin would say he was being too lenient. Shifting in the city went against the rules—unless it was absolutely necessary to save a human. But they'd ridded New Orleans of one more demon, hadn't they? Who gave a shit what his cousin would've said?

"Who's covering the bar tonight?" He motioned with his head for Chase to follow.

"Amber. She had a vision it'd be a busy night, so she let me go early."

The hair on the back of his neck stood on end at the mention of his sister. Her gift of premonition proved useful in the battle against the demons, but it wasn't always accurate. "Any details?"

"Nah. Just said she had a feeling."

"We need to get back." Luke picked up the pace, stomping through the mud toward the city. Chase followed on his heels.

"Noah and Cade are there. She's safe."

She better be. Chase would have to be out of his mind to leave Luke's little sister alone at the bar. She couldn't protect herself if anything... He stopped the thought right there. Only the eldest offspring of werewolf couples could shift, and Amber was as defenseless as a human. So was Melissa, his former fiancée. She'd been a second-born were, and he'd let her get killed three years ago.

He couldn't bear it if he lost another vulnerable female he loved. "I'm not worried about her," he lied. "I need to get my truck."

"Where you headed?" Chase asked.

"We're going to the morgue."

CHAPTER FOUR

JIMMY HANCOCK SAT ALONE ON THE PORCH OF THE two-room cabin in the swamp, watching the neon-blue glow of the bug zapper. Mosquitoes the size of horseflies encircled the glimmering death trap. One by one, the brave insects would venture into the light they were so enamored of. And one by one, they'd die in a sharp pulse and a *zap*. Occasionally, the light of death would draw in a gray moth. It took more than a quick singe to kill those. The rapid flicker and *buzz, buzz, buzz...zap,* made Jimmy's skin crawl.

What did it feel like for the moth? It must've been worse than for the mosquito.

He wrung his hands and stared at the puddle of sweat on the floor beneath them. It was nothing compared to the amount his once-white T-shirt had absorbed from his pits and back. The thick mass of trees around the cabin blocked any chance of a breeze, but even that wouldn't have helped. Jimmy's nerves were making him sweat.

His younger brother should have been home hours ago, and Jimmy didn't know what to do. He could go looking for him, but what if someone found the cabin? All the work they'd done would be exposed. Or worse… destroyed. What would Ross do to him then?

Another moth met its fate with a crackling *zap*. Jimmy cringed. He'd prefer the bug zapper any day to what his brother could do to him. What Ross *would* do to him.

He looked at the scar on his left palm. A thick black scab covered the thin line he'd opened the night before. He was supposed to open it again tonight, but not without Ross.

Jimmy couldn't control the demons. His brother did that part, so what was he supposed to do? He couldn't very well conjure one on his own. But if he didn't, he'd be in deep shit. His heart raced at the thought of the shit he'd be in. He must've screwed up already. Why else wouldn't Ross be home? Jimmy had done something wrong. It was his fault; it always was. He was only human.

Ross was the blessed one. Being half demon made him special. Jimmy wasn't special. He was a stupid idiot. He was lucky to have Ross as a brother. Damn lucky. And that's all Jimmy was. He wasn't smart. Wasn't handsome. He didn't have any friends because nobody liked a stupid idiot. Jimmy was lucky. That was all. And he was okay with that.

He opened the screen door and stepped inside the main room of the cabin. An old, rusty stove, sink, and ice box lined one wall, creating the small kitchen. A dilapidated futon leaned against another. That was where Jimmy slept. He was lucky to have such a soft place to sleep. He'd been real good that week when Ross brought it home for him. How long had it been? Fifteen years? Jimmy hadn't been good since.

He ran his hand along the wooden altar in the middle

of the room, and his scar tingled. He didn't know why it did that. He picked up the ceremonial knife in his right hand. It was really a kitchen knife Ross had scratched some symbols into. Jimmy knew that, but Ross said the symbols made it special, so it wasn't just a kitchen knife anymore.

He held it up to the light. "*Hmpf.* Still looks like a kitchen knife."

"*Put it down, you stupid idiot.*"

"Huh? What?" The knife clanked on the linoleum floor. "Ross? That you?" With a trembling hand, he picked up the blade and put it back on the altar. He searched the room, but he couldn't see his brother.

"Where are you? On the porch?" He threw open the screen door, and it slammed against the wall with a loud *crack*. Jimmy jumped. No Ross.

"Ross?" Oh, no. His brother had seen him with the knife. He probably thought Jimmy was about to do something stupid again. "I...I wasn't gonna do it yet. I was waiting for you. I...I...I didn't know when you were coming back."

He tried to swallow, but it felt like his heart was lodged in his throat. It couldn't have been in his throat, though. It was beating in his chest like a race horse's hooves pounding the ground. He tentatively took a step back, bracing himself for the blow his brother was sure to give him. Would it be the head or the gut this time?

When nothing happened, he took another step back... Then another. With a maniacal squeal, he leapt to the futon and curled into a ball. He squeezed his eyes shut and mumbled into the dust-filled cushion. "I'm sorry, Ross. I'm so sorry. I screwed up again. I'm sorry."

"*Shut up, moron.*"

Cold shivers ran down his spine. Where was his brother?

"Get up and get a hold of yourself. You have to do something for me."

Jimmy turned his head slightly and opened one eye a slit. No one was there. He opened the other eye and raised his head. "Where? I can't see you."

"Of course you can't, dimwit. I'm dead."

CHAPTER FIVE

"WHAT DO YOU MEAN YOU CAN'T FIND IT?" MACEY balled her hands into fists as the lab tech blinked at her. She wanted to slap the annoyed expression off the kid's face. Of course, she wouldn't *actually* slap him, but the thought entered her mind, and she considered it. He couldn't have been more than twenty—with his acne-covered face and scrawny arms—and was obviously new to the job. "You *lost* the body?"

The tech sighed and rolled his eyes. "*I* didn't lose it." He tapped on the clipboard. "Says right here it should be in locker fifty-seven."

"But it isn't."

"Nope." The tech pulled up his social media account on the computer.

Macey snapped her fingers. "Hello?"

He slowly turned his head toward her, keeping his gaze on the monitor until the last second. "Yeah?" He flicked his eyes toward her before focusing on the computer again.

"If the body isn't in locker fifty-seven, then where is it?"

The guy shrugged. "How should I know? My shift just started twenty minutes ago." He clicked the play button on a video post, and a kitten wearing a top hat danced across the screen.

Macey's nails cut into her palms as she tried to maintain her composure. He was a kid. She shouldn't take his lack of respect personally. "I need you to…"

Click. Click. Click. He ignored her. With every muscle in her body tensed, she reached across the counter and switched off the monitor. She put her hands on her hips and glared at him.

The tech crossed his arms over his chest and glared back. "Look, lady. I dunno what you want *me* to do. It's not my problem."

Lady? She took a deep breath and let it out ever so slowly. *Ten. Nine. Eight. Seven.* She had to keep her cool. *Six. Five. Four…Keep your voice low, Mace…Three. Two… One.* She put on her biggest fake smile and took one more breath before she spoke.

"I realize you're new here, but let's get a few things straight. First, my name's not Lady. I introduced myself as Carpenter. *Detective* Carpenter. You saw my credentials, so I expect to be addressed accordingly. Second, you are the tech on duty, so, yes, it is your problem." Her blood boiled at the blasé expression on the kid's face. Who did he think he was? "Third, when an officer requests to see a body, you have to produce it. If it isn't where the log states, you need to *find* it."

The sound of the door opening behind her stopped Macey's rant. Bryce sauntered to her side. "I figured you'd have been in and out of here already. How goes it?"

Macey let out a cynical chuckle. "I would have been if this young man would do his job and find the body."

"Find it?" Bryce cut his gaze toward the tech. "Where is it?"

He shrugged. "I dunno. Not where it's supposed to be."

Bryce furrowed his brow. "Then go look for it."

The tech let out a long sigh and nodded. "Yes, sir." He rose from his seat and shuffled out the back door.

"Sir? You've been here for thirty seconds, he calls you sir and does what you ask. I've been here for fifteen minutes arguing with the little bastard, and what do I get? 'Look, *lady.* I dunno what you want me to do.' Jeez!"

Bryce shook his head. "You're a girl. And a little thing at that."

"It doesn't matter."

"It *shouldn't* matter. But it does. No one said it would be easy, Mace. You know that."

She closed her eyes and rolled her head from side to side, stretching her sore neck. The pain in her temple that had been threatening her earlier had turned into a full blown headache. "I've worked hard to earn the respect of the boys at the station. Even the Chief respects me. Why's it so hard for people like this kid to?"

"Why do you let it bother you?"

That was a good question, with a long list of answers. After being abandoned by her family at such an early age, she rarely felt like she belonged anywhere. Her life was a never-ending balancing act, trying to prove her worth while keeping everyone at a safe distance to avoid getting hurt. But standing under the fluorescent lights of the stark white morgue, waiting for a disrespectful kid to find a missing body, wasn't the time or place for a pity party. She'd thrown enough of those in her lifetime.

"No reason, I guess."

Luke and Chase sat in the cab of the pick-up and stared at the back door of the morgue. A single security camera hung loose from its mount, the frayed wiring sticking out of the device rendering it inoperable. They'd have no problem picking the lock and getting in, but finding the body without being caught might prove difficult.

"What's the plan, man? Just run in and grab it?" Chase circled his shoulders as if loosening up for a fight.

"Right. And not get caught. You ready?" Luke didn't wait for an answer. He stepped out of the truck and closed the door, searching the area for witnesses. They were alone. With long strides, he made his way to the door, Chase close behind. He pulled his lock-picking tools out of his back pocket, and within seconds, the door opened. As he peered inside, a scrawny kid with messy orange hair slammed a drawer shut and sulked out of the room.

"Now," he whispered, and they slinked inside. Bright fluorescent lights illuminated the cold, dreary room. Rows of metal doors lined three of the walls, their two-inch thickness the only thing separating the living from the dead. A lone steel table stood in the center of the room—probably where they did the autopsies. The stale smell of death lingered in the air.

Luke shivered. He'd done more than his share of killing animals, but that was for food. Dead humans were another story. How anyone could work in such a dismal place, he'd never understand. Why would someone want to be surrounded by death all night? The sour look on Chase's face said he probably thought the same thing.

Luke pointed to his nose, an indication for them to use their senses to find the body, rather than opening every drawer. Chase nodded, and they stepped farther into the room.

"You're sure you checked every locker?" A female voice floated in from down the hallway, and Luke held his breath. He'd recognize Macey Carpenter's melodic cadence anywhere, and though his mind told him he needed to move, his body betrayed him, freezing him to the spot. What was it about this woman that had him aching to know her?

Chase knocked him on the shoulder, bringing him back to the present. They needed to get the hell out of there. Now. Macey's voice drifted closer; they'd never make it to the back door. There was no time to escape. Nowhere to hide, except…

Chase yanked open an empty drawer and crawled inside. Luke's heart threatened to beat a hole through his chest. He couldn't stand being inside an elevator, much less a body locker. But what other choice did he have? He spun around and found number fifty-nine ajar. He peeked inside. No body.

He could do it. But the space was so small…Would he be able to breathe?

"I opened them all twice." The door knob twisted.

Now or never. He slid inside and the door closed behind him, the *click* of the latch sounding so final, his breath caught. Total darkness engulfed him. Utterly still. Cold. One twitch would give away his location, not that he could've moved a muscle if he'd wanted to. The confined space had him paralyzed with dread.

He closed his eyes and took several long, deep breaths, trying to slow his pulse. Now was not the time to panic.

"Well, it didn't get up and walk away. Where's fifty-seven?" Macey's boot heels thudded across the tile, the sound echoing in Luke's constricted chamber like a hammer driving nails into a coffin.

"It's over here," a male said. "But, I told you. I opened it twice already. It's not there."

The *clack* of the latch and the sound of metal sliding on metal sent his heart racing again. They were so close to finding him.

The *bang* of the drawer slamming shut shook the wall of lockers. Luke held his breath.

"Let me see the report." He heard Detective Carpenter flipping through the pages, sighing heavily as the clip-board clanked on metal. "Joseph filed it. He's been here longer than I've been on the force. He doesn't make mistakes like this."

"Don't look at me." The male again. "I just got here. He handed me the folder, asked me to enter it, and left."

"No one's blaming you," an older male with a deeper voice responded. "But we do need to get this figured out. Fast."

"You're sure it wasn't transferred?" Annoyance edged Macey's words.

"There are two ways in and out of the building, and no one has taken a body out the front door since I got here." The younger male sounded indignant as he stomped across the room. "The back door locks automatically, and Joseph and I are the only ones with the key." He banged on something metal. "It's closed tight."

Luke allowed himself a small sigh of relief. At least they'd closed the door behind themselves when they broke in.

"Is there a security camera?" Macey's voice sounded closer, and Luke's head spun. Either she'd find him soon or he'd have a heart attack in this confined space. He clenched every muscle in his body to stop himself from shaking. *Please get this over with.*

The younger man sighed. "It's been broken for a week."

"Dammit. You're sure no one stuck the body in an adjacent locker by accident?" Macey again. Another drawer slid open. "Not in fifty-six."

Shit. His pulse pounded in his ears. The combination of fears called on his flight instinct. His beast begged to take over, the primal urge to shift and get the hell out of there overwhelming him. *Not now...*

"What about fifty-eight?" The drawer next to him slid open.

It took every ounce of control to tame his beast. He could not shift. Not there. He clenched his trembling hands into fists and fought to breathe. The air in his chamber grew heavy. He couldn't get enough of it into his lungs. He would suffocate if he didn't get out of there fast.

The adjacent door slammed shut. Was his next? The sharp screech of fingernails sliding across metal. A slight jiggle of the latch. He could practically feel her hand resting on the handle of his drawer. He closed his eyes, willing her to let go.

"Did you check fifty-nine?"

This was it. He swallowed hard.

"You know, boss. I think we need to call Joseph," The older man said. "Maybe he can shed some light on it."

"You're right." The handle clicked as she released it. "Let's get him on the phone." Her footsteps thudded across the room. A door opened and closed again.

Silence.

He couldn't wait another second. Fumbling his arms over his head, he gave the door a solid push.

It didn't move. *Crap!*

He pushed it harder. Still nothing.

Cold sweat trickled down his forehead, stinging his eyes. He was trapped. He ran his hands across the metal, searching for a latch to release him from the frigid tomb. The damn things only opened from the outside. He pressed his boots against the end of the chamber for leverage and slammed both fists against the door.

It didn't budge. That was it. He was going to suffocate. There was no way out, and he would die an excruciatingly slow death trapped inside a meat locker in the morgue. No…It couldn't happen. He banged frantically on the door, using all his strength to will it open. With his feet against the wall, he gave it a thrust with all his might, and the door flung open. His momentum sent the drawer shooting out, his body flying off the platform and crashing to the floor.

With a smack, his breath *whooshed* from his lungs. Pain shot through his limbs, and he gasped for air. He was free. Momentarily blinded by the overhead lights, he rubbed his eyes and shot to his feet. His entire body trembled, no longer with the need to shift, but with sheer terror.

"Dude, you okay?" Chase must've opened the latch.

"The door wouldn't open," Luke muttered.

"You closed it all the way." Chase chuckled under his breath.

"Yeah." Luke ran a hand through his sweat-soaked hair. With the racket he'd made, he was surprised no one had come running back into the room. It was time to jet. "I'm good. The body's not here."

"So I heard." Chase motioned toward the exit.

Luke paused and inhaled deeply. "I don't smell it in

here either." He followed Chase out the door and jogged to his truck. He couldn't get away from that place fast enough. What kind of alpha gave in to irrational fears like that? He needed to get his act together if he ever wanted to be pack leader. Taking one last look at the closed door, he peeled out of the parking lot.

With the morgue in the rearview mirror, Chase turned to him. "You think it already...woke up?"

Luke sighed. "God, I hope not."

CHAPTER SIX

JIMMY WAS A HERO. HIS BROTHER WOULD BE SO proud of him. He just knew it. He'd gotten Ross's body out of that place, and no one even saw him do it. He beat those flea-bag werewolves and that pretty cop too.

He grinned as he thought about what their faces must've looked like when they noticed his brother was gone. They didn't have a clue. Even the werewolves didn't pick up his scent as he hid out in the dumpster behind the morgue until they'd left. They'd run out the back door so fast, you'd have thought they'd seen a zombie or something.

"Who's the idiot now?" Jimmy shoved his brother's body over the edge of the dumpster and cringed when it thudded on the ground. Ross was dead. He couldn't feel that, could he? Jimmy swallowed. He hoped he couldn't.

He didn't know where Ross's ghost was. He'd said something about checking on a host and a birth—whatever that meant. It was confusing. He was supposed to get the body and bring it to the shack in the swamp. If he thought about anything else for too long, he'd get distracted. And the last thing his brother had told him before he left was *don't get distracted.*

He heaved his large frame from the dumpster to the ground and picked up the sack that held his brother. Good thing Jimmy was strong, because his brother was heavy. And it was a good thing he'd found that big duffle bag last spring. He'd had to fold him up just right, but Ross's body fit perfectly in the sack. It zipped up and everything.

With a proud grin stretching across his face, Jimmy slung the bag over his shoulder and trudged across the street. As long as he could make it to the forest without being seen, he'd be fine. He might even make himself a bed of leaves to sleep on the rest of the night. It had taken him two hours to walk to the morgue. It would take even longer to get home.

He stepped behind a fat tree trunk and gently dropped the duffle bag. That's what he'd do. He'd get some rest and go home in the morning. Ross would be so proud of him that he wouldn't mind waiting.

CHAPTER SEVEN

O'MALLEY'S PUB DIDN'T LOOK LIKE MUCH. SMALL. Quiet. Exactly the kind of place Macey needed to clear her mind. She'd walked by the bar dozens of times, always ignoring the urge to step inside. Something about the run-down building called to her. Beckoned her to open up and let it tell its story. That was the reason she'd steered clear of the establishment. Any structure that called that strongly had to be bad news.

And she didn't need any more of that.

The only lead on the case had disappeared. Now, she had nothing. No one at the morgue knew anything. They remembered checking the body in, and it ended there. She reported the broken camera to the head of security, but it wouldn't help with this case. If someone had taken the corpse out the back door, they'd never know.

She put her hands on her hips and shifted her weight from side to side. A change of scenery would help clear her mind. O'Malley's couldn't be *that* bad. Biting her bottom lip, she took a deep breath and pushed open the door. She braced herself for the onslaught of memories into her psyche. A building this old had to have an interesting past, and even without opening herself up to them, she expected the stories to hit her like a wall.

Nothing happened.

Hmm...Kinda disappointing. A smile tugged at the corner of her mouth. Maybe she could actually relax tonight. It was her night off, after all. She deserved a break, even one she'd been forced to take.

She adjusted her bun and smiled at the bartender. With his tattoos and piercings, he had a rough appearance, but the way he grinned gave away his sweet personality. He raised his head to acknowledge her. "What can I get you?"

Macey made her way to a stool at the corner of the bar. "Abita?"

"Sure thing." He filled the glass and set it in front of her, then went back to washing dishes. A news program played on the sole television, but it sat too far away to read the closed captioning.

The phone rang, and the man crossed the bar to pick up the receiver as Macey took a long drink of her beer. The icy bubbles tickled her throat on the way down to her stomach. It'd been way too long since she'd savored the malty goodness. Too long since she'd savored—or even enjoyed—anything. She'd been so caught up in the case; it was all she thought about. If the Chief hadn't insisted she take the night off after the body disappeared, she'd have been thinking about it now.

Damn it. It was still on her mind. After the fitful sleep she'd endured that morning, she needed to loosen up. The bartender hung up, punched in some numbers, and spoke to someone else briefly. The sparkle in his eye disappeared after the phone call, and he shuffled toward her, tensing his jaw and grumbling something under his breath.

"Everything okay?" She absently rubbed the condensation off the glass with her finger.

The bartender wiped the counter with a rag. "Yeah. It's…a family thing." His head snapped up when a side door opened, and he hurried over to the hunk that entered the room.

Wow. Macey scooted closer to the corner of the bar so she could watch the exchange without being seen. The man who entered from the back of the pub stood at least three inches taller than the bartender. He ran a hand through long, wavy, caramel locks, and his black T-shirt stretched tight across muscular pecs when he moved. His sapphire eyes held brotherly concern as he looked at the other man. "What's up?"

"Bekah's damn sitter canceled on her again, and she's gotta go to work. Amber's not due in for another two hours, and—"

The taller man raised a hand to stop him. "It's okay, Chase. Go do what you gotta do. I'll cover."

They walked toward the bar, and Macey gulped her beer to cool the fire that stirred in her core. She gripped the nearly empty mug with both hands and swallowed down a giggle. Had the alcohol already gone to her head? She chewed her bottom lip and focused on the tiny bubbles in her beverage, trying to make her eavesdropping less obvious.

"You sure, man?" The bartender reached into his pocket and pulled out a set of keys. "You've been on site all day."

"Go take care of your niece." He lifted the hinged part

of the bar and stepped inside. Macey chugged what was left of her drink.

"Thanks, and I think the lady needs another round." His glittering smile returned as he bounded out the front door.

Macey took a deep breath and forced herself to make eye contact with the gorgeous man.

"What are you drink...ing?" A look of recognition flashed in his eyes before he composed himself.

"I...uh..." A lump in her throat had formed in the half second she'd caught his gaze. She cleared her voice. "Abita, please."

The corners of his eyes crinkled as he smiled. "Have you ever tried Blue Moon? I know Abita's the local favorite, but it's got nothing on this one." He poured the drink without waiting for a response and set it down in front of her.

"Well, no...but I..." Macey stumbled over her words. What the hell was wrong with her? She was a confident, kick-ass detective, but in half a minute, this guy had turned her into a babbling idiot.

He squeezed an orange slice and dropped it into the glass. "On me. If you don't like it, I'll buy your next Abita."

Fair enough. She picked up the beer and took a swig. It was smooth, like liquid gold, and the burst of citrus made her taste buds dance. "Wow. That is good." Finally, she'd found her voice. "Looks like you're off the hook. I'll keep the Blue Moon." She took another drink and toyed with the glass as her heart pounded hard against her chest.

"This your first time in?" His deep-blue eyes drew her in, and she had to look away.

"Yeah. I've lived here most of my life, though. I guess I

don't get out much." *Good job, Mace. Way to sound pathetic.*

He chuckled. "Well, welcome." His gaze locked with hers for what felt like an eternity, holding her still, making her forget how to breathe. How did he do that? "I'm Luke Mason, by the way." He held out his hand to shake. "My old man owns the bar."

She hesitated to take his hand. Something inside her screamed to stop. Instinct told her this was the beginning of something bigger than she could imagine, but she chided herself. It was only a handshake. She reached across the bar and shook.

As soon as her skin brushed his, a buzzing sensation shot up her arm, making her hairs stand on end. It paused at her elbow, stinging like she'd hit her funny bone, before it lurched up to her shoulder. It spread through her body in a jolt, and she jumped. *What the hell?*

He gave her a quizzical look. "Interesting."

"Sorry." She jerked her hand away and rubbed her palm on her jeans. "I'm Macey. I must've built up some static electricity or something. You kinda shocked me."

"You shocked me too." Luke ran his hands through his hair and tied it at the nape of his neck with a band. "Do you want a menu? I recommend the steak. Made the marinade myself."

"You cook?"

"Does that surprise you?" His grin sent her heart racing again. What was wrong with her?

"I guess not. I'll stick to the beer, though. Thanks." She tugged on her bottom lip as she watched him wash his hands, pull a lemon out of the small fridge under the bar, and begin cutting it.

The muscles in his forearms flexed and extended with

each chop of the knife. Her gaze traveled up to his biceps, where a thin, pink line scarred his otherwise perfect skin. His black T-shirt blocked her view of his obviously muscular shoulder, and warmth pulsed from her core out to her fingertips and toes. Was it the beer or the amazingly hot man across the bar making her feel this way?

Whatever it was, she needed a distraction, so she turned her attention to the video trivia machine at the end of the bar and dropped in a quarter. She touched the screen for eighties pop culture and began answering questions about music and movies from the decade. Her second beer was half empty, and she hadn't been in the bar half an hour.

She sipped her drink, occasionally stealing glances of the sexy bartender, as more and more patrons filled the bar. By the time she drained the glass, people wearing small white stickers on their shirts had packed the establishment, and Luke had filled three rows of plastic cups with ice on the bar in front of her. "What's going on?" she asked.

"Haunted French Quarter tours. They happen every night at six and eight."

"Ghost tours?" She chuckled.

He shrugged and poured a drink that looked like red Kool-Aid into the cups—New Orleans' infamous hurricanes. "My dad thought it would help with business."

She traced her finger along the rim of her empty glass. "Does it?"

"At six and eight. Excuse me." Luke stepped toward a group of customers and handed a patron two of the drinks. He reached for another plastic cup and glanced at Macey. Then he stopped, picked up a beer mug, filled it, and slid it toward her.

She would have thanked him, but he turned away to help the onslaught of customers getting ready for the tour. The once dark, quiet bar now bustled with activity. People filled every chair, lined the walls, and chattered incessantly. She popped another quarter into the machine. Luckily, the tour started in fifteen minutes. She could hang on until then. In the meantime, at least she could enjoy the view.

Luke finished serving the customers, and as the last one left the bar, he turned to face her. He looked at her quizzically, slightly cocking his head to the side. He narrowed his eyes and focused on her so hard, the rest of the world slipped away. Was he judging her? Checking her out? Whatever he was doing, it made her palms sweat and her heart race. He went utterly still.

Then, he inhaled deeply and shook his head like he didn't believe something. He dropped his arms, and his smile returned, as if that awkward moment never happened.

"So, Macey…You're a detective, right? I think I've seen you on TV a few times."

"Yeah." She grimaced. Never one for the spotlight, she'd managed to keep her face off the evening news for years, letting her charismatic partner handle all the on-screen interviews. With the nature of this case, though, NOPD decided to be politically correct and have a woman on screen for a change. Lucky Macey.

And now Luke knew who she was. When men found out her occupation, some of them bolted immediately. It took a strong man to handle an equally strong woman, and it would've been nice if he'd gotten to know her personality before her reputation.

Wait. What was she thinking? It didn't matter what this guy thought of her; she wasn't looking for a relationship. She had no intention of setting herself up to be hurt again. Still, something about Luke drew her in.

"You've got quite a rep," he said. "I mean…you bust a lot of bad guys."

"I know. But it's my night off…" She batted her lashes, hoping he'd get the message that she didn't want to talk about work. He didn't.

"Can you tell someone is a criminal by looking at him?"

"There are certain qualities I look for, but I've learned not to judge a personality by the package." She took another sip of beer and let her gaze travel from his face down his muscular chest to his pants. "No matter how tempting the package may be." *Crap.* She didn't mean to say that last part out loud. Heat crept up her cheeks as she cleared her throat. "Why? Do you have something you want to confess?"

He chuckled and leaned toward her. "If I did, you'd have to beat it out of me." He winked before standing up straight and crossing his arms. Was he flirting with her? One way to find out.

"You'd like that, wouldn't you?"

The corner of his mouth pulled into a crooked grin. "Maybe."

He *was* flirting. A fluttering sensation formed in her stomach, like butterfly wings beating against a net. She leaned her elbows on the bar, resting her chin on her fist. "Hmm…"

He scratched behind his ear. "Anyway…you're working on the rape cases right? How's that going? Any leads?"

"Ha. I *had* a lead…until the body walked out of the morgue." *Crap!* What was her problem tonight? Was it the man? Or the beer? Whatever it was, she needed keep herself in check before she jeopardized her job.

His eyes widened in surprise. "You lost a body?"

"*I* didn't lose it. But…just…forget I said anything. I'm not supposed to talk about it." She gazed into his eyes, willing him to understand. "Please?"

He raised his hands in a show of innocence. "Okay. I didn't hear a thing."

***

Nothing he didn't already know, anyway. He probably could've gotten her to say more, but he didn't want to take advantage of her. She wasn't drunk, but she was obviously buzzed. And, damn, she was cute.

"Good. Because this case is tough enough. I don't need to lose my job over it."

He couldn't help but grin at the beautiful woman before him as she reached behind her head and loosened the bun at the nape of her neck. Silky blonde hair flowed over her shoulders, accentuating the delicate dip at the base of her throat in the center of her collar bone.

His mouth watered as he imagined his lips pressed against the indention and the sweet taste of her skin as he trailed kisses across her chest. "Wow."

"What?" She shoved the hair band into her purse and pushed her beer away. "I think I've had enough."

"Your hair is pretty. You should wear it down more."

"Oh." Her gaze shifted to the bar, and she blushed. "Thanks. I would, but…it gets in the way at work. I've been thinking about cutting it—"

"Don't."

She looked into his eyes, and a sly grin curved her lips.

"Is that an order? Because I don't like being told what to do."

He slid his gaze down to her tempting mouth and lingered there a moment too long. What would those lips feel like pressed against his? "Just a suggestion."

"Suggestions I can handle."

What the hell was he doing? He needed to stop flirting with her. No matter how hot an inferno she lit inside his core, she was human for Christ's sake.

Or was she?

When he'd touched her, some kind of magic had shot up his arm. Possibly a witch. For a split second, he'd felt the electricity of a were…but she couldn't be. There was no way a were could live in the Quarter for as long as she had without the pack knowing. Rogues were required to register.

If she wasn't a werewolf, he didn't need to waste his time. But the longer she sat there in front of him, the less he cared about pack laws. When he became alpha, he could make his own laws.

Damn it. No! She'd gotten too close already. To the crimes. To the demons. Her job was to figure out what was happening, and his was to keep her from discovering the truth.

Her jingling cell phone pulled him back to reality. She dug in her purse and held the device to her ear. "Hey, Bryce." She mouthed the words *It's my partner* to Luke.

Even if she hadn't told him, she had the volume on her phone up so loud, he could hear every word Bryce said.

"Listen, Mace. We've got an issue with the first victim."

Macey rolled her eyes. "Oh, c'mon, Bryce. It's my night off. Yours too. Can't someone else handle it?"

"*They are, but…she's dead. Ripped open…and eaten. Her entire abdomen.*"

"Come again?"

"*That's all I know. On my way to the scene now. 857 Masters Street. Meet you there?*"

She ran her hand over her face from her forehead down to her chin. "Actually, could you come pick me up? I'm at O'Malley's on St. Philip."

"*Are you drunk, Mace? Do you need to sit this one out?*"

"Hell no. You know me better than that. I've had a few, and I don't want to drive, that's all."

"*Be there in ten.*"

She shoved her phone into her purse. "Sorry about that. Guess it's not my night off after all." Sliding off her stool, she hesitated, tugging on her bottom lip. "I have to go. How much do I owe?"

"It's on me tonight. It was nice to meet you, Macey." He held out his hand.

"Thank you." When they shook, the same buzzing electricity shuddered up his arm. Definitely some kind of magic. He held on too long. After the conversation he'd overheard, his instinct told him not to let her go. To protect her above all else. But what could he do? She wasn't his to protect, no matter what his wolf wanted.

Her eyes widened as she pulled her hand away. "I'd like to see you again sometime."

The energy faded, and a new heat flushed his system at the thought. He'd like to see her again too. Naked. In his bedroom… But he couldn't. His duty to the pack came first. "I'm sure we'll run into each other again." Even if he couldn't be with her, he'd be damned if he'd let any harm come to her.

Her expression dropped, the light in her eyes fading, as she turned for the exit. "Um…yeah. See you."

As soon as the door closed behind her, Luke hopped over the bar and called for one of the guys in the back to cover for him. There was no way he'd make it to the scene before Macey. Even if he did, the place would be crawling with cops. Two hundred pack members, and they still didn't have a man on the inside. He shook his head and bounded for his truck.

From the sound of it, whatever ate that woman had come from inside her.

CHAPTER EIGHT

JIMMY'S BODY FELT LIKE LEAD. HIS MUSCLES ACHED, and he trudged along like he was moving in slow motion. He'd carried his brother's body across the swamp and all the way to their house. It took him all day. He didn't mean to sleep so long, but that bed he'd made in the leaves was so comfy.

Ross would be mad. But maybe, since Jimmy had the body, his brother would forgive him.

A thick layer of mud covered his sopping wet boots. Dead leaves crunched under his steps as he hoofed it through the last few yards to the front door. It wasn't dark out yet, but heavy clouds covered the sun, casting an eerie haze over the already spooky house. Jimmy shivered. He didn't like living in the swamp. A small apartment in the city, with people all around, would have been nice. He liked people. But Ross insisted on the swamp because it gave them privacy. Being half demon, he needed his space.

But Jimmy didn't. The only reason he didn't leave was because when Ross was born, he'd eaten Momma. He said if Jimmy ever tried to run away, he'd eat him too. Jimmy swallowed hard. He didn't want to get eaten.

Still, he didn't like being alone. He had a dog once, but a gator ate it. He didn't get any more pets. As long as he stayed by himself, nobody got eaten.

He dragged the sack up the front steps and flung open the screen door. "Ross? You here?"

He took a tentative step inside and dropped the body bag at his feet. "Ross?"

"I'm here."

"Oh, good. For a minute I thought somebody—" Before he could finish his sentence, something crashed into him, knocking him to the floor. Jimmy stared up into the bright-red eyes of what looked like a ten-year-old boy. But Jimmy knew better. This wasn't a boy. He smiled and tried to get up as the boy backed away.

"Hey there! I didn't know we had a visitor. What's your name?"

The boy snarled, baring sharp teeth, and leapt toward Jimmy. Jimmy was about to scream when the boy stopped in mid-air and catapulted to the floor like he'd been hit. Jimmy screamed anyway.

The boy got up, dusted off his too-big trousers and crossed his arms. "I'm sorry. I didn't know you were Master's brother."

Jimmy's mouth fell open, so he snapped it shut. His brother hated it when he gaped. "Master?"

"He means me, you idiot. I should've let him tear you up. What the hell took you so long?"

Jimmy didn't know what to say. So many questions ran through his mind, but he knew he'd get in trouble for asking something stupid. "You were heavy." That was the truth. He couldn't get in trouble for telling the truth.

The impact of a hand across his face made his head jerk to the side. Pressure built in his eye like it would explode, and his cheek stung. Was it wrong to say Ross was heavy?

"It doesn't matter now. I don't want it anymore."

Confusion made Jimmy's thoughts tumble. "You don't want your body? But how will you—" He received another blow, this time to his gut. He doubled over as the air *whooshed* out of his lungs.

"Does it feel like I need a body?"

He coughed. "No, sir. It doesn't."

"Good. I don't have enough energy to knock any more sense into you. Besides, I can use your body when I need it."

"How can you—" A piercing pain shot through Jimmy's body, like he'd been stabbed with a million straight pins all at once. For a moment, he couldn't breathe. He stood frozen in the sensation of his skin being turned inside out. Then the pain stopped just as suddenly as it had started. His arms moved up and down, and he jumped. His body crouched and leapt into the air, but he wasn't controlling it. He tried to speak, but his mouth wouldn't move. All he could do was think. *What's happening? Why am I doing this?*

"Because I'm controlling you." He felt his mouth form the words, but they didn't come from his brain. It was almost his own voice, but Ross was speaking. "It's a little trick I figured out while I was waiting for you to get back. Fun, huh?"

Not really.

"Sure it is. And get used to it, because I like it. You and I are gonna have some fun. Maybe we'll go into town tonight and find a woman."

Oh, no. He can hear everything I think.

"Damn right, I can. Good thing you don't think much."

The sharp, tearing sensation returned, but this time it felt like the pins were pushing from the inside out. As Ross ripped himself from his body, Jimmy collapsed to the floor, gasping for breath. He ran his hands over his arms, patting his body to make sure his skin was still there.

"I...I didn't like that, Ross."

"Neither did the boy here. He's only a day old, but he's a lot stronger than you. You're easier to control." Ross laughed. *"That's no surprise."*

"What are you going to do with him?" Jimmy gestured to the boy who stood silently against the wall. Though, calling him a boy was a stretch. He'd be full grown in a couple of days, just like Ross had been.

"He's gonna be my eyes in the city. I'm gonna turn him loose and let him wreak his havoc or do whatever the hell he wants to, as long as he keeps an eye on those damn werewolves."

At that, the boy bolted through the house and out the door. Jimmy wanted to ask a question. He knew he shouldn't, but he really wanted to know. "Why are we doing this? Calling demons and stuff?"

"You're doing it because I told you to. I'm doing it because...I'm bored. I'm tired of living in the swamp. I'm going to run this city one day, and all its magic will be mine."

He was able to ask that question without getting punished. He started to smile, but stopped himself. Maybe he could ask some more.

"What do the demons do after we call them?"

"They rape and murder. What else, moron? Then we get more half breeds like the boy."

"Why?"

"Because they obey me. And the more evil there is in the world, the better. Once I get enough of them, I'll build an army. Then I'll get rid of those damn werewolves, and every magical being in the city will answer to me."

CHAPTER NINE

MACEY MUNCHED ON A BEAR CLAW DURING THE fifteen-minute drive from the French Quarter, down the dusty country road, to the victim's home. She hadn't been drunk when Bryce called her, but a little food in her belly would sober her up if any tipsiness remained in her system.

The comfort food also helped ease the sting of rejection. She must've read Luke wrong. His glittering smile and flirtatious conversation couldn't have been what she'd thought. He probably flirted with all the customers. A guy that good-looking…Women probably went to that bar for the view of Luke alone. It was just as well. Getting involved with a man like that was the last thing she needed. No matter how much she'd wanted it at the time.

She swallowed the last of the pastry and reached for the cup of joe Bryce had so thoughtfully picked up for her on the way. She took a sip and wistfully stared out the window.

Her partner broke the silence. "You know, I expected you to be stumbling over your feet when I picked you up.

But you only had three? I've seen you drink way more than that and be fine."

Macey took another sip of her coffee and put it in the cup holder. "I'm sure my BAL is over the legal limit. It was high enough to screw up my judgment of the bartender, anyway."

Bryce flicked his gaze over to Macey for a second. "Do I want to know?"

She sighed and ran her hands through her hair, pulling it into a low ponytail. Holding a rubber band in her mouth, she twisted her mane into a tight bun. "It's just..." She spoke with the band between her teeth. "I really thought he liked me." Yanking the elastic out of her mouth, she twisted it in her hair. "He smiled and flirted. I thought he was flirting."

Bryce glanced at her with raised eyebrows.

"He was definitely flirting, Bryce. Ugh! Why do I care? I shouldn't care. I don't *need* a man." Honestly, she didn't even *want* one. As long as she didn't open herself up to anyone, no one could get close enough to hurt her.

"How do you know he's not interested?"

"Because I told him I wanted to see him again, and he said, 'I'm sure I'll see you around,' or something like that. He blew me off."

Bryce drew in a long breath. "Well, then he's an idiot, Mace. Forget about him."

"You're right. It's not like I ever have to see him again. I just won't go to that bar anymore." She inhaled deeply and closed her eyes, pushing the thoughts of Luke and his amazing biceps out of her head.

The sedan chugged down the dirt road, jolting over bumps and through potholes. The seatbelt pressed into her lap, each bouncing bump making the need to pee over-whelm her.

"Are we there yet?"

Bryce chuckled. "Don't make me turn this car around, young lady. We'll be there when we get there."

Macey groaned. "Seriously. I need to pee. If you see a store, you have to stop."

Her partner grinned silently as he made a sharp left turn into a driveway. "We're here. If the bathroom's been cleared, you can go. Otherwise…you'll have hold it."

Her mouth fell open. "You want me to pee in the victim's house? At the crime scene?" She got out of the car and slammed the door. "You're nuts. I can't do that."

"Suit yourself." He shrugged and shuffled toward the house.

Macey glared at his back, but she followed. It was only three beers. She could hold it.

Monstrous pine trees towered over the small yard, creating a canopy across the walkway. The usually-green needles appeared as black silhouettes against the darkening sky. Gravel crunched beneath her flip-flops—not the shoes she'd have chosen for police work, but she didn't have time to change. Her denim capris clung to her skin, and she fought the urge to pop the button to relieve some of the pressure on her bladder.

Four stone steps led up to the entrance of the white Creole-style cottage, and green shutters framed the windows. Two men in blue greeted Macey and Bryce at the front door. "Victim's in the back yard," one of them said. "There's blood in the kitchen. Trails out the back door."

"Thanks." She smiled at the man and brushed past him into the small living room. Beige Berber carpet lined the floor from white wall to white wall. A canary yellow sofa sat across from a small television. Various trinkets lined the built-in bookshelves, all evenly and meticulously spaced. Nothing appeared to be out of place. No sign of a struggle so far.

Bryce cleared his throat and pointed his thumb toward an open door. "Bathroom's clear."

"Bryce!"

"Just saying. I'd use it." He grinned and took the lead as they headed into the kitchen. The chrome sink and faucet shined in the brightness cast from the recessed lighting. The cabinets gleamed a pristine white, and a large bouquet of sunflowers overflowed a blue vase on the center of the island. Except for the bloody hand print lying bright red against the pale gray granite, it was the most cheerful kitchen Macey had ever seen.

Bryce laughed.

"What?" She shifted her weight and fought the urge to bolt to the bathroom.

"You're doing the pee pee dance, Mace. Go use the toilet."

She glanced down at the awkward position she was standing in. "Oh, fine. But you better not tell anyone."

He drew a cross over his heart and pretended to zip his lips.

Macey ducked in and out of the restroom as fast as she could, and no one noticed her using the crime scene facilities. Men were lucky. Any tree would do when they had the urge. She trekked through the house and onto the back porch where Bryce stood, talking with a uniform.

"Feel better?" the man asked. Her partner tried to muffle his laughter.

"Not funny, Bryce." Her face burned with embarrassment, and she punched him on the shoulder. She had to be as red as a beet. She'd get him back, though. One way or another.

Down the steps and to the right lay the body of the first victim in the string of crimes. Her limbs were contorted, like she'd fallen and writhed in pain as whatever attacked her turned her into a meal. Macey peered over the railing at the bloody sight. The woman's abdomen was nearly nonexistent. She'd almost been chewed in half, but her still intact spine glistened white in the harsh, artificial light that had been set up to illuminate the scene.

The blood-soaked ground looked black beneath the mauled body, and bits of flesh lay scattered around the yard. Macey covered her mouth and fought the urge to vomit. She had to get a closer look, but this image would surely invade her nightmares. She followed Bryce down the stairs and stopped a few feet away from the victim.

The coroner was crouched by the body, and he rose to his feet when the detectives approached. He peeled the soiled latex gloves from his fingers and tossed them into a bag before he spoke. "Stomach and uterus are completely gone. What's left of the other organs is shredded to bits."

Macey's gaze darted from the victim to the examiner. "Any idea what could have done this?"

The man shrugged. "Something hungry. Or someone completely twisted. She's been here nearly twenty-four hours. That's all I know."

"Thank you." She glanced at the body again. Could the same creature that attacked the rapists have been responsible for the carnage here? If so, why would it have come back for the woman? Nothing about this case made sense. Turning to Bryce, she took a deep breath and immediately wished she hadn't. The stale scent of death mixed with flesh on the verge of decay made her stomach turn. "Do you think a *person* did this?"

He looked at the body and grimaced. "I sure hope not, but who knows? Do your thing, and maybe you'll get something."

She pursed her lips. Her ability hadn't helped so far, but she'd give it a try. She trotted up the porch steps and put her hand against the wall. The old cottage's secrets danced through her mind as fleeting images and short movies. She saw a Creole woman giving birth, a couple cooing over a baby, a soldier heading off to war as his wife cried over a cradle. Other images flitted in and out of her consciousness too quickly for her to grab onto. What was the house trying to tell her? Where was the victim's energy?

Macey took a deep breath to clear her mind. Then she closed her eyes and focused on the victim, willing her energy to come forward. A single picture flashed through her senses: the victim standing sideways in front of a mirror with her hand on her pregnant belly. Macey tried to grab hold of the picture, to make it stay so she could explore it. But it flitted away as quickly as it had come.

She dropped her hand and exhaled a sigh. It didn't make sense. The victim wasn't pregnant. Macey had spoken to her a few weeks earlier. She didn't have any children, according to the police report, but the woman in the vision was at least eight months along. Maybe she'd had a miscarriage at one time?

"He's here."

Macey jerked her head around at the whisper. It sounded as if someone stood right beside her. "What?" She scanned the scene, but she stood alone on the porch. The rest of the people there were men, and the whisper had been female.

A prickling sensation made the hairs on the back of her neck rise. A static electrical charge had her body humming. Was it the woman's spirit? It had to be. Like in the courtyard a few days prior, the spirit's energy danced around her...so close, but she couldn't grab onto it.

"I heard you," Macey whispered, so no one would hear her talking to a ghost. "What happened to you?"

She strained to hear the spirit again, but nothing happened. The energy dissipated, leaving Macey alone. Had she imagined it? She turned to report what she'd seen to Bryce, but movement in the line of trees behind the house caught her eye. The shadow of a man darted from behind a trunk and disappeared into the thicket.

What if it was the killer? If anyone was sick enough to do something like this, he'd probably return to the scene. Or was it a ghost? In the darkness, it was hard to tell. Macey slipped off the porch and tiptoed through the grass toward the woods, careful not to draw attention to herself.

She crept past the tree line and swept the area with her vision. She didn't see anything unusual, but the crunch of a breaking branch drew her attention deeper into the forest. She reached for her gun, but she didn't have it. Her heart pounded, the sound thrumming in her ears, as icy adrenaline flushed through her system. Her muscles tensed, and she tried to slow her breathing. What was she thinking heading into the woods unarmed and unprepared? If she called for backup now, whoever—or whatever—she was tracking would surely bolt. She was already here. She could handle it.

The figure took off, sprinting through the trees. She caught a glimpse of it—tall, broad shoulders, definitely masculine—before he disappeared into the thickness. Macey gave chase, running in the general direction he'd gone. She dodged tree stumps and stumbled over roots, nearly losing a flip flop, before she stopped.

She'd lost him.

"Where the hell did you go?" Standing utterly still, she held her breath and hoped a sound of his movement would betray his location. A soft breeze tickled her skin, and she inhaled deeply. The only scent that danced on the wind was the putrid death of the scene behind her. She crept forward through the brush, taking care to place each step with precision. The last thing she needed was a broken branch piercing the thin, floppy sole of her shoe.

A noise to her right made her heart leap. She stumbled back and caught herself on a tree trunk as a flock of quails squawked and flew from their nests. She swallowed and wiped the sweat from her brow. *Get a grip, Mace.*

As she continued to inch ahead, a thick, frigid gust of air enveloped her. It pricked at her body like thousands of dry pine needles piercing her skin. Ice formed in her veins as the atmosphere around her closed in, choked and heavy, with an aura of something…familiar. It slithered up her arms and swirled around her head as it made its presence known—the spirit from the courtyard. Instinct told her to bolt, but she tried to stay calm as whatever—or whoever—continued to torment her. If it was the rapist whose body went missing, maybe she could communicate with him.

"Who are you?" She gritted her teeth as the pricking sensation grew stronger. "What do you want?"

She strained to hear the faint chuckle that danced through her head.

"I want you, Detective."

"What the hell?" The voice had come from inside her

head. With one sharp rip, the spirit entered her body. She'd never been possessed, but she knew without a doubt the ghost had gotten inside her. She could feel it rolling through her limbs, trying to control her mind. She couldn't move herself, but her head jerked toward a sound to her right.

A sharp exhale. A rustling in the brush. Her pulse thrummed in her ears and her stomach dropped as a creature appeared from the shadows. Shiny caramel-colored fur rolled over its muscular haunches as the biggest wolf she'd ever seen stepped toward her. It crept slowly, lowering its head and peering at her with piercing blue eyes.

"Not another one," the voice echoed.

Though the intelligent look in the wolf's gaze intrigued her, Macey didn't hesitate when it bared its teeth and growled a warning. Spirit or no spirit, she needed to get the hell out of there.

She clenched her fists and opened her mind like she did when she read an object. The rapist's face, with a snarling grin, flashed before her. The same man whose body went missing from the morgue. Without thinking, she grabbed on to the image and forced the parasite from her consciousness. Sharp pain ripped through her pores like she was sweating nails as the spirit left her body and circled above her head.

"Another time then."

She didn't have time to consider what had happened, and instead backed up carefully, never taking her gaze off the sapphire canine eyes. Something about the wolf seemed familiar, but she'd never seen it before. Had she dreamed of it? Seen it in one of her visions?

She inhaled sharply as the creature took another step

toward her. Was this animal responsible for the horrific scene she so desperately wished to return to? If so, would she be its next victim? One foot behind the other, grasping at branches and tree trunks for support, she edged her way toward the house. When she reached the clearing, the wolf bowed its head and bounded away, deeper into the forest.

Once it was out of sight, Macey turned on her heels and sprinted for the house. She ran past Bryce and the body, took the stairs two at a time, and stopped on the porch. Heaving giant breaths, she leaned her hands against the railing and fought the urge to vomit yet a second time. What the hell had happened?

"You okay, Mace? You're white as milk." Bryce trotted to her side and placed his palm on her back. The warmth of his touch slowed her breathing enough for her to speak. But should she tell him about the spirit? Not yet. Not until she had time to process it.

"The woods. Back there." She pointed to the thicket behind the house. "A wolf." She turned to face her partner, resting her backside against the wooden rail. "I saw something in the forest. When I went to check it out, a wolf was checking me out."

"Are you hurt?" Bryce looked her over, concern dancing in his gaze.

"No. It growled at me, and I backed away. Do you think it could've…"

"Without a doubt. Wolves don't normally attack people, but if they're hungry, sick, or frightened enough, they will. Is it still out there?"

"No. It ran off as soon as I got to the clearing." Finally catching her breath, she shuffled across the porch to look at the body. "I don't know, Bryce. Why would a wolf just eat her abdomen?" *And why would the ghost of a rapist be hanging out in the woods?* "Wouldn't it go for the throat first…you know…to kill its prey?"

He shoved his hands into his pockets. "I don't know. But right now, it's all we've got. I'll let the coroner know to be looking for teeth marks and animal hair. And next time…let me know before you take off like that. We're partners."

She stiffened. "I had it under control."

"You also could've been eaten. No need to take chances like that when you've got a partner you can depend on. Sometimes it's okay to ask for help."

She smiled and patted his shoulder. "Thanks. I'll remember that." *But I can take care of myself.*

Luke watched from the shadows as Macey climbed into the car with her partner. Had he imagined her eyes? When she'd frozen and started talking to the air in the forest, she seemed to…change. At first, she'd almost appeared to be in pain. Then her eyes had glowed red for a minute…

Nah. Couldn't have.

They hadn't been the same deep crimson of a demon. They had only seemed a little red, hadn't they? It was a glare; that was all.

Whatever it was, he hated scaring her like that. But being in the forest alone with who-knew-how-many demons on the loose was dangerous. Deadly. He hadn't thought about it at the time—his main goal had been Macey's safety—but showing her his wolf form might have helped with the case.

At least the cops would be looking for an animal now rather than a murderer. And it might have bought him enough time to find the halfling that ripped its way out of the poor woman's stomach before it caused any more trouble.

He jogged to his truck, which he'd parked at the last restaurant before the road turned to dirt, and ran a mental to-do list. He'd have to get James to check on the other females to be sure none of them were pregnant. The weres had stopped most of the demons before they could spill their seed, but he needed to be sure. The half demon body from the morgue was still missing, but there wasn't anything he could do about that. The fiend would either come back or he wouldn't.

Luke needed to get some rest. All the demon hunting had made him lose focus on his regular job, and the deadline for the current building renovation his crew was working on was only a week away.

And on top of all that, he had to figure out what to do about his growing feelings for the sexy detective. If he could act on instinct, he'd take her to his house and keep her there until he vanquished every last demon. The intense urge to protect her barely overshadowed the *other* urges he felt every time he looked at her.

But the pack came first. Always.

He growled as he started the truck. What was he going to do about that woman?

CHAPTER TEN

MACEY SAT ALONE IN A CORNER BOOTH AT THE Gumbo Place, perusing the menu as she sipped an iced sweet tea. After the gory scene she'd witnessed last night, and the nightmares that followed, the fact she even had an appetite this evening should have surprised her. But she'd tucked the ghastly incident into a compartment in the back of her mind, like she always did, and now her mouth watered at all the delicious temptations the menu offered.

Whatever had happened to her in the woods was a memory now. The spirit hadn't tried to contact her since. In fact, she hadn't sensed *any* spirits since the incident. The day had been so normal, she'd begun to doubt if her ghostly encounter had even happened.

Scooting to her right to avoid the tear in the faded, red vinyl seat, she scanned the restaurant, making note of her surroundings. Booths lined the walls of the large, open dining area, with tables scattered about the center. Zydeco music piped through the speakers, muffling the incessant hum of the overhead fluorescent lights, and patrons occupied four of the tables: a man at the table next to her, a couple in a booth by the window, and two families across the room.

The ambience wasn't much, but this place had the best fried crawfish tails and étouffée in town. She ordered a dish that contained both her favorites and glanced up when the front door swung open. Her breath caught as Luke stepped across the threshold. He'd tied his light-brown hair back in a band, and a tight, heather gray T-shirt stretched across his chest. An intricate tattoo on his bicep peeked from beneath his sleeve. Heat flushed her cheeks as the image of him shirtless skittered through her mind. Did he have any more tattoos?

He looked right at her. Macey averted her gaze, staring intently at her hands folded on the table. Maybe he didn't catch her looking. She ignored him as long as was politely possible, but when his approach was obviously directed to her, she lifted her eyes and smiled.

"Hi, Macey. Is this seat taken?" He gestured to the bench across from her.

She shook her head. A minute motion, but he must've picked up on it because he slid into the seat and folded his hands on the table to match her posture. The waitress approached and set a glass of tea in front of him.

"Good evening, Luke." She grinned at him and offered a menu, but he waved it away.

"I'll have the same as the beautiful lady here."

The waitress shrugged and shot a heated glance at Macey. "Suit yourself." She turned on her heel and strutted away.

What was that about? Wait...had Luke called her beautiful? She hardly knew the man, but the words he'd uttered shot thrilling tingles to her core. He shouldn't have affected her that way. Not that soon. And especially not after he'd blown her off the way he had. She smoothed her hair toward her bun, hoping to smooth the thoughts from her head. "You don't even know what I ordered."

He raised a shoulder in a dismissive shrug. "I trust your taste. Everything's good here anyway."

She raised an eyebrow. "Oh, you trust me, do you?"

He cleared his voice. "I said I trust your taste."

"Mmm-hmm."

Leaning back in the booth, he stretched his arm across the back of the seat. "If you don't mind my asking, why are you alone again? No friends to hang out with?" He winked as if to show he was joking, but the truth of his statement stung.

"Honestly? I've always been kind of a loner." Her ears burned with embarrassment, but she didn't know why. Her lack of a social life was no secret at the station. She kept everyone but her parents at arm's length. She'd turned down so many invitations, her coworkers rarely asked her to hang out anymore. This virtual stranger's opinion shouldn't have mattered so much to her.

But it did.

He put his hands on the table and leaned forward. "I'm sorry. I didn't mean any—"

"It's okay." Her hard shrug made her bounce in her seat. "I've never really felt like I fit in anywhere. I've gotten used to it."

She picked up her glass and gulped down the contents, hoping to end the conversation. Their food arriving saved her from the awkward moment, and from Luke's response.

The waitress set the plates down and touched Luke's elbow. "It's good to see you again."

He inclined his head toward her. "You as well, Jackie. This is all we need." He all but dismissed her. She pursed her lips, trained her gaze on the floor, and scurried away. The pair obviously had some sort of history, though Macey didn't dare ask. She didn't want to know if they'd dated. For some reason, the image of Luke in the arms of that woman—of any woman—made her shudder. Possessiveness clutched at her heart, but why? He didn't belong to her any more than the man at the table next to them.

And she didn't want him. Why did she have to keep reminding herself of that?

Luke looked at the plate in front of him. "Good choice. One of my favorites." The corner of his mouth pulled into a wicked grin. "Of course, I like *everything* here."

His gaze locked with hers, and her heart stuttered. Was he implying he liked her? Surely he wasn't. She scooped a forkful of étouffée into her mouth and savored the flavor explosion on her tongue. The zing of spicy crawfish danced on her taste buds, and she closed her eyes to relish the moment. Opening them again, she found him grinning at her.

"What?" She wiped her mouth with the napkin.

"Nothing." He picked up his fork and pushed the food around on his plate. "You really enjoy your food, don't you?"

"I savor the things that bring me pleasure."

"Words to live by."

Luke stabbed the crawfish tails and shoved them into his mouth. What the hell was he doing flirting with the detective again? He was either out of his mind or masochistic, but he couldn't help it. The more he got to know her, the more enamored of her he became. He adored everything about her, from the way she closed her eyes with each bite she took to the way her brow furrowed when she caught him staring at her.

When werewolves found their fate-bound mates, they felt an instant connection. Others had described it as an overpowering sense of possessiveness. Protectiveness. A basal instinct to grab hold of the other person and never let her go. A feeling of completeness that could only be achieved with the person as his mate.

In the past, werewolves couldn't mate with anyone but their fate-bound, and if they didn't find the one they connected with on that primal level, they spent their lives alone. The law was meant to ensure the strength of the species, but with so few weres finding that deep connection with another, the threat of extinction forced the congress to change the law.

Now they could mate with anyone they chose, but they had to mate for life. Unless they were part of the alpha bloodline. No dilution allowed.

Sitting there, looking at Macey, Luke felt that instant connection. Hell, he'd felt it the moment she touched him at the bar. The protectiveness. The completeness. She was meant to be his.

But she was a human, damn it. She couldn't be his fate-bound mate...or even his regular mate. When he saw her sitting in this booth, he should've turned around and walked out the door. He was wasting his time and leading her on, but he couldn't help himself. The woman was magnetic.

If he were honest with himself, he'd admit Macey was the reason he came to this damn restaurant in the first place. He'd been tailing her for weeks, hiding evidence and trying to throw her off the trail of the demons, and he knew her schedule like clockwork. Tonight was Gumbo Place night, and he'd wandered there on autopilot, subconsciously hoping to get a glimpse of her. He hadn't planned on joining her for dinner, but here he was, enjoying every second of it.

"You said your dad owns the bar? And you work there?" The melodic cadence of her voice roused him from his thoughts.

He blinked as the question registered. "Yeah. I mean… my dad owns it, but I don't technically work there. I'm a contractor."

"Oh, that's cool. So, you do remodeling and stuff."

"And stuff." He chuckled. "You have a way of simplifying things."

"You have to in my line of work. There are only three things that motivate people." She ticked them off on her fingers. "Money, power, and love."

"And, which one motivates you, Ms. Carpenter?"

She grinned slyly. "I guess that depends on the situation."

He finished the last bite of his food and rested his elbow on the table. The silence must have made her uncomfortable because she babbled through the rest of her answer.

"I mean…I'm okay money-wise. And power? I guess I have more than I need."

"So all that's missing is love." As soon as the words left his lips, he wished he could take them back. Love was one thing he couldn't offer her.

She shifted in her seat to sit on her hands. "I…yeah. But it's…Who am I kidding? It's missing." She let out a half-hearted laugh and cast her gaze to the table.

He'd done it again—hit a sore spot with her for the second time in one night. *Real smooth.* Maybe he could change the subject. He cleared his voice. "Do you have family close by? Brothers or sisters?"

She sat up straight and inhaled slowly before she spoke. "My adoptive parents live in Metairie. My biological parents died when I was young. I had…" She put her fingers to her lips. "I don't know why I'm telling you this. It's not something I talk about." Folding her hands on the table, she gazed up at him with sad eyes.

Instinct told him to comfort her, but what could he do? It was an ancient pain she held deep in her heart. It would take more than a few kind words from him to help her heal. He placed his palm over her petite hands, almost covering them completely. Vibrating energy seeped from her skin, snaking up his arms, and she sucked in a sharp breath as the fine blonde hairs on her arms stood on end. He followed the trail of goose bumps over her shoulder and up the delicate curve of her neck. She licked her lips. That tiny flick of her tongue had him groaning inwardly, his mouth watering with the need to taste her. He released her hands and fisted his in his lap. The need to pull her into his arms and kiss away the pain overwhelmed him.

She possessed some sort of magic, but he couldn't figure out what kind. Did Macey even know? She didn't act like any sort of magical being. And if normal humans had adopted her, not knowing…Thoughts raced through his head, but he needed to focus on the present.

"I'm sorry," he said. "We don't have to talk about anything you don't want to."

"It's okay." She rubbed her hands together and gazed at them quizzically.

She must've felt his energy too. A pure human would never notice it.

A smile brightened her face as she dropped her hands into her lap. "You're easy to talk to. I don't mind, actually."

Leaning his elbow on the table, he rested his chin on his hand. "Do you still see your parents often?"

"Two or three times a month."

"Must be nice. I see my folks nearly every day. It gets old."

She inclined her head and looked at his arm. "Hey, what's your tattoo of?"

"It's kind of like a family crest." He lifted his sleeve and slid his arm toward her.

"It's beautiful." She traced her finger across the design and yanked her hand away as a jolt of energy shot straight to his heart. She looked at her fingers, furrowed her brow, and looked at him. "Why does that happen?"

"What?"

"Please tell me you feel it too. Every time I touch you, it's like...I get shocked."

He considered lying, saying he didn't feel a thing. But the way her gaze implored him, he had to admit it. "I do. I guess we have a spark between us." He chuckled, trying to play it off. He felt more than magic of the supernatural kind. The chemistry between the two of them was undeniable.

She smiled, the delicate curve of her lips sending his heart into overdrive. "It does feel that way, doesn't it?"

"Yes, it does."

They stared at each other for a moment, and he lost himself in the emerald sea of her eyes. She was a witch. Or maybe some type of fae. She had to be. Could an alpha werewolf mate with a witch? Would her magic be enough to produce werewolf offspring? He'd have to do some research. Maybe somewhere along the family lines…It would explain how the younger siblings got their powers —like his sister who could see the future in her visions. But how could he find out if Macey truly possessed magic? "Can I ask you something?"

"Why not? I've already told you my dirty little secret."

"I'd hardly call it dirty."

She shrugged and folded her arms on the table. "Shoot."

"Do you know anything about…er, do you believe in magic?"

She stopped breathing for a moment. Straightening her spine, she opened her mouth as if to speak, but shut it with a *click*. "Why? What have you heard?"

Not the response I was expecting. "Nothing. I just wondered if you do."

She pursed her lips into a thin line as her brows drew together. "I…don't know. Do you?"

"Sure. Why not? I'm curious about your response, though. Should I have heard something?"

She took a deep breath and blew it out hard. "I can't believe I'm telling you this." Leaning forward, she lowered her voice to just above a whisper. "There might be a rumor going around that I can talk to the dead. Some people say that's how I close so many cases—that I can communicate with the victims."

He tried to hide the surprise in his eyes by blinking.

Macey held up her hands. "It isn't true. I can't really talk to dead people."

"How do you solve so many cases, then?"

She bristled. "What? You don't think I'm capable of capturing criminals with my brains and wit? Because I'm a woman I have to have some kind of magical powers to do my job?" She flung her hands about as she spoke; he'd hit sore spot number three. Or was it number four? He'd lost count.

"Macey, I have no doubt that you are the best detective New Orleans has. You're one of the smartest people I've met. My question had nothing to do with you being a woman."

Her shoulders dropped as her anger tempered. "I'm sorry. I feel like I have to defend myself a lot...to get respect. It's hard being a woman in a man's field."

"I'm sure it is." And he would have loved to let her vent; he could've listened to her voice for hours. At the moment, though, he needed to figure out her magic. "But you can't communicate with the dead at all? It's just a rumor?"

She hugged herself with her left arm and tugged at her bottom lip with her right hand, an adorable nervous habit. "I can't. But I can sort of sense things, I guess."

"The dead?"

"Sort of."

"Amazing." She was a necromancer. Or a psychic medium. He couldn't fight the smile that tugged at his lips. There was hope for them yet.

Macey snorted. "Hardly. I can't control it, and it only helps sometimes. Mostly after the energy's had time to..."

He raised his eyebrows.

"When it's had time to soak into an object. If I can touch something—usually a building—that's when I can sense things."

"That makes sense."

She cocked an eyebrow. "Does it? I'm glad you understand because it baffles and annoys the hell out of me. But, listen. I have to get back to work." She reached for the check he hadn't noticed the waitress deliver. The plates had been cleared as well, but he'd been so focused on the sexy detective, the rest of the world had slipped away.

That was fine with him, anyway. The waitress was one of several pack members after his affections. His upcoming pack leader status appealed to the weaker wolves. As his father's retirement date inched closer, the number of ladies vying for his attention had gone from zero to about fifteen.

"Let me take care of that." He pulled the ticket from her hand.

"That won't be necessary." She slapped a twenty on the table. "That should cover my part."

He sighed and laid a few bills on the table to cover the rest of the check. How many times could he offend her in one night? She was a strong, independent woman, and that was only one of the many things that made her so attractive. As they stood, he reached for her hand, expecting her to jerk away when the electricity surged between them.

Instead, she inhaled a sharp breath, glancing at their entwined fingers, before smiling at him. Hand in hand, they shuffled out the door.

His heart thudded a beat of exhilaration. Had he found his mate? The likelihood of a simple psychic being powerful enough to bear a were-child was slim, but he felt so much more power coming from her. A sliver of hope was all he needed. He'd start researching the family lines as soon as he got home. There had to be a way to make this work.

Sticky summer heat caressed his skin as they strolled up the street. A bead of sweat rolled between Macey's breasts, and he had to tear his gaze away before she caught him looking. What he'd have given to be that drop of moisture...

"Thank you for the company. It was nice." She paused at the intersection and blinked up at him. "I have to go this way." She pointed to the left.

"It was my pleasure, Macey. I enjoyed it."

"I guess I'll see you around?"

His stomach tightened. Hopefully she didn't notice his sweat-slickened palms. "It would be easier for me to find you if you gave me your number."

Her smile widened. "Okay." She recited the digits as he clumsily punched them into his phone with his right hand. He favored his left, but he wasn't ready to let her go.

"Got it. I'll let you get to work now." He leaned down and pressed his lips to her cheek. Her skin was warm and slightly salty. A shiver ran down his spine as the urge to take her mouth with his rose through his core. Her breath caught, but she didn't move away. He lingered there, his lips barely brushing her skin as she tightened her grip on his hand and turned to meet his mouth.

He hesitated, gazing into her emerald irises and reveling in the warmth of her breath on his skin. She closed her eyes and touched her mouth to his. Liquid warmth flowed to his core as he wrapped his arms around her waist and pulled her body closer. She melted into his embrace, her body conforming to his in a way that felt so damn right. He shuddered, slipping his tongue between her lips, and she moaned softly, the vibration of her voice sending a wave of electricity through his body. He had to pull away, or he'd never let her go.

He stroked her cheek with the back of his hand and memorized the hungriness in her eyes. He could get used to her looking at him like that every day. "I'll see you soon, Macey."

Macey couldn't help but grin as she made her way up Conti Street toward the police station. *What a way to start the night.* Her logical mind told her not to get excited. Letting people in, getting close, led to heartache. But she couldn't deny the way her body reacted when she was near Luke. It was almost as if some other-worldly force drew her to him. He'd talked about believing in magic, and that's how this connection she had with him felt.

Maybe it wouldn't hurt to let Luke get a little closer. Let him satisfy her physical desires without getting her heart involved. She'd managed to keep the rest of her emotions compartmentalized since she was a kid; she could keep it casual with Luke, couldn't she? Lord knew it had been a while since she'd had any kind of satisfaction…

She strolled into her office and dropped her purse into her desk drawer before firing up her computer.

"What are you smiling at?" Bryce leaned in the doorway and crossed his arms.

"Nothing you'd be interested in, trust me." She logged into her e-mail and pretended to focus on the screen, but her grin widened.

"As long as it doesn't have anything to do with your date with BOB, I'm all ears." He pushed off the wall and sauntered into the room.

Macey leaned back and spun in her seat to face him. "I did have a date, but not with BOB."

He plopped into the chair across from her desk. "It's about damn time."

CHAPTER ELEVEN

LUKE MANAGED A GRUMBLED, "HELLO," AS HE shuffled past the morning bartender. Six a.m. was too damn early to start work. Too early for a bar to open, too, but his old man had the crazy idea they should serve breakfast. To Luke, a bar was a bar. Drinks, beer, maybe some hot wings or cheese fries...They didn't need to serve anything else.

But the bar didn't belong to him, and as soon as his dad retired for good, it would fall into his sister's hands. Luke's contracting business was lucrative enough, and he was about to become alpha. He didn't need the hassle of running the bar too.

If he became alpha. The archaic law that he had to have a mate would be the death of him if he couldn't figure out a way to get the pack to accept Macey. He barely knew the woman, but she already had his heart in her hands.

And he was running out of time.

He ground his teeth. His heart didn't matter to the pack, but he *would* become alpha. It was his duty. His birthright. He shouldn't have to give up his dream of waking up to a woman he loved every morning in order to fulfill his destiny. With the intense connection he felt with Macey, he couldn't imagine falling in love with anyone else.

A grin tugged at the corner of his mouth as he imagined waking up with her, seeing her silky blonde mane tousled from a night of lovemaking. Her sleepy smile greeting him as he rolled over to embrace her.

He rubbed his eyes to wipe away the image. *Focus, man.* His first order of business was to register the new rogue who'd just come into town. He powered up his MacBook and glanced at the clock. The rogue's appointment was at six-fifteen. Hopefully, she wouldn't be late. His men were already on site at the remodel, and they needed all the help they could get.

After his dinner with Macey last night, he'd joined Chase and James on a demon hunt, so he hadn't had time to research the family lines for magic, but that occupied the next spot on his list...after he handled the pack business, caught up on the remodel, and took a second to breathe.

At ten past six, someone knocked on the office door. Luke double-clicked the shortcut to open the pack database and picked up his coffee. "It's open."

He raised the cup to his lips and nearly spilled it in his lap when the tall blonde stepped through the threshold. She had wavy, shoulder-length hair, and long bangs framed her bright-green eyes. If he didn't know any better, he'd have said this felt like a set-up.

"Are you Luke?"

He stared at her. His predicament was no secret, and word could have spread to the neighboring packs that the soon-to-be-alpha was in the market for a mate. But to send someone disguised as a rogue could be grounds to start a war. He dismissed that idea as quickly as it formed. No pack would be that stupid.

"Is this a bad time? I can come back later."

He rubbed a hand over his face. "No, no. Sorry. I'm Luke. You must be Alexis Gentry." He stood and held out a hand to shake, and when she accepted, the familiar tingle of werewolf shimmied up his arm.

"Have a seat. Do you have a driver's license or ID, so I can enter your info into the database?" The chair creaked as he sank into it again. He really needed to get the WD-40 after it.

The woman reached into her pocket and pulled out a small piece of plastic. Sliding it across the desk, she avoided looking into Luke's eyes and rubbed the back of her neck. "You're staring at me."

He picked up the ID and turned toward the computer screen. Holding the card in one hand, he tried to focus on typing the information with the other. The rogue was beautiful, no doubt about that. And he couldn't ignore the coincidence that she showed up now, as his deadline to select a mate was fast approaching. While he doubted another pack sent her, he wouldn't put it past his old man to send in a new "rogue" every day until he'd chosen one.

But this woman didn't hold a candle to Macey. In fact, he couldn't get the sexy detective off his mind. He needed to see her again. Soon.

He huffed and handed the card back to her. "How long do you plan to stay in New Orleans?"

She raised one shoulder and stared at her ID card. "I don't know. It depends on how things work out. A few months, maybe?"

"Good enough for me. What brings you here?"

Alexis put her card in her pocket and fiddled with the buttons on her shirt. When she spoke, her voice sounded strained. "Oh, I just like to move around a lot. I get bored, I guess."

She wasn't telling him everything, but he didn't have time to pry the answers out of her. If his old man had sent her, the most harm done was the waste of her time. If she was hiding something else…one of his men could keep an eye on her; he needed to get to work. "How long have you been rogue, and why did you leave your pack?"

She straightened in her chair and folded her hands in her lap. "I've never belonged to a pack. My parents were rogues, and I've been on my own since the change came." Her gaze steadied, locking with his as if challenging him to judge her.

Luke held her gaze until she looked away. "All right. I've got all your info. Do you have a place to stay?"

"Yes. One of your pack members gave me the name of a boarding house. I'll stay there until I get my feet back under me."

"Good. I have to get to work now. If you need anything else…" He rose and motioned toward the door.

Alexis stood and stepped toward the exit. "Actually, I could really use a job."

He blinked at her. Most rogues wanted nothing to do with the pack. They especially didn't want help. Every now and then a needy one would pass through, but he never understood why someone so willing to accept pack support would want to be on her own. "What can you do?"

She shoved her hands in her pockets. "This and that.

Mostly carpentry, plumbing, a little auto work. I can usually fix whatever I get my hands on."

He raised an eyebrow. If she was telling the truth, this rogue could come in handy. "I'm a contractor. My crew is working on a remodel on Decatur. If you're any good, we could use some help. I'm heading there now."

"Oh, I'm good." She grinned. "What's the address?"

He scribbled on a scrap of paper and handed it to her.

"I'll be there in half an hour. And...thank you." She nodded her head and stepped through the door.

Luke did a few more things at the office, and by the time he arrived at the work site, Alexis stood in the parking lot, waiting for him.

"What took you so long, boss?" She grinned and playfully punched him on the shoulder. "Your boys here didn't believe you'd offered me a job."

"We didn't believe a rogue would accept help her first day in town." James approached Luke and lowered his voice. "Is she legit?"

"Yeah. I hired her." Though her casual way of addressing him tempted him to regret his decision. She had a rogue attitude, and if she planned to stick around, she'd have to learn the pecking order. Still, something about her didn't sit quite right with him. "Show her the ropes," he said to James. "I've got to go over the plans with the client."

"Sure thing." James led Alexis into the building.

After his meeting with the client, Luke checked in on the rogue from time to time, but apparently he'd worried for nothing. She fit right in with his team, pulled her weight, and didn't get in anyone's way. Any doubts he'd had about hiring her had washed away by the day's end. And her lack of...interest in him quelled his worry about his old man's matchmaker games. Then again, his dad probably had another female waiting in the wing if Alexis didn't work out.

As the crew put their equipment away and headed to their vehicles, Alexis dusted her hands off on her pants and strode toward Luke. "Same time tomorrow?" She flashed an anticipatory grin.

"Yeah. Good work today."

"See you tomorrow, boss." She turned and strode toward her beat-up Honda Civic.

Luke checked his watch. Seven fifteen. Macey would either be at home or the coffee shop she frequented in the evenings before work. She'd been on his mind all day; it wouldn't hurt to swing by and see if she was out. Maybe he could get her to elaborate on her ability to read objects. Then he might be able to figure out exactly what kind of magic she possessed and whether or not it would be strong enough for her to be his mate.

Macey pulled into a parking space at her favorite coffee shop and slid out of the driver's seat. After her dinner with Luke, last night had been alarmingly quiet. Nothing even remotely related to the case had required her attention, and while she didn't wish for another incident, a break that led to solving the case would have been nice. She'd have to do some more digging. Maybe look into recent cult activity in the area.

She paced through the parking lot toward the entrance, acutely aware of a man following behind her. With everything that had happened the past few weeks… and being this close to an alley…her senses were on high alert. She turned to greet the man and assess if he presented a threat.

Her heart dipped into her stomach as she gazed into Luke's bright-blue eyes. "What are you doing here?"

He grinned. "I felt like having a cup of coffee after work. You?"

"Same...but before work. My shift starts in two hours."

His gaze traveled from her eyes to her mouth, and back up again.

She tugged on her bottom lip, trying to think of something to say to ease the tension. It had only been twenty-four hours since she'd seen him, but she'd thought about him so much it felt like days. "You keep showing up like this, and I might start thinking you're following me."

Luke inclined his head and opened the door. "How about that coffee?"

"Okay."

A single barista stood behind the counter of the dimly lit shop. Sleek blue hair hung over her face, and a dozen earrings glinted in her ears. She put down her book and stepped toward the cash register. Macey ordered a decaf latte. Luke took his coffee black. They sat at a table by the window, and he reached across to take her hand. Tingling electricity shot up her arm, and his eyes gleamed devilishly as he gave her a knowing smile. She was getting used to the spark, but she would never get used to the way the rest of her body reacted to his touch. What was it about this man that got her so worked up?

"That's a beautiful bracelet." He ran his finger across the hammered copper band adorning her wrist. "I like the stones. Are they turquoise?"

"Yeah. It belonged to my biological mother."

"Oh?"

Why did she tell him that? She seemed to dredge up her tragic past every time she talked to him. "I don't remember her. I was three when my parents died."

He laced his fingers through hers and stared deeply into her eyes. "What happened to them?"

"Car crash. That's what I was told, anyway."

"You don't believe it?"

"I do. It's on the official report, but…"

He raised an eyebrow, urging her to finish.

She let out a nervous laugh. "I don't know what it is about you, but I always seem to spill my guts anytime you're around. I'm sorry. I don't mean to burden you with my life story."

He leaned forward, resting his elbows on the table. "It's not a burden. I want to know everything about you. So it's on the report, but…"

"But I've always had this weird feeling there's more to the story. I don't know. I did some research, and everything checks out, so…" She shrugged. "At least I know why they're gone. My sister…" She clamped her lips together. When would she learn to keep her mouth shut?

He leaned toward her. "You have a sister?"

She sucked in a breath and blew it out hard. She'd already opened the can; she might as well deal with the worms. "She ran away when we were in our third or fourth foster home. One day, everything was fine. Then she was just…gone. She didn't even say goodbye." A tear slid down her cheek, and she brushed it away. "I'm sorry. I don't think I've ever told anyone this. I didn't realize it still hurt so much."

Tightening his grip on her hand, he placed his other one on top of hers. She needed to pull herself together before she turned into a blubbering mess. Straightening, she wiped beneath her eyes. "My new parents adopted me not long after that, and they brought me here. All's well that ends well, right?"

The concern in his gaze felt way too heavy. "Do you know where she is now?"

A familiar pang of sadness shot through her chest. "I've been angry with her for so long; I've never tried to find her. But let's not talk about that, okay?" There were a million better ways to spend time with a guy as hot as Luke, and none of them involved crying over her tragic past. She locked the unwanted emotions away in the vault in the back of her mind and forced a smile. "What about you? Tell me something I don't know about Luke."

He chuckled and stared at their entwined fingers. "Well, I—"

"Excuse me." The barista approached their table. "Aren't you that detective? The one they keep interviewing on TV?"

Macey pulled her hand from Luke's and sat up straight. This was why she preferred to avoid the cameras. "Yes, I am. But I'm not at liberty to discuss an open case."

"That's okay." The barista grabbed a chair and joined them at the table. "You don't have to talk about it. Just listen. I have a theory."

"A theory." Macey looked at Luke who shrugged and crossed his arms. Everyone had a theory about it, and she'd have to hear this girl out if her time with Luke was to continue in peace.

"Yeah." The barista's eyes sparkled with excitement. "Werewolves."

Luke coughed.

Macey turned to the girl. "Your theory is werewolves?" She was nuts. There was no other way to describe her.

"Yes. See, all the women say they were raped, right? And that an animal or something killed the attacker. But what if the animal and the attacker were the same person? What if the werewolf assaulted the girl while he was in human form, and then he turned into a wolf and ran off?"

Macey *had* seen a wolf in the woods near that woman's house. Could it be possible that...no. She'd have to be nuts herself to even entertain the preposterous idea.

"Would you look at the time?" Luke tapped an imaginary watch on his wrist. "I didn't realize how late it was. I've got an early morning tomorrow, so we better get going." He rose from his chair, stepped around the barista, and offered Macey his hand.

"Yeah. You're right." Macey stood and looked at the girl. "Thanks for the coffee."

Luke led her out the door and around the corner of the building. Macey's car sat alone in the lot. "Well, that was weird." He ran a hand through his hair.

"Actually, I get that a lot. People with theories, I mean. Not werewolves. That was a first." She leaned her back against the car door and gazed up at him.

A sly smile curved his lips as he took a step toward her. "Werewolves. That's ridiculous." He leaned in closer, resting a hand against the car near her shoulder.

Her pulse sprinted. "Crazy." She could feel the heat radiating from his body. Her fingers twitched with the urge to run her hands up his chest and wrap them around his shoulders, but she resisted. She didn't want to get involved with anyone, but she wanted Luke so badly she could taste it.

Oh, to taste *him*...

"I wonder where she'd get an idea like that." He stroked her cheek with his thumb, and her breath hitched, her skin tingling where he touched her.

"I have no idea." Her heart pounded harder as he lowered his face to hers, their lips mere centimeters apart. Should she do this? It had been ages since she'd been with a man, and the way Luke touched her had her aching for more.

"You're so beautiful, Macey." His warm breath tickled her skin, and his mouth took hers. His lips were soft, the kiss firm, determined. He started to move away, but she slid her hand behind his neck, urging him to stay. She *needed* to do this.

A low moan resonated from his chest as he wrapped his arms around her and pulled her body close to his. She ran her hands over his arms and down his back, exploring every bulge and cut of his muscular frame. He broke away from the kiss to gaze into her eyes, his sapphire irises pooling with desire.

His voice was husky as he spoke. "I should probably let you get to work." He brushed his lips to her cheek, her jaw, her neck. When he reached her collarbone, he inhaled deeply, as if he were drinking in her essence. She shivered as he kissed the dip at the base of her throat and glided his mouth up to her earlobe.

"I've got a little over an hour, so I was planning to head home first. My place is just a few blocks away, if you wanted to come over." What was she thinking? This was only their second date, and she was already inviting him over? She needed to start thinking with her head and not her hormones.

Luke grinned wickedly. "Oh, I would love to, but..." He pressed against her, his arousal rubbing her hip. His lips brushed hers as he traced his fingers down her arms to hold her hands. "Not until we've had a proper date. A planned one." He leaned in and touched his lips to her ear. "And I'll need more than an hour with you."

His words seemed to suck the breath right from her lungs. She swallowed the thickness from her throat. "You would actually have to call me then. To plan a proper date."

He grinned. "I will tomorrow. I promise."

"I'm going to hold you to that."

"I never break a promise." He tugged her into a tight embrace. "I'll see you soon, Macey." The syllables of her name rolled off his tongue like music, weakening her knees.

Her chest ached at the thought of him leaving so soon. "Do you need a ride?"

"Nah. It's a glorious night. I think I'll walk." He kissed her once more and strolled away.

Macey bit her bottom lip as he sauntered out of the parking lot. He turned to wave goodbye before disappearing around the corner, and she let out a breath. How had she won the affections of such a scrumptious man? Her whole body tingled with the thoughts of how their next date might end. In her bed. Or maybe in his.

She couldn't wipe the grin off her face as she drove home and opened the front door. Her cat, Thor, greeted her with a hiss and darted under the sofa.

"Well, hello to you too, mister." She bent down and tried to coax the brown tabby out, but he met her with a swipe of his paw. "Are you jealous, Thor?"

The cat mewed.

"Well, you're going to have to get used to it. You aren't the only man in my life anymore."

CHAPTER TWELVE

"Detective Carpenter, it's so good to see you."
Macey's father grinned as she approached.

"Oh, hush, Dad. I made detective years ago. How long
is it going to take for you to get over it?" She skipped up
the concrete path and threw herself into her father's arms.
He squeezed her in a bear hug and kissed the top of her
head.

"I'm just so darn proud of you, daughter. I'll never get
over it."

"And the neighbors never hear the end of it. Come
here." Macey's mother, Jenny, gave her a hug, wrapped her
arm around her daughter, and walked her inside the small
brick house.

The scent of oregano and thyme mixed with beef and
carrots made Macey's mouth water. Her mom had made a
pot roast—Macey's favorite. She followed the enticing
aroma into the kitchen and lifted the lid on the slow
cooker. Steam wafted out, tickling her senses and making
her stomach growl. "Mmm…How much longer until
dinner?"

Her mom took the lid, closing the pot and shooing Macey away from the food. "Another fifteen minutes or so." She took a large bowl out of the cabinet and handed her several bags of chopped vegetables. "Here, mix the salad for me and tell me what's new with you. Any more trouble with…you know?"

Macey cringed. Her mother knew all about her ability, but she wished she hadn't told her about the spirit trying to possess her—or whatever had happened. All it did was worry her. "No. I'm sure it was my imagination. Forget I said anything about it."

Jenny pursed her lips and pulled a loaf of fresh, baked bread out of the oven. "Anything else going on?"

A grin curved Macey's mouth as she poured the cucumbers into the bowl. "Well, I've had a couple of dates."

Her mother paused and turned to Macey. "And how did they go?"

She dumped the bell peppers and carrots on top of the lettuce and tossed it around in the bowl. Her heart raced, and fresh adrenaline pumped through her body as she relived the surreal experience. "It was…weird. He's so easy to talk to. I told him way more than I should have."

"It's about time you opened up to someone."

"It's scary, though. You know?"

Her mom smiled. "I know you have reservations when it comes to relationships, but you deserve to be happy. Go ahead and enjoy it."

Macey grinned. Maybe her mom was right. She did deserve to be happy. Maybe it was time she opened up the gates to her heavily guarded heart and let someone in. "He's such a gentleman. He's got caramel-colored hair and gorgeous blue eyes."

"What's his name?"

"Luke Mason. He's so—"

"How do you know Luke Mason?" A musical voice drifted into the room, followed by a rotund, elderly woman with curly gray hair and dark brown eyes. She glided across the kitchen as if her feet didn't touch the floor beneath her long, burnt-orange skirt.

"Roberta! I didn't hear you come in." Jenny wiped her hands on a dish cloth and hugged the woman.

"William let me in. Your husband is such a charmer." Her smile lit up her face, and her eyes twinkled as she turned her attention to Macey. "You must be Macey. Your mother has told me so much about you."

Macey held out her hand to shake, but Roberta pushed it away, pulling her into a big hug instead. Macey tentatively hugged her back, patting her on the shoulder until she released her hold. She glanced at her mother, who smiled and busied herself with preparing the meal.

"Come. Sit." Roberta motioned for Macey to follow her to the dining room table.

Macey hesitated, looking at her mother.

"Go ahead," Jenny said. "Dinner's almost ready. I'll bring it to the table."

She followed Roberta, settling into a chair opposite her at the table. The woman's smile was so dazzling, she couldn't help but smile in return.

Roberta folded her hands on the table. "How do you know Luke?"

Heat rose to Macey's cheeks. "We kinda had a date last night." She picked at imaginary lint on her shirt, afraid to look in Roberta's eyes. Would this woman tell him what she said?

"Hmm…" Roberta picked up the small, red glasses

that hung from a beaded chain around her neck and settled them on her nose. She narrowed a long and intense gaze at Macey. Then, she closed her eyes and inhaled deeply, absently nodding her head. The uncomfortable moment lasted no more than half a minute, but Macey's palms starting sweating.

"Interesting," Roberta muttered as she opened her eyes.

What had that been about? The woman seemed to have almost slipped into a trance. Desperate to change the subject, Macey shifted in her seat and asked, "How do you know my mom?"

Roberta's demeanor shifted back to cheerfulness. "I teach a meditation class at the civic center. Jenny joined a few weeks ago."

"That's cool." She had no idea her mother was into meditation. Maybe she needed to visit more often.

"It's been such an eye opening experience." The sound of her mother's voice startled her, and she jumped.

"God, Mom. I need to put a bell on you. You scared me!"

"Sorry, sweetheart." Jenny set the table with plates, silverware, and full glasses of sweet tea. Then she scurried to the kitchen and brought out the food. "Soup's on," she called over her shoulder to William.

With dinner on the table, they loaded their plates and began eating. The potatoes melted in Macey's mouth, and she had to remind herself to slow down. She didn't get home-cooking like this very often, and it was so good, she wanted to shovel it all in.

"Macey." Roberta dabbed the napkin at the corners of her mouth. "Your mother asked me to come over to talk to you about the trouble you had with a spirit. It seems you have an undeveloped gift you may need help with."

"Mom!" Macey glared at her mother. Her ability had always been their secret—she didn't want anyone to think she was a freak.

Jenny shrugged. "I was worried about you. Roberta is a psychic medium, so I thought she could help."

That explained the strange behavior. Macey's ears burned with embarrassment or anger—she didn't know which. Her mother had no right to share her secret. If Macey wanted to tell people, that was her business. But to go around telling complete strangers? What would the guys at work think of her if they found out?

She turned to Roberta and spoke through clenched teeth. "I don't know what my mother told you about my *ability*, but I'm handling it fine. And I'd appreciate it if you didn't talk about it to anyone else. My job depends on my sanity...or people perceiving me as sane."

Dropping her napkin on her plate, Macey rose to her feet and stormed out of the dining room. She wanted to slam the door behind her as she left the house, but she refrained from the childish action. Instead, she carefully clicked it shut, dropped down on the front steps, and sat with her head in her hands.

She'd overreacted, but embarrassment stopped her from going back inside. Her mother should've warned her. If she would have let her know why she'd invited Roberta, Macey would've had time to process. To avoid acting like she did. What a fool she'd made of herself. She needed to apologize to Roberta, at least.

She was about to do just that when the door opened and Roberta stepped onto the porch. Macey stood and leaned against the hand rail. "I'm sorry, Roberta. It's not something I tell many people, and you caught me off guard."

Roberta held up a finger. "No need to apologize. It can be hard accepting a gift you don't understand." She folded Macey's hand into her arm. "Let's walk."

They strolled up the driveway, and Macey led her to a walking trail through a wooded area behind the neighborhood. Massive oak trees created a canopy over the gravel path, their leaves dappling the sunlight on the ground. A gentle breeze rustled the branches, stirring the scent of earth and arbor in the air. Roberta's jolly demeanor slipped away, turning serious as she began to speak.

"There are things in this world that aren't as they seem. Some of us are gifted enough to see things as they are. Most of us are not. How long have you had the ability to read objects, Macey?"

She shrugged. "I don't know. As long as I can remember."

They paused at a bridge that crossed a narrow stream. "And you haven't sought help in developing it. Why?"

"My dad doesn't believe in it, so he won't talk about it. And, Mom…she taught me to keep it to myself. That's why it threw me off when she told you."

Roberta's musical laugh danced on the breeze. "Jenny is opening her mind to many things. I'm sorry it came so late. It must have been very hard keeping it to yourself."

"Not really. I've told a few people…People I trust. Some believe me, some don't."

"Luke believes you."

She pulled her hand from Roberta's grip. She'd trusted Luke, and to think he'd discussed her ability behind her back caused a sharp pain in her chest. How stupid of her to talk about herself with a man she barely knew. "How do you... Did you talk to him? How do you know him?"

"We run in similar circles, so to speak." She smiled knowingly. "He didn't share your secret with me, but I know him and I know he believes you."

Macey let out her breath as relief loosened the tightness in her chest.

Roberta stepped onto the bridge and turned to her. "Running water increases a spirit's ability to manifest. Were you near a stream when it happened?"

"It's possible, but I didn't see one. I was out in the woods...kinda like this." She spun in a circle, her senses suddenly heightened at the similarity of the scene. A warm breeze caressed her skin, and birds chirped in the trees above. Nothing out of the ordinary. No ghosts dancing in the wind. She turned to find Roberta staring at her.

"That's good. You should always pay attention to your surroundings."

Macey laughed. "As a cop, I always do. But now I have to pay attention to things I can't see?" She sat on the edge of the bridge. "It really happened, didn't it? I think I convinced myself it didn't."

Roberta eased down next to her. "It did, indeed. I sensed the remnants of its essence in you when we hugged. And I sense it is near now, though I can't tell where. Somehow, it's blocking me."

Macey swallowed. "It's here?"

"It's following you. And it's powerful."

"Well, crap." Just what she needed. As if her ability wasn't freaky enough, now she had a real ghost haunting her.

"Do you know what it wants?" Roberta asked.

She sighed and rubbed her temples. "It could only be

after one thing. It wants to stop me. Have you heard about the case I'm working in the Quarter?"

Roberta raised her eyebrows. "I have."

"It's the ghost of one of the perpetrators. The one whose body we found." She rubbed her arms, suddenly chilled by the reality. "I saw his face when he got… inside me."

Her eyes tightened briefly before she forced a half-smile. "Try not to worry. You're strong, Macey. If you fought it out once, you can do it again."

She threw up her arms. "Well, that's great. I have to spend the rest of my life on the lookout for an evil spirit who wants to possess me? Do you think it'll leave me alone once I solve the case? *If* I solve the case?"

"If?"

"Well, so far, nothing in this case makes sense."

"That's because you're looking at it from a strictly human perspective. You need to open your mind to other possibilities."

"What kind of possibilities?" Werewolves? No, thanks. She'd already heard that one.

Roberta sighed and brushed a stray strand of hair from Macey's face, a motherly gesture that put her fears at ease. She could trust this woman. She felt it in her bones.

"There's only so much I can tell you. But if you'll allow me to help you develop your gift, the secrets will reveal themselves to you."

"But if you know something that will help solve the case, you have to—"

"I know what I know. This case is bigger than you, child. Truly solving it will change your life forever. I can help you if you are open to it. Are you ready?"

Macey chewed the inside of her cheek. Did she want

her life changed? Did she have choice? "I guess so. Can you help me get rid of this spirit that's stalking me too?"

"I'm afraid only you can get rid of it for good."

An icy entity snaked around Macy's legs, spiraling up to her ear. *"You'll never get rid of me."* She jumped to her feet, spinning around, trying to locate the spirit.

"Roberta?" Her voice came out as a breathy whisper.

"It's here, isn't it?" Roberta said. "It's still blocking me. Don't let it in." She rose to her feet and stepped to Macey's side.

"Now, where did we leave off? Oh, yeah. I was trying to get inside you."

Her body trembled as the familiar prickling sensation covered her skin. "How do I keep it out?" Panic tipped in her voice.

"Same way you did last time, child. Use your mind to put up a shield."

Macey imagined a bubble of white light surrounding her body. She tensed her muscles, pushing back as the spirit tried to enter her. The sensation of a million needles lodged in her skin, the spirit pressing them in, her will pushing them out.

"Don't listen to that damn witch. I'm going to get inside you, so you might as well stop fighting."

"I won't let you in." She pushed back with all her might, gritting her teeth as sweat beaded on her forehead. A metal curtain slammed down in her mind, shutting the spirit out. Her body trembled, fatigue setting in and threatening to crumble the wall she'd so forcefully built. Then, the pricking stopped. The darkness that had closed in around her dissipated, lifting a weight off her chest.

"I'll get you another way, then." The spirit swirled

around her in frantic circles before shooting up into the air.

Dizzy and drained, she leaned her hand against a tree trunk, trying to catch her ragged breath. "Did you hear what he said?"

Roberta put a hand on her shoulder. "I couldn't hear a thing. He was only talking to you."

In his wolf form, Luke crouched in the brush a few yards away from Macey. Initially, he'd berated himself for following her, but now he was glad he did. Something was tormenting her, though he couldn't wrap his mind around what it was. A regular spirit didn't have that kind of power, and once a demon was vanquished, it went straight to hell. It couldn't hang around in spirit form. Unless...

It had to be the half-demon James had killed a few days ago. But why wouldn't it have reincarnated its own body? Was it more powerful this way? A low growl rumbled in his chest. That explained why her eyes had turned red. The bastard had already gotten inside her.

Lying on his stomach, he inched forward on his haunches to get a better view of the scene. Macey leaned against a thick oak, her head tipped back so it rested against the tree. Long, golden hair flowed over her bare shoulders, cascading down to the center of her lavender tank top. Luke's chest tightened. So beautiful. Delicate. The fragility of human life made his heart ache.

The witch stood next to her, stroking her arm in comfort.

"He said he'd get to me another way." Macey's voice trembled as she spoke.

"You'll have to keep your guard up, then," Roberta said.

Macey shivered and whipped her head around. "He's here. I can feel him."

Luke rose onto his paws. He sensed the demon too. Scanning the scene, his gaze fixed on a branch, as thick as his thigh, swaying above the women. The air was stagnant; no breeze could've caused the movement. The branch pressed down, then snapped up as if it were pushed. He growled a warning.

Still out of sight, he crept closer, his gaze shifting from Macey to the tree. What the hell was the demon doing? Spirits weren't strong enough to move—

Before he could finish the thought, instinct took over. He leapt from his hiding place and bounded toward the women. Macey let out a yelp as he plowed into them, knocking them out of the line of the falling branch.

The bough crashed to the ground, splitting in half with a thundering *crack*. With the women safe, Luke prowled the area, howling a warning to the fiend. No one messed with his woman.

He lifted his muzzle, inhaling the coppery tinge of fresh blood. Macey was hurt. His stomach dropped, and he turned slowly to the pair. Roberta sat where she'd landed, dusting dirt and leaves from her skirt. Macey sat frozen, her gaze locked on his wolf form. Had she even noticed the gash on her thigh? Blood ran in ribbons over her knee, turning black as the ground absorbed it.

Luke cautiously took another step forward to examine her. Other than the cut on her leg, she seemed to be okay. He lowered his head and whimpered, trying his best to show Macey he wouldn't hurt her. It didn't work.

She grasped Roberta's shirt, never taking her gaze off him. "Roberta...I think we're about to get eaten."

"Oh, nonsense. It's just a wolf, and it saved our lives. Sit still until it goes away." Roberta looked into his eyes and raised an eyebrow as she spoke to Macey. "Do you sense the spirit, dear?"

Macey shook her head. "N-n...no. I think it's gone."

"Okay, then. We're safe." She looked at the cut on Macey's leg. "You've got a little scratch from your fall." She turned to Luke. "Nothing a salve and a bandage won't fix. I'm sure the wolf will leave now." She emphasized the last two words as if making sure he got the point.

He couldn't do anything else, so he blew a hard breath through his nose, turned, and ran into the woods. He'd have to trust Macey's intuition that the fiend had left. He didn't sense it there, but that didn't mean anything. It was only half demon, and it didn't have a goddamn body.

What the hell were they doing out in the woods again? Roberta, of all people, should've realized the danger Macey was in. That's if she knew it was a demon spirit.

When he first saw Macey with the witch, he'd thought he had it all figured out. That Macey was a witch as well, and she'd been holding back when they talked at the restaurant. But given the nature of the women's conversation, he wasn't sure now.

Could she really possess so much power and not even realize it? Growing up in the magical community, Luke couldn't fathom having no one to talk to about his abilities. Of course, the breadth of his abilities consisted of turning into a wolf on command and changing back into a human. Macey could read energy. And apparently be possessed by it.

He broke into a sprint, bounding through the forest

with long strides, leaves crunching and twigs snapping under his massive paws. He needed to watch her more closely. To protect her. The thought of that fiend hurting her was enough to drive him mad. He'd already failed one woman. It wouldn't happen again.

At least she'd have Roberta coaching her now. Roberta was the most powerful witch he knew. She was a member of the local coven, but she didn't get involved in their politics. If anyone could train Macey to use her gifts, she could. The idea relaxed him a little, but he had to be extra vigilant to make sure his woman stayed safe.

His woman. He already thought of her that way, but she wasn't his yet. He still didn't know if it was possible for an alpha to mate with a non-were. He'd have to find out soon.

CHAPTER THIRTEEN

Two days passed with no word from Luke. Macey's elation after their dates deflated into a feeling of emptiness. And, they *had* been dates. Though they didn't start out that way, by the end of each evening, they were definitely in date mode. He'd even kissed her, for goodness sake! Then she'd invited him back to her house…

But he'd turned her down.

She gripped the steering wheel so tightly her knuckles turned white as she drove up Chartres Avenue. In the passenger seat, Bryce sat oblivious to the inner torment storming inside her.

"You trying to choke it to death?" Her partner nodded toward Macey's hands. Maybe he wasn't completely oblivious. "What's up, boss?"

She relaxed her death grip and let out a long sigh. "When two people have a…date…and they have a really good time…and the guy says he'll call, how long should it take?"

Bryce shook his head and mumbled, "Sorry I asked." He took a deep breath and peered thoughtfully out the window. "You're asking *me* for dating advice? The perpetual bachelor?" His goofy grin helped lighten the mood.

The tension in Macey's chest eased its grip. "You're the only guy I trust. The only person I can talk to."

He sighed. "Okay. How long has it been?"

"Two days." When she said it out loud, it didn't sound nearly as long as it felt.

Bryce laughed. "That's nothing, Mace. Give the boy time. He's probably trying to figure out what to say when he calls. Patience, grasshopper."

"It's hard to be patient after..." Heat flushed her cheeks at the memory of the kiss. Did she want to share all the juicy details with her partner?

"After?"

She huffed and fiddled with the AC controls. She had goose bumps thinking about the way she fit so perfectly into Luke's arms. At the personal information she'd shared so willingly with him. "He was easy to talk to. I told him a lot of things I don't normally tell people. He probably thinks I'm a freak now. That's why he hasn't called."

Bryce shifted in his seat to face her. "He doesn't think you're a freak." He tapped his finger against his chin, his eyes growing wide. "You're falling for this guy, aren't you?"

"What? Don't be ridiculous." She tried to laugh off the accusation. "I just...like him a little."

"Your confidence is slipping. I've never heard you question what a man thinks about you."

That's because I've never cared. "Okay, I like him a lot. Happy? He's different..." Cool relief flooded her system as a call came over the radio. At least she didn't have to talk about Luke anymore. Unfortunately, the call confirmed another murder.

Macey floored it, and five minutes later they arrived at the scene. As they approached the historic mansion-turned-apartment-building, the sharp, coppery scent of blood crept to her senses. In her line of work, she should've been used to the aromas of death. But the smell singed her nostrils. She paused in front of the structure, leaning her hand against the beige wood. Flipping open her notebook, she pretended to read as the images and energy stored in the building flowed through her fingertips and into her mind. She shuffled through the pictures, but found nothing of use. Maybe she'd get something inside the victim's apartment.

A steady stream of light from a gas lantern illuminated the sidewalk in front of the building. A glass fixture enclosed the flame, so the wind couldn't blow out the fire. Yet, the lantern in front of Macey flickered as if a breeze blew by. The flame danced, rising and falling as it shimmied in the non-existent wind. Even if the fire were exposed, the night hung dead still. Not even the slightest breeze alleviated the heavy, southern heat that clung to her skin like a wet blanket.

The flame stilled as the breeze circled Macey, raising goose bumps on the back of her neck. Was it another spirit trying to contact her? If so, it needed to try harder. She wasn't a psychic.

"The victim's this way." A uniformed officer motioned for them to follow him into an alley. A crowd had gathered behind the police tape, and they had to weave their way through to get to the courtyard and the body.

Macey swallowed down the bile that formed in the back of her throat as the stench assaulted her. What she would have given to have a man's nose. The smell never bothered them. Bryce wandered off to talk to another officer while she approached the body. She stifled a gasp as her gaze landed on the lifeless eyes staring into the night sky.

Another rape victim. Just like the last one, her abdomen was obliterated. But nothing ate this woman. The shot gun that lay at her feet was responsible for tearing the enormous gash through her stomach and out her back. Bits of flesh and bone lay scattered about the woman's head, no doubt the remnants of what blew out her back when she was shot. But why would the murderer leave the weapon lying at her feet?

She turned to the officer next to her. "Witnesses?"

"No one saw the shooter. Her roommate's out of town, but neighbors heard the shot. Only one fired."

"One was all it took," she muttered under her breath. "Has her apartment been searched?"

"Yes, ma'am. No evidence of a struggle. Victim was a neat freak, for sure. Carpets looked freshly vacuumed. The only interesting thing we turned up so far was this." He handed her a plastic bag containing a single slip of paper.

Macey squinted to read the pristine handwriting in the dark. Two lines centered on the page read:

I have to get rid of the devil inside me.
This is the only way I know how.

Macey returned the evidence to the officer. This wasn't a murder. It was a suicide.

The devil inside me... Was the woman possessed? Could the spirit that had tried to contact her earlier be the victim or the "devil" inside her? Too many questions clouded her mind.

"I've seen enough. How 'bout you, boss?" Bryce said.

"Yeah, me too." She raised her voice so the others would hear. "Pack it up, boys." As the myriad of questions spun through her head, she followed her partner toward the alley where the crowd was finally dispersing.

"I think I'm gonna hang behind and...you know."

A slow smile raised the corners of his mouth. "I figured as much. You always get that puzzled look on your face. I'll catch a ride back to the station and take care of the paperwork. Our shift's almost over anyway."

As Bryce strode off toward the other officers, Macey turned back to the scene. The coroner's men were already packing up to take the body to the morgue, but it was just as well. Macey was looking for spirits. Or at least the energy they left behind.

Inside, the victim's apartment appeared as the officer had described. Pristine. The trails left by a vacuum cleaner lined up evenly across the light beige carpet. Framed photographs on the mantle suggested the woman had many friends and a boyfriend. Macey rested her hand against the brick fireplace and closed her eyes. Happy images of the victim's life played in her mind like old home movies. She was rarely alone. Always surrounded by friends and family. And love. Only the most recent memories contained any sort of dismay.

"What am I missing?" Macey investigated the rest of the apartment, but couldn't find any physical evidence. No spirits tried to contact her. She made her way down the stairs and exited the building. She should go home. Bryce was taking care of the paperwork; there was no need for her to return to the station. But could she sleep after witnessing a gruesome scene like that?

She sighed. Of course she could. She'd lock the images away in the vault in the back of her mind where she kept every horrendous act she'd encountered. Before she left, she'd give her ability one last try. She meandered to the front of the building near the gas lamp that had flickered. That had to have been a spirit trying to contact her earlier.

As she rested her hand against the wood, a familiar silhouette flashing in the corner of her eye caught her attention. It had the same broad shoulders as the one she thought she'd seen in the woods at the other scene. He stood in a doorway across the alley, the backlighting making it impossible for her to discern his features. She stepped toward the figure, and he bolted from his position.

Damn it! She'd seen him. Luke dashed up the alley, walking as fast as he could. To run would only bring more attention to himself. He'd just had to get a closer look, hadn't he? If he'd have stayed in the shadows like he normally did, she would've walked right past him. James had beaten the officers to the scene and had already removed the bits of shattered fetus from the body, incinerating the flesh to conceal the evidence. Luke had no business getting so close. Or hanging around as long as he had. His emotions were making him sloppy.

"Excuse me, sir. Sir, stop!"

Busted. He slowly turned around and raised his hands in mock surrender. "Hey, Macey. Don't shoot."

She dropped her hands to her sides, and her mouth hung open. "Luke?" With three purposeful strides, she closed the distance between them. "Why were you running away from me?"

"I…" He huffed a hard sigh. *Might as well tell her the*

truth. A little of it, anyway. "I didn't want you to think I was following you. You've already accused me of it once."

Redness rose on her cheeks, and she gazed at the ground. "Were you? Or…what are you doing here?"

He shrugged and shoved his hands into his pockets. "I saw the crowd and was curious. I might have lingered a little longer because you were there." That wasn't exactly a lie.

"Oh." She tilted her head and narrowed her eyes. "Do you ever go north of the Quarter? Masters Street area?"

"Can't say that I do." He would have to be more careful.

"No. I guess not."

Awkward silence hung between them. Her mouth opened a few times as if she were going to speak, but the words didn't come. As he watched the movement of her lips, all he could think about was how they'd felt pressed to his: soft, warm, moist. He could almost taste them.

"I'm sorry I haven't called you," he finally said. "I've been tied up with work." *And killing demons.*

"It's okay." She waved away his apology.

He took her hand and laced his fingers through hers. "No, it's not. I shouldn't have left you waiting like that."

Sucking in a sharp breath, she swallowed hard as she inched closer to his body. She glanced around at the empty alley and angled her head up toward his. Her pink tongue glided over her lips before she spoke. "You're here now."

He groaned. Did she have any idea how sexy she was? Of course she did, and she used it to her full advantage. He shouldn't have been pursuing her yet. Not until he had all the facts and had presented them to his father. He'd spent the past two days researching the family lines to see if there was any chance Macey could be his mate. A handful of cases existed where wolves had mated with other magic beings and still had were offspring. Mostly witches, mages, and fae, though—never with a simple psychic.

But Macey was more than that. Her power coursed through him every time they touched, taunting him with its mystery. And there was more magic in her. It had been suppressed long ago, or never formed, but surely he could help her chip away at whatever held it back. Then he could fulfill his duty as alpha and follow his heart as a man.

And right at that moment, with Macey's luscious lips parted and ready, he was all man. He leaned in and took her mouth in a gentle kiss. Her warm velvet lips sent tingling energy shooting straight to his heart. He expected her to pull away, but she leaned into the kiss, pressing her soft curves against his body and wrapping her arms around his waist. He cradled the back of her neck with his hand and slipped his tongue into her honey-sweet mouth. If only her hair hung loose; he'd have loved to tangle his hands in her silky locks.

He tilted his head back to look into her eyes. What thoughts swam behind those emerald pools? Did she feel like she'd known him forever, the way he felt about her? They were meant to be together. Could she sense it too? He hadn't spoken to her in two days, but the time and distance melted away as he held her in his arms.

Sighing, she leaned her head against his chest. "I was beginning to think you weren't interested in me."

How could she think such a thing? He placed his hands on her shoulders and gently pushed her away, so he could look at her. "I am *very* interested in you, but my life is complicated, and—"

She touched her index finger against his lips. "It's okay."

He grabbed her hand and playfully bit her finger. "Would you stop saying that? There's no excuse for my behavior, and I need to make it up to you. How about we get out of this alley? Can I buy you a cup of coffee? Or do you need to go back to work?"

She grinned. "Actually, my shift just ended, and coffee sounds fantastic." She looked at her watch and furrowed her brow. "Don't you have to be at work in a few hours? It's late for someone with a day job."

"I'm a big boy. I'll be okay." Werewolves didn't need as much sleep as humans, anyway.

"Well, all right then. My car's across the street. Do you want to follow me?"

"Actually, my truck's at home. I was out for a walk when I...uh...saw the commotion." He shoved his hands in his pockets and prayed she'd buy his story. Who went for a walk at one in the morning?

"Hmm..." Her emerald eyes narrowed briefly before a sly smile curved her lips. "Night owl, huh? Me too. C'mon, I'll drive."

———

Macey climbed into the driver's seat, and Luke slid in next to her. As soon as he closed the door, a static charge seemed to build in the confined space, drawing her toward him, making her palms sweat. She cranked up the AC and held her hands in front of the vents to dry them.

Luke buckled his seatbelt and chuckled. "Nervous?" He nodded to her hands.

She yanked them away from the vents and wiped them on her pants. "Not nervous. I don't know how to describe it. You...make me feel things."

"You make me feel things too." He caught her gaze, and the overwhelming urge to reach across the console and pull his mouth to hers consumed her. Something about Luke awakened a long-forgotten primal instinct deep inside her. The question was, could she keep her heart guarded while satisfying those instincts?

He reached for her hand and held it between both of his. "I have a confession."

"Uh oh. That doesn't sound good."

He took a deep breath and blew it out hard. "I *was* following you tonight."

Her heart paused for a moment before giving one solid slam against her chest, and a red flag planted itself firmly in the center of her brain. But Luke wasn't a stalker. His actions may have been questionable, but for some unknown reason, she trusted him down to her core. *Hear the man out, Mace. Surely he has a good reason.* "Why were you following me?"

"We have a police scanner at the bar. It's a...hobby of my old man's. When I heard the report come through, I figured you'd be at the scene, so I came out to see you. After not calling you for two days, I thought my apology would be more believable in person."

"Oh, that's nice of you." A little weird, but nice. "But, if you wanted to see me, why did you run from me?"

He let out an embarrassed chuckle and gazed at their entwined hands. "Once I got here, I realized how creepy it was, so I tried to get away before you found out it was me."

She chewed her bottom lip. So he wasn't the most suave person on the planet; neither was she. Plucking the red flag from her mind, she tossed it aside. "I see."

"I needed to see you again. I thought it would be a romantic gesture, but it turned out to be stalkerish." He shrugged. "With all our chance encounters, and your detective mind, I thought you might be suspicious. Better to come clean now, right?" He chuckled. "I just made things weird, didn't I?"

"Yes." Though, honestly, every time Luke was near, her brain seemed to shut down and let her hormones take over. The coincidence hadn't seemed odd at the time, but she may have been suspicious later, when her brain started working again. She squeezed his hand. "It's okay. I like weird."

Coming to a crime scene to see her was a strange choice, but no one had ever shown so much interest in her. She could forgive his lack of judgment this time. Besides, with his warm, musky scent filling the car and that strange energy dancing between them, all she could think about was what he would look like with his clothes lying on the floor beside the bed.

His shoulders moved away from his ears as his tension released. "That's good to know." He leaned across the console, as far as the seatbelt would allow, and stroked the back of his fingers down her cheek. "I'd like to kiss you now, if that's okay."

She didn't bother with an answer. Unhooking her seatbelt, she leaned into him, crushing her mouth to his. She shouldn't have been doing this. She didn't want to get involved with a man.

Damn it, why did her brain have to turn on now? She needed to plant her butt back in her seat and end this before he got close enough to hurt her. It would be the logical thing to do.

But as he cupped his hand behind her neck and slipped his tongue between her lips, her logic flew out the window right along with her inhibitions. Red flag? What red flag? She wanted this man.

And she could have him in a physical sense without getting her heart involved, couldn't she? It was worth a try.

She held his face in her hands and touched her forehead to his. "How about that coffee?"

"I've got a Keurig at my place…three blocks away."

She closed her eyes as a shudder ran through her entire body. "Show me the way."

Shoving the voice of reason into the vault, she drove to Luke's house and followed him inside. As soon as he shut the front door, she grabbed him by the shoulders and took his mouth again. If she stopped to think about what she was doing, she'd talk herself out it.

A growl emanated from Luke's chest as he slid his arms around her waist and held her close. The evidence of his desire pressed into her stomach, and she glided her hand between their bodies to rub him through his jeans.

He sucked in a sharp breath. "Are you sure you want to do this? We haven't even had a proper date."

It was just sex. As long as she could convince herself it didn't mean anything more, she'd be fine. This basal, primal urge she felt to possess him, to make him hers, was physical…nothing more. Grabbing his shirt by the hem, she yanked it over his head. Her mouth watered as she ran her hands along his firm chest, down his defined abs, and popped the button on his jeans.

He gripped her hips. "Can I take that as a yes?"

"Yes." *God, yes.*

He tugged her to the bedroom, took a condom from a drawer, and then tossed it on the nightstand. The nagging voice of reason tried to escape from the vault, warning her she was getting in too deep, but she locked it away.

The hunger in his eyes was unlike anything she'd seen, and as she undressed before him, his pupils dilated with desire. "Christ, Macey, you're gorgeous."

She unhooked her bra and dropped it on the floor, and another growl rumbled from his chest, awakening every feminine urge inside her body.

"Take your hair down."

She yanked the band from her hair, letting it spiral out of its knot and tumble over her shoulders. Then she slid down his zipper and pushed his pants and underwear to the floor.

Holy moly, he was huge.

"I need you, Luke." God, did she need him. She grabbed the condom and pushed him onto the bed. Forget about foreplay. It had been three years since she'd been with a man, and with Luke's dick hard and ready, she couldn't wait any longer.

She rolled the condom down his length and straddled him. Using her hand to guide him to her center, she sheathed him, moaning as his girth filled her completely. Never in her life had she felt so much desire, so much sheer need, emanating from somewhere deep inside her being. In this moment, he belonged to her...and she belonged to him.

Sliding his hands up her thighs, he clutched her hips and guided her up and down his thick cock. The electricity she normally felt when she touched him increased one hundred fold, rocketing through her body and setting her soul ablaze. She wanted to go slow, to make the searing intensity last, but as she moved her hips, the delicious friction of him sliding in and out sent her too close to the edge. With her hands on his chest, her nails digging into his skin, she lost herself to the moment. To the man.

He locked eyes with her, and licking his thumb, he pressed it to her clit, rubbing her sensitive nub in circles, sending more fire coursing through her veins. She couldn't take any more. Her orgasm ripped through her body, sending a shock of pleasure from her womb to her toes. Her legs trembled, and she collapsed on top of him, gasping for breath, burying her face in his neck.

He held onto her, moving his hips, each thrust sending another electric jolt of ecstasy through her system. He groaned as his own orgasm overtook him, showering her neck and shoulder in kisses, nipping at her sensitive skin as he found his release.

As her breathing slowed, she raised her head to look at him. His satisfied smile tugged at her heart, but the bright-red scratches trailing down his chest made her stomach drop. "I'm so sorry." She slid onto her side and ran her finger over the marks. "I hurt you."

"Nah. I'm fine." He rubbed a hand over his pecs. "They're already fading; no harm done." Rising onto an elbow, he kissed her cheek before whispering into her ear, "I liked it."

His breath against her skin made her shiver, and her stomach flip-flopped at his playful words. The marks faded before her eyes, turning into light pink lines before disappearing completely. She must not have scratched him as hard as she'd thought. She looked into his eyes, and her heart raced into overdrive. "I...liked it too."

Rolling onto her back, she stared at the ceiling. What had she just done? She'd acted like an animal, letting her primal desires overtake her, acting on instinct rather than listening to reason. For the first time in her life, she felt a sense of completeness. Something about being here with Luke felt so good...so *right*.

Luke slid out of bed and tossed the condom in the trash, and a smile tugged at Macey's lips. He was all smooth skin and hard muscle, and his backside looked as good as his front. Maybe she should let her instincts take over more often.

He climbed back into bed and pulled her close, and she allowed herself to get lost in the comfort of his embrace. Though he was nearly a foot taller than her, their bodies fit together perfectly, as if they were made for each other.

He pressed his lips to the top of her head, and his chest vibrated as he spoke. "If this is what I get for stalking you, I'll have to do it more often."

She propped her head on her hand and grinned. "Next time, I want a proper date first."

"So there will be a next time?"

She bit her bottom lip. If she had her way, there would be lots of next times. "I hope so."

"Good."

She laid her head on his shoulder. What was she saying? If she started going on dates with him, she'd start feeling things she didn't want to feel. She'd already opened up to him way more than she should have, and those feelings she didn't want to feel were starting to creep into her heart.

So much for the need being purely physical. Coldness flashed through her core, and she sat up. This couldn't be happening, could it? She swallowed the lump from her throat. The feelings weren't creeping; they'd slammed into her chest like a sucker-punch before she even had time to react.

"Where are you going?" He took her hand.

Good question. She had to get away or she would drown if she didn't come up for air. "You have to get up in a few hours. I should let you sleep."

He rose onto his elbows. "I'd sleep better with you curled up next to me."

His grin melted her heart, soothing her frazzled nerves. Something about his presence calmed her, making her want to stay in bed with him all night and all day tomorrow. But she couldn't. He needed to sleep, and she needed some alone time so she could sort out her emotions, decide what these strange new feelings meant. "I'm not tired. I work nights, remember?"

"I'll stay up with you then."

She smiled and rested a hand on his chest. The familiar tingle shimmied up her arm, and she was tempted to slide her fingers beneath the sheets. His smooth skin and intoxicating scent beckoned her to stay, but she fought the urge. She needed to gather her scattered thoughts and figure out if she was capable of letting Luke in.

Sliding out of bed, she picked up her clothes and dressed. "I'd rather you get some sleep, so maybe you'll remember to call me and ask me out on that date you keep promising me."

He sighed as he rolled out of bed and pulled on his underwear. "Let me at least walk you to the door."

He kissed her as she left and stood in the doorway until she got in her car and backed out of the driveway. Her chest tightened as she shifted into drive and headed home. She was in way over her head with this man. He was sweet, sexy, amazing in bed...

She'd built a fortress around her heart, but she may have found a man worth lowering the drawbridge for.

Luke only got three hours of sleep, but he woke the next morning feeling more refreshed and lively than he had in ages. Making love to Macey had been better than he could've imagined...and he'd imagined it plenty of times. It was a shame she took off the way she did, but he didn't want to push her to stay. Neither of them had planned on the night ending with them in bed together, but he was so damn glad it had.

He could've lain there all morning imagining her beautiful face. The way her warm, supple body would feel against his as they cuddled the day away. But he had a job to do and a pack to run. *Damn responsibility.* After last night, there was no doubt in his mind Macey was the one for him. She was his fate-bound; it didn't matter that she wasn't a werewolf. He couldn't deny fate.

The first order of business would be to convince the current alpha that Macey was an acceptable mate. Once his old man was on board, everyone else would follow.

After getting ready for work, he skipped down the stairs. Bypassing his truck, he took advantage of the gorgeous morning and walked to the job site. It was only six blocks away, and his body buzzed with excited energy. The morning sun hadn't risen high enough to peek over the buildings in the Quarter, so he was spared from the sweltering heat that would soon fry the dew from the grass. Jackson Square bustled with activity as the local artists and entertainers hurried to set up their displays as the tourists ventured out of their hotel rooms. Fortune tellers set up folding tables on the sidewalk, and painters hung their creations on the wrought iron fence that enclosed the grassy park. Luke waved at a man encrusted in gold paint from head to toe. He smiled to reveal a set of matching gold teeth.

A line of people had already formed outside Café Du Monde as they waited for their taste of the venue's famous beignets and café au lait. The sweet scent of fried pastries beckoned to him, and he almost stopped in for his own French donut smothered in powdered sugar.

But the pair of glowing red eyes watching him in the distance drew his attention away from the café. Luke stopped cold and returned the stare. *Christ! These things aren't supposed to be out in the daytime.*

A low growl resonated in his chest as he crept toward the fiend. The demon's wicked grin revealed a set of perfectly white, human teeth. Luke paused and eyed the creature. It looked too human to be a creature from hell. He angled his nose upward and inhaled a deep breath. The distinct demon-like smell of rotting flesh floated on the breeze. It was the half-demon born of the first victim. It had to be. He appeared to be a teenager, which put him at the right developmental age for a halfling.

Luke took two more tentative steps forward. When the demon merely sneered, he sprinted, barreling through the crowd toward the fiend. The halfling spun around and dashed away, cutting in and out of groups of tourists before darting into the French Market.

Luke cursed and skidded to a stop at the entrance to the bazaar. Row after row of tables filled with every kind of merchandise imaginable lined the shopping pavilion.

People meandered up and down the columns of parcels, and the demon blended right in. At Luke's height, he could see over most of the patrons' heads, but the fiend was nowhere to be found.

Luke clambered his way through the market, checking the eyes of every male he passed. None were red. The demon was probably half-way to his hideout before Luke made it to the end of the pavilion. Exhaling a deflated sigh, he made a left on St. Philip to head to the bar. His civilian work would have to wait.

CHAPTER FOURTEEN

"What the hell is that bag doing here? People can probably smell it a mile away. Are you trying to get us caught?"

Jimmy curled into a ball on the corner of his futon. He didn't know where in the room his brother was, but the gash on his forehead hadn't healed from the last time Ross had struck him. He didn't want to get hit again.

"You never told me what to do with it. I…thought you might still want it." He ducked his head between his forearms and held his breath, waiting for the blow that never came. Instead, a cool breeze rustled through his hair.

"Don't worry, brother. I'm not going to hit you again. We need your face to heal for what I have planned."

Jimmy peeked his head up and looked around the room. He would never get used to his brother not having a body. It just wasn't right. He wished Ross would get back into his old body and leave him alone. Jimmy didn't like the way it felt to have his brother inside him. He didn't know what Ross had planned, but he was sure he wouldn't like it either.

Jimmy cringed before asking his next question. He hated asking questions because they were always stupid, and stupid questions got stupid answers. Or punches to the gut. "What should I do with you...uh...the bag?"

"Burn it...No. That would draw too much attention. Go find a cinder block to tie it to, and sink it in the swamp. It's no use to me now."

"Yes, sir. I'll do it right now." Jimmy swung the pungent bag over his shoulder, relieved to be getting rid of the awful smell. It probably wouldn't have been a good idea for Ross to go back into his old body now that it was so stinky.

He turned to leave, and the door swung open, smacking him in the nose. An explosion of pain shot through his face, but Jimmy forced his watery eyes to focus on the boy who came in. Though he was only a few days old now, the boy looked more like a man to Jimmy. Ross wouldn't give him a name, though, so all he could call him was boy.

The boy strutted into the shack and gave Jimmy a mean look. He didn't even say he was sorry for smacking him in the face. "Master?" the boy called. "Master, I saw the wolf."

"What?" Ross growled. *"When?"*

The boy stood straight as a rod with his hands by his side. "A few moments ago, Master. I came here right away."

A pan flew across the room, missing the boy's head by two feet. Jimmy cringed. If Ross had been aiming for Jimmy, he wouldn't have missed. Ross liked the boy better than he liked him. It wasn't fair.

"What do you have to report?"

"The wolf was with the cop last night. I saw her leaving his house. I think they're working together."

"The cop, huh? I'm not worried about her; she'll be easy to handle. It's those damn wolves that keep killing my demons. Although…" An icy breeze whirled around Jimmy, making him sick to his stomach. He didn't want Ross inside him again. Maybe if he tensed all his muscles, he could squeeze him out.

A hollow laugh echoed through the small shack. *"If the wolf is spending so much time with her, they must have more going on."*

"What do you mean, Master?"

Jimmy stood there. He was glad the boy asked the question that almost slipped from his mouth.

"They're lovers. You two are both too naïve for your own good. We can get to him through her. Jimmy! Why are you still here?"

"I'm sorry." Jimmy shuffled out the door to bury his brother's body. Whatever Ross was planning, Jimmy wouldn't want to do it. Maybe he would stay away for a very long time. Maybe he just wouldn't go back.

But if he didn't, where would he go?

CHAPTER FIFTEEN

"Absolutely not, son. You're alpha."

Luke sighed and ran a hand through his hair. The video call with his parents wasn't going as well as he'd hoped. "Technically, Dad, you're alpha. I'm still second."

"You know what I mean. You'll be alpha as soon as you find a mate, and it's not going to be the cop. Psychic or not, she isn't a werewolf."

"But I've researched—" He glanced at the door and lowered his voice to avoid any unwelcome eavesdroppers. Trying to control his frustration, he fisted his hands on the desk. "I've researched the family history. Our line has mixed with fae and other magical creatures for centuries. Macey is powerful. I can feel it."

"You feel it with your cock."

"Marcus!" his mother interjected. "Mind your words." She looked at her son through the computer screen. "You love this girl, don't you?"

He sucked in a sharp breath. If being in love meant wanting nothing more than to make the other person happy—to spend every day of the rest of his life with her

—then, yeah. Sure it was way too soon to call it love, but he couldn't deny his deep, primal desire to protect her, provide for her. Werewolf or not, she was his fate-bound. "She's the only one I can even consider taking as a mate."

"Well, you're gonna have to *consider* someone else," his father said. "What about that new rogue?"

Luke huffed. "Nice try, but no. And don't bother sending another one. It won't work."

"You think we sent her to you?" His mom looked appalled.

"Didn't you?"

"No, son. We didn't." His father crossed his arms. "But since she's there, you ought to consider—"

"No, Dad. She's not an option."

"Neither is the cop."

Luke ground his teeth. Why did his old man have to be such a hard ass? He drummed his fingers on the desk, trying to keep his heart from racing out of control. Mating with anyone but Macey was…unimaginable. Maybe he could appeal to his mother's sensitivity. "Mom, you understand, right?"

She smiled sadly and folded her hands in her lap. "I do, sweetheart. In any other case, I'd say your happiness comes first. But your father has a point. You're going to be alpha. You can't dilute the bloodline by mating with a non-were."

He fisted his hands to stop his fingers from trembling, but nothing could halt the frantic sprint of his heart. If his own mother wasn't on his side…

He stopped the thought before it could form. There had to be another way. A life without Macey wouldn't be worth living. "You know, it's still just a fifty-fifty chance my offspring will be able to succeed me. What if my first born is a girl? Alphas have to be male, so—"

His father sighed. "Werewolves only, son."

"But—"

Marcus raised his hand to stop him. "Werewolves only."

They said their goodbyes, and Luke slammed the MacBook shut. He wasn't ready to give up, but damn it, his mother was right. He couldn't take a chance in diluting the bloodline. Too many weres were mating with humans as it was. An alpha couldn't add to the weakening of the species.

He pressed his index finger and thumb to the bridge of his nose and closed his eyes to stave off the impending headache that threatened from behind his temples. Pushing his love life to the back burner for the time being, he rose from his chair and followed the murmur of voices down the hall to the meeting room.

He pushed open the door, and a hush fell across the crowd. Nearly thirty pack members lowered their heads to greet him, already giving Luke the respect of an alpha. Though the meeting was open to everyone, he didn't expect anyone but the ten people on the demon hunting team to show. The pack must've been more concerned about the demon issue than he'd thought.

As he strode to the front of the room, everyone settled into the metal folding chairs that circled the space. Everyone, except his cousin. Stephen stood next to Luke, his arms crossed over his chest, a scowl on his face. The sharp sting of tension mixed with jealousy radiated from Stephen's body. He wanted to be in control so badly, it showed in every move he made.

Luke scanned the crowd, acknowledging each person's

attendance with a nod of his head. His heart stuttered when he met Alexis's familiar gaze. If his old man hadn't sent her as a potential mate, what the hell was she doing at a pack meeting?

"First of all, I want to thank you all for coming. And I want those of you who aren't on the demon team to know that we have the situation under control."

"Do you?" An older were stood. "I'm afraid to let my daughters out of the house at night."

Luke bristled at the man's tone. "No weres have been attacked."

"Not yet. My girls are second and third born. They can't shift, so they have no way to protect themselves."

"We're all scared to death," a woman said.

"No incidents have been reported in the last week. My men have stopped three demons before they had the chance to find victims."

The man laughed cynically. "But have you stopped the person who's summoning them? Do you even know who he is?" He sat down and crossed his arms, murmuring to the woman next to him. Stephen shifted his weight as if he wanted to speak.

Luke took a deep breath. He'd had no idea his pack was this worried, and he should have. His mind had been so wrapped up in thoughts of Macey, he'd been neglecting his people. What the hell was his problem? He needed to get his mind off the sexy detective and focus on his duties. Hell, he needed to get his mind off women all together. As if to drive his point home, he caught Alexis's gaze. She pursed her lips and gave him a sympathetic look.

He needed to get this meeting under control. Get rid of the demons. Make things normal again. Then he could focus on making Macey his mate. He still had close to two weeks before his old man's retirement. He could do it all by then.

"I don't know who's summoning the demons," he said, "but I know how we can find out."

The whispering quieted as everyone focused on Luke. Stephen's mouth dropped open, and he clicked it shut. "When were you going to share this information with me?" he asked so quietly only Luke could hear.

Luke chuckled. "Right about now." He faced the crowd and raised his voice so they all could hear. "I saw the half-demon child this morning. He reeks of hell and has the same red eyes; he won't be hard to find again. With the whole team on the lookout, we'll find him and track him to his hideout. He'll lead us straight to his master; I'd put money on it."

From the whispers he overheard in the crowd, they seemed satisfied...for now. Leave it to Stephen to raise another concern. "What about the cops? That female detective is getting too close."

"No one needs to worry about the cops. I'm taking care of the detective." *And setting myself up for a major heartbreak.*

Stephen turned to Luke. "And just what are you doing about her?"

Luke fisted his hands and gritted his teeth. If the pack knew his true feelings for Macey, he'd lose their respect. "I befriended her. I'm giving her misinformation and guiding her away from the truth."

"You *befriended* her? You mean you're screwing her." Venom oozed from Stephen's voice. "You reek of human."

"It's strictly business. My relationship with Macey Carpenter goes no further than ensuring our secrets stay safe." He cringed inwardly. He hated lying to the pack, but what else could he do? Tell them he was in love with a human?

He scanned the crowd for their reactions. Most nodded their approval or whispered amongst themselves, but Alexis furrowed her brow and squirmed in her seat. Was she glaring at him? Surely not. Even rogues knew to respect an alpha. She shifted her gaze to the floor and chewed her bottom lip.

Before dismissing the meeting, he described the halfling in more detail, making sure everyone knew to be on the lookout. When the room cleared, Luke made his way to the bar for a beer. Lord knew he needed one after the week he'd had.

Chase poured him a brew as he plopped down on a stool. Most of the pack had left the bar, but a few people occupied the tables around the room. Alexis leaned against the wall in the back, talking to another female. He caught her gaze and nodded a hello. She responded by pursing her lips and giving him a curt nod in return.

Chase mixed a drink for a customer and turned to Luke. "Look, man. I know it's none of my business, but..."

Luke raised an eyebrow at his friend. "Then why are you asking?"

"There's more to the story with you and the detective, isn't there?"

He closed his eyes for a long blink. When he opened them, Chase stared intently at him.

"I'm asking because you're my friend. And I've seen the way you look at her."

Luke leaned forward, lowering his voice. "This is between you and me."

Chase nodded.

"She's amazing, man. I don't know what I'm going to do about it, but, yeah. I'm falling for her hard. As far as the pack's concerned, though, it's business. That's probably all it'll turn out to be anyway." He swallowed down the sour taste that formed in the back of his throat.

"I never thought I'd see the day you fell for a human."

Luke downed his beer and slid the glass to Chase. "Me neither. But duty comes first." Maybe if he said it out loud enough, he could convince himself it was true.

"Right." Chase clapped him on the shoulder. "Who needs happiness when you've got duty?"

The front door swung open, and both men snapped their heads toward the entrance. James barreled through and skidded to a stop in front of Luke. With one hand on the bar, he heaved in a few breaths before straightening his posture. "I got another one. He was already on top of her, but I got him."

"Damn it!" Luke slammed his fist on the bar and rose to his feet. "Did it rape her?"

James shook his head. "I don't know. Possibly. Your girl is probably on her way to the scene now."

"Shit! All right. Let's go."

"Hey, Luke." Alexis's voice came from just behind his shoulder. How long had she been standing there?

"Make it fast. I have to go." He stalked toward the door, and Alexis followed.

"Let me go with you. I…want to help."

He paused to give her a once over. If she had a motive, he couldn't sense it. And he didn't have time to argue with her. "Stay in the shadows, and keep up. Don't let the cops see you."

He glimpsed a grin curving her lips before he turned and bolted out the door.

CHAPTER SIXTEEN

"It's about time we had another one." Bryce floored it and sped toward the crime scene. "It's been so quiet these past few days, I thought our cult had skipped town."

Macey groaned and gripped the door handle as the car lurched over the bumps on the narrow French Quarter road. He weaved around parked cars, blasting the siren to alert pedestrians to get out of their way. These streets weren't made for Bryce's kind of driving. Next shift, she'd have to be sure she was behind the wheel. "Do you think it's one group doing all this? That they're organized?"

Her partner shrugged. "Beats me. But they always seem to happen the same way."

"What about the animal that saves them? How do you explain that? And the body? And the ash? It doesn't add up."

Bryce turned left on St. Louise and headed toward Dauphine. "You're not still hung up on all that paranormal crap are you? Monsters don't exist, Mace. Not the supernatural kind anyway."

Macey crossed her arms and let out a long sigh. A month ago, she would've agreed with him, but that was before a mysterious animal started attacking rapists and turning them into ash. Ghosts were real, weren't they? So, why couldn't there be some kind of monster or spirit out there wreaking havoc? Why not werewolves, like the barista suggested? That would explain the strange wolf she'd encountered twice now. And why Roberta didn't seem the least bit scared of it.

What am I thinking? Monsters? Werewolves? She needed to focus on the facts. The answers had to be there in the evidence. But the evidence kept disappearing: first the attackers themselves, then the body from the morgue, and now the ash from the lab. Looking at facts and thinking like a detective was getting them nowhere in this case. Maybe it was time she opened her mind to other possibilities.

Could she convince her partner? "How do you know monsters don't exist?"

He chuckled. "Because I've never seen one."

"You've never seen God, and you believe He exists."

"That's different."

"How?"

"Because He's God. If monsters and vampires and werewolves were real, we'd know about them, Mace. C'mon. You have to think logically." He parked against a curb and unlatched his seatbelt.

Macey put her hand on his shoulder. "Thinking logically isn't helping solve this case. All I'm saying is that maybe we need to be a little more open-minded."

"Right. You crack open your mind. I'm going to look at the evidence." He got out of the car and slammed the door.

Great. Now he thinks I'm crazy. If she couldn't get her own partner to consider the possibility, she certainly couldn't expect anyone else to believe her. Except, maybe Luke. The way he'd asked if she believed in magic made it sound like he believed. And he was so accepting of her ability when she'd told him about it. It didn't even faze him that she might be able to talk to spirits. Did he know something?

She laughed at herself and got out of the car. Maybe she really was going crazy. Even if Luke did believe in monsters and magic, she couldn't discuss the case with him…no matter how close the two of them were getting. No, she needed to get him out of her mind for the time being and focus on the evidence. Bryce was right.

They were the first to arrive on the scene, and Macey rushed to the woman who cowered in the corner of the alley. With her knees pulled up to her chest, her matted brown hair swinging forward to cover her face as she buried it in her arms, the woman looked more like a terrified child. Macey's chest tightened as she approached the victim.

"Ma'am, are you okay?" Of course she wasn't okay. What a stupid question. "An ambulance is on its way. I'm Detective Macey Carpenter."

The woman scuttled away as Macey stepped closer, curling into an even tighter ball.

Macey squatted to her level. "I'm not going to hurt you. Can you tell me your name?" She glanced at her partner, who pointed to a pile of ash a few feet away. Macey nodded and returned her attention to the victim.

"Jessica." The woman wiped her face with the back of her hand and loosened her posture tentatively.

"Okay, Jessica. Can you please tell me what happened? Were you raped?"

Jessica sucked in a shaky breath. "No, thank God. He just beat me up pretty bad." She burst into tears and hid her face in her hands.

Macey put her arm around the victim, who shivered in the August heat. Sirens in the distance blared, getting louder as the ambulance approached the scene. She didn't have much time to talk to the woman privately. "What happened after he beat you?"

"He was trying to get my panties off when…" Jessica rubbed her face and shook her head. "It's crazy, but a big dog or something attacked him."

"A dog? What did it look like?"

"I don't know. It happened so fast. It was like…I heard a growl. No, it was more like a snarl, you know?" She looked at Macey, who nodded her head. "And one minute the guy was on me, but the next he was rolling on the ground with the dog. Then the dog took off, and I guess it dragged the guy with it. I don't know."

She'd heard the story what, seven or eight times now? It was the same as the other victims, but they'd never described the animal as a dog. Could it have been the wolf she'd seen before? What on Earth would an animal like that be doing in the French Quarter? Absolutely nothing about this case made sense.

The woman sobbed uncontrollably, and Macey gently rubbed her back. The ambulance doors opened and closed. She had to hurry. "I know this is hard, Jessica. But can you tell me what the dog looked like? Could it have been a wolf?"

"I guess so. It was gray, I think. Or black, maybe. But

it was big. Way bigger than any dog I've seen. If it was a wolf, it was a monster of one."

"And you didn't see what happened to the man who attacked you?"

"No. I think the animal carried him off."

Macey smiled sympathetically and stood as the EMTs scurried over to check Jessica's vitals. "Thank you. That's exactly what I needed to know."

Luke, James, and Alexis watched from the shadows as Macey scooped up the demon ash and sealed it in an evidence bag. She handed the bag to an officer, slipped off her blue latex gloves and placed her hand against the wall. She must've been trying to pick up the energy of the scene from the building. Hopefully she wouldn't get anything useful.

"Looks like I'll be breaking into the lab again," James said.

Luke tore his gaze away from the beautiful detective to look at his friend. "At least you know your way around now. I've got it from here; you can go patrol. Alexis, you can head back too."

James nodded and took off up the alley. Alexis hesitated, her gaze shifting from the scene to Luke. "I'd like to stick around, if that's okay. I really want to help."

Luke furrowed his brow and narrowed his eyes at her. What was she up to? He preferred to be alone so he wouldn't feel the need to hide his feelings for Macey. But getting to know Alexis better was probably a good idea. If his old man really didn't send her, she must've had some other motive for wanting to be involved in the demon issue.

"Why are you taking all this interest in the pack? You thinking of joining?"

As she watched the detectives gather evidence, a look of sadness fell across her face. "I don't know. I like it here. I just figured you could use all the help you could get with your demon problem."

"Have you fought demons before?"

"No. But I'd like to learn." She turned to him and smiled. "If you need another person on the team, I'll volunteer."

"Let me think about it." What would the rest of the team think about working with a rogue? They'd accepted her on the job site, but carpentry wasn't demon hunting. He doubted they'd approve. Rogues didn't care about anything but themselves, but Alexis wasn't like any rogue he'd ever met. As he watched her watching the scene, she seemed to take a genuine interest in what happened. If only he could get inside her head and figure out why she cared so much. "What's your story?"

She sucked in a sharp breath. "I don't have a story. Why?"

"You're holding something back."

Her gaze landed on the detective. "I've told you everything you need to know." She looked at Luke, glanced back at the scene, and stepped away. "Well, it looks like you've got this under control. I'm going to jet."

"Okay…" Before he could say goodbye, she trotted down the street.

"Hey, Mace." Bryce paused before opening the car door.

Macey dropped her bag in the trunk, slammed it shut, and stepped to the passenger side. "Yeah?"

"Listen, I'm sorry about the way I acted in the car earlier."

She gave him a tight grin and slid into her seat.

Bryce got in the car and started the engine. "I don't believe in that stuff, and to hear you talking about it like it's real... It scares me."

Macey scoffed. "Nothing scares you, Bryce. You're a big, bad detective, remember?" She grinned, hoping to ease the tension that filled the car like static electricity.

"Now, hear me out." He gripped the steering wheel so hard his knuckles turned white. "I was thinking about what you said, and...Well, what if you're right? What then?"

She tugged on her bottom lip as Bryce kneaded the steering wheel like dough. "I don't know," she said. "But I did get a little more info out of the victim this time. She described the animal as a wolf."

"A wolf? Like the one you saw in the woods?"

"The coloring was different, but yeah. I think there might be a pack of wolves attacking people."

Bryce raised an eyebrow at her. "But—"

"I haven't figured out what they have to do with the case, but it's a start. Maybe they can sense the victims' fear, and they're attracted to it. Or maybe all the women have something in common. I don't know, but it's something to look into."

He let out a long breath. "So it's not a monster. Just a wolf. I'll give animal control a call."

As if on cue, Macey's cell phone rang. Another detective on the scene of another assault outside the Quarter.

"Looks like our night is just getting started. Head over to the Hilton on Canal."

"Another one?"

When they arrived at the hotel, they took the elevator up to the fifteenth floor. "This doesn't seem right," she said to Bryce. "All the others have been in the alley or on a small street. Our guys don't operate in hotel rooms."

The elevator door slid open, and they stepped into a deserted hallway. A pair of guards stood outside the victim's door. Macey nodded to the men and stepped through the threshold. The basic hotel room held a king-sized bed in the center, a flat screen TV on a table, and a small desk in the corner. The twisted bed sheets lay half-pulled to the floor. Pens, a notepad, and a lamp lay scattered about the room. Obvious signs of a struggle.

The victim sat on a chair near the window. A sketch artist's pencil flew fervently across the page as she described the attacker. Her face was a mask of blankness, her shuddering breaths the only clue to the earthquake that must have been crumbling inside her.

Macey spotted the detective who'd called and motioned for him to talk to her. "What happened here?" she asked.

The man shoved a small notepad into his jacket pocket. "Sexual assault. Victim said she met the guy in a bar. He followed her and forced his way into her room. Did his thing and left."

"Why did you call me? This doesn't sound anything like the other cases."

The detective cut his gaze toward the victim and lowered his voice. "She said the attacker had red eyes."

Jimmy peeled the blood-stained T-shirt over his head, used it to wipe the clammy sweat from his face, and hung it on the arm of the futon to dry. His whole body felt raw, like he'd been dragged naked across the asphalt while tied to the back of a truck. He hadn't, of course. But that's what he felt like. Was it from Ross's spirit ripping its way in and out of his body? Or was it because of what Ross had made him do?

The back of his mouth tasted sour like vomit, and his muscles ached from the explosion of excitement he'd just experienced. Did he enjoy it?

A little.

He didn't want to hurt that girl. But Ross was controlling his body, so he couldn't help it. He could feel it, though. And it felt good. Jimmy had never made love to a woman before. He'd wanted to make love to her. When Ross had used Jimmy's body to talk to the girl, it was exciting. He said some clever things and made her laugh. Jimmy could never say such clever things on his own because he was a stupid idiot. But Ross was smart, and he made smart words come out of Jimmy's stupid mouth.

The girl liked Jimmy. Well, she liked Ross inside Jimmy's body, but that was close enough. When it was time to leave, Jimmy was sure the girl was going to say yes to sex. But when Ross made him ask if he could walk her to her hotel room, she said no.

"That's okay," Ross had said in Jimmy's mind. *"We're still gonna screw her."*

But she had said no, so Jimmy didn't want to do it anymore. Ross made him follow her and push his way into her room. Jimmy was strong on his own, but Ross made him stronger. The girl tried to put up a fight, but Ross made Jimmy smack her in the face. She screamed and stumbled backwards into the room, falling on top of the bed...right where Ross wanted her. She kicked and bit, but Jimmy's body was too strong.

Jimmy squeezed his eyes shut and curled up in a ball on the futon. "Why did you make me do that, Ross? She said no."

A cool breeze snaked up his arm and whispered into his ear, "*Shut up, moron. You liked it. I can hear your thoughts, remember?*"

Tremors shook his body as a deep sob escaped his throat. "I liked the way it felt. I didn't like hurting that girl."

CHAPTER SEVENTEEN

Luke was ready for his date with Macey by six o'clock, but he wasn't picking her up until eight. She had him so wound up, he couldn't stop his leg from bouncing under the kitchen table. He got up and paced the room. He needed a distraction, something to occupy his mind for the next two hours until he saw her again.

Why the hell was he so nervous? He'd gone out with her before; he'd made love to her for Christ's sake. Maybe the nerves were a warning from his subconscious to guard his heart. Nah, it was too late for that. His heart belonged to Macey, even though his old man had made it clear she was off limits. But he couldn't help himself. He had to see her again. He was still holding on to that tiny sliver of hope that things could work out.

He switched on the TV and flipped through the channels to the local evening news. A little doom and gloom would keep his brain busy while he waited. He plopped down on the sofa and rested his feet on the coffee table, but the screen didn't distract him from his thoughts. This was their first real date. The times before had been spontaneous…well, he'd followed her on purpose, but what had happened afterward had been spontaneous. This date had been planned. He'd called her and asked her out, and she'd said yes. And that made it so much more real.

He focused on the television. A journalist stood outside a hotel on Canal Street, her grim expression revealing the seriousness of the story she reported. He turned up the volume.

"…though the circumstances are different in last night's attack, the perpetrator had one thing in common with the others. The victim claimed he had red eyes."

"Shit!" Luke jumped to his feet. Why didn't he know about this one yet? A police composite sketch filled the screen, and he snapped a picture of it with his phone. Either the demons were getting smarter, taking their victims indoors, or this was the human who'd been summoning them. He had to warn the pack.

As he entered the bar, Chase and Stephen stood near the TV, the volume blasting to drown out the music. Another reporter told the same story on a different channel.

"You see this, man?" Chase said. "It's all over the news. Can't believe we missed one."

Stephen crossed his arms, tightening his jaw. "We wouldn't have missed it if I were in charge. Maybe we need to call your daddy, so a *real* alpha can handle this."

Luke glared at his cousin, holding eye contact to exert his dominance. Stephen returned his gaze, challenging him with his stare. Tension thickened between them as Luke took a step forward. The last thing they needed was to fight amongst themselves when they shared a common goal, but an alpha had to take every challenge seriously.

"Don't you have some accounting to do in the back?" Luke said. "I'm sure if you walk away now, I can forget this ever happened."

Fear flashed in Stephen's eyes, his resolve seeming to waver, but he didn't tear his gaze away from Luke's. He fisted his hands at his sides and gritted his teeth.

Luke took another step forward. "Or are we going to have a problem?"

Stephen let out his breath in a slow hiss, his challenging posture deflating. "No. We're good." He dropped his gaze to the floor, ending the confrontation.

Luke turned to Chase. "I'm texting you the police sketch. Send it to everyone on the team. This guy's M.O. is different, and that makes me think it might be the leader."

Chase's phone chimed. "Got it. You headed out for your date?"

"Is it that obvious?"

"Shirt's ironed. No holes in your jeans." He shrugged. "Pretty damn obvious."

Stephen stepped from behind the bar. "You're going out with the cop?"

"Yeah. I am. Got a problem with that?"

"Alphas can't mate with humans."

"I'm well aware of that."

Stephen shook his head and stormed through the door to the office.

Chase grinned. "Seems like he'd be happy if you mated with a human. With you out of the way, he'd be free to run his reign of terror."

Luke sank onto a barstool, a heaviness sinking in his

heart. "She's not going to be my mate." And that was the truth, wasn't it? No matter how strongly he cared for Macey, she wasn't a werewolf.

"Then why are you going out with her?"

He traced the wood grain on the bar. "You know…to lead her away from the truth. Keep her from finding out too much."

Chase raised an eyebrow. "Uh huh."

"What am I supposed to do, man? She's incredible. I can't let a girl like her get away." He drummed his fingers on the wood. There had to be something he could do…

Macey freshened up her makeup for the fourth time and sipped a glass of chardonnay. Liquid relaxation pooled in her core and flowed out to her limbs, a welcome relief from the tension she'd carried in her muscles all day. Luke said he'd pick her up at eight, and she'd been a nervous wreck since he'd called. Butterflies flitted in her stomach just thinking about him.

An actual planned date with the man of her dreams. Wait…was he the man of her dreams? He was all she thought about, so he must be.

Thor jumped onto the bathroom counter and mewed for her attention. She stroked his soft brown fur, and his body vibrated with a satisfied purr.

She finished her wine, letting the soothing liquid calm her nerves. Running her fingers through her hair, she tousled the roots to give it volume. Luke had mentioned he liked her hair down. Would he remember saying that? Would he think she was trying too hard? Maybe she should put it up. She'd be more comfortable in her usual bun anyway.

She reached for her brush, and the doorbell rang. *Crap! He's here.* Thor jumped from the counter and darted under her bed. Macey checked her reflection one last time and padded into the living room. "Coming."

She opened the door, and her breath caught at the sight of him. He wore dark jeans and a deep blue shirt that matched his eyes. A crooked grin lit up his face as he offered her a bouquet of lemon-yellow daisies.

"They match your dress."

"Hmm?" She took the flowers and inhaled their sweet fragrance. "Oh, yeah. I guess they do. Thank you. Do you want to come inside?"

He shoved his hands in his pockets and rocked back on his heels. "Actually, we have a dinner reservation at eight-fifteen, so we should get going."

"Okay. Let me put these in some water." She trotted to the kitchen, shoved the bouquet in an empty vase and grabbed her purse. She'd worry about the water later. Right now, the only thing on her mind was the gorgeous hunk on her doorstep.

"Where are we going?" she asked as he opened the truck door for her.

"Captain Boudreaux's, if that's okay with you." He closed the door behind her and got in the driver's seat.

"Sounds wonderful."

They rode in silence up St. Charles, Luke kneading the steering wheel while Macey's leg bounced up and down. She rested her hand on her knee to stop the movement and tried to think of something to say. He'd always been so easy to talk to before, but now he seemed different.

Distracted. She tugged on her bottom lip and swallowed the dryness out of her mouth.

"Is everything okay? You're quiet tonight," she said.

He glanced at her and relaxed his grip on the steering wheel. "Yeah. I've got a lot on my mind."

"Do you want to talk about it?"

"Nah." He reached for her hand, and all the tension drained from her body. How could a simple touch have such an effect on her?

"You look beautiful. I love it when you wear your hair down." He slid his hand up the back of her neck, his fingers combing through her hair. Her heart stuttered at the intimacy of his touch, and heat pooled below her navel. He glanced at her with palpable hunger in his eyes before returning his hand to the steering wheel. It was a good thing he hadn't come inside when she'd asked. They probably wouldn't have made it out of the house.

When they arrived at the restaurant, a line of people stretched out the door and around the corner of the Victorian style structure. Lavender and white striped awnings hung above the windows, matching the purple siding and white trim of the building.

"Looks like we'll be waiting a while," Macey said.

Luke grinned. "No worries. They know me here." He led her past the line of hungry patrons and ushered her through the door.

"Local celebrity?"

"Nah. I did the remodel after the last hurricane. They got eight feet of water inside. Almost tore the place down, but my team was able to restore it. The manager's a friend of mine."

As they entered the dining room, Macey's breath

caught. Vaulted ceilings revealed exposed wood beams stained dark chocolate brown. Crystal chandeliers hung from above, filling the room with pale, warm light. Framed black-and-white photos of famous New Orleans buildings adorned an exposed brick wall, obviously original to the nineteenth-century structure. How many stories could this old building tell? And they'd almost torn it down.

"You did all this? It's beautiful." She picked up a menu.

"Me and a crew of thirty men." He scanned the room, eyes gleaming. "I'm glad we were able to restore it. Our city's so rich in history. It breaks my heart when we have to bulldoze a building."

She grinned at him.

"What?"

"Nothing. It's…you have a soft side. Artistic. I wasn't expecting it." She folded her menu on the table and took a sip of water.

"Well, you're a lot different than I expected too."

She raised an eyebrow and rested her hands on the table. "And how did you expect me to be?" She braced herself for his answer, unsure if she really wanted to know.

"Cocky. All business. You know the type." He reached for her hands across the table. "But you're not like that at all."

Electricity tingled up her arms. Her heart fluttered, and she leaned in, the urge to close the distance between them overwhelming. "What am I like then?"

He leaned in to match her posture and held her with a piercing gaze. "Kind. Caring. Beautiful. Amazing…in the bedroom and out."

It took every ounce of control she could muster to keep herself from climbing over the table and throwing herself into his arms. Simply touching him sent her body into overdrive. She leaned back and fanned herself with the menu. "Is it hot in here?"

A sly smile curved his lips. "No, I think it's just you."

The rest of their dinner went by in a blur. She was so caught up in this incredible man, she'd forgotten what she ordered by the time the food arrived. The line still stretched out the door as they left the restaurant, and they strolled hand-in-hand down Frenchman Street.

They stopped in front of a squat brown building with a red door. A saxophone's sad wail drifted to the street from somewhere inside. Live music was abundant in this part of town, tucked away from the flashy neon lights and cover music of Bourbon Street. A simple wooden sign above the door advertised the name of the establishment: Louie's. This was the street locals went to for live music. None of those annoying hawkers trying to lure people into bars with the promise of cheap, watered down drinks and scantily-clad women.

"Do you like Blues? Or Jazz?" Luke asked.

"Love it."

"Good." He opened the door and led her inside.

A dozen people filled the chairs of the small room. Strings of pale white lights hung from low ceilings, giving the establishment a cozy feel. A sax, a bass, and a baby grand piano sat upon a tiny stage, their players belting out a soulful rendition of "Do You Know What It Means To Miss New Orleans." Luke led her to an empty table near the stage and wrapped his arm around her shoulders. He absently traced his fingers along her skin as he hummed along to the tune.

The band finished the number and announced a short break as a rough-looking man approached Luke. His jeans were torn and paint-stained, his shirt yellowing with sweat. His unkempt hair was greasy, and anger filled his eyes. He didn't speak, but his hands clenched into fists at his sides as he stared at Luke.

Luke sighed. "Will you excuse me for a minute, Macey?"

"Sure." She watched the exchange, though she couldn't hear what they said. The man's sharp gestures and accusing posture would have intimidated most people. Luke kept his cool, though she could tell he was agitated. He said something that appeared to appease the man, gave him a tight smile, and returned to the table.

"Sorry about that. Work drama." He settled in next to her and took her hand.

"Everything okay?"

"It will be. So, do you—"

The piano player clapped Luke on the shoulder. "Luke, my man. Long time, no see."

"Hey, Benny." He stood and shook the man's hand. Benny was a rotund character with leathery skin and canyons etched into his forehead. His bright brown eyes crinkled when he smiled.

"My old bones need a longer rest, but these guys ain't gonna let me have it." He pointed a thumb at the other musicians on stage. "Think you could take over the keys for a song or two to give my joints a break?" He splayed his gnarled fingers, cracked his knuckles, and winked at Macey.

Luke grinned. "Anything for you, Uncle Ben."

Macey arched an eyebrow. "You play?"

"A little."

Was there anything this man couldn't do? Luke slid onto the bench behind the piano, and Benny took the microphone, crooning "Sitting on the Dock of the Bay" while Luke's fingers flew across the keys like a professional.

Macey had to remind herself to breathe. Musicians had always made her heart swoon. There was something undeniably sexy about a man who could express his emotions through song. If she wasn't careful, she'd end up falling in love with this one.

He finished the song and took his seat next to her, resting his hand on her knee. His palm warmed her skin, and she leaned into his side. "You're good."

He chuckled. "My mom wanted to make sure I was a well-rounded person."

"Good for her."

His thumb tapped a rhythm on her leg. "Hey, you want to get out of here? Go have a cup of coffee someplace quiet?"

"I've got coffee at my place, and it's quiet. Want to go there?"

He looked at her, his smoldering gaze traveling from her eyes to her lips, down her body, and up again. "Yeah. I do."

"Here we are." Her voice cracked as she spoke, and she bit her bottom lip. Her cheeks flushed pink as she blinked those emerald eyes and opened the front door. "Come on in. So, this is my living room, obviously." She was cute when she was nervous. She stared at him, apparently waiting for a response, so he had to tear his gaze away from her little yellow sundress to survey the room.

Wood floors. White sofa. Teal pillows. "It's nice." He

stepped toward her, sliding his arm around her waist. "But I'd rather look at you."

He lowered his head to kiss her, but a brown cat jumped onto the sofa and hissed. With its back arched and ears flat, the feline screeched a challenging meow.

Luke straightened his spine and eyed the furry creature. "You have a cat."

"Sorry. I don't know what's gotten into him. He's been acting weird lately. Shoo, Thor. Get down." She waved her arms at the cat, and it darted under the sofa.

He chuckled. "God of thunder, huh?"

"He may be small, but he's mighty."

The cat glared at him from under the couch. Luke sighed. Werewolves had a distinct animal scent. Though it was imperceptible to humans, other animals recognized it immediately. The cat didn't approve. "I'm more of a dog person myself."

"So am I, but don't tell Thor that." She bent down to look at the feline. "Cats are easier to take care of. Since I work so much, I needed a pet that didn't mind being alone."

"It's okay. I don't mind cats." He knelt and rested his forearms on the floor, palms flat in a submissive gesture. If his pack could see him bowing down to a cat, they'd never let him live it down. But he needed to win over the pet if he wanted to keep the woman.

"Come on, Thor. I won't hurt you."

The cat inched forward.

"That's a good kitty."

Thor slinked from under the couch and eyed him warily.

Luke blew out a breath and rolled over on his back, allowing the cat to jump onto his chest. *This is so demeaning.* Thor stared at him triumphantly and licked his paws.

"See? We're buddies now, right, Thor?" He scooped the cat into his arms and stood, scratching its ears.

"Well, how about that?" Macey took Thor from his grasp and put him on the floor. "Do you want me to make some coffee?"

He stepped toward her and traced his fingers along her jawline, raising her chin. Leaning in, he hovered his lips over hers, letting the anticipation build, fueling the fire in his heart. Heat radiated from her skin, awakening a primal desire deep inside him. He crushed his mouth to hers.

She moaned, wrapping her arms around his waist, molding her body to his. He wanted her. He wanted her more than he'd wanted anything his entire life, and she was his for the taking. She tugged at his shirt, leaving trails of fire on his skin as she slid it over his head. Desire pooled in her eyes as she ran her hands over his body and licked her lips. Her dress strap slipped off her shoulder, and he groaned, trailing kisses up and down her neck. She reached behind her back and tugged down her zipper.

His phone rang, but he ignored it, focusing instead on her sensuous curves as her little yellow sundress dropped to the floor. He glided his hands along her body and gripped her hips, pulling her against him.

His phone rang again. He groaned and fished it from his pocket to find Chase's name lighting up the screen. Cupping Macey's cheek in his hand, he pressed a tender kiss to her lips. "Hold that thought. This will only take a minute."

He held the phone to his ear. "This had better be important."

"We've got a problem." Chase's voice sounded grim.

"Danny called an emergency meeting. There's a crowd at the bar."

"What?" He stepped away from Macey. "He doesn't have the authority."

"He saw you with the detective tonight. Rumors are flying that you're choosing a human over the pack. People are scared."

Damn it. He thought he'd appeased his pack member at the jazz club when he'd assured him he was trying to lead Macey astray. Apparently things were worse than he'd thought. "I'll be there in ten. Can you hold down the fort 'til then?"

"I'll do my best."

Macey picked up her dress. "Where are you going?"

The disappointment in her eyes tugged at his heart, and he wanted nothing more than to finish what they'd started. To take her to bed and make love to her all night long.

But as much as he wanted to be with this woman right now…forever…he couldn't. His pack was scared. Of the demons and of the possibility that Stephen could become alpha if Luke didn't get his act together. James wasn't the only one who'd threatened to go rogue if Luke let Stephen lead, and now it seemed the sentiment was spreading.

He was letting his heart get in the way of his duty, and it was about to tear his pack apart.

"It's a work emergency." He pulled his shirt over his head.

"At eleven o'clock at night?"

"I'm sorry." He kissed her on the cheek and opened the front door. "There are some things I need to take care of. I might be busy for a few days, but I promise I'll call you as soon as I can."

She furrowed her brow. "I don't understand."

What the hell was he doing? He had to make a choice between the woman he loved and his pack, and there was no right answer. He wanted both. He *needed* both. "I'll call you in a few days. I'm sorry."

CHAPTER EIGHTEEN

Jimmy held the ceremonial kitchen knife in his sweaty right hand and tried to keep it from trembling. The cut always hurt more when his hands shook. He wasn't scared. Ross had already made him summon so many demons, he was used to the pain. Jimmy's hands were shaking because he was mad.

He glared at the boy lying on his futon. That was Jimmy's futon, and the boy had stolen it. His back ached from sleeping on the floor, and he had bruises on his hips from where the bones dug into the hard linoleum. His brother said the boy was more useful. Smarter. Jimmy was a stupid idiot, and stupid idiots slept on the floor.

"What are you waiting for, dimwit? Do I have to possess you and summon the demon myself?" Ross's voice came from everywhere and nowhere all at once.

"No, please. I'll do it." He pressed the blade against his palm, only wincing a little as a fresh ribbon of blood pooled in his hand. He held it over the altar, counting as three drops fell into the ceremonial bowl. It looked like a cereal bowl to Jimmy, but he'd learned not to argue with his brother.

He whispered the special chant Ross had made him memorize. It took him two weeks to learn the chant because he was stupid and didn't know how to read. He'd learned a little before Momma died, but once she was gone, he didn't go to school anymore. He knew the chant now though, and he whispered it fast so he could move away. This was the scary part.

He grabbed a towel to stop the bleeding and clambered into the corner as a big mass of billowing black smoke swirled out of the bowl. All the air seemed to be sucked out of the room, ripped from his lungs like he was sitting inside a vacuum. The smoke spread out, hovering below the ceiling like thick carpet before tumbling back toward the bowl. A demon with bright red eyes and shiny black skin crouched on the altar and stared at Jimmy like it wanted to eat him. Jimmy's whole body shook, and his heart pounded like it was going to explode out of his chest. He *really* didn't want to get eaten. Sometimes the demons looked like mean people, with human colored skin. This one was slick like a snake, and twice as scary.

Ross said his own chant in a language Jimmy didn't understand, and the demon shot out the door. Jimmy whimpered.

"Why are you scared, idiot? I told you I won't let them hurt you. Only a pure human can raise a demon. You're special, brother."

Special? Jimmy was special? He must be if Ross said he was. His mouth curled into a smile, so he covered it with his hand.

"It's okay to smile. You did good. Now, get over there and raise another one."

"Another one? But I'm tired, Ross. Calling demons makes my tummy hurt, and it gives me a headache. Can't that be enough for today?"

A blow to his head knocked him to the ground. Jimmy clutched his eye, trying to hold it in because it felt like it was going to pop right out of his head. He was stupid. He deserved to be hit.

"As long as those damn wolves keep killing my demons, you'll keep raising more. And that bitch detective. I saw your face all over the evening news yesterday, and I know she was behind that. We've gotta take her out."

"Isn't she dating that werewolf? Won't they all be protecting her?" Jimmy braced himself for another strike, but it didn't come.

"You're right. You may not be as stupid as I thought you were."

Jimmy's mouth tried to pull into another smile, but he fought it this time. He could tell by the tone of his brother's voice that he wasn't going to like what Ross said next.

"I think it's time for us to pay Detective Carpenter a visit. But, first, we're gonna need a lot more demons."

CHAPTER NINETEEN

MACEY AND ROBERTA SAT IN A SWING ON HER MOM'S front porch, sipping tea and trying to build Macey's powers. She took a deep breath and focused on the energy trapped inside an antique clock.

"It was in a Creole plantation. A young slave girl used to dust it every day, but she knocked it off the shelf once." Macey read the energy, relaying the melancholy story of the artifact to her teacher.

Roberta nodded encouragingly. "That's good. Now, I want you to see if you can release the energy."

"What do you mean?"

"When you touch the clock, you see a story. You understand why the item makes you feel a certain way. For most people, all they get is the feeling. This clock brings sadness into the home, but most don't know why. If you can release the energy into the universe, you'll be cleansing the item so someone else can enjoy its beauty without feeling the sadness that comes along with it."

Macey looked at the clock, turning it over in her hands. "You can do that?"

"I can, yes. And I think you can too, if you try. Find the energy inside the clock, and coax it out. Set it free."

Macey turned her focus to the clock and the energy that swirled inside it. She imagined opening the clock and warm, white light flowing through it, whisking the negativity away. An electric pulse radiated through her hands as the slave girl, and the horrible beatings she'd endured, broke free from the artifact and floated away. Then, nothing. She rested her hand on the clock, searching for a trace of the energy, for the story, but it was gone. "That's it? It's that easy?"

Roberta smiled. "For you, it seems it is."

"Huh." If she'd known using her ability could be that simple, she'd have sought out help a long time ago. "Thanks." She tugged on her bottom lip and stared at the clock. If only everything were this easy. "Have you seen Luke around lately?"

"I can't say that I have. Is there a problem?"

"He had to leave abruptly on our last date, and I haven't heard from him in a few days. He said he had a work emergency, but…"

Roberta inhaled deeply, and an unreadable expression fell across her features. "I'm sure there's nothing to worry about, child. He's probably behind on a deadline; give him time."

"Yeah." That's probably all it was. How many times had she pulled twenty-hour shifts when she'd been working on an important case? He probably worked all day, and then crashed from exhaustion as soon as he got home. It made sense. Still…he could've at least sent her a text by now.

"You're right." She had another question that had been burning in her mind. "I've been meaning to ask…Why weren't you afraid of that wolf the other day? Do you have some sort of animal power too?" Or were werewolves really a possibility? At this point, the idea made as much sense as any other theory she'd heard about the case.

She laughed. "I suppose you could say that. The wolves are our friends." She clamped her mouth shut, pressing her lips into a tight smile.

"Okay." Roberta was a mysterious woman, for sure.

"Same time tomorrow, then?" The old woman heaved herself from the swing and straightened her skirt.

"Sounds good."

Macey handed Roberta the clock and said goodbye. Maybe her power could be of some use after all. Maybe not on the case, but at least it was good for something. The attackers had been quiet for several days, but it was only a matter of time before he—they—it—whatever it was struck again. The spirit that had tormented her was quiet too, and she wondered again if the two were related.

She wondered a lot lately. Thought about the case incessantly. Anything to keep her mind occupied, her thoughts away from Luke and the strange way he'd left.

"Macey, dear." Jenny stepped onto the porch and sat next to her daughter. "It's not that I don't love you being here, hon. But...don't you think Thor is getting lonely? You've slept here after work three days in a row."

She waved her hand dismissively and picked up her tea. "He's a cat, Mom. I stop by the house every day to make sure he's okay." *Please don't ask me about Luke.* "I better get ready for work."

She hopped off the swing and shuffled inside.

Her mom followed. "It's about that boy, isn't it? Did he break up with you?"

She groaned. "He's not a boy; he's a grown man, and he didn't break up with me. He's been busy."

"Have you tried calling him?"

"No, and I'm not going to. If he wants to see me again, he'll call me." And if he didn't, that was fine too. That's what she'd keep telling herself, anyway. It was her own fault for letting him in. For getting close. She'd ignored all the warnings her logical mind had thrown at her, and look where it had landed her. Missing him. She could hold on to the hope that he'd call for a few more days, but then what? Admit that yet another person she cared about had abandoned her? That she wasn't worthy of love?

Her mom rubbed her hand on Macey's back. "Men are complicated creatures. I won't even pretend to understand them. But there are other fish in the sea, right? Someone better will come along."

"I don't want another fish. I want Luke."

Luke sulked into O'Malley's and slid onto a barstool. He needed to get his shit together. The demon activity had been quiet the past few days, so there wasn't much to distract him from his thoughts. Every time he closed his eyes, he saw Macey's face. He'd purposely spent the last three days away from her to appease his pack. They needed the reassurance that he wouldn't let them down…that he *would* be the next alpha…but, damn it, why did he have to hurt Macey in the process?

His fingers itched with the desire to dial her number every time he looked at his phone. But as soon as he heard her melodic voice, he'd have to see her again. He wouldn't be able to help himself. What the hell was he going to do?

Chase slid him a beer, and Luke gulped it down. His mom would lecture him about daytime drinking, but he'd say it was her fault for raising him in a bar. Besides, it was the only thing that dulled the pain in his heart. His folks would be home in a few days, and the pressure to find a mate would pick up again. His dad's retirement would happen on the next full moon, but did it have to be at the cost of Luke's happiness?

"Slow day at the office?" Chase asked.

"You could say that." He should've been on site, helping his team, but he couldn't focus on anything but figuring out a way to make Macey his mate.

"What did you decide to do about your detective?"

Luke laid his palms flat on the bar and stared at his fingers. Only days ago, those fingers had caressed her supple body, twisted in her silky hair. They tingled with the memories. "I'm thinking about petitioning the council." They probably had more knowledge on the issue of weres mating with other magical beings. But a no from the council would be a conclusive no, and he wasn't sure he could handle something so final. At the moment, he at least had a shred of hope that his dad would change his mind.

Chase arched an eyebrow. "You sure you want to go over your old man's head? The pack bond's already volatile."

He closed his eyes and let out a low growl. "You're right. Even if they approved her as my mate, I'd lose the pack's trust if I disobeyed the alpha. I'll either make him change his mind or I'll have to break it off with her." His chest ached at the thought.

"I'm sorry, man."

"My duty to the pack comes first."

Stephen stepped through the office door and strutted to the bar. "It's about time you acted like an alpha. I was starting to think you *wanted* to be second the rest of your life."

Luke squeezed his hands into fists. "Don't start with me."

"Seriously, though, cuz. I'm sorry you couldn't make it work with your human. It would've been nice to have a cop on our side."

"What cop?" Alexis asked as she entered the bar, followed by a couple of Luke's employees. "What are you talking about?"

Damn it. Who else was going to eavesdrop on this conversation? He should've kept his mouth shut. Now the whole pack was in his personal business. Alexis was out of line questioning her superior like that. Being a rogue was no excuse for not following pack rules. The two workers sat at a table in the back, but Alexis lingered by the bar, waiting for an answer. When he didn't give her one, she glared at him before shifting her gaze to his cousin. What the hell was her problem?

Stephen wiggled his eyebrows and grinned. "Our soon-to-be alpha is going to stop screwing the detective." He leaned on the bar, resting his chin on his hand to feign interest. "How are we ever going to keep her off our trail now?"

A low growl resonated from Luke's chest, warning his cousin to back off. He didn't need this kind of disrespect. Especially in front of a rogue.

"You've really been screwing Macey?" Alexis sounded incredulous.

Luke turned to face her. "How I run my pack is not your concern, rogue."

She bristled. "It is when you're hurting innocent people. You can't use a woman, lead her on like that, to serve your *pack's* purpose." She spat the word pack in disgust. "Macey has feelings. She's not some pawn in your demon hunting game."

Luke rose to his feet, straightening to his full height. "You're a rogue. Why do you care so much about what happens in *my pack?*"

"I don't care about your pack. I care about my *sister.*" Her eyes flashed like she'd said more than she intended, but she set her jaw and gave him a challenging look.

"You..." He stammered, squeezing his eyes shut, clutching the edge of the bar to steady himself. His chest tightened, and he had to remind himself to breathe. Did he hear her right? "Macey is your sister?" His voice came out as a raspy whisper.

Alexis raised her chin. "Yes, she is."

Luke turned to Chase, who raised his eyebrows. If Macey was Alexis's sister, that meant she was...

"She's your *biological* sister? You have the same parents? The same blood?"

She crossed her arms. "That's generally what 'sister' means."

"Looks like we finally got our man on the inside," Stephen grumbled under his breath.

"Goddammit!" Luke pointed a finger at Alexis. "Stay here until I get back. I'm not done with you."

He stormed out of the bar and stopped on the sidewalk, resting his hand against the wall, heaving heavy breaths as his eyes adjusted to the blinding sunlight.

Macey was a werewolf.

Why hadn't he made the connection before? She'd told him she had an older sister. Macey had powers like other second-born weres. Hell, he'd even detected a hint of werewolf in her energy the first time he'd touched her, but he'd dismissed it—his ego insisting no werewolf could live in the Quarter without his knowledge. How could he have been so stupid? It made so much sense when he pieced it all together. Alexis was the sister who'd abandoned her in foster care.

He had to talk to Macey. He could make things right.

He jogged up St. Philip Street and made a left on Burgundy. He'd knock on her door and tell her everything. They *could* be together. Elation filled his heart, inflating his chest with joy. It was two in the afternoon. Would Macey be up? He'd wake her if she wasn't. This was too important to wait.

He lifted his face to the cloudless sky, letting the sunlight warm his skin as he trotted along the sidewalk. The answer to all his problems had come to him in the form of a cumbersome rogue. Who would've thought?

He chuckled as he rounded the corner, but the bookcase he plowed into cut his laugh short. He grunted as his knee made contact with the edge of the shelf, shooting stinging pain down his shin, and he knelt to pick up the second-hand novels he'd scattered on the sidewalk. The store clerk stepped outside, and he smiled at her as he returned the last book to the case and continued on his way. Nothing would spoil his mood today.

He could finally fulfill his duty as alpha *and* spend the rest of his life with his fate-bound mate.

But would Macey still want him after he'd blown her off? His run slowed to a walk. Would she be willing to open her heart to him after the way he'd acted? He had to find out. He'd beg if he had to.

He bounded up her front steps and pounded on the door. "Macey? Macey, it's Luke. Open up please." The seconds ticked by into an eternity as he waited for her to answer. He knocked again. *Please be home.* He held his breath as the lock rattled and the door cracked open.

Macey's face appeared between the door and the jamb. "Luke?"

"I need to talk to you. Can I come in? Please?"

She studied him for a moment, as if trying to decide whether or not she wanted to talk. Finally, she sighed and opened the door. "Come on."

The cool air of her living room made him shiver. Or was it his excitement? He wasn't sure. He closed the door behind him, blocking out the summer heat, and stared at her, another kind of heat pooling in his core. She was barefoot, wearing a silky green robe, and she'd piled her hair on top of her head in a messy twist. A few silky strands hung down around her face, framing her sparkling eyes. He'd always fantasized about what she'd look like if he woke up next to her. She was more stunning than he'd imagined.

"Well?" She picked up a coffee mug and settled onto the sofa, curling one leg underneath her.

"I'm sorry." He sat on the edge of the couch and turned his body to face her. "The way I acted was inexcusable, and I hope you can find it in your heart to forgive me."

She gazed into her mug and inhaled deeply. "Thank you for the apology. Is that all you needed?" She set her cup down and started to get up.

He reached for her arm. "That's not all."

She sat down and pulled her arm from his grasp. Thor jumped into her lap, and she held him close, stroking his fur.

"See, the thing is...oh, Macey, there's so much I need to tell you. I don't know where to start." He raked his hand through his hair, desperately trying to gather his thoughts.

She stared at her cat. "You can start with explaining why you ran off. One minute things were going great, and then you bolted." She lifted her gaze to meet his, and the pain in her eyes pierced his heart. "What happened?"

"It really was an emergency, but it wasn't for work. It was..." He let out his breath in a huff. How could he make this right? "Let me start this way. Your power? Your ability to read objects and sense spirits is real."

She squinted her eyes. "I know. Roberta has been helping me develop it."

"Roberta. Yes. She has powers, too, but they're different. So magic is real."

"What are you getting at?" She put the cat on the floor and crossed her arms.

"So, if you have powers, and Roberta has different powers...then other people could have even more different powers. Like me."

She raised an eyebrow. "You have powers?"

"Kind of. Yes."

"And what does that have to do with you running out on me?"

"It's complicated."

"And why haven't you called? Or at least texted?" She flung her arms about, irritated. "I was starting to think I'd never hear from you again."

He folded his hands in his lap and swallowed. There

was no easy way to say it. "You've seen a wolf in the woods twice now, haven't you? A light-brown one? It knocked you out from under a falling tree branch."

She gaped at him. "How did you know that?"

He tapped his fist against his chest. "That wolf was me. I'm a werewolf."

She stared at him, blinking. He waited for her to respond, but she just narrowed her eyes and stared.

"I know it sounds crazy, but it's true, Macey. That's why I ran off that night. The emergency had to do with the pack, and I didn't think I could tell you about it, but I was wrong. I don't want to keep secrets from you. I want you to know everything." He took her hands in his, and she didn't pull away. "I want to be with you, Macey. If you'll have me."

She opened her mouth to speak but snapped it shut again. Her gaze fell to their entwined hands and rose to meet his. "You're a werewolf? That's a real thing?"

"Yeah."

She let out a cynical laugh and shook her head. "So, I'm not going crazy then?"

"No, you're not. I'll prove it to you. Wait here." Heart thudding in his chest, he paced to the next room and shifted. Seeing his wolf form would be shocking enough. He'd save letting her watch the transformation for another time. Slowly, he padded into the living room, lowered his head submissively, and approached her.

"Oh, my God!" She folded both legs onto the couch and balled herself up in the corner. He crept toward her and rested his chin on the cushion, trying his best to look harmless. He whimpered, begging her to relax. If she could accept this part of him—all of him—they could spend the rest of their lives together. His stomach fluttered at the thought of spending forever with Macey.

Slowly, her muscles began to unwind; her eyes held an incredulous expression. "Luke? Is that really you?" She uncurled herself and tentatively reached a hand toward his head. "Can you talk?"

He stared at her. He could understand everything she said, but a wolf's mouth couldn't form human words.

"I guess not." She rested her hand on top of his head and stroked his fur. "You're so soft." Tilting her head, she studied him. Slowly, all traces of fear drained from her eyes, and she smiled. "I'm not crazy. This is…amazing."

He hopped onto the couch and licked her face.

She laughed. "Okay, enough of that, mister." She stroked a hand down his shoulder and shook her head. "You're really a werewolf. No wonder Roberta wasn't afraid of you. She knew."

The knot in his chest released, and he jumped down and trotted out of the room to shift back to human form. She was already taking things much better than he'd expected.

She giggled as he stepped back into the room. "So when those women claimed a big animal saved them from the attackers…that was you?"

"Well, me and my team."

"There's more of you? More werewolves?" She giggled again, covering her mouth with her hand. "It feels so weird saying that."

He smiled. "There's a whole pack in New Orleans. About two hundred of us."

"Two *hundred*?" She tugged her bottom lip. "But, the rapist. Who?"

"Demons."

Her mouth fell open. "Demons?"

He sank onto the sofa next to her. Closer this time, but still not close enough. "Yeah. Someone has been summoning them. We're working on finding the bastard and putting a stop to all this."

He could practically see the gears turning in her head as she shook it, narrowing her eyes, trying to understand. "But how come no one knows about you? How do you keep two hundred people hidden?"

"We're not hidden. We're regular people, who happen to have some special abilities. We try to keep it a secret." Silence stretched between them like an infinite sea. What thoughts were tumbling through her mind? He could only imagine the emotions she must have been enduring, but relief seemed to be somewhere at the top of the list. He wanted to scoop her into his arms and tell her everything would be fine now. To wrap her in comfort and reassurance. But she needed time to process, and he could give her that too.

Finally, she spoke. "And that's why you freaked out on me? Because you're a werewolf, and you thought I couldn't handle it?"

He knelt on the floor in front of her and grasped her hands. "I'm so sorry, Macey. Can you find it in your heart to give me another chance?"

She searched his eyes, and his chest tightened as he prayed she'd find what she needed. Tugging him onto the sofa, she held his face in her hands. A smile spread across her own, reaching all the way to her eyes. "I think I can."

He kissed her. Deep and slow. Passionate heat built in his chest, its flames licking out to set his body on fire. She'd taken him back, and he would never lose her again.

"Just promise me one thing," she said as she snaked

her arms around the back of his neck. "No more secrets, okay?"

He swallowed. "Well, there is one more thing you need to know."

She pulled back, eyeing him warily. "What's that?"

"It'll be easier to explain it at the bar. That's our base. Can you go there with me?"

She hesitated, folding her hands in her lap. "All right. Let me get dressed."

A thousand emotions danced through Macey's heart as they approached O'Malley's Pub, but relief topped them all. Relief that Luke still wanted her. That she wasn't going crazy. The case was solvable now that she had some answers. It was all starting to make sense. She had hundreds of questions to ask him, but for now, she relished the elation of holding his hand.

"There's a hierarchy in the pack, a lot like regular wolves. We have an alpha who's in charge, and everyone answers to him."

"So he's like a king?" They turned right on St. Philip and stepped around a young man playing his guitar on the sidewalk. She dropped some change into his instrument case and wrapped her arm around Luke's bicep.

"Not really a king. More like a boss. The president of the company. But the alpha is determined by bloodline, so I guess king works too. All alphas have to be descendants of the first family."

"Okay." She shook her head. It was hard to believe this was all real, but she'd seen it with her own eyes. What would her partner think now?

"When the alpha dies or retires, if his son is a full werewolf, he takes over. Otherwise, the oldest first family male steps in."

"Full? You can be half a werewolf?"

He smiled and kissed the top of her head. "Only the firstborn child of a werewolf couple can actually shift. The younger siblings are born with special abilities—my sister has premonitions—but they can't turn into wolves."

"Interesting. And what would happen if a werewolf and a human had a baby together? Would the baby be a werewolf? Or half a werewolf?" She bit her lip. What was she thinking asking a loaded question like that? They'd just solidified their relationship, and she was already asking about their babies?

"There's a fifty-fifty chance the children will be weres. Mating with humans dilutes the bloodlines." He looked at her with an expression she didn't understand. Regret, maybe? If he married her, would he be shunned for not producing werewolf offspring?

They stopped outside the pub door, and he turned to face her. "That's the reason I ran off that night. Some weres do mate with humans, but the son of the alpha can't." He pinned her with an intense gaze, searching her eyes for understanding.

A heaviness settled in her core as the realization dawned on her. "You're the son...of the alpha?"

"Yeah."

She froze, a wave of nausea rolling through her stomach. Was all this for nothing? The revelation of his secret, her acceptance of his supernatural existence...and she couldn't be with him because he was werewolf royalty? "But I'm human, Luke."

He tucked a strand of hair behind her ear and gently

kissed her cheek. His mouth lingered by her ear, his warm breath tickling her skin. "You're a werewolf, Macey."

She shook her head. "No."

"Yes. Your abilities? The way you can read energy? It's because you're a were."

She crossed her arms over her tightening chest. "I think I would know if I turned into a wolf."

He raised his eyebrows. "Only the first-born child can shift."

She covered her mouth. "My sister." Her head spun. She leaned into Luke for support, trying to understand what he was telling her. "But she ran away. How could she —? How did you—?"

He wrapped his arm around her shoulders and led her into the pub. "She's here, Macey. Alexis is here."

As Macey's gaze landed on the woman at the bar, the entire room became a vacuum, sucking the air from her lungs. She fisted her hands at her sides, using the burn of her nails biting into her palms to keep herself steady. Thoughts raced through her mind, turning her into a whirlwind of emotions…none of them pleasant.

She wasn't the gangly teenager Macey remembered, but the woman at the bar was definitely her sister. She laughed at something the bartender had said, but as soon as their eyes met, Alexis's face went slack with shock. She stumbled to her feet and pressed her back against the bar, gripping with her hands as if she needed to steady herself. "Macey."

Macey hadn't seen her sister in twenty years. What was she supposed to say? She rubbed the back of her neck and focused on the sensation of Luke's hand resting on her back, grounding her.

Alexis looked from Macey to Luke and back again. "Macey, I was going to find you—"

"Don't, Alexis. Just…don't." All the resentment she'd felt toward her sister bubbled to the surface, tainting her words with venom. She counted backward from ten, but this was an ancient anger that couldn't be quelled with tricks. "After all these years…you show up in *my* city, and you don't even have the guts to talk to me? You must have known I was here."

Alexis took a step toward her. "I did. That's why I came."

"Shut up. You don't get to talk to me." She couldn't deal with this. Not now. "I'm going home."

"Wait, Macey." Luke grasped her arm, but she yanked it away.

"I want to go home."

He followed her out the door as she stomped into the street. She fumed with anger. Her hands balled into fists, nails cutting into her skin again. *Focus on the physical pain. It hurts less than the betrayal.* She struggled to breathe. What did all this mean? Her sister was here, in New Orleans, and she was a werewolf. She'd only just found out werewolves existed, and now she was related to one?

Luke approached her tentatively. "Can I walk with you?"

She sucked in a deep, shaky breath and blew it out hard. "Yeah." She shook her head. "I…why didn't you warn me? I wasn't prepared for a shock like that."

He laced his fingers through hers and gave her a sheepish look. "I'm sorry. I thought it would be a good surprise to see her. I screwed up again, didn't I?"

"Yeah, you did." His touch calmed her. His intentions had been in the right place; she couldn't be mad at him.

"But…it's okay. I need some time to process all this. I've got so many thoughts and emotions swirling around inside me, and I don't know how to sort it all out."

"Do you want me to come over? We can talk about it. I'll answer as many questions for you as I can."

She chewed her bottom lip, contemplating his offer. "Okay."

They walked three blocks to her house, and Thor greeted them at the door. He purred and wound his way through their legs, stopping to rub his head against Luke's calf.

"Looks like you won him over," she said.

Luke scratched the cat behind the ears. "Yeah, don't tell anybody how I gained his trust. I'm about to be alpha. I can't go around submitting to cats."

"It's weird he was never afraid of me."

"Why is that weird?"

"I'm assuming he didn't like you at first because he could sense you're a werewolf, right?"

"Sure. He's got animal instincts. He could smell the wolf inside me."

"So, why couldn't he smell the one in me?"

An amused grin curved his lips. "There is no wolf inside you. You're all woman."

She let out her breath in a huff. "I don't understand."

"You have the werewolf gene, but since you're second born, it's dormant. You're a carrier, but you don't have any canine traits yourself."

"So I'll never turn into a wolf?"

He shook his head.

That's a relief, but… "Why do I have a bloodhound's sense of smell?"

He shrugged. "Lucky, I guess. Like any other were,

your blood is sacred. It's where your magic lives, and it shouldn't be taken lightly."

"Sacred?" A sinking feeling formed in her stomach. "I've donated blood before. Did I spread my magic? Or could I have hurt someone?"

His eyebrows scrunched together as he considered her questions. "I don't think so. Like I said, your werewolf gene is dormant; it shouldn't be a problem. The receiver's own white blood cells would have been able to destroy the foreign substance, so I wouldn't worry about it. I hope you won't donate again, though. Our laws forbid it."

Jeez. Special werewolf laws? She shook her head and motioned for him to sit on the sofa. "You've got a lot of explaining to do. Want a beer?"

"Yeah."

She popped the tops on two Blue Moons and tossed the lids in the trash. They landed on the wilted, brown flowers he'd given her on their date, so she pushed them farther down in the bin and laid a napkin over them. This was a fresh start. She didn't need a reminder of the trouble they'd been through.

He grinned as she sat next to him and offered him the brew. "I thought Abita was your favorite."

"You changed my mind." She held up her bottle. "Here's to starting over. Truthfully this time." They clinked the glass necks together and took a long drink. The frosty bubbles soothed the tightness in her throat and warmed her from the inside out.

Luke took her hand. "I will tell you everything you want to know."

They talked for hours, Macey listening intently as he explained the origin of the New Orleans werewolves and the way the pack worked. The politics confused her, but she tried to grasp the concepts. She must have had a glazed look in her eyes because he stopped and smiled at her, cupping her cheek in his hand.

"This must sound so strange to you. You're taking it like a champ."

"Really? Maybe once the shock wears off, I'm going to have a heart attack." She put her hand on his, leaning her face into his palm. The tingling energy that used to frighten her now provided comfort. Warmth.

"So this electric feeling is because you're a werewolf? And it will always be there?"

"It's like a paranormal calling card of sorts. All magical beings have a certain energy they radiate. Generally, you get used to it, but it's stronger with you. Stronger than I've ever felt with anyone. And different."

"I like it."

He leaned forward and pressed his lips to hers. Her pulse quickened, a different kind of energy racing through her veins.

"That spark though," he whispered, his mouth hovering over hers, "is only ours." He winked and pulled away. "Do you have any more questions? Or is that enough weirdness for one day?"

She shook her head. That was definitely enough. "I guess I should talk to Alexis."

"I can give you the number she registered with, if you want to call her."

Macey nodded. "I can't believe she's a werewolf."

"Technically, you are too. And so is your boyfriend."

There was no explanation for the way she felt about this man, and she wasn't going to question it anymore. If magic and werewolves were real, maybe this seemingly otherworldly force that drew her to him was real too. She gazed at the hopeful longing in his eyes as her heart flip-flopped in her chest. She'd finally found a place she belonged. "You're my boyfriend?"

"I'd like to be. If that's okay with you."

"I think we can work something out." Desire pooled below her navel, and her fingers twitched with the need to feel the sinew beneath his shirt.

As if he read her mind, he traced his fingertips along her jawline, leaving a trail of heat on her skin that tingled with energy. He hooked his finger under her chin and leaned in so close she could feel the warmth of his breath on her lips. He stayed there, letting the anticipation build until she thought she'd have to throw herself at him. She closed her eyes and inched closer to him. Electricity danced between their lips as he slowly leaned in and took her mouth with his.

His tongue slipped out to taste her, licking her upper lip, then moving down to trace her lower one. Every muscle in her body relaxed as she melted into his embrace. "I think that's been enough talk."

The corner of his mouth tugged into a wicked grin. "I agree." He stood, pulling her body to his, pressing the evidence of his own desire against her stomach and taking her mouth once more. She snaked her hands over the ripples of his abs, memorizing every cut of muscle with her fingers. He was warm and hard. All over. Never in her life had she desired a man this much, and it was all she could do to keep her knees from buckling beneath her.

He kissed along her jaw, trailing his lips up to her earlobe, down her neck, and across her collar bone. She slipped her hands beneath his shirt, kneading the tight muscles as she worked her way up to his chest. When his lips caressed the top of her breast in the dip of her V-neck shirt, shivers ran down her spine. She dug her nails into his skin, and a soft moan escaped her lips.

He scooped her into his arms, frantically kissing her as if she might slip away if he stopped. "Bedroom?" he breathed into her mouth.

"Down the hall on the left."

He carried her into the bedroom and stopped in the doorway. Soft sunlight filtered through the sheer white drapes covering the bay window, casting a golden glow on the alabaster bedspread. She slid from his arms and beckoned him into the room. Climbing onto the mattress, she held out her arms, inviting him in, but he stood by the bed with an expression of awe in his eyes. "You're so beautiful, Macey. I could stare at you all day."

"I can think of a lot more fun things to do, but that would require you climbing into bed with me." She rose to her knees, hooked her finger in the waistband of his jeans and pulled him toward her. Her gaze fixed on the bulge beneath his zipper, and she stroked her palm across the mound. He sucked in a sharp breath, and she clutched the bottom of his shirt, yanking it up over his head.

He caught her wrists in his hands, and she dropped his shirt on the floor. "Are you sure you want to do this? You've been through a lot today." His gaze was so intense, she almost second guessed herself. But his grip on her, though gentle, aroused a primal need inside her. His broad shoulders and perfectly chiseled stomach had her entire body aching with the need to feel him on top of her, inside her, becoming part of her.

"I want you to take me."

He cocked an eyebrow and released her hands. "You don't have to ask me twice."

She unbuttoned her shirt and slid it over her shoulders. "I didn't plan to."

"And if I'd hesitated?" His grin widened as he climbed onto the bed and laid her on her back.

"You wouldn't have." Desire filled her to the core, tightening her womb and making her mouth go dry as she reached behind her back, unsnapped her bra, and tossed it on the floor.

In an instant, he was on her, pressing his body against hers, taking her mouth in a passionate kiss. He trailed his lips down her neck, his tongue flicking out to taste her skin as he explored her breasts with his hands.

He moved down, tasting and caressing every inch of her bare skin. Every nerve in her body sung with electricity as his lips inched closer to her navel. He looked at her with passion-drunk eyes as he undid the button on her pants and slowly slid down the zipper. He worked the clothing over her hips, tossed it on the floor, and sat up to look at her. "You are the most beautiful woman I have ever seen."

He said it with such conviction, she believed every word. She bit her lip, anticipation tightening in her core as he removed his jeans. He cupped her breasts, teasing the sensitive nipples with his thumbs, and her breath hitched as he slid his hand down her body to caress between her legs.

She took his length in her hand, and he moaned.

She stroked up and down, reveling in his masculine groans and the way his body reacted to her touch. Who knew she could derive so much pleasure from making him feel good? His eyes closed as he tipped his head back and let his breath out in a hiss. He put his hand on hers to still her stroking. "If you don't slow down, this is going to be over before it starts."

She released her grip. "Well, we wouldn't want that now, would we?"

"No, we wouldn't. Let's take it slow this time."

She craved making him orgasm as much as she craved feeling her own, but she relented, lying back and letting him take the lead.

He trailed his lips from her belly button, across her hip and down her inner thigh, his velvet touch raising goose bumps on her skin. She spread her legs, offering herself to him to do with as he pleased, allowing herself to be vulnerable if only for the moment. As he flicked out his tongue to stroke her folds, fire shot through her core.

Fisting the sheets in her hands, she let out a soft moan. She'd have to let him have his way more often.

"You taste even better than I imagined." His voice vibrated across her sensitive center, tightening her stomach, making her ache for more.

Gripping her hips, he circled his tongue around her clit, sending waves of ecstasy pulsing through her body. He slipped one finger inside her, then another, moving them in, out, and around until she lost control.

She cried out, tossing her head back and tangling her fingers in his hair as the orgasm ripped through her body. "Oh my God, Luke! I need you inside me." She heaved heavy breaths as he slowed his stroking and gazed up at her hungrily.

"Yes, ma'am."

She reached across to her nightstand drawer and grabbed a condom.

He slid the rubber down his shaft and pressed it against her opening. His smoldering gaze locked with hers, and he pushed inside slowly, deliberately, stretching her to the point of pleasurable pain. She gasped as he filled her, and he slid back out, until only the tip remained inside her. He held it there, staring at her with so much adoration in his eyes her breath stilled in her chest. A thousand thoughts rushed through her mind, but she couldn't form the words she wanted to say.

He crushed his mouth to hers as he plunged inside her, and she gave herself to him. Fully. Utterly. Completely. She was done holding back. She'd spent her entire life guarding her heart, but from this moment on it belonged to Luke. She had to relinquish it because she wanted every part of him—body, heart, and soul.

He moaned, hooking his hands behind her shoulders and thrusting his hips. Each plunge sent electric tingles pulsing through her middle. He roamed his tongue over her shoulders and up her neck until he found her mouth again. He groaned against her lips as his rhythm increased, pushing her closer and closer to orgasm.

"You're incredible." His breath tickled her ear.

She tried to utter a response, but hearing his raspy voice, thick with passion, sent her over the edge again. Her orgasm overtook her, sending wave after wave of pulsing pleasure rocketing through her body.

As he found his own release, he relaxed on top of her and nuzzled his face into her hair. With a deep inhale, he rolled to his side and pulled her into his arms, grazing his lips across her forehead, her nose, her mouth.

"You are amazing."

She nuzzled into his chest and sighed. "You were pretty awesome, yourself." Though awesome didn't begin to describe what she'd just experienced. Astounding. Incredible. Mind-blowing. The best sex of her life. But it had been so much more than sex. So much raw emotion. So much…dare she say it? Love.

After cleaning up and snuggling under the covers, Luke dozed off in the warmth of Macey's embrace. The way she fit in his arms. The way he fit inside her. Everything about her was so…right. He had no doubt in his mind that she truly was his fate-bound. His soul mate. They were destined to be together.

As he lay on his back, she traced the cut of his muscles with her soft fingertips, and he opened his eyes sleepily and smiled at the beautiful creature in his arms.

A werewolf after all.

I love you. The words trembled on the tip of his tongue, but he bit them back. She'd been through so much today, he didn't want to overwhelm her.

"I'm curious." She propped her head on her hand. "Since I'm not a full werewolf, would our…" Her cheeks flushed pink, and she pretended to inspect her fingernails. "Never mind."

Rolling onto his side, he rested his hand on her hip. "Would our children be full werewolves?" His heart pounded, a smile stretching across his face. She was already thinking about their future; he couldn't imagine a life without her.

She pulled her hair over her shoulder, nervously combing it with her fingers, avoiding his gaze. "Yeah. I mean, not that I'm thinking about stuff like that."

"It doesn't matter whether or not you can shift. You've got were blood, so our first child would be full. The second would be like you."

Drawing her eyebrows together, she looked at him. "The second?"

He shrugged. "And the third and fourth."

Her eyes widened. "Four?"

He chuckled. "How many kids do you want then? Five?"

She playfully hit him in the face with a pillow. "Stop it. I don't know." She snuggled down into his side. "What time is it?"

He kissed her head before glancing at the clock on her nightstand. "Seven."

"Ugh. I have to go to work soon."

He held her tighter, unwilling to let her go so soon after he'd finally made her his. Lying there naked with her warm body pressed against him…he couldn't think of anywhere he'd rather be. If only he could make the moment last forever.

She sat up to stretch, and the sheet fell away, revealing her creamy breasts and perfect pink nipples. His cock went instantly hard, and he pulled her on top of him for another kiss. He could get used to waking up to this every day.

CHAPTER TWENTY

"Well, our rapist has definitely gotten smarter," Bryce said to Macey as they left yet another hotel room. "He's getting them out of the alleys, anyway."

"Yeah." It didn't make sense. This victim had given the same description of the attacker—he appeared completely human aside from the red eyes. And these weren't random attacks like the others. This guy met his victims in bars, charmed them, seduced them into trusting him. Maybe the incidents were unrelated. Maybe this attacker wasn't a demon.

Bryce cracked his knuckles as they stepped onto Bourbon Street. Later in the day, rap and hip hop music from various bars would mix with classic rock to form a cacophony of drunken sound, and inebriated tourists would stumble through the street in search of their next drinks. But this early in the morning, the only people milling about were the locals on their way to their jobs and the workers washing the streets.

"You pick up anything with your spirit sensors?" he asked. "Any paranormal theories about this one?"

"I think it's just a man. Probably wearing contacts. You know how people like to let their freak flags fly here. Normally, no one would bat an eye at a pair of red eyes."

Bryce rolled his neck as if the stress of the case was getting to him. It was getting to all of them. "And the ones from the alleys?"

She shrugged. "Same. Probably a group of men…a cult or a fraternity." Now that she knew the truth, she understood why Luke had tried so hard to cover it up. She'd be on a fast track to the looney bin if she tried to convince the police they were searching for demons. Better to play it down and let the werewolves take care of the problem.

"So, no evil spirits or monsters then?"

She forced a smile. "Come on, Bryce. You have to think logically. Those things don't exist."

"I'm glad you've come to your senses. Hey, want to grab a bite to eat before you head home?"

An icy breeze snaked up her arm, wrapping tightly around her neck. She froze. For a moment, she couldn't breathe as frigid tendrils of dread encased her racing heart. Then the entity released its hold and whispered in her ear. *"Did you think I'd forgotten about you?"* The sinister voice was unmistakable—the same spirit that had tormented her before. It had to be connected somehow.

"I'm coming for you." The spirit's energy circled her one more time before flitting away on the breeze. She reached out with her mind to find it, but the entity's essence dissipated as quickly as it had formed.

"Macey?" Bryce waved a hand in front of her face. "Did you hear me?"

She blinked. "Yeah. Sorry. I was…lost in thought."

"Everything okay?"

She forced another smile and nodded. "I'm fine. I'm not very hungry. Thanks for the invite, though."

He arched an eyebrow and looked at her skeptically. "No problem, boss. Take care of yourself."

The sun barely peaked above the horizon as she made her way toward St. Philip and O'Malley's Pub. Why a bar needed to be open at six in the morning was beyond her, but Luke asked her to stop by when she got off work. She quickened her steps as the anticipation of seeing him again built.

The spirit had rattled her, but since Roberta had helped her develop her powers, she was confident she could keep it out of her head. Still, she needed to let Luke know what was going on. She should have mentioned the spirit before, but it took a while for her brain to catch up with everything he'd revealed to her. Maybe he could figure out what the dead guy had to do with the demons.

She entered O'Malley's and made her way to the bar. The place sat empty, except for the tattooed bartender slicing lemons on the countertop. Her mind flashed back to the night she met Luke, to the image of his biceps flexing and contracting as he did the very same thing. She remembered the first time she'd felt that magical jolt of energy from his touch—a feeling she'd grown to love so much. Her stomach flitted at the memories, and she shivered.

"Not much business in the early morning, I guess?"

The bartender grinned. "Not of the human variety. I don't think we've been properly introduced. I'm Chase."

"Hi. I'm Macey."

His grin widened. "I know. Luke's told me all about you."

Heat flushed her cheeks, and her heart did a giddy

little flip-flop. Luke was talking about her? She regained her composure before she spoke. "All good things, I hope."

He winked. "Of course. Luke's in the back. I'll call him for you." Chase picked up the phone and made the call as a dark-haired man with deep brown eyes entered the room. He narrowed his gaze at her and strode toward the bar, stopping two feet in front of her.

"Well, well. If it isn't our fearless leader's new plaything." He raked his gaze over her body and cocked an eyebrow as he stared at her chest. "I can see why he likes you."

Refusing to take the bait, she fisted her hands at her sides and counted backward from ten. She would not let this asshole get to her.

Chase hung up the phone. "Dude, that's Luke's girlfriend. Show some respect."

"Oh, I could respect her all night long." He slinked past her, his serpent-like gaze boring into her as he stepped behind the bar.

She locked eyes with the snaky brunet, daring him to make another comment. She'd dealt with plenty of men like him before. Misogynistic jerks who thought they needed to keep women in their place. If he was trying to intimidate her, it wasn't working.

Chase shifted uncomfortably, his gaze flicking between Macey and the man. "Luke's finishing up. He'll be out in a few minutes. Can I get you anything while you wait?"

She ignored the snake and beamed a smile at the bartender. "Thanks, Chase. I'm fine."

The jerk ran his tongue over his teeth. "Yes, you are."

"Stephen…" Chase's voice was heavy with warning.

Stephen straightened his spine and eyed the bartender. "You need to remember your place." He returned his sickly stare to Macey's chest. "If you ever want to know what a real man tastes like, you come give me a lick, darlin'."

Her stomach churned in disgust, but she maintained her poise. She smoothed her hair into her bun and leaned her forearm on the bar. "Stephen, I'd sooner lick the sludge off the Bourbon Street sidewalk than get my tongue anywhere near you."

Chase laughed and slapped Stephen on the shoulder. "Sounds like you need to remember *your* place, buddy… and your mate."

He balked, but she was just getting started. Her entire career, she'd had to deal with disrespect. Condescension. She was sick of trying to prove her worth to men. "Luke is more man than you'll ever be. He—"

The front door swung open and a pair of college-age guys staggered in. The blond seemed to be drunk already —or still drunk from the night before. His friend looked rough, with messy hair and a crumpled blue shirt, but at least he could walk straight.

"C'mon, man. Let's go," blue shirt said.

"Hold on. Hold on. I need another beer." Blondie swaggered up to the bar. "Gimme a Coors Light."

An amused smile lit on Chase's lips. "We don't serve Coors here."

"Why the hell not?" He cut his gaze over to Macey and straightened his posture as if he just noticed she was there. "Hey there, sweetheart." He moved behind her and rubbed her shoulders.

Not another one. She stiffened as his fingers kneaded her muscles, and when he started to glide his hands over her shoulders and onto her chest, she grabbed him by the wrist. In one swift movement, she pivoted around and wrenched his arm behind his back, pinning his head to the bar.

"Ow."

Without loosening her grip, she leaned down to speak to him face-to-face. Her years on the police force had taught her to keep her voice calm and steady—a whisper was much more intimidating than a shout. "I just got off work, and I really don't want to haul your drunk ass down to the station right now. So I'll make you a deal. I'm going to let you go, you're going to take your friend and walk out of this bar, and we'll pretend like this never happened. Go back to your hotel room and sleep it off. Okay?"

Fear widened his eyes as his gaze darted about the room. "Yes, ma'am. I'm sorry."

She released him, and he grabbed his friend and scurried to the door.

"Go to your hotel."

"Yes, ma'am."

"Hot damn." Chase gave her a slow round of applause. Stephen gritted his teeth and glared at her as she settled onto a barstool.

"Impressive." The bartender nodded his approval.

Macey shrugged. "Not really." She'd dealt with worse. "Why don't you serve Coors Light here? It's pretty popular, isn't it?"

Chase chuckled. "Because it's also called the Silver Bullet."

It took her a moment to catch on. "Oh...Wait. That's a real thing? Can a silver bullet really kill a werewolf?"

"A silver bullet can kill anything if it hits the right spot." Chase grabbed a rag and wiped the counter where the drunk guy had been pinned. "But no. That's a myth. Silver doesn't hurt werewolves." He held up his right hand to show her a silver ring on his finger. "Not serving the beer is part of the so-called joke." He nodded to the cardboard *Employees and Werewolves Only* sign on the door.

Her cheeks flushed with embarrassment. Of course it was a myth. She was almost afraid to ask her next question. "What about full moons?"

Chase smiled wistfully. "Our wolves are more powerful under a full moon, and the urge to shift is stronger. Lunar cycles affect us, but they don't control us like the movies would have you believe."

"I guess I've still got a lot to learn."

"Oh, yeah." Stephen grumbled as he lifted the hinged part of the bar and headed toward the back. Luke stepped through the swinging door as Stephen opened it. "I thought you said she'd be useful." He shoved past Luke to get through the door.

Luke's face lit up as soon as he looked at her, and he strutted forward to greet her. "Hello, beautiful." He swept her in his arms and spun her around. "How was work?"

"Fine. What did he mean by useful?"

He shook his head. "Ignore my cousin. He has an inferiority complex."

"He's your cousin?" The two men looked nothing alike. Their personalities were even more different. How could Luke be related to a guy like that?

"Unfortunately." He trailed the back of his fingers across her cheek and planted a firm yet inviting kiss on her lips. Her head swam with desire. She slid her hands behind his neck and pulled him closer, deepening the kiss. She couldn't get enough of this man. His tongue brushed hers, and a shudder ran through her body, weakening her knees.

Chase cleared his throat.

Luke smiled. "Sorry, man. I can't seem to keep my hands off her." He turned his smoldering gaze back on her. "Ready to go?"

Boy, was she. But once they made it to his house, she'd lose the ability to think straight. "Before we leave, there's something I need to tell you."

A crooked smile lifted one corner of his mouth. "Uh oh. That doesn't sound good. It's not going to be the 'it's not you, it's me' speech already, is it?" He said it jokingly, but she detected a hint of apprehension in his voice.

She laced her fingers through his to ease his concern. "It's nothing like that." She glanced at Chase, who stared at the ceiling, doing a terrible job of pretending not to listen. "There's a spirit that's been bothering me."

The bartender raised his eyebrows and looked at Luke.

"I thought you couldn't talk to spirits." Luke eased onto a barstool and tightened his grip on her hand.

"I can't, normally. But this one talks to me."

His jaw tightened, concern etching lines in his forehead. "Is it the same one from the woods? When that tree branch almost…"

"Yes. And I know who he is, but I can't figure out how he's connected to all this."

A vein in his neck throbbed, and anxiety tightened his eyes. "Who is he?"

"Do you remember that body that went missing from the morgue?"

The men exchanged a knowing glance, and Luke nodded.

"It's him. He's been following me to the crime scenes, but I can't figure out why. Or how he's communicating with me…trying to get inside me. I can't talk to spirits."

He took a deep breath. "He's not just a spirit. He's a halfling."

"What's that?"

"Half human, half demon. He should've reincarnated into that missing body, but he's chosen to stay in spirit form instead."

"Well, that explains a lot." The werewolves hadn't accidentally killed a human criminal. They'd killed a monster.

"Are you certain it's the same guy from the morgue?"

She nodded. "I saw his face when he got inside my head. Right before I forced him out."

Anger flashed in his eyes before he softened his gaze. "Don't worry, beautiful. I won't let him hurt you." He traced his fingers across her forehead and kissed her cheek. "I will keep you safe. Always."

While the gesture was sweet, she certainly didn't need coddling. "I'm not worried. He only got inside me once, and I know how to keep him out now."

"Still. Just know that I'm here…that we're all here…" He glanced at the bartender. "To protect you."

Chase chuckled under his breath. "Like she needs it."

Luke ignored his friend's comment and wrapped his arms around her. "You've had a long night working. Let's go back to my place, and I'll take you to bed."

Her heart pounded at the thought, and she slid her arms around his waist. "Okay, but I do need to sleep *sometime* today."

"Oh, I know." He nuzzled her neck, his teeth lightly grazing her skin and sending goose bumps running down her arm. "And I promise I'll let you." He moved to the other side of her neck and trailed his tongue up to her earlobe. His breath warmed her skin, raising goose bumps on the other arm. "After I have my way with you."

"Here we are." Luke led Macey through the door and into the living room. "It's not much when you see it in the daylight, is it?"

She smiled as her gaze danced about the room. "It's nice. Cozy."

An empty beer bottle sat next to a crumpled chip bag on the coffee table, and he whisked them away to the trash. "Sorry about the mess."

"It's not messy."

She was right. That was the only piece of trash lying out, but he straightened the pillows on the couch anyway. They'd already shared themselves intimately, but something about having her in his house made him feel more vulnerable. Her presence seemed to fill the room with warmth, turning his eating and sleeping quarters into a place he'd like her to call home.

Clasping her hands behind her back, she bit her bottom lip and gazed up at him. His cock swelled at the sight of those hooded emerald eyes, and when her tongue flicked out to moisten her lips, his heart nearly beat out of his chest.

"So, about that *way* you wanted to have with me." She untied the knot in her hair, and it spilled around her shoulders.

Dear lord, he could have taken her right there on the living room floor. Just watching the rise and fall of her breasts as she breathed was enough to make him lose control. But he intended to make this moment last. "I've been out hunting all night. I could use a shower."

She stepped toward him and ran a finger down his chest, stopping at the waistband of his jeans. He held his breath as she popped the button and slid the zipper down. Another wave of heat flashed through his groin as she slipped her hand into his pants to grip his shaft, his body shuddering at the feel of her soft fingers wrapped around him.

"I'm feeling a little dirty, myself. Mind if I join you?"

He cupped her face in his hands and slid his fingers into her hair. "Let's go clean you up then."

"Okay." She smiled, keeping a firm grip on his dick.

"You might want to let me go, so I can walk." He laughed and tugged her hand from his pants before leading her into the bathroom.

Leaving their clothes in a heap on the floor, they stepped into the shower. Rivulets of moisture rolled down Macey's skin, sliding over her sensuous curves before falling to the ground. She was a hot, wet goddess standing before him, and all he could do was stare. "You're so beautiful. I really could just look at you all day."

A sly grin curved her pink lips. "And I really *couldn't* let you do that. I need you to touch me."

A low growl resonated in his chest as he lathered his hands and slid them over her body. Her soft skin was a stark contrast to his calloused hands, but the look in her eyes said she enjoyed his touch. Her breath hitched when his thumb brushed her nipple, and he cupped her breasts in his hands. She closed her eyes and moaned softly as he pinched the pink pearls between his fingers, hardening them with his touch.

He continued washing her, sliding his hands over her stomach, down one leg and up the other, and when his fingers reached the sensitive nub between her legs, she gasped. He slipped a finger inside her tight, wet warmth, and she moaned. Good God, how he loved this woman.

He reveled in the sensuous sounds that escaped her lips as he caressed her.

She trembled as he rubbed her clit, her breaths becoming rapid and shallow. "Luke, I can't...I can't stand up."

"Hold on to me, baby."

She clutched his shoulders and pressed her head to his chest as she came. The sounds she made. The way her entire body shuddered with her orgasm. It was the most beautiful thing he'd ever seen. A sight he needed to see every day for the rest of his life.

Her breathing slowed, and she looked at him with mischief in her eyes. "You're still dirty. We need to fix that." The water beat down on his back as she lathered her hands and slid them down his chest, his stomach, his legs. Her skin felt like velvet rubbing against his, her magic energy mixing with the sparks of passion igniting in his core.

She knelt to the ground and took his length in her hand, circling her tongue around the tip. Fire shot through his veins as she took him into her mouth and gazed up at him. Never looking away, she moved her mouth up and down his cock, taking more and more of him in with each stroke of her lips. His stomach clenched as his orgasm built, but he put his hands on her shoulders to stop her.

"I need to make love to you. Right now." His voice was raw with need.

She released her hold and ran her hot tongue from base to tip before rising to her feet and kissing him. Grabbing his neck, she hooked her legs around his waist and pressed her slick, wet body against him. He fumbled to turn off the water and carried her to the bedroom to toss her onto the bed. He needed to be inside her. To fill her. To feel her.

He grabbed a condom from the drawer, and she yanked it from his hands, ripping open the package. "Lie down." Her command thrilled him, and he did as he was told. She straddled him and gave his cock a final lick before sliding on the condom and guiding him to her folds. Sweet elation engulfed him as she sheathed him.

Beads of water dripped from the ends of her hair, falling onto his stomach and rolling toward the place where their bodies joined. His gaze followed the trail, and he memorized the look, the sensation, of becoming one with the woman he loved.

"You feel so good inside me, Luke." She rocked her hips, gliding up and down his shaft, slowly at first, but increasing steadily as she held his gaze. Her hooded eyes. Her soft moans. He could feel her need as if it were his own—passionate, lustful, full of emotion. She ran her hands over his chest, her gentle caress making his entire body ache for her. For them. He belonged to Macey...in this moment and forever. Though neither of them had said the words aloud, she loved him too. He could see it in her eyes. Feel it in the way she touched him.

Her movements quickened, her breathing growing shallow, and she tossed back her head and cried out as the climax overtook her. Seeing her writhing in pleasure as she rode him sent him over the edge. His own orgasm exploded, and he ground his hips against her, thrusting deeper and deeper inside her.

As their rhythm slowed, she leaned forward, laying her breasts to his chest, touching her lips to his. His heart swelled with so much love for the woman in his arms, and he knew, without a shadow of a doubt, she was meant to be his mate. His wife. A satisfied *mmm* escaped her lips as she rolled off him and snuggled into his side.

As she started to doze, he slid out of bed. She reached for him, and his chest tightened at the gesture.

"Where are you going?"

"I need to throw this away. I'll be right back." He tossed the condom in the trash and closed the drapes.

She rolled onto her back. "Don't do that. I can barely keep my eyes open as it is."

"Then close them." He slid back into bed and held her in his arms. "Sleep here today. With me."

She snuggled her back into his front and tugged his arm around her chest. "I have to see my sister this afternoon." The sleepiness in her voice had him hard all over again. He could imagine falling asleep with her in his arms every day. Waking up wrapped in her warmth.

"What time do you need to get up? I'll set an alarm."

"Noon?"

"Consider it done." He kissed her neck as she relaxed in his arms and slipped into blissful sleep.

CHAPTER TWENTY-ONE

MACEY SHUFFLED INTO JACKSON SQUARE AND FOUND her sister sitting on a bench facing the St. Louis Cathedral. Alexis smiled tentatively and lifted a hand to wave. She wore beige cargo pants and a fitted green tank top that revealed her muscular arms. Her nails were short, but clean, her hands calloused like she worked a manual labor job. Macey returned her smile and sat next to her.

She'd only texted her sister, not having the courage to speak to her on the phone. Now that they were face to face, she still didn't know what to say. She stared up at the eighteenth-century church and collected her thoughts. The shock of seeing Alexis after all these years had subsided, and now she wanted answers. "Why did you come here?"

Alexis stared straight ahead. "To find you."

Macey examined the cathedral façade, with its triple steeples towering over the square. She stared at the clock below the middle steeple, ticking away the hours, and contemplated all the years they'd lost. So much time gone. Their relationship had crumbled into nothing. Could they rebuild it? "How long have you been in New Orleans?"

"A few weeks."

She inhaled a deep breath and held it. A few weeks… and her sister hadn't bothered to contact her. "How did you know I was here?"

"I saw you on the news." She finally looked at her. "Macey, I came as soon as I learned you were here. I was going to talk to you myself. I just needed time to figure out what to say."

It had been twenty years; a few weeks didn't make much of a difference. She had her sister back, and that was the important thing. So why did it still hurt so much?

A bead of sweat rolled down Macey's neck, and she wiped it away. "You abandoned me. Why come back now?"

"I changed, Macey. I turned into a werewolf, for Christ's sake. What was I supposed to do? I didn't know what was happening to me. Mom and Dad never prepared me."

Her jaw tightened. "They died."

"I…" Alexis sighed. "I know. I'm not blaming them, but put yourself in my place for a second. Imagine being thirteen years old, having no knowledge that any type of magic exists, much less flows through your own veins. I freaked. I'm sorry."

She had a point. At thirteen, Macey's biggest concern was getting rid of the zit on her nose before taking her yearbook picture. Her sister turned into a werewolf. Still… "You could've come back for me once you figured it out."

"I did." Alexis rested her elbow on the back of the bench. "By the time I found some help and came back, you'd already been adopted. I tried to find out where they'd taken you, but I couldn't get to your records. I was only thirteen. I was a child too."

Her chest tightened. "You came back for me?" All these years Macey thought her sister had abandoned her without a second thought. But she hadn't. Not on purpose, anyway.

Alexis smiled. "Of course, I did. You're my little sister. I love you."

"I love you too." A glimmer of the bond they'd shared as children sparked in her core. Perhaps they could rebuild their relationship.

"Yoo hoo. Macey." A melodic voice drifted on the air. Macey looked up to see Roberta, dressed in a long brown skirt and a colorful blouse, sitting at a small folding table and shuffling a stack of tarot cards.

She turned to her sister. "Come here. I want you to meet someone." They stepped around a juggler performing for a small crowd and passed two women in similar gypsy clothes with signs claiming they could read the future. Jackson Square overflowed with faux fortune tellers, so seeing Roberta came as a surprise.

They sat in the chairs at Roberta's table. "I didn't know people with real powers set up booths here," Macey said.

"There are a few of us." She nodded to an older man holding a crystal ball.

"This is my sister, Alexis." Macey leaned in and lowered her voice. "She's a werewolf."

A knowing smile brightened the old woman's face. "So the truth has revealed itself to you."

Macey glanced sideways at Alexis. "It's about time."

"And Luke?" Roberta asked.

Warmth bloomed in Macey's heart at the mention of

his name, and she couldn't fight the smile that curved her lips. "He's good. Luke is…amazing."

Roberta patted Macey's hand in a motherly gesture. "Have you heard from our spirit friend?"

Macey gazed at the stack of tarot cards lying on the table. The thick card stock had yellowed with age, and the edges were frayed. "Yeah, actually. Yesterday…he said he was coming for me." She explained the demon spirit to her sister.

"Sounds like a halfling if his spirit is able to torment you like that," Alexis said. "He'll be hard to kill."

"Especially since he's already dead." Macey traced her finger across the top card, and crackling magical energy seeped into her skin. How many magical things had she touched in her life and written the sensations off as her imagination?

"A werewolf can kill a demon easily," Alexis said. "But a half-demon spirit? It would take a medium to capture something like that."

Roberta smiled. "Macey can do it."

A heavy feeling sank in her stomach. "I cannot." She'd learned how to release energy from an object a few days ago. She didn't have the power to fight a demon.

"The method is the same." Roberta picked up the stack of cards and laid a few of them on the table. A slight smile tugged at her lips before she scooped them up and returned them to the deck. "If you can release energy, you can capture it too."

Macey shook her head. "How?"

"Do the process in reverse. And if you can find out the spirit's name, that will help. A named thing is a tamed thing." Roberta shuffled the cards again. "Luke has an exceptional demon hunting team, dear. You'll be a great asset."

"An asset." Could she help them fight the demons? She'd busted plenty of human monsters since she became a cop, but demons? She chewed her bottom lip. Well, why not? She was a werewolf, after all. "Roberta, why didn't you tell me Luke was a werewolf? If you knew all along…"

"It wasn't my secret to tell, child. Think about how you felt when your mother told me yours."

"Oh." When she put it that way, it made sense. She probably wouldn't have believed her anyway.

Roberta rummaged through her bag and pulled out a rough, oval-shaped crystal, about the size of a potato. A kaleidoscope of colors sparkled in the translucent white stone as she turned it over in her hands. "I use it for releasing energy, but you can also use it to trap your spirit." She offered it to Macey.

She held up her hands. "Oh, I can't."

"Please, take it."

Macey sighed and slipped the rock into her purse. Her mentor made it sound so easy. Hopefully it would be. Trapping a demon spirit wasn't something she could practice beforehand. "Thanks, but…I'm not sure I'll know what to do."

"You will when the time comes." Roberta's gaze was intense, almost as if she were willing the information into Macey's mind. "Now, if you ladies will excuse me, I need to see some paying customers."

Macey and her sister walked up St. Ann and crossed Decatur toward Café Du Monde. They climbed the steps near the iconic green and white coffee shop and peered out over the Mississippi river. Barges drifted by in the distance, and a steamboat churned up the mucky water with its paddle wheel near the shore.

"I'm sorry for blowing up at you in the bar." Macey reached out to touch her sister's arm, but let her hand fall to her side. The anger and resentment she'd felt toward her had quelled, but having Alexis back in her life would take some getting used to. "If I had known you were going to be there, maybe I would have behaved differently. Luke thought it would be a nice surprise."

Alexis ground her teeth. "I understand. It was a huge shock." She chewed her bottom lip and stared at the ground. "Listen. There's something you need to know about Luke."

"He's in line to be the next alpha." That infectious smile returned to her lips. "I know what I'm getting into."

"No. Not that. He…" She shoved her hands in her pockets and kicked at the dirt on the concrete. "I don't know a nice way to say this, so I'm not going to sugar-coat it. He's only been dating you to feed you lies and throw you off the case." She looked at Macey, sadness filling her eyes.

Heat spread from Macey's neck up to her cheeks like fingers of fire burning a building. Why would her sister say such a thing? "That's not true. He told me everything. I know all about the demons and the werewolves, and we're still together. We're seeing each other tonight."

Alexis raised her hands. "I know. But I went to a pack meeting, and that's what he told us. He was keeping you occupied until they could defeat all the demons. He's been using you."

Macey crossed her arms, dread clutching at her heart. She refused to believe it.

"And when they found out you were my sister…that

you were a werewolf too, they decided to use you as their 'person on the inside.' You're the only werewolf cop in New Orleans, so you can cover up their tracks for them."

Macey's nails dug into her arms. Every muscle in her body tensed at the accusations her sister made. Could Luke be using her? Was all the tenderness, all the passion, just a ploy to get her to cover up the pack's tracks? She shook her head. "Luke would never…" Would he? Spikes of doubt began to bore into her mind. Was that what Stephen meant when he mentioned her being useful?

"He did. I was there when he said it."

How could she have been so naïve? Looking back on the path of their relationship, Alexis's words made sense. Luke had deceived her, then left her. But when he found out she was a werewolf, and he could still use her, he'd come running back. And she'd accepted him with open arms like a fool.

Tears welled in her eyes. "I see."

Alexis wrapped her arms around her. "I'm sorry, Macey. I hate being the one to tell you this, but I don't want to see you get hurt."

"Too late." She pulled away from her sister's embrace.

"Stephen said Luke was screwing you to keep you occupied. Did you sleep with him?"

"Worse. I gave him my heart."

Pity softened her eyes. "Oh, Macey."

"I have to go." She hurried down the steps and crossed the street into Jackson Square. This was her own fault. She'd let her guard down. She'd been distracted by his piercing eyes and sexy body, and she'd opened up to him. Made herself vulnerable. A mistake she wouldn't make again. There was a reason she'd guarded her heart so heavily all these years, and she was stupid to think Luke would be any different. People left. She was never worth sticking around for, and she still wasn't.

How long was he planning to string her along? Just until they'd vanquished the demons? Or would he keep using her until he tired of her?

She wiped her tears and straightened her spine. Love wasn't in the cards for her, and that was fine. She was done playing the fool.

As she passed in front of a candy store, the shop owner yelled at what appeared to be a homeless man, then he hit him on the head with a thick stick of summer sausage. The poor guy cowered in the corner, trying to inch his way toward the door, but the shop owner's relentless berating continued.

Tucking her emotions into the vault, Macey welcomed the distraction and stepped inside to flash her badge. "Is there a problem here?"

The homeless man whimpered.

"Every week," the shop keeper shouted. "Every week he comes in here and eats my samples. Every time he buys nothing!"

The cowering man covered his face and peeked at her through his fingers. Tears filled his frightened, brown eyes, tugging at Macey's heartstrings.

"Okay. How about I take him outside and have a talk with him?" she said to the shopkeeper.

"Tell him not to come back! Idiot!"

"Okay." She cautiously approached the man and touched his elbow. He recoiled. "Sir? Do you want to come take a walk with me?"

He ran his hand under his nose and wiped it on his sweat-stained shirt. "Please don't hit me." His bottom lip trembled as he spoke.

"I'm not going to hurt you. Come on. Let's take a walk." She ushered the man outside and guided him away from the store. She sat him on a park bench and waited for his sniveling to subside before speaking. "What happened in there?"

He wiped his nose and dried his eyes on his shirt sleeve. "I was hungry. I thought it was free." He sighed. "I'm a stupid idiot."

"No. No, you're not. That wasn't nice of the shop-keeper to call you that." She sat down next to him. Aside from his dirty clothes and greasy hair, something about the man wasn't quite right. Like his elevator didn't go all the way to the top. He almost seemed drunk, but she couldn't smell any traces of alcohol.

"Oh, I am. My brother told me so." He appeared to be about thirty years old, but he had the speech pattern of a six-year-old. His stomach growled, and he hit it with his fist. "Sometimes, if I punch it, I can make the roaring stop."

"When was the last time you ate?"

"The candy in the shop." He pointed.

"I mean a meal. Something that filled you up?"

He shrugged. "My brother brings me food sometimes. Well, he used to."

"Sometimes? Wait here." She trotted to the food vendor a few feet away and bought two hot dogs, a bag of chips, and a bottle of water. The man's innocent gaze flitted about the park like a little boy's would. He smiled when he saw a dog pretending to be passed out on the street, a hurricane glass lying on its stomach and a patty of fake vomit near its mouth.

"That's a smart dog," he said as Macey returned to the bench. "It's not really asleep. It's just playing like it is."

She offered him the food and sat beside him. Though she was certain she'd never seen him before, his oddly familiar face pricked at her mind, raising the hairs on the back of her neck. She stifled a gasp as she realized where she'd seen him. She pulled out her phone and found the image of the police sketch. His features were similar to the rapist. It wasn't an exact match, but this was only an artist's rendition based on someone else's description. It could be the same man.

He inhaled each hotdog in two bites, then started on the bag of chips. How long had it been since his last meal? He certainly didn't act like a rapist. The women had described him as charming. Smooth. This was a child in a man's body. And he had brown eyes, not red. The guy in the sketch was most likely half demon. This man definitely was not. "What's your name?"

He finished the chips and chugged the water. "My name is Jimmy."

"Well, it's nice to meet you, Jimmy. I'm Macey."

"Thank you for the food, Miss Macey. That will keep my tummy quiet for a long time."

"My pleasure. Jimmy, do you come here often? The shopkeeper said he sees you every week."

"Oh, yes, ma'am. Mondays are my free days. I get to come here every Monday."

She tilted her head. "But it's not Monday."

"Oh, my brother told me to meet him here today. He said we're going to do something fun. I hope we can go to the aquarium. I want to see the fishies." He clapped his hands.

"Do you have somewhere to stay? A bed to sleep in?"

He nodded. "Yes ma'am. I have a futon. My brother got it for me when I was really good."

"Does your brother live with you?"

"Yes, ma'am. Well, kinda."

"Kinda?" She pulled a pen and a slip of paper out of her purse. She'd have to do some research on this brother of his. "What's his name?"

Jimmy's eyes grew wide. "Oh, I...I'm really not supposed to talk about him. I...I'm not supposed to talk to people at all." He jumped off the bench and tripped over his feet, falling back down. "I have to go." He clambered to his feet again. "Thank you, Miss Macey, for the food. You're a real nice lady." He turned on his heel and disappeared into the crowd.

"Well, that was strange." Macey picked up the food wrappers and tossed them in a trash bin. There was no way that guy was the rapist. He probably couldn't even operate a toaster, much less a woman's body.

CHAPTER TWENTY-TWO

As Luke strolled up St. Philip, the evening sun dipped into the horizon, painting the sky in shades of pink and purple. The afternoon clouds had dissipated, and the French Quarter buildings cast long stripes of shade across the pavement. The steamy scent of fresh rain drifted up from the puddles in the street.

He'd had the urge to dial Macey's number all afternoon, but she was spending time with her sister. He'd see her soon enough. As he approached the bar, he hesitated to go in. His mind was so wrapped up in his sexy detective —and she was *his* now—he didn't want to think about werewolf business.

But he had to. With Macey's help, they wouldn't have to worry so much about the humans finding out about the demons, but they still needed to catch the bastard who was summoning the fiends. His parents would be home tomorrow. He'd be alpha in five days. He needed to wrap this up.

The chilled curtain of air separating the inside of O'Malley's from the outside blasted his skin. Chase had his arms full of half-drunk hurricanes, and he dumped the contents down the sink before tossing the plastic cups in the trash. Alexis sat at the bar, nursing a glass of whiskey, a grim expression occupying her face.

"How'd it go with Macey today?" Luke asked.

"Oh, fine." She glanced at him before turning her attention to her drink. "Trying to repair twenty years of damage won't be easy."

"At least you made a start."

She shrugged.

Chase poured Luke a beer and handed it to him. "You've got a spring in your step I haven't seen in a long time."

Luke grinned. His life was finally starting to fall into place. "I'm in love. What can I say?" And he planned to tell her tonight.

Alexis's head jerked up. "Love? But you said—"

"Hold on." Luke's phone vibrated in his pocket. His grin widened when Macey's name lit up the screen. "Hello, beautiful. How was your day?"

"You can stop now, Luke." Her voice was strained. Irritated.

"What can I stop?"

"Pretending you like me. I know, okay?"

He tightened his grip on the phone. "Preten—Macey, what are you talking about?"

"You've been using me to cover up the truth. That's why you're dating me. Well, you don't have to anymore. Okay? I'll be your 'man on the inside,' so you can stop the charade. I won't tell anyone about the werewolves or the demons. No one would believe me anyway."

"Where on Earth would you get an idea like that?" He

eyed the woman sitting at the bar, staring into her drink. He knew exactly where.

"Alexis told me everything."

His heart pounded like a sledgehammer as he glared at Macey's sister. "And you believe her?"

"Of course I do. She's my sister."

"Macey, none of that is true. Macey? Hello?"

Silence hung heavy on the other end. Final.

Angry heat rolled through his body as he dropped his phone into his pocket. He turned to Alexis. "What did you do, rogue?"

She shrank in on herself, wrapping her arms across her middle. "I...I was looking out for my sister. After what you said at the meeting, I thought you—"

"Well, you thought wrong." He raked his hands through his hair. "I'm not using her. I'm in love with her."

Alexis's mouth hung open, her bottom lip quivering. "I..."

He dialed Macey's number. Straight to voicemail. "Macey, Alexis was wrong. None of that is true. I...just... please call me." He pocketed his phone. "I've got to find her."

He strode toward the door, and James came flying through. "Demons. Three. On Rampart," he said between breaths.

"Shit. They aren't wasting any moonlight." Luke tensed. He *had* to hunt the demons, but Macey...

"I'll talk to her." Alexis downed the rest of her whiskey. "I'll make things right."

"You better."

Chase leapt over the bar, and the men rushed out into the night.

The French Quarter swarmed with people. They'd have

to herd the demons out of the city to have any chance of battling them unnoticed. James led them up St. Philip to Rampart and stopped. "They're on the move."

Luke inhaled deeply, sifting through the scents of the Quarter. It was faint, but underneath the sweet smells of magnolias and pralines and the sour tinge of alcohol, the putrid scent of death and decay lingered like a long-buried secret. "This way."

They darted down Dumaine and skidded to a stop on Royal. There, in the shadows, indistinguishable from the darkness, save for the gleaming red eyes, three demons lurked in an alley.

"One man on the roof," Chase said. "The other two at each end of the alley. We surround them and get them all at once. They won't know what hit them." He shifted his weight from foot to foot, his eyes gleaming in the gas light.

"You got lucky last time," Luke said. "We're not shifting in the city again. Too many witnesses."

James cracked his knuckles. "Witnesses that are about to become victims if we don't act fast."

"Right," Luke said. "Wait...what's this?"

A black-haired man approached the fiends and spoke to them. Luke couldn't make out their words over the chatter of tourists, but this guy had to be involved.

"That the bastard who's summoning them?" Chase clenched his fists.

The man turned his head and scanned the street with his own set of red eyes. Luke recognized him immediately. Though full-grown now, his face was unmistakable. "That's the halfling I saw last week."

The man pointed into the alley, and the demons' eyes followed his gaze. They slinked deeper into the shadows as the halfling turned and ran up Royal Street.

"Can you guys handle three on your own?" Luke asked.

"Are you kidding?" James bounced on the balls of his feet. "I was born for this."

"Good. I'm going to tail the halfling. See if he can show me where his master's hiding out."

Keeping his distance, Luke followed the man out of the Quarter. He slinked through the outlying neighborhoods and through the wards that still hadn't completely recovered from the last hurricane. Where was the fiend headed? With the last house behind him, Luke shifted into wolf form and stalked the halfling into the swamp.

Though he looked like a man, the half-demon moved with the speed and agility of an otherworldly creature. He leapt over fallen logs and ducked under low-hanging branches as if he had the entire forest memorized.

As the halfling approached a run-down shack situated on a piece of semi-dry land, Luke slowed his pace and ducked behind a tree. Crouching low, he belly-crawled closer to the structure. His back leg kicked a fallen tree branch, disturbing a nest of wild boar piglets. They snorted and squealed for their mother, scattering through the trees. The halfling snapped his head around at the sound and peered into the darkness.

Luke held his breath, anticipating the attack from the sow. Wild boars could be as mean as gators, especially the ones in the swamp. But the mother never came. Maybe she'd already been turned into someone's dinner. A piglet scurried past the halfling, and he sneered, picking up the squealing baby and carrying it inside.

Luke released his breath. The last thing he needed was for a pig to give him away. He crept closer to the shack and peeked through the window. A makeshift altar stood in the center of the room. It was nothing more than a wooden table covered in cloth and animal bones, but this had to be the place where the demons were summoned. He could just make out the designs drawn on a cereal bowl in the middle of the table. Black magic markings.

The halfling picked up the knife that lay beside the bowl and stabbed the piglet. It let out a piercing squeal before flailing and going limp in his hand. Luke didn't stick around to watch the rest. He could've easily taken out the demon spawn on his own, but the signs of struggle would let his master know he'd been found. He'd wait until the bastard was home and end this thing once and for all.

Macey took her frozen dinner out of the microwave and settled on the couch with a glass of chardonnay. Thor sat on the other end of the sofa and flicked his tail triumphantly.

"Don't look so smug." She eyed her cat. "He fooled you too."

She flipped on the television and shoveled a spoonful of mac and cheese into her mouth. Luke planned to take her to a new Italian restaurant in the Garden District tonight. It would have been better than the cardboard pasta and runny, half-frozen cheese sauce she was currently eating. *Stop it, Mace. Don't think about him.*

That was easier said than done. The harder she tried to get the image of his deep blue eyes and caramel hair out of her mind, the more vivid the picture became. She sighed and put the bowl on the coffee table. She'd get over him.

Her life was fine before she met him, and it would be fine with him gone too. He had too many responsibilities, anyway. His job, running his pack, hunting demons. She was busy too…

And Thor would have missed their Saturday night Netflix binges.

She could think of a thousand reasons why not being with Luke was the best decision she could've made. As long as she kept her distance, he'd never have the chance to abandon her. This time, she was the one who left. The relationship ended because *she* wanted it to, and she would keep reminding herself of that until it stopped hurting.

She finished her dinner and set the bowl in the sink. Thor curled up in her lap, and she sipped her wine as she started season two of her new favorite show.

A knock on the door made her heart jump. Could it be Luke? So what if it was? He'd only fill her head with more lies, and she wasn't sure she had the strength to resist him. She'd probably fall for whatever story he fed her, so she'd better not answer the door.

The knock sounded again. "Miss Macey? Are you home?"

That wasn't Luke. She set Thor on the floor and tiptoed to the door.

Another knock. "Miss Macey? It's Jimmy."

The guy from the candy store? How on Earth did he know where she lived? She looked through the peep hole, and sure enough, Jimmy stood on the porch. He wore clean clothes, and his hair had been combed, but it was definitely him. She unlatched the lock, but kept the chain in place, and opened the door a crack. "What are you doing here, Jimmy?"

"I'm sorry, Miss Macey. My brother made me do it."

He squeezed his eyes shut, a tense, pained expression masking his face, as a garbled yelp came from somewhere deep inside. His body shuddered, and a sinister smile curved his lips. He sucked in a deep breath and slowly opened his eyes.

Blood red eyes.

Macey gasped and stumbled back, trying to close the door, but he stuck his foot in the jamb. He slammed his shoulder against the door with inhuman strength, snapping the security chain in half. Thor hissed and darted into the bedroom as Macey backed into a table, knocking over a lamp and shattering it on the floor.

Jimmy wrapped his long fingers around her neck and pinned her against the wall. "You were kind to my brother today."

Brother? His voice was the same, but different. It no longer held the childish intonation it had earlier in the day. And his eyes...

"He likes you now." He slammed her onto the floor, and the air *whooshed* out of her lungs.

She gasped for breath. "Jimmy? What are you doing?"

"I'm not Jimmy."

She tried to scoot away, but he was on her in an instant, straddling her, pinning her to the ground. Her shoulder blades dug into the wood, sending piercing pain shooting into her arms.

"I was going to have some fun with you before I killed you, but now that my idiot brother has taken a liking to you, I won't. I don't want to damage his mind too much. Such a shame. You are a pretty little thing." He thrust his hips against her as he spoke. "He begged me not to kill you. 'Miss Macey's a real nice lady,'" he said in a mocking tone. "A nice lady who's been getting in my way long enough."

He stood, lifting her off the ground by the shoulders, her feet dangling three inches above the wood. "You see…" With his hand around her neck, he slammed her into the wall. Her head knocked against drywall, and her vision swam with stars. Clawing at his hand, she tried to peel his fingers from her throat, but he held her with otherworldly strength. The strength of a demon. The brother who terrorized Jimmy was the half-demon spirt who'd been taunting her.

"You see, *Miss Macey*, I've got a plan. I'm going to run this city. And I am trying to build an army of halflings to help me do it. But you and your werewolf friends are making my life difficult. How can my demons impregnate enough women to build an army, when the werewolves keep killing them?"

She tried to speak, but his grip crushed her windpipe. She could barely breathe, but she refused to be his next victim. If only she could reach her pistol; she'd left it on the kitchen counter with her badge. She clutched his arm and managed a strangled, "Please."

The demon in Jimmy's body sighed and shook his head. "I have to use a body to kill you, since I don't have one of my own. Making that branch fall on you took all the energy I had. It took hours for me to recover after that. Spirit energy isn't infinite, I'm afraid." He squeezed her throat tighter. "This way is much more efficient."

She couldn't breathe. Her vision tunneled, blackness closing in around her, when he suddenly let her go. She clutched her neck as she gasped for breath. Blinking away the darkness, she found Thor climbing up the man's back, his teeth slicing into his neck.

She took the chance and stumbled into the kitchen, throwing herself at her firearm. Jimmy flung Thor across the foyer and roared as he came barreling into the room.

Macey raised her gun and fired. The bullet burrowed into his shoulder. Jimmy fell against the wall and slid down. He reached for the wound and pulled away a shaking hand covered in blood. His bottom lip quivered.

"You bitch." The voice bellowed from every corner of the room. *"I need that body."*

She swung the gun around, frantically searching for the source of the sound.

"Miss Macey?" The childish tone returned to Jimmy's voice. He stood up and swayed on his feet. "I don't feel so good."

"Run, you moron. If you pass out here, I swear I'll kill you myself."

"I'm sorry, Miss Macey. You really are a nice lady." He stumbled into the living room and out the door. Thor hissed and darted into the kitchen.

The last thing Macey saw was a cast iron pan flying across the room, striking her head with splitting pain.

CHAPTER TWENTY-THREE

LUKE SHIFTED TO HUMAN FORM BEFORE HE REACHED the city. He stopped by the bar, but his hunters were still on patrol. Macey didn't pick up her phone, so he tried Alexis. No answer. Could they be at Macey's house? It wouldn't hurt to look.

He stepped out into the humid night and headed toward her home. At worst, he could at least let her know what was about to go down in the swamp, so they could concoct a cover story to satisfy the police. At best, Alexis would have convinced her she was wrong, and Macey would throw herself into his arms as soon as he knocked on the door. His chest tightened. He could only hope for the best.

As he turned the corner on Barracks, he caught a whiff of rotting flesh as a black mass dropped from a rooftop into an alley. *Damn demons.* His reunion with Macey would have to wait.

With his back pressed against the wall, Luke peered into the alley to see what the fiend was up to. This was a residential street; attracted to the masses, demons usually stuck to the crowded areas. More victims. Easier targets.

This demon crouched in a shadow, rubbing its knobby hands together, and staring up at a balcony. Tendrils of ivy crawled across the cast iron railing and climbed up the poles. Soft rock music played from a speaker on a table, where a glass of soda sat, untouched, the ice melting in the heat. A girl stretched out on a chaise lounge; she couldn't have been more than fourteen. She punched in something on her cell phone, and the blue light illuminated an amused grin, her innocent eyes sparkling as she laughed.

The demon's nostrils flared. That thing could scale the balcony railing in a single leap. He had to stop it, but it was against the rules to shift in the city. Aside from piercing the heart, the only other way to kill a demon was to cut its head off. He scanned the area for something sharp. Nothing.

He could fight it in human form. Wrestle with it. Try to make it run. It rocked to the balls of its feet like it was about to jump.

Screw the rules. These were desperate times.

Luke leapt toward the demon, shifting in midair, bringing his massive claws down on…nothing. The fiend had disappeared, leaving behind nothing but a dissipating cloud of black smoke. *What the hell?* Demons couldn't disappear.

A maniacal cackle emanated from the balcony. The girl screamed. The fiend clung to the railing like a monkey, taunting Luke and scaring the girl to death. She scrambled back, curling into a ball and pressing herself against the wall. She glanced at the open door and focused on the demon.

Luke rocked back on his haunches and launched

himself up. He swiped at the fiend, slicing a massive claw through its thick, leathery skin. It let out an ear-piercing squeal and lost its balance on the railing. Hanging from one arm, it let out a snake-like hiss. Luke growled in return.

The girl's shrill scream echoed through night as she stumbled off her chair and darted inside, slamming the door. The fiend looked up at the balcony and glared down at Luke. Its lips peeled back over dagger-like fangs in a sick attempt at a smile. Then, it disappeared in another cloud of smoke.

Shit! Luke ducked into the alley and shifted into human form. Where had the bastard gone? The girl's entire body trembled as she peeked through the curtains and clutched her phone in her hand. It hadn't followed her inside.

A freakish cackle sounded from down the street as the fiend jumped onto another rooftop. Luke gave chase, following it as it leapt from building to building, leading Luke up Chartres, closer and closer to Basin Street.

The demon jumped to the street and plowed through a group of people on a vampire tour. They squealed in surprise, laughing at their own reactions, probably thinking the fiend was part of the show. Luke slowed his pace as he wove through the crowd, trying not to draw any more attention to the chase. As soon as he broke from the mass, he sprinted after the beast. He wouldn't let this one get away.

"Smells like death around here. Need some help?" Chase and James caught up, flanking Luke on either side.

Luke pointed to the rooftop where the demon returned. "Tried to get a teenage girl on Barracks."

"The bastard," James said.

The demon darted across Basin street, weaving through traffic like a crazed animal. Drivers slammed on their brakes and honked their horns at what probably looked like a shadow to them.

The men followed, using the confusion in the traffic jam to their advantage and racing across the street. The demon scaled the wall of St. Louis Cemetery Number One and disappeared into the graveyard.

"Damn, that sucker's fast." Chase tried the gate. "Locked."

"Step aside, boys, and give me some cover." James took a lock-picking kit out of his pocket and stepped toward the gate. Luke and Chase stood in front of him, blocking him from view.

He tried to act casual, but so much adrenaline coursed through Luke's veins, he doubted he was pulling it off. "Make it quick," he said through clenched teeth as he nodded at a couple passing by. They slowed as they approached the cemetery gate—probably tourists wanting to experience the graveyard and all its spooky mysteries at night. But the St. Louis cemetery closed at dusk, and even daytime entry required a licensed tour guide. Breaking in was completely illegal, and completely necessary.

He straightened his spine and looked the man in the eyes. His girlfriend grabbed at his arm like she was nervous. "Evening," Luke said.

The man's eyes widened, a hint of fear draining the color from his face as he quickened his pace and hurried past.

"Got it. We're in." James popped the lock, and the others followed him inside the walls.

Stepping into the cemetery was like entering another world. Towering tombs rose from the ground in classic

Spanish style. Row after row of white stucco structures housed the remains of generations of New Orleans residents. Most were well-kept, with elaborate statues adorning the crypts and long lists of names etched into plaques dating to the seventeen hundreds. Others had crumbled with decay, decades of weather eating away at the stucco, exposing the brick and mortar underneath.

"Welcome to the city of the dead," Luke mumbled.

"The demon could be anywhere," Chase said.

"We'll find him." James crept up the walkway, peering between each row of tombs. "Heeere demon, demon, demon," he called. "Come to papa, you disgusting piece of hell trash."

A shadow darted by in Luke's peripheral vision, and he took off after it. He sprinted up a row of tombs and made a left.

Dead end. No demon.

He backed out and continued up the path.

"Over here," James yelled.

Luke followed his voice across the cemetery and found the fiend perched atop an enormous mausoleum, like a hideous, living gargoyle. It peeled back its lips in a putrid smile and cackled wildly before disappearing in a cloud of smoke.

"What the hell?" Chase rubbed his eyes. "I've never seen one do that."

"I forgot to mention that," Luke said. "This one's gonna be harder to kill."

James grinned. "You mean more fun. Let's get this bastard." He shifted into wolf form and loped down the path. Chase and Luke shifted and took off in opposite directions. There'd be no more talk, but in wolf form, they had an almost telepathic form of communication. They couldn't exactly read each other's minds, but they always knew what the other was thinking.

Chase growled, and Luke turned a corner to find his friend face to face with the demon. It sneered as Chase leapt for it, disappearing in a poof before the wolf could make contact. It reappeared on a tomb four feet away, only to vanish and show up behind him. The fiend was toying with them.

James swiped at the creature, but it disappeared. Its teeth sank into Luke's shoulder before he even realized it was on his back. He howled and rolled, knocking the demon to the ground. Luke latched onto its leg, and it let out a screeching wail. It clawed the ground, trying to free itself from Luke's jaws.

They had it.

Chase pounced. Luke's teeth snapped together. The creature was gone.

It reformed two feet away, dragging its mangled leg and leaving a trail of smoking, black blood. The wolves circled it, closing in, growling. The fiend tried to disappear again, but the injury had zapped its strength. Fear filled its wild, red eyes as Luke stepped forward and swiped a claw across its heart. This time, the cloud of smoke turned into a pile of ash. They sent the demon back to hell.

The men shifted to human form and slipped out of the cemetery, locking the gate behind them.

"What a night," James said as they made their way into the French Quarter. "That one made six, all in a span of a few hours."

"I wonder what else he's going to throw at us tonight." Chase said.

"It's our turn to throw something at him." Luke glanced at his friends. "I know where the bastard lives."

"Macey?"

Macey's eyes fluttered open at the sound of her sister's voice. The kitchen lights pierced her eyes like daggers, and her stomach roiled at the pounding pain in her head. The cold tile floor chilled through her shirt, but it didn't stop the sweat from beading on her forehead. She rolled onto her side and clutched a cabinet, pulling herself into a sitting position.

"In here." Her voice came out as a croak. Her throat felt like she'd swallowed a desert. Glass crunched under Alexis's shoes, her pounding footsteps quickening like a jackhammer in Macey's skull.

"Macey!" Alexis dropped to her knees and reached out like she wanted to comfort her sister, but she hesitated. "Are you okay?"

Macey's vision wavered, but she managed to find her voice. "I'll survive. Help me up."

Alexis lifted her by the arm and steadied her on her feet. But as soon as she let go, the world turned on its side. Macey caught herself on the edge of the table, and her sister helped her into a chair.

"An ambulance is on its way," Alexis said.

"No. No hospitals. I just hit my head. I'll be okay."

"You could have a concussion."

Macey blinked away the stars in her vision and focused on her sister. "I'm fine."

Alexis crossed her arms. "You're going. I made the call when I found your front door open."

A fresh wave of nausea rolled through Macey's stomach. Maybe it wouldn't hurt to get her head checked. "Okay. Did you see Thor? My cat?"

"He hissed at me and ran down the hall." Alexis pulled a chair next to her and sat down. Her jaw flexed, the sound of her teeth grinding like crunching gravel in Macey's skull. Concern filled her sister's gaze as she reached out and gingerly brushed her fingers across the knot on Macey's head. She closed her eyes. "Who did this to you?"

CHAPTER TWENTY-FOUR

"Hold still, you insolent fool." Ross's voice sounded like it came from inside Jimmy's head, but his brother wasn't possessing him. He squirmed under the boy's weight and screamed when the boy stuck his fingers into his wound. Ross wouldn't squirm or scream. Only stupid idiots did that.

The bullet made a squishy sucking sound as the boy pulled it out, and fire shot down Jimmy's arm. It wasn't really fire, but that's what it felt like. The real fire burned in the stove, crackling like a monster trying to escape a prison.

The boy wasn't a boy anymore. He was a full-grown man the same size as Jimmy, and he had no trouble pinning Jimmy to the floor. He stuck a long metal rod into the fire and poured alcohol into the hole in Jimmy's arm. Fresh flames seemed to engulf him, stinging like a thousand wasps.

"What are you gonna do with that poker?" Jimmy's voice sounded tiny.

"He's going to cauterize the wound. We can't have you bleeding out; I still need you."

"What's a cot-trize?"

"Cauterize, you idiot. Make it stop bleeding."

"Oh." It would be nice if it stopped bleeding. Maybe it would stop hurting too. "Is Miss Macey okay? You didn't kill her, did you?"

"If you wouldn't have gone and got yourself shot, I would have. Without a body, I barely had enough strength to knock her out."

Good. Miss Macey didn't deserve to die.

"Next time I see that bitch, she's dead."

Next time he saw her, Jimmy would fight back against his brother. He couldn't let Miss Macey get hurt. She was a nice lady. The nicest lady he'd ever met, besides Momma.

The boy who wasn't a boy smiled and pulled the poker out of the flames. The tip of the stick glowed red hot, and Jimmy squeezed his eyes shut. His heart pounded in his chest, and his wound bled harder.

The poker plunged into his shoulder, and he screamed. Then everything went black.

CHAPTER TWENTY-FIVE

"So, anyway, I was wrong. I'm sorry I screwed things up with you and Luke." Alexis brushed the hair out of Macey's face and sat on the edge of the hospital bed. A clock on the wall ticked the seconds away as the IV drip tried to keep time. The computer monitoring Macey's vitals hummed, quietly beeping every few seconds.

"Thanks for clearing that up." She patted her sister's hand.

The blood pressure cuff inflated, squeezing her bicep tightly before slowly, rhythmically releasing its grip as the pain medication relaxed her, easing the throbbing in her head to a dull ache. But it did nothing for the ache in her heart. She didn't know what to believe anymore. Did Luke care for her? Or was he using her? Maybe it was a little of both. Either way, she'd broken her sacred rule: don't let anyone get close enough to hurt her. It was time to repair the fortress walls she'd allowed Luke to break down.

"Do you think you'll get back together?"

Macey sighed. "I don't know. I've always had a hard time opening up to people, ever since…you know."

Alexis stared at her hands and sucked in a shaky breath. "I'm sorry."

"I know. And I understand why you did it now. I'm not blaming you. But it's going to take some time for me to learn to trust someone again. And Luke..." She shook her head. "I don't know. I've let my guard down too many times with him. He makes me want to open up and share everything about myself."

"Isn't that a good thing?"

"Not for me. I was vulnerable. If it was so easy for me to be *that* hurt over a misunderstanding, then I was in way over my head. I've never gotten so close to someone so fast. And now I know why."

A knock sounded on the door, and Bryce sauntered into to the room. He set a bouquet of pink roses on the table beside the bed and smiled at Macey. "How you feeling, boss?"

"A little headache. Any sign of the perp?"

"Not yet. Got word in at all the hospitals and urgent care clinics to let us know of any patients with shoulder wounds. Nothing so far."

Macey let out a sigh of relief. She'd given the first responders a false description of Jimmy and denied any knowledge of the attacker's identity. She'd even told them he wore a mask. "That's too bad."

Bryce's smile widened, and he ran a hand through his hair as if he just noticed someone else was in the room. "Hi there. I'm Bryce, Macey's partner." He reached across the bed to shake her sister's hand.

Alexis grinned as her cheeks flushed pink. "I'm Alexis. I'm...uh..." She looked at Macey, uncertainty causing her brow to furrow.

"She's my sister," Macey said.

Bryce stopped shaking her hand, but he didn't let it go. "I didn't know you had a sister, Mace." His gaze lingered on Alexis.

"It's a long story."

"Well, I better get going." Alexis slid her hand out of Bryce's grasp. "I'll check on Thor. Make sure he's okay. That's one hell of a cat."

"He deserves a medal," Macey said.

Alexis touched her fingertips to Macey's shoulder. "You'll be okay?"

The concern in her sister's voice touched her heart. She wasn't sure what to do about Luke, but she was glad to have Alexis back. "Yeah. Surprisingly, it wasn't a concussion. I'm sure I'll be released soon."

"I'll call you later. It was nice meeting you, Bryce." She smiled at him and slipped out the door.

Bryce stood there with his hands in his pockets, a goofy grin on his face as he watched her leave. "She's pretty."

Macey glared at him. "Don't even think about it."

He raised his hands. "What? I wasn't thinking."

"You never are. That's the problem."

He pulled up a chair next to the bed. "Is she single?"

She rolled her eyes. "She's not the type that wants to be your 'little woman,' making gumbo in the kitchen and having your babies."

"C'mon. You know I was kidding about that."

"She's off limits."

"Okay, boss. Whatever you say." He leaned his elbows on his knees, clasping his hands. "Do you really think this was a random attack? Nothing to do with the case?"

She cringed. Lying to her partner made her sick to her stomach, but what choice did she have? She had no idea how to cover everything up and solve the case in a way that would satisfy both the police and the werewolves. She needed to talk to Luke, but her chest tightened just thinking about him. "I don't know about random. I've put away plenty of bad guys, so someone could've been out for revenge. He wore a mask, so it could've been anyone. But I don't think it was the rapist." She smoothed the sheets over her stomach, trying to keep the bile from creeping up her throat. "He didn't seem interested in getting my clothes off. He wanted me dead. End of story."

"Well, I'm sure he'll turn up. He couldn't get too far with a wound like that. You're one tough little lady." He winked, always trying to get a rise out of her.

She was about to respond with a sarcastic comeback when the door flew open, thudding against the wall. Luke rushed in, his eyes wild with concern, and he threw himself onto the bed. "Oh, thank God." He stroked her hair and held her face in his hands. "I'm so sorry, Macey. Are you okay? What happened?" He kissed her forehead and both her cheeks.

She gripped the blankets in her fists to stop her arms from wrapping around his shoulders. Every fiber of her being ached to hold him, but she fought it. She would not lose her heart again. "I'm fine."

Bryce cleared his throat, and Luke looked up at him. His gaze danced between the flowers and her partner before landing back on Macey.

"Have you met Bryce?" she asked.

"Not officially." Luke shook his hand and focused his attention on Macey. "I'm so sorry, Macey. This is all my fault. I should have been there to protect you from that..." He cut his gaze over to Bryce. "That asshole."

She stiffened. "I don't need protection." Was that why

he was concerned? Not because she was hurt, but because he felt guilty?

Bryce stood and shoved his hands in his pockets. "Don't let her size fool you. She's pretty good at protecting herself."

"No." Luke shook his head. "I should have been there for you."

"Well." Bryce shuffled toward the door. "I'll let you two work this out on your own. I'll call you if I hear anything, boss."

Bryce closed the door, and Macey glared at Luke. "I did fine on my own."

Luke looked at her incredulously. "He knocked you out. You're in the hospital."

"I'm alive, aren't I? I shot him and came out with nothing more than a headache." Did he honestly think she was that helpless? That he needed to spend every waking moment by her side to protect her from the bad guys? She'd been fighting bad guys without him for years.

"I…" He let out a heavy sigh.

"Why are you even here, Luke? What do you want?" Anger seethed in her voice, and anger was good. Anger would keep her heart hardened.

He took her hand in his and stroked it. "Isn't it obvious? Those things Alexis told you weren't true."

She looked at her hand resting in his. The warmth of his touch. The familiar energy dancing on her skin. How could something so bad for her feel so right? *Anger. Focus on the anger.* "You said them, though."

"I know. I did it to appease the pack. To keep things under control. But I didn't mean a word of it. She told you that, right?"

Macey's throat thickened. Her eyes stung with tears.

Why did her resolve dissolve into nothing around him? He knew her weaknesses. How to press every button to keep her wrapped around his finger. Tears shimmered in his sapphire eyes, and she wanted nothing more than to throw her arms around his neck and let him back in.

But she couldn't. She had to be strong this time. Her heart might not survive another beating from a man like Luke. "She told me, but…"

"But?"

"But I don't know." She pulled her hand from his grasp and hugged herself. "I don't know what to believe anymore."

His hands clenched into fists on the blanket. "Damn it, Macey. I love you. Believe that."

She sucked in a shaky breath and hugged herself tighter. She did believe him. The emotion in his eyes spoke volumes above the words, but it didn't mean he'd stay. Her sister and her parents had loved her, but they'd abandoned her anyway. Love may have been a glue that held people together, but life could always tear them apart.

"Detective Carpenter?" A nurse poked her head through the doorway and knocked before entering the room. "You're being released. Just sign here, and you're free to leave." She looked at Luke. "Do you have a ride?"

"Yeah, I'll take her home," Luke said before she could answer.

The nurse removed the IV and disconnected her from the monitoring equipment before handing her a plastic bag. "Here are your clothes. Let me know if you need anything else."

As the nurse left the room, Macey swung her legs over the side of the bed. Her head still hurt, but at least she could get out of this suffocating hospital room. Luke watched her as she pulled her clothes from the bag and started to untie her gown. "Do you mind turning around?" she said.

"Yeah. Sure." His voice was barely a whisper, made thick by the tears he tried to hold back. He turned his back to her and fiddled with his hands as if he wasn't sure what to do with them.

He'd seen her naked before. He'd touched every inch of her body. But now she felt vulnerable, exposed in front of this man who knew way too much about her. She dressed quickly and cleared her throat to let him know she was done.

When he turned around, light glistened off the dampness of his cheeks. "I love you, Macey."

"I know. But the way I reacted when Alexis told me those things scared me to death. It's not you. *I* scared *myself*. I'm not used to being close to people."

He shoved his hands in his pockets and let out a dry chuckle. "Great. The 'it's not you, it's me' speech. Classic."

Why did her heart feel like it was being ripped from her chest? "I just need some time."

"Take all the time you need. I'm not going anywhere."

───

As long as she made up her mind within the next few days, he'd be fine. While his dad's retirement date wasn't technically set in stone, it would take an act of congress to change it. Literally. His father had filed for retirement with the werewolf national congress three and a half years ago. An alpha resigning voluntarily wasn't taken lightly, and he had to file for permission years in advance. He had to prove he had an acceptable successor, and a second in line in case the first one didn't work out.

Three and a half years ago, Luke had been engaged to Melissa. As the oldest male of the bloodline after Luke, Stephen had been the obvious second choice. No one ever expected him to actually be in the running for alpha, and now he was—if Luke couldn't get his act together. If he couldn't convince Macey they belonged together, he only had two options. Mate with someone he didn't love or let the pack fall into Stephen's hands. Neither option was acceptable. He couldn't let his twisted, power-hungry cousin tear apart the pack. And he could never love another woman. He'd thought he loved Melissa, but she hadn't been his fate-bound. Hell, he'd never fathomed the depths of love he was capable of until he met Macey.

She was his fate-bound. Now, if he could just convince her.

He pulled up to the curb in front of Macey's house and shut off the engine.

"Thanks for the ride." She reached for the door handle.

"Macey."

She froze, her hand trembling on the latch. "I should go."

"We don't have to talk about us...until you're ready. But we do need to talk about what happened. It was him, wasn't it? The guy from the sketch?"

She chewed her bottom lip and stared out the window. "I think you better come inside."

Glass crunched under his boots when he stepped through the door. A white ceramic lamp lay shattered on the floor, and a cracked dent marred the drywall at Macey's head level. If the guy had knocked her unconscious, he could've killed her easily. Snapped her neck. Crushed her windpipe.

His stomach twisted. He'd come so close to losing her. All the blood in his head plunged to his feet, making the room spin, before a flash of anger singed through his veins. Anger at the attacker, but more than anything, anger at himself for letting it happen. "Christ! What did that bastard do to you?"

"It's fine." She grabbed a broom from the closet and swept up the mess. "He didn't know what he was doing."

"He didn't know?" How hard had she hit her head to think the man didn't know he was trying to kill her?

She continued her frantic sweeping, keeping her gaze trained on the floor.

"Macey." He put his hand on the broom to stop her. "Come sit down. Talk to me."

She tugged on her bottom lip as her gaze darted about the room. "Luke, I…"

"Hey." He took the broom from her hand and leaned it against the wall. "It's business, okay? No matter your feelings for me, we're on the same team. We're going to have to work together, so put your detective cap on and talk to me like a cop. Right now, I'm just the alpha, and you're a police officer, and we're trying to solve a case."

Her posture relaxed, the tension draining from her muscles as she stepped toward the sofa. A slight smile curved one side of her mouth, and the sparkle almost returned to her eyes. "But you're not the alpha."

"Not yet." His arms ached to hold her as she sank onto the couch. Days ago, she'd been his. Now she was like a stunning statue in a museum. Cold and untouchable. But not completely. That small smile, that tiny glimmer, gave him hope. She could be his again.

He sat on the opposite end of the sofa, not nearly as close as he wanted to be. "What did you mean when you said he didn't know what he was doing?"

Her fingers brushed the knot on her head. "He was the rapist. But he wasn't. He did it, but he didn't mean to."

He looked at her, hoping his silence would encourage her to explain. She wasn't making any sense at all.

She let out an exasperated sigh. "The man in that picture—the man who beat me up last night—he was possessed by a demon."

"A demon?"

"Yeah."

"How do you know?"

"Because it was the same demon that tried to possess me. The halfling that went missing from the morgue."

He raised an eyebrow. "You're sure?"

"It's him. He's the hotel room rapist. He's using his brother, possessing him so he can assault women and do whatever else."

He nodded. "And summon more demons. He was a halfling. His brother must be human. He's using his brother's blood to summon the fiends." Luke's heart pounded. It was all starting to make sense. "We've got him, Macey. I know where the bastard lives. We can take out him and his brother." He wanted to hug her. To sweep her up in his arms and kiss her. He refrained.

She shook her head. "You can't."

"Oh, yes we can. Werewolves were born to hunt demons. We can take them both down."

"You can't hurt his brother. Jimmy is innocent."

Luke scoffed. "Innocent, my ass. He's been summoning demons. Only a pure human can do that."

"You don't understand. Jimmy is…special. He's like a

little boy stuck in a man's body. His brother abuses him into submission." She looked at him with pleading eyes. "He needs help, Luke."

Crap. "Well, that complicates things, doesn't it?"

She yawned. "I guess it does."

"You've been up all night. You should get some rest. I'll stay with you...I mean, I'll stay in the living room...so you can sleep."

She cocked an eyebrow. "I'll sleep fine without you here. Don't you have some demons to chase?"

"Not in the middle of the day. It's okay. I can stay and keep you safe."

Her nostrils flared. "I don't need you to keep me safe. I'm going to take a nap, and then I'm going to go to work."

"You're recovering from an attack. You shouldn't be going to work."

She stood and marched toward the door. "You shouldn't be telling me what to do. I appreciate the ride home, but now it's time for you to leave."

He'd done it again. The mere suggestion that she might need help always seemed to set her off. He should've known better by now to tread carefully around that subject. Standing, he cautiously approached her. He needed to defuse the situation before he walked out the door. He couldn't leave her mad at him...didn't want to leave her at all.

"I'm sorry. You're right, I'm being overprotective. I just...I came so close to losing you. I'm afraid for it to happen again."

He took a step closer and cupped her face in his hand. For a moment, she nuzzled into his touch, closing her eyes like she was giving in. Then she stiffened.

"You don't h…have me anymore." Her voice trembled as she spoke.

He dropped his hand to his side. "I know. But that doesn't mean I won't fight for you."

She took a deep, shuddering breath. "When I allow myself to get close to anyone, something always happens. Life always finds a way to take away the ones I love."

He reached for her hand, lacing his fingers through hers, his heart hammering at her use of that word. She didn't pull away. "Life never gives guarantees, but I can. I promise you this, Macey. I will love you with every fiber of my being for as long as I'm alive, and I will do everything in my power to stand by your side forever, no matter what life has in mind."

"I'm scared."

"I know. But don't be so afraid of dying that you never learn to live." He squeezed her hand and kissed her softly on the cheek. Her breath hitched when his lips brushed her face. Was it the supernatural energy or merely from his touch? "Please lock the door. And don't answer it for anyone."

She nodded and closed the door. He caught it with his hand just before it shut. He couldn't mask the pain of his breaking heart. "Come back to me, Macey. Please."

"I need more time. I'm sorry."

CHAPTER TWENTY-SIX

MACEY GAZED AT THE OBLONG CRYSTAL ROBERTA HAD given her. It weighed heavy in her hands, its uneven edges rough against her skin. *You'll know what to do when the time comes.* Hopefully, Roberta was right. Releasing energy from objects had become so easy, once she learned what to do. Would trapping a ghost be as simple? *Just do the same thing, in reverse.* She could do that, couldn't she? She had to. This was the weapon for stopping the demon spirit, and Macey had to wield it.

She sighed and dropped the stone into her purse before shoving it in her desk drawer. If Luke would even let her get close to the fiend. He had this crazy idea that she was a helpless damsel in distress who wouldn't be safe without a big bad werewolf watching out for her. Never mind that she was a police detective who fought human monsters every day. What was his problem?

She slammed the drawer shut and toyed with her copper bracelet. Had her mother been a full werewolf who could shift? Or her father? Her life would certainly have been different if her parents had survived. Maybe she wouldn't be so terrified of loving Luke if they had. Then again, she probably wouldn't have even met him.

Her chest ached with the thoughts. *Focus on one thing at a time.* Right now, the most important thing was stopping the demon spirit and getting Jimmy the help he needed. Fixing her heart would have to wait.

"You okay, boss?" Bryce leaned in the doorway and took a bite of his Snickers bar. "I didn't expect you back tonight."

"I'm fine. Needed to get out of the house. Keep my mind busy."

He pushed off the door and sauntered toward her desk, dropping a Hershey Special Dark bar in front of her as he sat in a chair. "I hear women like chocolate when they're having man trouble." He winked.

"I…" She started to push the candy away but hesitated. The sweet chocolaty scent filled her nose, making her mouth water. "What the hell." She opened the wrapper and placed a square of chocolate on her tongue. Her eyelids closed as the bittersweet goodness melted, relaxing the tension in her shoulders. When she opened her eyes, Bryce grinned at her.

"Wanna talk about it?" he asked.

"Not really."

"Whew." He pretended to wipe sweat from his forehead. "Good."

Macey rolled her eyes.

"Can we talk about your pretty sister?" He wiggled his eyebrows.

"No."

"Well, it was worth a shot. Listen, Mace, I'm pushing them real hard to find the guy that attacked you, but they're coming up with nothing. Have you remembered any more details? Anything at all that could help our boys out?"

Her face tightened. She tried to relax into a neutral expression, but her heart rate kicked up, and her palms went slick with sweat. She looked him in the eyes, forcing herself to hold his gaze as she spoke. "I've told you everything I remember."

He squinted at her, studying her. Bryce could spot a lie a mile away before it even rounded the corner. He wouldn't buy it, but he might let it slide. "And you're not holding anything back? Nothing else is going on? That Luke guy—"

"Luke did not hurt me, so don't even go there." *Not physically, anyway.*

"Okay. But if you ever need any help with him…"

"It's not like that. I promise."

"But if it ever is."

She reached across the desk and patted his hand. "Thanks, Bryce."

The tune of Taylor Swift's "Shake It Off" drifted up from Bryce's pants. He grinned as he fished his phone out of his pocket. "Like my ringtone? It's new."

Macey laughed and leaned back in her chair. If only she could shake it off like Taylor. She trusted her partner. She hadn't opened up to him about everything in her life, but he knew a lot. And he'd been around for five years. Maybe Luke… She didn't have time to finish her thought.

"Got another one. Over on Esplanade. Let's go."

Luke brushed off his shirt and tied back his hair. His parents had arrived at the Louis Armstrong International

Airport that afternoon, and his dad waited for him in the office. Dread tightened his chest. He'd hoped to have the demon infestation taken care of before his old man got home. He could imagine the disappointment his father must have felt to learn Luke hadn't taken care of the problem.

He hadn't seen his folks in two months, and he'd hoped their reunion would consist of a nice dinner and maybe a few souvenirs. His dad wanted to get straight to business.

He opened the door to find Marcus sitting behind the desk, a casual smile lighting his face as he stroked his wife's hand. Luke's mom perched on the edge of the bureau, toying with a tiny Eiffel Tower figure. She set the trinket on the desk and rushed toward Luke, wrapping her arms around him.

"Welcome home, Mom. How was your trip?"

"It was wonderful. I can't wait to tell you all about it."

"Hey, Dad." Luke reached across the desk to shake his father's hand.

"Sit down, son." Marcus's face was serious. "I'm concerned."

Luke sank into the chair and gripped the smooth, wooden arm rests. The disappointment in the old man's eyes stung. He'd failed him.

"I expected a debriefing from you first, but I wasn't home ten minutes before your cousin knocked on my door." Marcus folded his hands on the table and leaned forward, resting his weight on his arms. The chair creaked with his movement. Luke's mother settled into the chair next to him and clasped her hands in her lap.

Luke cleared his throat. "I've got the demon situation under control. I have a plan. I—"

"That's not what I'm worried about. I have no doubt you'll clean up that mess before the week is through."

He exhaled. He hadn't failed his father. Not yet. "Then what did Stephen want, if not to tattle on my lack of progress?"

His father held his eyes with a steely gaze. "He wants to be alpha, son. Rumor has it you haven't selected a mate. You know you can't be alpha unless you're mated to another werewolf."

Luke rubbed the back of his neck. "I have chosen one."

His dad crossed his arms over his chest. "The cop? I heard she dumped you."

Good news sure did travel fast in the wolf pack. "She just needs time. She'll come around."

"We don't have time."

His mom patted his hand. "I was ecstatic when I heard Macey was a were. I really was. But if she doesn't want to be with you…"

He jerked his hand away. "She does. I love her, and I know she loves me. She's scared. That's all. Macey *will* come back to me."

His old man leaned back in his chair. "And if she doesn't? I won't have Stephen tearing this pack apart."

Luke shot out of the chair, knocking it over. "He won't." He clenched his fists by his sides and raked in a ragged breath. "I *will* be alpha."

"Then you'd better choose an alternative mate. You're running out of time. After Stephen left, three different women knocked on my door offering to be your mate. The pack doesn't want your cousin to lead it. You have plenty of choices, son."

He swallowed down the sour taste bubbling from his

throat. Choosing anyone but Macey was unthinkable. "I'll tell you what. If I can't win Macey back before the dead-line...you can choose one for me. Anybody you want. It doesn't matter."

"Oh, honey." His mom's eyes held sadness, her voice pity. "We can't choose a life partner for you."

"Sure you can. If it isn't Macey, it might as well be anyone. It won't matter to me, because I'll never love anyone else. I'll do my duty. I'll run this pack, and I'll have offspring. But my heart will always belong to Macey." He reached for the doorknob. "I'm going to get her back. She just has to learn to trust me."

His mom smiled. "Then you need to learn to trust her."

Jimmy woke up to a throbbing pain in his shoulder. His back ached from sleeping on the floor, and his hair was soaked through with sweat. "Hello?" he called out into the shack.

No one answered.

"Ross? Boy?"

Silence.

He peeled himself off the floor and gingerly touched his wound. A big white blister surrounded by an angry red welt covered the hole where Miss Macey's bullet had hit him. It wasn't bleeding anymore, but it sure did hurt.

Miss Macey had looked so frightened when he went to her house. Ross had used him to scare the nice lady, and he'd tried to kill her too. Jimmy didn't like scaring or killing. Or being used. Hopefully Miss Macey was okay, but Ross would keep going after her until she was dead.

He was sure of that. He wouldn't use Jimmy to do it, though. Jimmy would fight back.

His stomach growled, and the memory of those hotdogs made his mouth water. Maybe he could help Miss Macey. No one had ever been so nice to him, except for Momma. He picked at the scar on his palm. Ross had killed Momma. Jimmy wouldn't let him kill Miss Macey too.

CHAPTER TWENTY-SEVEN

As Macey climbed the creaky wooden steps toward the victim's apartment, she ran her hand along the cracked brick wall. Images of the building's history shuffled through her mind like a slide show of secrets to which only she was privy. A few weeks ago, the barrage of images would've overwhelmed her. Now that Roberta had helped develop her gift, she could easily grab hold of any image she chose and soak in the energy, the story, the building held.

She grinned as she watched the image of two young boys in knickers and suspenders sliding down the stairs on an old board like they were riding a sled. They hooped and hollered and crashed at the bottom, then ran back up and slid down again.

Would her own children be as rambunctious as these boys one day? Would they look like her, with small statures and pale hair? Or would they favor Luke?

She shook herself. *Don't think like that.* She needed to focus on the case. One step at a time.

"You okay?" Bryce paused at the top of the stairs; Macey had stopped mid-flight.

"Yeah. Just…reading." She continued her ascent.

Bryce raised his eyebrows. "Anything helpful?"

She shook her head and brushed past him. The victim's apartment showed no sign of struggle. A rainbow of pillows lined the sofa, each one tilted at a perfect diagonal and carefully laid in place. The shelves held rows of neatly stacked books, and a stick of burning incense filled the room with patchouli. Strings of orange beads hung over the doorway to the balcony, and Macey stepped through to find the victim sipping juice on a lawn chair.

The woman had dark brown eyes that crinkled in the corners when she smiled. "You must be the great Detective Carpenter. I've heard about you." She offered her hand, and Macey shook it.

A soft tingle buzzed up her arm, and Macey narrowed her eyes. The woman wasn't a werewolf; the sensation felt different. But she possessed some sort of magic. A small cut marred her forehead, and a clay pot lay smashed on the floor. Here had been the struggle.

"You seem awfully calm for being the victim of an attempted sexual assault, Miss…" She flipped through her notes to find the woman's name.

"Natasha."

"Natasha, can you tell me what happened?"

The woman waved her hand dismissively. "It was nothing a little voodoo magic couldn't take care of."

"Voodoo?" Bryce tried to step onto the balcony, but he got tangled in the beads hanging in the doorway. He stumbled and spun around and finally made it out the door.

Natasha glanced at him and focused on Macey. "That demon messed with the wrong priestess is all I'm saying."

"Demon, huh?" Bryce chuckled. "Let me guess. Red eyes?"

"Yeah," Macey said. "We've been getting a lot of reports of a guy wearing red contacts harassing women. It was probably him."

Natasha glared at Macey, her gaze heavy, full of warning. "I know a demon when I see one. You should too."

Macey stepped toward her partner and lowered her voice. "Why don't you let me handle this. Maybe I can talk some sense into her. You know…woman to woman."

"Gotcha, boss. I'll be right inside." Bryce swatted at the hanging beads and stepped through the door.

Macey pulled a chair up next to Natasha. "The demon," she whispered. "What did it look like?"

"Oh, you believe me now, do you?" Natasha spoke loudly, leaning back and crossing her arms.

"Shh…I do, but they don't." She nodded toward the men in the apartment. "Did you kill it?"

Natasha laughed. "Kill it? Nah. I can send a spirit on to the next plane, but I ain't mastered demon slaying. I sure did scare it off, though."

"Which way did it go?"

"Took off up the street there." She pointed. "He's probably still hanging around. I pissed him off, so he'll be back. You can count on that."

"Maybe you should stay inside tonight." Macey leaned over the balcony, scanning the shadows below. If only her werewolf blood enhanced her vision like it did her sense of smell. All she could see was darkness.

"I ain't afraid of no demon. The neighbors heard the commotion and called you, but I done blessed this place and set up a charm. Ain't no evil getting back in here tonight."

"All right. Just—" Something stirred in the corner of her vision. Two blocks away, a shadow morphed into a human-like form and slinked down the street. "That's it, isn't it?"

Natasha leaned forward. "Mm-hmm. That's a demon if I ever seen one. Check out them eyes."

The fiend turned its head, and crimson eyes flashed like glowing embers. Where were the werewolves? They were supposed to be stopping these things. Macey darted into the apartment and shoved past the officers in the living room.

"Where you headed?" Bryce called as she dashed through the door.

"I'll be right back. Stay here." She bounded down the steps and sprinted as soon as her feet hit the pavement. "Hey! Stop!"

The demon turned around and peeled its lips back into a reptilian sneer. It hissed and darted down an alley into the shadows. Macey veered around the corner and skidded to a stop. Dead end. She had it trapped.

The creature crouched by the wall, rocking side to side on its claw-like feet. It made a screeching sound like metal scraping metal and arched its back like a cat. Macey raised her gun. Head or heart? Would a bullet even kill a demon? She hesitated, hovering her sights between its eyes. No. It had to be the heart.

The demon screeched again, and another assaulting wail answered it. Macey jerked her head around as a second demon dropped into the alley from the rooftop above. Her heart jack hammered in her chest. The *whooshing* of her pulse pounded in her ears. She pointed her gun at the first demon. Then the second. What could she do? They had her pinned in.

They crept toward her, inching closer, their crimson eyes bleeding hate. The second fiend sprang, leaping toward Macey and knocking the gun out of her hand. It skidded to the feet of the first demon, who picked it up and tossed it aside.

The demons slithered closer, the odor of death and garbage emanating from their pores and assaulting Macey's senses. She stumbled back and tripped over a broken piece of wrought iron railing. She fell to the ground and quickly sprang to her feet, gripping the metal stake in her hand.

She couldn't breathe. Fear gripped her heart like a steel fist as she waved the pole at the fiends. If she was going down, she'd go down fighting. "Back off."

A massive, sandy colored wolf dropped into the alley from above. Without warning, it leapt toward a demon and clamped its jaws on the fiend's neck. Macey didn't hesitate. She charged at the second demon and drove the metal spike straight through its heart. The devil exploded into a billowing cloud of ash as the stake clattered on the cobblestone.

Macey gasped and stumbled back against the wall. The werewolf grunted, standing over the ashes of the other fiend. It nudged Macey's pistol with its nose, sliding the gun across the stones. Macey crept forward and picked it up.

"Thanks for your help. I know you're not Luke. Who are you?"

The wolf glanced down the alley toward the street and blew out a hard breath. It shifted its gaze back to Macey as its body began to vibrate. A shimmery mist enveloped it, and it transformed into a woman.

Macey blinked. "Alexis?"

She rushed toward her sister and embraced her. "Macey! Are you okay?"

"Yeah. I'm fine. But…your clothes." She ran her hands over Alexis's shirt sleeves. The wolf wasn't wearing a teal T-shirt and jeans, but when it morphed into her sister, she was fully clothed. "How?"

She shrugged. "Magic, I suppose. Whatever I'm wearing…or carrying in my pockets…gets absorbed in the shift. When I shift back, everything's in its place."

"That's…weird."

"It's always been this way."

"Well, how about that?" She shook her head. "When did you start chasing demons?"

Alexis dropped her arms by her sides. "I don't…officially. Luke won't let me on the team since I'm not a pack member. But I figured y'all needed all the help you could get."

"Thanks. You saved my life."

"Hardly. You slayed that demon like a pro." She wrapped an arm around Macey's shoulders. "You can take care of yourself, little sis."

Macey sighed. "I'm glad someone thinks so. Walk with me. I need to get back to my partner."

"Luke being over-protective?" Alexis followed her sister out of the alley.

"He's treating me like I'm helpless. I have one little altercation, and suddenly he thinks I can't be alone anymore."

"You have to remember…he's an alpha male. About to be *the* alpha male. It's in his nature to be protective."

Macey slowed her pace as they approached Natasha's building. "I know. You're right, but…"

"But you're scared."

"Terrified."

"I get it." Alexis nodded toward Bryce coming down the stairs. "There's your partner. You'd better get back to work. I'll call you later."

Macey jogged to the building and arrived as Bryce reached the street. Natasha still sat on her balcony, sipping her glass of juice and smiling smugly.

"Thanks, Natasha," Macey called up to her. "It's taken care of. You have a good night."

Natasha waved. "Yes, ma'am. I knew you could do it."

"What was that about?" Bryce said as they walked to his car.

Macey grinned. "It's a girl thing. You wouldn't understand."

Chase leaned against the wall outside Jean Lafitte's Blacksmith Shop. With his hands shoved in his pockets and one leg crossed in front of the other, he appeared calm, casual. To a human, he looked like a normal guy hanging out in the French Quarter. But Luke knew better. Chase's attentive eyes scanned the scene, raking back and forth across the shadows in the distance. He was hunting demons.

The old Blacksmith Shop-turned-bar was a popular place for ghost tours to stop and give the tourists a break. Built in the 1700s, it was one of the oldest buildings in the Quarter. Two attic windows jutted up from the sagging, shingled roof, and a brick and mortar chimney rose between them. Three shuttered doors stood open on the building front, and patrons filed in and out as they got their drinks and returned to their tours. The structure's sordid history alone would be enough to attract creatures from hell. The crowd swarming inside and spilling out onto the sidewalk made it all the more appealing.

"Quiet night." Luke sauntered toward his friend.

"Yeah." Chase smiled, but it didn't reach his eyes. He inhaled and opened his mouth like he was going to say something, but he shook his head instead. Luke leaned against the wall and shoved his hands in his pockets to mirror Chase's posture.

Chase glanced at him with a strange expression and focused back on the shadows. "How'd the debriefing go with your old man?"

Luke exhaled sharply and ran his hand over his face. "Not good, man."

"Not happy about the demon situation?"

"No. I've got a plan for that. We're going to take these suckers out tomorrow afternoon." He told Chase about the new information Macey had given him. "Soon as I find someone who can trap the halfling spirit, we're good to go."

"What's the problem then?"

"It's Stephen. Knocked on the old man's door as soon as he found out they were home."

Chase shook his head. "He's chomping at the bit to be alpha. Dude wants it bad. I hope he doesn't do anything stupid."

"He won't."

Chase hesitated, kicking at the dust on the ground. "He's not going to get the chance to be alpha is he?" He raised his eyes to meet Luke's, and they were tight with worry. "You'll mate?"

"C'mon, man. You know me better than that." He let

out a cynical laugh. "I told my folks if I couldn't get Macey back before the deadline, they could choose someone for me."

Chase raised an eyebrow. "You'd go through with that?"

"As long as the mate understands it's just business, yeah. I'll do what I have to do for the good of the pack. But honestly?" He let his gaze drift toward the shadows as his throat thickened. "It *has* to be Macey. It *will* be."

"Yeah. Speaking of Macey and our quiet night, I talked to Alexis a few minutes ago."

A feeling of dread sank in his gut as he gave him his full attention. "What happened? Is Macey okay?"

"She's fine. But…a pair of demons cornered your girl in an alley. Alexis fought them off, sent them back to hell."

His stomach turned. "Holy shit. It must've happened when I was meeting with my parents. Goddammit! I should've been there to protect her. I've got to go check on her."

Chase put a hand on Luke's arm. "Slow down, Lancelot. Your princess walked away without a scratch."

Luke balled his hands into fists. His muscles tightened with the urge to run to her. To comfort her. But what good would that do? She didn't want to see him. He inhaled deeply and tried to relax.

"Look," Chase said, "I know you worry about her after what happened to Melissa."

"I worry about any were who can't shift. They're defenseless."

"Some may be, but Macey isn't one of them. She's a badass detective who takes down monsters on a daily basis. So the monsters she's used to are human. So what? Sometimes those are the worst kind."

Luke huffed. His friend had a point.

"I don't know much about women, but I'm pretty sure you rushing in to scold her for doing her job isn't going to help your case. Think about the things that attracted you to her in the first place. Her independence? Spunk? Confidence? Those things aren't going to disappear because you're in her life. They make her who she is. Macey doesn't need a knight in shining armor. She needs a partner."

"Damn it, Chase. Why do you have to make so much sense?"

He grinned. "Someone's got to keep you in line."

Across the street, the shadows moved. A drunk woman leaned against the wall near an alley entrance, her friends ignoring her as she doubled over and dry heaved. A fiend had found its target. Luke nodded toward the demon. "Looks like we'll have an interesting night after all."

CHAPTER TWENTY-EIGHT

Luke got up at dawn and headed to Café Beignet to meet Roberta. He could take care of the living halfling and the human, but he needed a medium to trap the demon spirit. Roberta would know who could help.

He turned onto Bourbon Street and headed toward Musical Legends Park. The café was located in the rear of the square. Foamy liquid flowed down the sidewalks and cascaded into the storm drains, and he inhaled the clean scent of soap. This was the best Bourbon Street would smell all day. Every morning, before the sun came up, a crew washed the streets in the French Quarter. Especially this one. The bubbly mixture rinsed away most of the beer, urine, and vomit the tourists had deposited the night before, but it wouldn't be long before the foul scents returned. As soon as the revelers finished nursing their hangovers, they'd start the party over again.

Laissez les bon temps roulez. Let the good times roll. It was the theme of the Big Easy, and he understood the appeal. He'd done his share of partying, and he couldn't imagine a greater city than New Orleans.

As he entered the park, he spotted Roberta sitting on an upstairs patio, sipping from a paper cup. Alexis sat next to her at the small, wrought iron table. What the hell was she doing there? Roberta waved, smiling brightly. Alexis swallowed hard and averted her gaze. At least she realized she was overstepping her boundaries.

"Thanks for meeting me, Roberta." Luke settled into a chair across from the women. "Alexis." He nodded.

The corners of Roberta's eyes crinkled, deepening her crow's feet into canyons. "Anything I can do to help my friends." She passed a knowing glance to Alexis.

Luke stiffened. Pack members couldn't keep secrets from the alpha. Normally he could demand they tell him whatever secret they shared. But these women weren't pack…and he didn't technically hold the alpha title yet. He'd have to coax it out of them gently.

"What are you doing here, Alexis?" Okay, maybe not so gently, but the woman had been a thorn in his side from the beginning.

She sat up straight. "Roberta invited me."

"She's as much a part of this mess as you are," Roberta said.

His jaw tightened as he glared at Macey's sister. She did look out for her family; he'd give her that. "Fine." He shifted his gaze to Roberta. "I need a medium."

Roberta started to answer, but remained silent as a waiter delivered a cup of black coffee for Luke and three orders of beignets. He hadn't planned on eating, but he couldn't resist the sugary pastries. He tore one in half and shoved the French donut into his mouth. Powdered sugar floated down, dusting the table and his pants in white.

Amusement turned up the corners of Roberta's mouth. "You have a medium. A powerful one."

"Who?" Luke sipped his coffee to wash down the pastry.

"Macey," Alexis said.

He choked, spilling hot liquid down the front of his shirt. He slammed the Styrofoam cup on the table, sloshing the coffee everywhere. Roberta handed him a stack of napkins, and he dabbed at the stain on his shirt. "No way."

"Why not?" Alexis's challenging tone grated on his nerves.

"She's the best one for the job," Roberta said. "Her powers are effortless. She's a natural."

Luke shook his head. Macey wasn't getting anywhere near that demon again. "There has to be someone else. I won't put her in harm's way. She knows virtually nothing about the supernatural world. She can't shift. She's defenseless against these monsters."

Alexis crossed her arms. "Defenseless? She killed a demon last night. I think she can handle herself around monsters."

He froze. The napkin fell to the table. "She…killed one? Chase said that you…"

"I didn't tell him the whole story. She was fierce, Luke. She rammed a piece of wrought iron fence right through its heart. She probably could've taken on both of them if I hadn't shown up to help."

His mouth hung open in disbelief. Thoughts tumbled through his mind as he tried to comprehend. "She killed it?"

"I'm telling you," Alexis said, "she can take care of herself. And she can trap this spirit. You need to give her a chance."

Maybe she could handle it. She was strong. The strongest woman he knew. "I… She…"

"She's a detective, dear," Roberta said. "It's her job to be in harm's way. She needs to end this as much as you do. Let her."

He ground his teeth and swallowed hard. A weight the size of a bowling ball formed in his stomach as he took a deep breath and nodded. "Bring her to the bar at eleven, then we'll head to the swamp."

Alexis stood. "I'm coming too."

"Damn right you are." His team could handle the halfling and the human. Alexis would help him protect Macey.

Luke brought Chase and James up to speed on the situation while he waited for Macey and Alexis to arrive. Stephen insisted on tagging along, but he probably only wanted to impress the alpha. He'd shown no interest in the demon hunting team before the old man came back.

"Don't kill the human," Luke said. "He's innocent."

"Are you kidding me?" Stephen crossed his arms. "He's been summoning *demons*."

Luke sighed. This part would take some convincing… for all of them. He wasn't sure he believed in the guy's innocence himself, but Macey insisted. "He's a few cards short of a full deck, okay? Macey says he's like a kid in a man's body, and his brother's been forcing him to do it."

Stephen's lip curved in disgust. "Macey? Now we're taking orders from a human outside the pack?"

"You know she's not human." Luke stood and stepped around the desk, asserting his dominance.

Stephen widened his stance. "She's not pack."

"She will be."

"Some alpha you're gonna be. Taking orders from a woman."

Luke slammed his forearm against Stephen's chest, pinning him to the wall. Heat rolled through his body, his beast begging to take over and fight. It might take an ass-kicking to keep his cousin in line, but now wasn't the time. He took a deep breath, and spoke in a low growl. "I *will* be alpha. And *I'm* giving the orders. You better learn to accept that." He leaned in, pressing the air from his cousin's lungs. "Show some respect."

He released him, and Stephen slumped against the wall, rubbing his chest. He mumbled something under his breath, but Luke ignored him. It was eleven o'clock. The women had arrived.

Luke stepped through the swinging door into the bar to find Alexis and Macey chatting with his sister. Macey wore dark jeans and a fitted black T-shirt that hugged her curves in all the right places. Her face was clean of makeup, and she'd tied her hair back into a bun. Her gun sat holstered on her hip, while a black messenger bag hung across her body on the other side. His heart flittered at the sight of her, his fingers twitching to untie her hair.

Her eyes lit up for a moment when they met his, but they quickly dimmed as she looked away. His chest ached, but he pushed the emotions aside. "Seen anything help-ful?" he asked Amber.

"It's fuzzy. You guys are clouding my visions with all that testosterone." She smiled and motioned for Luke to come closer. Leaning in, she whispered, "Watch your back today. I'm sensing friendly fire."

"Details?" He glanced at his cousin.

She shook her head. "Good luck."

He turned to his team. "I'll drive the women as close as we can get, and we'll walk the rest of the way. Meet us there."

"Got it," James said, and the three men darted out the door.

He motioned for Macey and Alexis to follow him to his truck, and they all climbed in. The air hung heavy, tension thickening the atmosphere as Luke scrambled for something to say. Conversations with Macey had always been so easy before, flowing effortlessly like they'd never run out of things to talk about. Now he was at a loss for words. He couldn't talk about them, so he settled for talking about her. "I hear you killed a demon on your own last night."

Macey glanced at him. "I did." Wariness in her voice drew out her words. She sat in the middle of the bench seat, close enough that he could feel the warmth radiating from her skin.

"That's...amazing." His hand slid off the steering wheel, and he instinctively reached for her knee. At the last second, he played off the movement by reaching for the AC controls to crank up the air. Luckily, she didn't notice his almost-mistake.

"You sound surprised," she said.

"I've never seen anybody who couldn't shift take one on before. You're tougher than I thought."

Her posture relaxed, and a smile played on her lips. He'd finally said something right. If only he could keep the conversation going, but it was time to get to work. He pulled his truck to the side of the road and rolled to a stop. "We'll have to walk from here."

"How will we know if the spirit is even there?" Alexis

asked a few minutes later as they trudged through the brush toward the shack.

"I'll sense it." Macey shivered. "I can always tell when it's around."

"Here's the plan," Luke said. "The guys will take care of the halfling. Alexis, you and I will guard Macey. Make sure nothing happens to her while she's trapping the demon. Once the demon's gone and Macey's safe, then we'll deal with the human."

"I don't need a bodyguard," Macey said.

"What if it possesses your friend again?" Luke said. "He knocked you out before; he can do it again."

Macey stopped and balled her hands into fists. She pressed her lips into a hard line and glared at him. "This has got to stop. Why do you treat me like I'm helpless? You want me to be your 'man on the inside,' but you don't want me close to the action. I'm not going to sit at home looking pretty while the boys fight all the bad guys. I'm one of the boys, Luke. I'm better than most of them."

What could he say? She was right. They were all right. Macey wasn't Melissa. He was letting his past control his future with the woman he loved. When he didn't respond, she turned on her heel and marched away. Alexis hurried to catch up to her.

"I had a fiancée once." He had to force the words over the lump in his throat. "Did you know that?"

Macey stopped and turned around.

"Well, it wasn't official. I didn't give her a ring yet, but we'd talked about it." He stepped toward her and ran a hand through his hair.

Her angry expression softened. "I had no idea."

He shrugged as a familiar ache formed in his chest. "She got killed because of me. We were supposed to go out to dinner that night, but I was working late on a construction site. Then I had to go to the bar to deal with some pack business. I canceled on her. That was the last time I talked to her."

"I'm so sorry." She tentatively stepped toward him. Her hands twitched like she wanted to offer him comfort, but she held it back.

"If I'd have gone home after work. If I'd have been there for her, those damn rogues wouldn't have kidnapped her." He dropped his gaze to the ground. "They found her body in an apartment in Shreveport. The rogues were dead too. Police said it looked like a drug deal gone awry, but Melissa wasn't into drugs." He shoved his hands into his pockets. "I could have protected her, but I didn't. I don't want to make that mistake again."

Macey's body trembled. She crossed and uncrossed her arms and shifted her weight from side to side.

"Please say something, Macey."

"Wait," Alexis said. "Melissa who?"

He tore his gaze away from Macey's shimmering eyes. "Taylor. Melissa Taylor."

Alexis stiffened. "I knew her." Her voice was a whisper. She shook her head. "Luke, she wasn't kidnapped."

"What are you talking about?"

Alexis took a deep breath and let it out slowly. "Melissa went to that apartment on her own that night. She knew those rogues."

His heart dropped into his stomach. "How do you know that?"

"Because I was supposed to be there too."

A wave of nausea rolled through him, and he gritted his teeth. "Explain."

"The rogues were dealers. It's how a lot of them make a

living." She looked at Macey. "Not me. I never sold drugs, but I was dating one of them. Melissa was with the other one. The police are right. It was a drug deal gone bad."

He shook his head in disbelief. Melissa wasn't cheating on him. No way...

"I knew she had another boyfriend in New Orleans," Alexis continued, "but I didn't know it was you. She talked about leaving the pack. She liked the freedom of being rogue. I'm sorry, Luke."

He blinked, his throat thickening as his mind scrambled to comprehend. Melissa hadn't been kidnapped. She'd been cheating on him. He swallowed, and the sensation of hot coal burned down his esophagus, settling in his stomach like a boulder. The woman he'd once thought he'd spend forever with had betrayed him...but he couldn't be angry with her. She'd paid the ultimate price for her infidelity, and he wouldn't wish that fate on anyone.

Macey ran to him, finally offering the comfort she'd been holding back. She wrapped her arms around his waist and pressed her head against his chest. He held her, letting her warmth loosen the knots in his core.

Though his mind didn't want to accept the betrayal, in his heart he knew it was true. The signs were there, if he were honest with himself. The new wardrobe, excessive trips to the salon, how careful she was to never leave her phone lying where he would see it. In the back of his mind, he'd suspected it. But her death had washed away his doubt, leaving a thick layer of guilt in its place.

Though he'd cared for Melissa deeply, he'd used his anger at himself to cope with her death, feeling the sadness, but never truly dealing with it. Now, he expected the emotion to slam into his chest, knocking the air from his lungs. Instead, he let out his breath slowly as a hundred-pound weight lifted off his shoulders. The guilt he'd carried for three years floated away, and he hugged Macey tighter.

"Looks like we've both been letting our pasts mess with our lives," she said.

He looked at Alexis. "Yeah, I guess we have."

Alexis raised her hands. "Hey, I'll take responsibility for Macey's issues, but I had nothing to do with Melissa's choices. You can't blame me for that."

Luke laughed. Guilt was a useless emotion that did nothing but weigh him down and hold him back. Now he was free. Free to mourn Melissa's death properly and free to finally move on. "I don't. I'm glad to know the truth. Now let's go kick some demon ass."

Macey pulled away and gazed up at him, a timid smile curving her pink lips. What he would have given to know what thoughts tumbled through her mind at that moment. But it wasn't the time for talk. They'd already wasted too much with his confession and Alexis's revelation. He laced his fingers through hers and led them to the shack.

"It's there, through the trees," he said. Dirty white paint peeled from the rotted wood structure, and a lopsided porch crumbled in front of the house. A screen door hung loose, unable to latch closed because the house sank at an odd angle.

Macey gasped. "That's where Jimmy lives? No wonder he's starving. They don't even have electricity."

"Yes, they do." Luke pointed to a red engine near the back door. "There's a generator there. And there's a solar panel on the roof. Somebody was smart enough to set that up."

"Well, it wasn't Jimmy." Defensiveness sharpened Macey's voice. How could she be so fond of the man who'd attacked her? "And he's not here anyway. Neither of them are."

"Took you long enough." Chase and the other men approached from the left. He looked at Luke's hand, holding Macey's, and grinned. "Looks like nobody's home."

"We can wait," Luke said.

Macey shook her head. "It's Monday."

"So?"

"Jimmy goes to the Quarter on Mondays. He'll be in Jackson Square."

Stephen stepped forward. "How do you know so much about the rapist? Seems suspicious to me." He looked at the other men. "How do we know this isn't a trap? She could be working with the fiends. Setting us up."

Luke opened his mouth to defend Macey, but she didn't need his help.

"He's not the rapist," she said. "If you'd take a minute to look through all that testosterone swirling behind your eyes, you'd see the facts. The spirit is the one we're after. I met Jimmy. He's as helpless as a child." She was feisty. And so goddamn sexy.

Stephen looked at Luke like he expected him to step in, but Luke just grinned. His woman could take care of herself. He accepted that now. The only thing left to do was make her his again.

"What's the plan then?" he said to Macey. "Do we wait it out? When will he be back?"

"I think I should go to Jackson Square and talk to him. He'll listen to me. Maybe he can help."

"All right. Chase, James, Stephen, stay here. Stake the

place out and call me if you see any action. Alexis and I will go with Macey back to the Quarter."

Stephen puffed out his chest. "You're seriously taking orders from that *woman?*"

Macey put her hands on her hips. "I think *he* gave the order. I merely made a suggestion."

Stephen narrowed his eyes in an icy glare, but he didn't say anything else. James bit his lip, and Chase rubbed his face, both trying to hide their smiles. Hopefully this was the extent of the "friendly fire" his sister warned him about. A sinking feeling in his gut told him there'd be more.

CHAPTER TWENTY-NINE

THE AUGUST SUN HUNG HIGH IN THE SKY, ROASTING Jackson Square. Sweat stung Macey's eyes, and she wiped it away as she scanned the crowd for Jimmy. She checked the candy store first, but the owner hadn't seen him. Just her luck, he'd learned his lesson and wouldn't go there again. Hopefully she'd find him somewhere in the Square.

Luke and Alexis sat on a bench under a tree in the park. His gaze followed her as she walked around the perimeter. Protecting her from a distance.

At least he was giving her room to breathe now. Showing some trust in her abilities. Possessiveness gripped at her heart to think he had been engaged before. That he had loved another woman. She shook her head. He'd had a life before her; she'd have been a fool to think he hadn't. Still, a ball of jealousy knotted in her stomach every time she pictured him in another woman's arms. What did that say about her?

Did she want him back? Of course she did. Every fiber of her being ached to be in his arms. But if she needed him that badly, could her heart survive losing him? She'd given herself to him so easily before, and fallen apart so desperately when she'd thought he was using her. She couldn't take that chance again.

Focus, Mace. Find Jimmy. She'd have time to think about her relationship with Luke when this was over. She meandered through the crowd, searching the faces until her gaze landed upon Jimmy's innocent, brown eyes. He sat on a bench, facing the St. Louis Cathedral, and beamed a smile at the juggler tossing flaming batons into the air.

She approached him cautiously, assuming a cheerful posture and smiling to disarm his fears. His eyes widened when he noticed her, his gaze darting about like he might be watched. Seemingly satisfied with his observation, he waved and trotted toward her.

"Hi, Miss Macey!" He stopped, and his face fell as his gaze locked on her gun. He placed his hand on his shoulder and winced.

"I'm not going to hurt you, Jimmy. Is your brother around?" She didn't sense the demon, but maybe Jimmy knew where it was.

"Oh, no. He's not here." When he pulled his hand away from his shoulder, his shirt stuck to the wound.

"How's your shoulder?"

His bottom lip trembled. "It hurts."

"I'm sorry I shot you. I was scared."

He nodded, fat tears pooling in his eyes. "It's okay, Miss Macey. Ross made me do mean things to you."

"Ross? Is that your brother's name?"

His eyes widened, and tears dripped onto his cheeks. He nodded.

"Did you go to the doctor to fix your shoulder?"

"Oh, no ma'am. I'm not allowed to see a doctor. The

boy cat-rized it for me."

"Cat-rized?"

"He burned it. To make it stop bleeding. It hurts really bad, but it doesn't bleed anymore. Just some green stuff comes out."

Macey cringed. "You mean cauterized?"

"That's what I said."

"What boy?"

"Ross made him. He's special like my brother. Half demon." His face pinched. "He lives with us now. He sleeps on my futon. I have to sleep on the floor because I'm not special."

"I think you're special." Her heart ached for the poor man, but she tried to keep her expression cheerful.

His eyes brightened. "You do?"

"You're very special, Jimmy, and I'd like to help you. Would you like to get away from your brother? To have a real bed to sleep in and food every day?"

"Oh, I would like that very much. But he won't let me leave. He said if I ever tried to go away, he'd eat me like he ate Momma."

"You mean when he was born?" Visions of the first victim's mangled torso made her stomach turn. Had Jimmy watched his brother claw his way out of his mother's womb? No wonder his brain didn't work quite right.

"Yes, ma'am. And I don't want to get eaten."

"I won't let him eat you. I promise I can keep you safe. Will you let me help you, Jimmy?" She placed a gentle hand on his good shoulder.

He looked at her hand, and confusion clouded his eyes. Had he ever been touched in a loving way? Probably not since his brother was born. "Okay, Miss Macey. You're a real nice lady."

"I have some friends with me. Do you want to meet them?"

He grinned like a child. "Friends? I don't have any friends."

"I'm your friend. Do you want to meet some more?"

"Yes, please!"

She led Jimmy through the park gates and introduced him to Luke and Alexis. He smiled timidly at her sister and waved, but when his eyes met Luke's, he cowered. He shuffled backward, tensing like he was about to bolt.

"What's wrong?" Macey asked.

"He…he's a werewolf. Werewolves are bad."

"No, Jimmy." She put her hand on his elbow. That bewildered expression crossed his face, but he relaxed under her touch. "Luke is my friend. Werewolves are good. He's going to help you too."

"But Ross says werewolves are bad. They keep killing his demons."

Luke grumbled under his breath, but he didn't say anything out loud. He was letting Macey take the lead. Trusting her. He pressed his lips into a tight smile.

"Do you think what your brother is doing is good?" Macey asked.

Jimmy hung his head and rubbed the back of his neck. "No, ma'am."

"We're going to stop him and find you a place to stay. Would you like that?"

"Yes, ma'am."

"How many halflings are there?" Luke asked. "We need to know what we're up against."

Jimmy's gaze darted about the square like he wasn't sure if he should answer. Finally, his frightened eyes locked with Macey's.

"It's okay. You can answer him."

"Well, there's one. Maybe two."

"Maybe?" Luke stood. The calmness in his voice sounded forced. His fists clenched and unclenched at his sides.

Jimmy stepped back, crossing his arms over his chest in an X—a defensive posture. "He's mad at me." He angled his body sideways, as if bracing for a blow.

"No one's mad at you, Jimmy." Macey mouthed the words *sit down* to Luke. He grunted, but he did what she asked. Alexis sank onto the bench next to him.

"What do you mean *maybe* two?" Macey said.

Jimmy relaxed his posture and scratched his ear. "Oh. He said he had to go see about a birth today. Last time he said that, he brought the boy home. I don't want another boy in our house. I want my futon back."

"I'm going to get you a real bed."

His face lit with a smile. "Then I won't go back. I don't want to raise any more demons. It makes me feel sick, but Ross said we have to raise a whole mess of them tonight. But if I stay with you, Miss Macey, you'll keep me safe, right? You won't let Ross eat me. You promised."

Luke ran his hand over his face. He was obviously losing patience with Jimmy, but Macey almost had all the information she needed.

"I will help you," she said. "But first I need you to go back, okay? And pretend like you never talked to me."

Jimmy knit his brow. "Why?"

"It's the only way to stop your brother from hurting more people."

His gaze fell to the ground as he shoved his hands in his pockets. "I don't want to hurt more people."

"Will you help me then?" She reached for his injured

hand and turned it palm up to see the scar. "Help me help you?"

He nodded.

"Good. Here's what I need you to do."

Luke crouched in the leaves behind a bush, eyeing the dilapidated shack. It had taken every ounce of self-control he could muster to stop himself from beating the crap out of that guy for what he did to Macey. Once he met him, though, he understood. There was no way Jimmy had done all this on his own.

He watched the man pacing back and forth across the window, muttering to himself incessantly, wringing his hands like his nerves were tearing him apart. "How do you know he's not going to spill the whole plan to his brother as soon as he sees him?"

"I don't," Macey said. "But he trusts me. And if we move in fast enough, he won't have a chance to tell him anything."

He peered into the trees behind the shack. His team had already shifted, preparing to take on the two halflings at his command. Alexis was somewhere nearby. She'd be watching Jimmy. Macey didn't want to hurt the guy, but he trusted Alexis to do what needed to be done if Macey's life was in danger.

Luke grudgingly remained in human form. If it were up to him, he'd shift like the others and tear into that cabin like a storm, but Macey wouldn't let him near Jimmy unless he stayed human. He sure as hell wasn't letting her go in alone.

"What will they do with the baby?" She stared straight ahead, not meeting his gaze.

"The halfling?"

"If it's an infant, I…" She shook her head.

"By the time they get it back here, it'll be a child. Halflings grow exponentially, reaching full size in a few days."

"A child." She still wouldn't look at him.

"It may look like a child, but he'll be pure evil. Trust me. The spirit you're going to capture started out the same way. And it's already killed the woman who gave birth to it."

She nodded.

He rubbed his hand in circles on her back, trying to reassure her, and she leaned into him, resting her head on his shoulder. Her hair smelled like strawberries. He wrapped his arms around her and kissed the top of her head, his pulse quickening, his chest aching at how perfect she felt in his arms.

"I've missed you," she said.

His breath hitched, his stomach fluttering like a thousand butterflies emerging from their cocoons. "I've been lost without you, Macey."

She pulled away and looked at him. A sadness filled her eyes that he didn't understand. He was hers if she wanted him. Why wouldn't she let him in?

He cupped her face in his hand, running his thumb across her soft skin. "After this is over, can we give it another try? Can we give *us* another try?"

She took a deep breath and let it out slowly. "Luke, I —" She stiffened, her eyes growing wide with fear. "He's here."

CHAPTER THIRTY

JIMMY JUST HAD TO ACT NATURAL. PRETEND LIKE everything was normal and go along with whatever Ross wanted. That's what Miss Macey had said to do. He stopped pacing to stare out the window. She said she'd be out there somewhere, and she'd come in to help him as soon as she could.

Footsteps sounded on the front porch, making Jimmy's heart beat like a racehorse. Was she here? Had she come to save him early? "Mi—" He slapped his hand over his mouth. The boy stepped inside, followed by another boy. This one looked like he was five years old, but Jimmy knew better. He still had blood on his face from eating his momma.

Jimmy shuddered. If the boys were here, his brother must've been close by. Sweat rolled down his back, making his shirt stick to his skin. He shivered. Where was Miss Macey?

"Are you ready, dimwit?"

The voice snaked around him, slithering into his head.

Jimmy swallowed down the sour taste in his mouth and nodded. "I guess so."

Bam! The blow to his head caught Jimmy off guard, and he stumbled into the altar. His face stung where Ross's spirit hit him. What if Ross hit Miss Macey?

"You guess so? Don't make me use up all my strength keeping you in line, idiot. We've got a lot to do tonight."

"Okay."

The boy and the little boy sat on Jimmy's futon. Something burned inside him. He ground his teeth, and his body tensed as he glared at them. But he would have a bed to sleep in tonight. Miss Macey promised. How would she fight Ross when she couldn't touch him but he could touch her? It wasn't fair.

Jimmy had an idea. His tummy did a little flip inside him, and he smiled.

"What are you so happy about?"

"I don't want to raise any demons."

This time the blow came to his stomach. He doubled over, clutching his middle, but he still smiled. If he could get Ross to use up all his energy now, he wouldn't be able to hurt Miss Macey or her friends.

"You'll do what I tell you to, you moron. Now pick up the knife and get busy."

"No." He braced himself for another beating, but it didn't come. An icy snake slithered up his body and whispered in his ear.

"What are you doing brother? You're acting suspicious."

"N…nothing. I just don't want to raise no more demons." His knees trembled, so he put his hand on the altar to hold himself steady.

A loud *bang* sounded in the swamp, and he jerked his head toward the sound. That was the signal. The boys were supposed to run outside to see what it was, and then the werewolves would get them. But the boys didn't move from Jimmy's futon.

"What was that?" Jimmy said. "M...maybe the boy and the little boy should go check."

"You'd like that, wouldn't you? Does it hurt your little feelings to see them sitting there? Or is something else going on? What are you scheming?"

"I'm not scheming n...nothing."

"You know I can get inside your head and see for myself, so you might as well tell me."

Jimmy clamped his mouth shut. He was a stupid idiot. He should have gone along with Ross's plans like Miss Macey had told him to do. Good ideas never popped into his head. Only bad ones. He was a moron. Now what was Miss Macey going to do? She couldn't fight Ross and the boys at the same time.

"Why can't you follow orders like the boy there? If you weren't so easy to possess, I'd have let him eat you a long time ago."

Jimmy's whole body trembled. He didn't want to get eaten. "I'm sorry, Ross. Please don't let him eat me."

A million tiny razor blades sliced through Jimmy's skin as Ross pushed his spirit inside him. He wanted to collapse to the floor and cry, but he couldn't control his own muscles anymore. He could feel his brother prodding through his brain, sifting through his memories like someone panning for gold. Jimmy tried not to think about anything, but he couldn't get the image of Miss Macey's face to go away. And thoughts of Miss Macey led to thoughts of her friends, and before he knew it, he'd spilled the whole plan.

"Werewolves?" Ross growled the words with Jimmy's mouth. "You're friends with werewolves now?"

Ross ripped himself from his brother's body, and Jimmy crumpled to the floor. He gasped for breath and rocked back and forth on the hard linoleum. What had he done? He was such a stupid idiot.

"Thanks for bringing them here, brother. We're on my turf now. Killing them all will be fun."

CHAPTER THIRTY-ONE

"GODDAMMIT. THEY AREN'T MOVING." *I KNEW THIS wouldn't work.* Luke refrained from saying the last part out loud for fear of alienating Macey more. But, damn it, they couldn't depend on that guy. "He must've told them the plan."

"It's not his fault," Macey said. "You saw how his eyes glowed for a few minutes. The spirit possessed him. Maybe he can read his mind while he's in there."

"Could he read your mind?" Alexis leaned against a tree a few yards away.

"I don't think so. I forced him out as soon as he got in."

"Whatever the method, he spilled the plan," Luke said.

She crossed her arms. "It wasn't his fault."

"Why do you keep defending him?"

"He needs help."

Luke took a deep breath and chose his words carefully. "If it comes down to your life or his…"

"I know. But it won't."

"So," Alexis said. "What do we do now?"

Luke signaled the rest of his team to join them, and the men approached in human form. They'd lost the element of surprise, but they outnumbered them. "Looks like we're going to have to bust in with our teeth bared. You guys take out the halflings; we'll get the spirit."

"What about the halflings' spirits?" Alexis asked. "Won't they be set free like Jimmy's brother?"

"I don't think so," Luke said. "They're too young. Not strong enough. As long as you decapitate the bodies, they shouldn't be a problem anymore." He turned to Macey. "You've got your gun. My teeth and claws are my weapons."

"I understand. If you think you need to shift…"

He took her hand and led her away from the pack. "Listen, Macey." He lowered his voice so only she could hear. "If anything happens in there…and we need to get away fast…I want you to climb on my back, and we'll run."

"I can run."

"Werewolves are faster. Please. Promise me?"

A sly grin curved her lips. "You want me to ride you?"

"Every day of my life." He took her face in his hands and kissed her. Firmly. With purpose. If she wouldn't let him tell her how he felt, he was going to show her. At first, she stiffened, but she didn't pull away. Her body relaxed, her lips softening to accept him. Hope bloomed in his core, and he held on to it. When this was over, she would be his.

Macey's head spun from the kiss as she tromped through the brush toward the shack. Her body had reacted against her will, reciprocating the passion. She hadn't had time to consider the consequences letting him back in might bring, and she didn't have time to think about it now. She pushed those emotions aside and followed the pack of wolves as they stalked the demons.

They were all huge, but Luke outweighed them by at least fifty pounds. He stayed close, on her left side, while Alexis flanked her on the right. Her sister may have been the smallest, but she'd seen her fight a demon. Alexis was just as strong as the others. Chase had brown fur, and James was a dappled gray. Stephen's fur was also gray, but so dark it seemed almost black.

An icy chill crept up Macey's spine, raising goose bumps on the back of her neck. A sharp prickling sensation pressed into her skin, and she froze. The demon was trying to enter her. She pushed back, slamming down the iron curtain of her will, forcing the demon away. "Nice try."

"It was worth a shot." The voice swirled around her head. *"It would've been fun to make you kill your friends. I'll still enjoy watching my boys do it."*

The halflings stepped out of the shack. The bigger one dragged Jimmy through the door and shoved him off the porch. The wolves fanned out to face them, but Luke stayed glued by her side.

Tears streamed down Jimmy's face. "I'm sorry, Miss Macey. Please don't let your friends eat me."

"No one's going to hurt you, Jimmy."

"Get them!"

On the spirit's command, the halflings hurled themselves at the wolves. The small one carried a knife, and he stabbed it into the brown wolf's shoulder. Chase yelped, and James's jaws clamped down on the halfling's neck. The knife fell to the ground as the boy went limp.

It was a demon. Not a boy. Macey had to remind herself she wasn't witnessing a child's death. The older halfling darted into the trees, and Chase and James tore off after it. Stephen lingered for a moment, his fiery gaze boring into Luke, before running after the others. Jimmy dropped to his knees, cowering in the dirt, and covered his face with his arms.

"Your wolves are making my life difficult. Time to get rid of your sister."

Before Macey could react, a log flew through the air, pummeling toward Alexis. It collided with her head, splitting in two with a horrendous crack. Her massive body crashed to the Earth, and dark red blood matted in her sandy fur.

"Alexis!" Macey rushed to her sister, dropping to her knees at her side. She laid her head against the wolf's chest. Relief washed through her at the gentle rise and fall of her ribcage.

"Now that she's out of the way, I can deal with you."

Macey shot to her feet and whirled around at the voice. Luke growled, his gaze darting about as he searched for the demon. Jimmy curled into a ball in the dirt and sobbed.

Anger lit a fire in the pit of her stomach, and she burned to destroy the demon. With one hand on the crystal in her messenger bag, she reached out with her mind. At first she felt only the emptiness of the crystal, a black hole devoid of energy. When she read objects, the energy came to her. Now she had to search for it in the atmosphere. *Do the process in reverse.*

She tore her focus away from the crystal and sifted through the air around her, like fanning the pages of a book. The demon was here somewhere. She could sense his presence, even in his silence. A fleeting tingle tickled her senses, and she reached for it with her mind. The spirit sifted through her fingers like sand through a sieve.

Alexis whimpered, her body shifting to human form. Luke prowled around her, his gaze darting from the trees to Jimmy and back again. Dried leaves crunched under his paws. A heron squawked from above.

She shook her head. *Focus, Macey. You can do this.* She reached out again and grabbed hold of the ghost, pulling with all her might. If she could hold on long enough, she could transfer its energy into the crystal and trap it inside. But her feeble attempt at catching the spirit failed. It slipped from her grasp and floated away laughing.

"You've learned a thing or two since we last met. So have I."

A gush of frigid air blasted past her, slamming into Jimmy. He rolled onto his back, a strained groan filtering through his clenched teeth. His body stiffened like a rod and went slack. His entire demeanor changed as Ross took over his form. He rose to his feet, standing tall with his shoulders back, chest proud. He strolled toward her, a confident gait replacing Jimmy's awkward walk. A ring of crimson glowed around his chocolate irises.

Luke lowered his head and bared his teeth, inching closer to Macey. She raised her gun.

"You won't shoot me." Jimmy's voice was confident. Not his own. "You promised to help my brother. To give him a real bed to sleep in."

Macey's eyes grew wide.

"Oh, yeah. I can hear his thoughts. He thinks you're

going to be his new mommy." Ross laughed. "But that's not what you had in mind, was it, bitch?"

Luke growled, rocking back on his haunches, preparing to launch himself.

"Don't," Macey whispered. "Don't hurt Jimmy."

"Don't hurt Jimmy," Ross said in a mocking tone. "Go ahead and kill him. It won't hurt me."

He was right. If she shot him again, or if Luke attacked, they'd only be hurting Jimmy. Ross could leave his body as quickly as he'd entered it, and then what? Could Macey grab his spirit and force him into the crystal? She'd never been able to grasp free-floating energy. But she could pull it out of an object. Maybe even out of a human. She needed to keep Ross just where he was.

"Come on, wolf man. Let's see what you're made of." Ross taunted Luke, feigning attacks left and right and then slipping away before getting within arm's reach. "No? You don't want a piece of me? How about if I take a piece of your girl?"

He lunged at her, knocking the gun from her hand. Before she could react, he gripped her neck and slammed her into the ground. The air *whooshed* from her lungs. She gasped for breath and clawed at his hands pressing against her trachea. *Not this again.* Lacing her arms between his, she scratched at his neck, prying his hands apart with her forearms. She would not let him hurt her again.

Luke barreled into him, sending him flying off her and into a tree. The rotted trunk split with the impact, and Jimmy's body slid to the ground. Luke pinned him down with his paws and snarled in his face.

"Don't hurt him!" She forced the raspy words through her bruised throat.

Ross laughed hysterically. "Jimmy is so scared right

now. If you could only hear the thoughts racing through his mind. Go ahead and bite him. Snap his head off. I can find another human to raise my demons."

"Jimmy." Macey rose to her feet, "I know you're in there. I'm going to help you."

"By giving him a heart attack," Ross said, still laughing. "His chest is about to explode."

"Luke, please. You're scaring him."

"Trust her." Alexis sat up, cradling her head in her hand. "She can do this."

Luke blew out a hard breath and reluctantly stepped away from the man. Ross pulled himself up by the tree trunk, struggling to straighten and carry his weight on his feet. He leaned against the tree, squeezing his eyes shut as if the world were spinning.

Macey leaned in close to Luke. "I can catch him, but you can't help me like this…as a wolf. Do you trust me?"

He held her gaze for a long moment. Then he looked at Ross, struggling to right himself. In answer to her question, he shifted to human form. "What do you need me to do?"

"Hold him still."

"Finally, a fair fight." Ross stumbled forward. "Man to man. Don't let the injury fool you. I make this body strong."

He hurled himself toward Luke with inhuman speed, planting his shoulder squarely in his stomach. Luke went down. Ross drew his arm back and punched him in the face.

"Jimmy!" Macey screamed. "Take control, Jimmy. You can do it."

Luke caught the next punch in his hand and twisted Ross's arm, throwing him to the ground. Ross jumped to his feet, but Luke tackled him, wrapping his arm around his neck. Alexis threw herself on top of Ross, pinning his legs to the ground.

"Do your thing, Macey, but make it fast. He's strong." Luke tightened his grip on his neck. Any more pressure, and it might snap.

Macey dropped to her knees and rested a hand on Jimmy's head, gripping the crystal in her other hand. She closed her eyes and let the images fill her mind. Ross was a foreign energy inside Jimmy's body, just like the energy she read in objects and buildings. Flashes of Ross's life, the atrocities he'd committed, played through her mind like a movie. She saw it all—the assaults, the murders, the beatings poor Jimmy had endured at the hands of his own brother. Her insides twisted with nausea as the bloody scenes flashed behind her eyes.

"You can't do this!" Ross started to tear away from Jimmy's body, but Macey caught him this time.

She opened herself, allowing his energy to flow through her. "Ross, I'm banishing you from this dimension. You won't hurt anyone ever again." Her head spun. Vertigo threatened to pull her under, but she held on. Jimmy's body fell slack as she took the sickening essence of the demon into herself and pushed it toward the crystal.

Roberta was right. She knew exactly what to do. With one final push, the demon's energy left her body and filled the stone. It fell from her hands as she collapsed into Luke's arms.

"Macey, are you okay?" Concern furrowed his brow as he stroked her face and held her.

Was she okay? Memories of the demon's energy raking through her body made her shudder. She opened her mind to the energy in the air, but she no longer sensed the demon. His essence now resided in Roberta's crystal.

"I'm fine." She smiled, letting the warmth of Luke's strong embrace slow her racing heart. "We did it."

He pulled her closer. *"You* did it. That was amazing."

Alexis picked up the stone and turned it over on her hands. She curled up her lip at the pale red glow. "What do we do with it now?"

"I know a certain Voodoo priestess who can take care of it," Macey said. "How's your head?"

Blood had left a sticky red trail down the side of her face, but it was already starting to dry. She shrugged. "Werewolves are fast healers. I'll go check on the guys." She slipped the stone into Macey's bag and trotted deeper into the woods, leaving her alone with Luke.

Being in his arms felt so right. Maybe it was shock, but as his sapphire eyes searched hers, she wanted to give him everything he needed. All he wanted was to love her, and for her to love him. If she thought about it too much, she'd pull away. Guard her heart.

For now, she rode the adrenaline, allowed herself to be caught in the moment, and she pressed her lips to his. His breath hitched as she kissed him, uncertainty making him hesitate. She slid her hands behind his neck and kissed him harder, letting him know that—at least for now—in his arms was exactly where she wanted to be.

A soft moan escaped his throat as his passion finally met hers. His tongue parted her lips, and she let him in. The salt of his skin mixed with the sweet taste of mint as their tongues tangled, their bodies molding together. Thoughts of caution tumbled through her mind, but she ignored them for now.

"Miss Macey?" Jimmy interrupted them.

Tearing her gaze away from Luke, she looked up at Jimmy, who stood over them, clutching his back. The skin around his eye swelled purple, and abrasions reddened his neck and arms.

"Is m…my brother gone?"

"Yes, he is. You're safe now."

The other werewolves in human form approached from the trees. The men froze. The situation must have looked dire, with Jimmy towering over them, Luke clutching Macey in his arms on the ground. Alexis stood between Chase and James, and she put her hands on their arms to stop them. Stephen didn't hesitate. He barreled toward them, catching Jimmy around the waist and plowing him down. Jimmy yelped as his body crashed to the ground.

"Stop it!" Macey yelled. "Get off him!" She scrambled to her feet and rushed toward them, but Luke stopped her. He calmly wrapped his arms around her, pulling her against his chest.

"Stand down, Stephen. It's over."

Stephen stopped wrestling, but kept Jimmy's shoulders pinned to the dirt. "He's one of them. We should rip his throat out and end this for good."

"He's innocent." Macey struggled to get to Jimmy, but Luke's hold was firm. "He was possessed."

"Get off him, Stephen." Authority flowed through Luke's voice, calm with a hint of warning around the edges.

Stephen narrowed his eyes, his gaze darting between Luke and Macey, as he rose to his feet and dusted off his shirt like he was dusting off Luke's threat. "No alpha should take orders from a woman."

Luke tensed, gripping Macey by the shoulders. "The

order comes from me."

"You're not qualified to give the orders." Stephen shifted, his body morphing into the black wolf.

Luke shoved Macey to the ground and sprang away from her, shifting in midair. She grunted as she hit the dirt. Something hard jabbed into her shoulder, and she reached her hand into the dead leaves to find it. Her gun. She shot to her feet and leveled the barrel at the black wolf. Jimmy scrambled behind her.

"Macey, don't." Alexis raced toward her.

The wolves squared off, snarling as they stalked circles around each other. Chase and James stepped back, their expressions grim.

"It's a challenge for rank." Alexis put her hand on the gun, lowering Macey's arms. "You can't interfere."

"What do you mean?"

"Luke's supposed to be the next alpha. Stephen wants to take his place."

Macey shook off her sister and pointed the gun at Stephen. "He can't do that."

"He can if he kills him."

"No." She tightened her grip on the gun, her finger hovering over the trigger.

"If you interfere, you'll jeopardize Luke's position. The alpha has to be the strongest. Now he has to prove it. If he has help, it will open him up to more threats. More challenges. He has to defeat Stephen on his own."

Her hands shook as she lowered her gun. "I won't let Stephen kill him."

"As long as the fight is between the two of them and no one else, you have to step aside."

She nodded. She'd let them fight it out, but Luke's

words echoed in her mind. *If it's between your life and his...* She gripped her gun at her side.

Stephen sprang, his massive paws connecting with Luke's chest. The wolves tumbled over each other, biting and clawing until Luke found his footing. He charged at Stephen, his jaws clamping down on his neck. The black wolf yelped, and Luke knocked him to the ground. Stephen flailed, prying his flesh from Luke's grip.

They squared off again. The black wolf's lips peeled back over his massive teeth in a ferocious snarl. Luke exhaled, shaking his head. He didn't want to fight. Macey didn't want him to fight. Maybe he'd never abandon her willingly, but he might not have a choice if Stephen won.

Stephen lunged again. Luke's teeth tore into his shoulder as he threw him to the ground. His black fur shone with blood, but he scrambled to his feet. He lunged, and again, Luke deflected him. The fight stretched on endlessly. They were evenly matched; comparable in strength, though Luke's size gave him an edge. Macey flinched each time teeth tore into flesh. She didn't want to watch, but she couldn't look away.

Jimmy stepped from behind her. "Stop it, you mean black wolf. Mr. Luke is my friend."

"Jimmy, no!" Macey tried to hold him back, but he waved his arms and limped toward the wolves.

"You leave Mr. Luke alone!"

For a moment, the fighting stopped. Both wolves stared at the crazy man flailing his arms and moving toward them. Macey held her breath. Stephen sprang, claws extended, knocking Jimmy to the ground. Luke barreled into the black wolf as his jaws were about to snap on Jimmy's face. Jimmy squealed and crab-walked backward, scrambling behind Macey again.

She tore her gaze away from the fight to be sure he was okay. "Did he hurt you?"

"A big scratch." His shirt was torn, and fresh blood oozed from his bullet wound.

"Put pressure on it. You'll be okay."

Stephen limped in circles around Luke. Blood gushed from his flank, soaking his leg and matting his fur. Aside from a small gash in his neck, Luke appeared uninjured. There was no way Stephen could win this fight. He must have realized it was over because his gaze suddenly locked on Macey.

He sprinted toward her, and she froze. Panic gripped her muscles, turning them to stone. Luke leapt and tried to tackle the black wolf, but he was too late. Stephen pummeled into Macey, knocking her to the ground. The impact of her head slamming into the dirt brought back her control. Stephen snarled, opening his jaws above her face. Hot saliva dripped onto her cheek. Her shoulders were pinned, but she managed to raise her gun just enough to press the barrel into his fur.

In the split second he reared back, preparing to snap her face off, she fired. His body stiffened, his eyes going wild, as he rolled off her. She scrambled back as Luke clamped down on his neck and dragged him farther away.

Alexis dropped to her knees and held her, frantically searching her for injury. "Are you okay?"

Macey trembled, clutching her sister's arm as she watched the fight. "Is he going to kill him?"

"Challenges are fights to the death."

Stephen lay on his right side. His left back leg hung limp, but the gushing blood from the bullet wound had already slowed to a trickle. Luke stood with both paws on the black wolf's chest, growling.

Macey cringed. She couldn't watch Luke kill him. Justified or not, Stephen was already down.

Luke lowered his head toward Stephen and blew out a hard breath. The black wolf turned, locking eyes with Luke. Luke's gaze narrowed, a silent warning that the fight was over. Stephen sucked in a ragged breath and exhaled a sigh. He laid down his head and closed his eyes.

Every muscle in Macey's body tensed as she waited for Luke to make a move. He could have easily ripped Stephen's throat out, and apparently would have been justified in doing it. Instead, he walked toward his friends, his tail held high, chest proud. Chase, James, and Alexis dropped to one knee, lowering their heads in acceptance of his dominance.

Luke shifted and wrapped Macey in his arms. She covered her mouth with her hand and leaned into him, a shudder rocking her body. He worried she'd be afraid of him after witnessing the challenge, but she buried her face in his chest and slid her arms around his waist.

"You didn't kill him." She pulled away to gaze into his eyes.

"Of course not." As much as he'd wanted to tear the bastard's throat out for attacking his fate-bound, he wouldn't have killed his cousin whether Macey was watching or not. Stephen had relented, and Luke wasn't capable of murder. Even if their laws allowed it.

Stephen groaned as he shifted into human form and clutched his leg. The bullet probably cracked his femur. It would be a while before he healed.

"Get him out of here," he said to Chase and James. The men lifted Stephen and carried him toward the city.

"Wait," Macey called. "They can't take him to the hospital. My bullet is in his leg."

"They won't," Luke said. "His body will eventually expel it. He won't need medical attention."

"He's a bad werewolf." Jimmy rubbed a hand up and down his arm like he was trying to comfort himself. Jumping into the middle of a werewolf fight proved his insanity. Hopefully he really was as harmless as Macey made him out to be.

She pulled from his embrace and turned to Jimmy. "Sometimes good people make bad choices. We all make mistakes." She looked at Luke, and his heart stuttered. Was she admitting leaving him was a mistake? He could only hope.

"Do I get to stay with you now?" Jimmy said. "You promised you'd give me a real bed."

"No, Jimmy. The police are looking for you. Ross made you do some really bad things." She reached for him, but he recoiled.

"Will they hurt me?"

"No. You need to tell them everything that happened. Then they'll take you to see a doctor, and you'll get to stay in a hospital. People will take care of you, and you'll have a bed to sleep in every night."

Luke started to protest, but she raised a hand to silence him. Was she crazy? She wanted him to tell the police everything?

"That's sounds real nice," Jimmy said. "And will you come to see me every day?"

She patted his back. "How about once a week?"

He blinked as if contemplating her offer. Then he smiled. "I guess that will be okay."

"Go with Alexis. She'll take you to the truck, and I'll be there soon. I need to talk to Luke for a minute."

"Okay, Miss Macey." He turned and followed Alexis out of the swamp.

As soon as he was out of earshot, Luke spoke, "He's going to expose us all."

She shook her head. "No one will believe him. As soon as he tells them his brother's spirit possessed him, and the werewolves saved him, they'll chalk him up as a lunatic and put him in an asylum."

He raised an eyebrow. "*That's* the bed you promised him?"

"It will feel like a luxury resort after the life he's been used to. I'm going to take care of him. I've got a doctor friend who will keep an eye on him and make sure he's treated right."

He stared at the amazing woman standing in front of him. They ended the reign of demons because of her. She even killed one without his help. She fought off a werewolf attack, and in the end, it was her plan that saved the day. He'd never doubt her abilities again. He could feel the goofy smile tugging at his lips, and he probably looked like an idiot staring at her. But he didn't care. She was incredible.

She rubbed the back of her neck, her cheeks flushing pink under his heated gaze. "We should go before Jimmy changes his mind."

He grabbed her hand. "Go out with me tonight. Let me take you to dinner."

"I'm going to have tons of paperwork to file. I'll probably be there all night dealing with Jimmy. I want to be sure he's handled gently."

"Tomorrow then. Give me one dinner. That's all I'm asking."

A symphony of crickets chirped in the night, filling the sultry air with music. Macey adjusted the shoulder strap of her bag, and dry leaves crunched under her feet as she moved. A frog croaked nearby. She stared at the ground as she considered his request and inhaled a deep breath. When she finally raised her gaze to his, she smiled.

"I guess one dinner won't hurt."

CHAPTER THIRTY-TWO

LUKE HELD MACEY'S HAND AS THEY STROLLED UP Dauphine toward her house. The sweetness of the strawberry cheesecake they'd shared still lingered on his lips, but the memory of Macey's taste was sweeter. A gentle breeze caressed his skin, easing the stifling summer heat, making the night air almost pleasant. A lone musician played a haunting tune on his saxophone, and Luke dropped a dollar into his instrument case. Even the sad music couldn't dull the spark of happiness in his heart.

They'd spent most of dinner talking about the case, and how Macey had spun it at the station to ensure their secret stayed safe. And even though the talk was work related, the familiar ease of their conversations had returned. She hadn't pulled away when he'd reached for her hand across the table at the restaurant, and walking with her now felt like the most natural thing in the world.

She leaned into his side and sighed contentedly. "Anyway, he's got a psych evaluation scheduled. As soon as he told them his dead brother made him do it all, they called a doctor."

"So the only mystery that remains is what happened to the body."

She laughed. "No. Jimmy took it."

"What?"

"Right out of the morgue."

"No way."

"If you could have seen the kid on duty when it happened, you wouldn't be so surprised. It's funny though. All this time, I assumed you'd taken it."

"I tried. It was already gone. You almost caught me too." He told her about sneaking in with Chase and climbing into a locker to hide. "You had your hand on the latch, but then you walked away."

She laughed as she climbed the steps to her door. "Well, that was a close call."

"Tell me about it." He shuddered. "I hate tight spaces."

She arched an eyebrow. "*All* tight spaces?"

"Pretty much."

A mischievous grin lit her face as she ran her hands up his chest and over his shoulders. "That's a shame."

His eyebrows raised as her words sank in, and blood rushed to his groin. "I suppose *some* tight spaces aren't so bad." The mere thought of being inside her again had him rock hard in seconds. And when she pressed her body against his, he couldn't help but groan as he kissed her.

She tasted sweet, a hint of strawberry lingering on her tongue, and he slid his hands down her back to cup her butt and pull her closer. The rest of the world slipped away as he held the woman he loved. Caught in the moment, he forgot they stood on her front porch until a passerby whistled and shouted, "Get a room." He chuckled and leaned his forehead to hers.

"Do you want to come inside?" she asked.

"I do."

She fumbled with the key, her trembling hands making it hard for her to find the lock. He rested his hand on her back to steady her, and she opened the door. The familiarity of the scene gave him pause. He wouldn't make the same mistake again. They'd talk first, before they got carried away. Macey pulled him inside, but he lingered near the door.

"What's wrong?" she asked.

"Before we do this, I need to know. Are we official? Are we a couple again?"

Her gaze fell to the floor. "Oh. I...don't know." She held her left arm with her right hand. A wall clock chimed. Thor rubbed against Luke's legs and purred. "He likes you."

A sour sensation twisted in his stomach as his heart rate kicked up. "Don't change the subject."

She let out a heavy sigh. "I don't think I'm ready for anything serious."

"Really? Then you're sending me some pretty mixed signals." He crossed his arms.

"I'm sorry. Sometimes I can't control myself with you." She bit her bottom lip and gazed up at him.

"I know the feeling."

"I like you, Luke. I do. But you know I'm scared. I was hoping we could take it slow. Just date for a while and see how it goes. No expectations." She picked up her cat and scratched it behind the ears.

"You call what happened on your porch slow?"

She shrugged. "I need some time."

A groan rumbled in his chest. He was going to have to tell her. "Time is the one thing I don't have." He'd hoped she'd fall in love without the pressure of a deadline, but he was out of options. "I'm set to become alpha in two days. If we're going to be together, I need a commitment from you before then."

She blinked. "Or what?"

"Or we can't be together. Ever."

She put the cat down and fisted her hands on her hips. "That's the most ridiculous thing I've ever heard."

"You're right. It is ridiculous, but it's the law." A stupid, archaic law that would be the death of him if he couldn't get through to her.

"So we can't be casually dating when you become alpha?"

He shook his head. "It has to be official."

She crossed and uncrossed her arms, shifting her weight from foot to foot. He could practically see the gears turning in her mind. "Can't you lie? Tell them we're committed, and give me time to think about it? You've lied to them about dating me before."

If only it were that easy. "That was different. You would have to commit before the pack. In a ceremony. It would be binding."

She rubbed the back of her neck. Her gaze darted about the room, looking at everything but him. "Binding."

"As it stands now, you're not officially part of the pack. Now that we know you're a were, you're considered rogue, like your sister. But if you want to be with me…and I *really* hope you do…you'll have to join the pack. And follow pack law."

"So this is an ultimatum? Your pack is going to force me to commit to you or we're through?"

"No one's forcing you. That's why I'm telling you this. I love you, and I want to spend the rest of my life with you…if you love me too. Do you love me, Macey?" His chest tightened. He held his breath and waited for the answer he didn't want to hear.

"I…" Her chin quivered. Confusion clouded her eyes as she finally looked at him. "I can't do this now. You need to leave."

"Macey…"

"I need time."

Letting out a heavy sigh, he rubbed his head. He wasn't above begging, but the stubborn set of her jaw told him now wasn't the time. Macey loved him, and if she thought she didn't, she was lying to herself. She was his fate-bound, damn it, but if he tried to tell her that now it would drive them even further apart. She'd realize it eventually on her own, but then it might be too late.

He fought off the sickening feeling churning in his stomach and opened the door, pausing in the threshold. "I hope two days is enough."

Macey locked the door behind him and sank onto her sofa. Thor jumped up next to her and mewed softly.

"I like him too, but what was I supposed to do?"

The cat sat down and blinked at her contemptuously.

"He can't force me to spend the rest of my life with him with only two days' notice. What if I'd said yes, and he changed his mind later and left me? Or what if something happened to him? Then I'd be stuck in the pack and forced to follow their rules for the rest of my life. I can't do it, Thor."

He licked his paw and wiped his face.

"And anyway, I'm sure he's exaggerating. How could

they stop him from dating me again after he becomes alpha? He'll be the one in charge; I'm sure he can do anything he wants. So we break up now, and maybe later we can try it again. It's the logical thing to do."

An impatient mewl sounded in Thor's throat.

"Oh, what do you know? You're just a cat."

She leaned back and closed her eyes. Two days. How could she make a decision like that in two days? She couldn't. She wouldn't. And that's all there was to it. Life would go back to normal, the way it used to be before Luke showed up. Everything would be fine.

She opened her eyes, her gaze landing on the black messenger bag lying on the foyer table. The crystal with Ross's spirit still rested inside. She shivered to think the half-demon soul may have heard her exchange with Luke. Tomorrow, she'd meet with Natasha and send the fiend to hell where he belonged. Tonight, she would do her best to not think about Luke.

Macey slung the messenger bag over her shoulder and walked out the door. The afternoon sun shone high in the cloudless sky, baking the city in relentless heat. Sweat immediately beaded on her forehead. She hurried across to the shady side of the street, resting her hand on her fabric bag. The only demon lurking in the shadows today was stuck inside Roberta's crystal. Hopefully she'd never have to see another one again.

Natasha sat on her balcony in a folding chair. An orange scarf circled her hair, thick braids sprouting from the center like a potted plant. Her red lips curved into a smile when she spotted Macey, and she waved. "Door's open. Come on in."

Macey's phone buzzed in her pocket as she climbed the stairs to Natasha's apartment. Another message from Luke. She'd programmed her phone to send his calls straight to voicemail after his third attempt to reach her this afternoon. If he didn't give up soon, she'd have to block his number all together. Still, the temptation to check the message had her fingers hovering over the screen.

She sighed and shoved the phone into her pocket. *Don't let him get to you, Mace.*

Even though Natasha had told her to come in, she knocked before opening the door. She looked forward to the relief of conditioned air, but the sticky breeze of a box fan blowing in the corner greeted her instead. Incense smoke hung in the humid air like fog, and she fanned it out of her face.

"I'm on the porch," Natasha called. "Come on out. I made some tea."

Macey stepped through the beaded curtain. "Hi, Natasha. Thanks for helping me with this."

"Ain't nothing. Sit down, have a drink." She offered her a tall glass of sweet tea.

Macey took a big gulp. The icy liquid slid down her throat, cooling her from the inside out. "Thank you." She set the glass on the table and pulled out the crystal. "Here he is. His name's Ross if that helps."

Natasha's face contorted with disgust as she eyed the stone. "That's a demon all right." She snatched the crystal from Macey's hands and dropped it into an empty clay pot on the floor. "I'll take care of it."

"Is there anything I can do to help? I want to make sure he can't come back."

Natasha straightened. "Not unless you're practiced in Voodoo rituals and know how to open the veil between worlds?"

Macey shook her head. "I'm sorry. I didn't mean—"

"Don't you worry, Detective. I said I'll take care of it."

"Please, call me Macey. This is strictly off the record. If the department found out…"

Natasha smiled and shuffled a deck of tarot cards. "I know how you werewolves like your privacy. I won't tell your secret. Never have."

Macey blinked at her. "How did you know?"

"I have a few powers of my own. I've been a part of this community my whole life, and I know how things work. Probably a lot better than you do. You're just coming into your powers, ain't you?"

Macey sipped her tea. Everything about the supernatural community was new to her, but admitting her own naivety was still difficult. "I'm learning to understand them. I've had them all my life."

"Mm-hmm. It ain't nothing to be ashamed of." She set the cards down and folded her hands in her lap. "Luke's a good guy, you know. You could do worse."

Macey swallowed. "You know Luke?"

She waved her hand in dismissal. "Everybody in our community knows who Luke is. Why anybody would dump him is beyond me."

"Wow. You are really good at reading people." Not that it was any of her business.

Natasha laughed. "I haven't read you yet, girl. I'm a good listener. Hair stylist by trade. I do Roberta's hair. Girl loves to gossip."

"Great." Her relationship with Luke—or lack thereof —was the subject of the supernatural community's gossip pool. *Fantastic.* "I appreciate your help with the spirit. If there's ever anything I can do for you, let me know." She started to stand, but Natasha closed her eyes and raised a finger in the air. Macey sank back onto the chair.

Natasha swayed from side to side, nodding her head. "Now I'm reading you."

"I really don't need to be read. I'm going to go now."

She opened her eyes. "Just like I thought." Her lips pressed into a disappointed line as she shook her head.

"What?"

"You think too much."

Macey scoffed. Like that was even possible. "Okay. Thanks again for your help."

"Your brain'll fool you. You need to listen to your heart more. It won't steer you wrong."

She forced a smile and stepped toward the doorway. "I think I'm doing fine."

"Don't believe everything you think."

CHAPTER THIRTY-THREE

THE SOUND OF A KEY IN HIS FRONT DOOR LOCK roused Luke from sleep. He grumbled and rolled over, squinting at the clock on his nightstand. As he blinked, the red digital display came into focus. Ten a.m. He'd been in bed since midnight.

"Good morning, sunshine. It's time to wake up." His mother's melodic voice drifted on the air, but he didn't respond. Maybe if he stayed silent, she'd go away and today wouldn't have to happen.

Sunlight filtered in through the mini-blinds, illuminating the dust motes floating in the air. If he lay still long enough, maybe he'd turn to dust and could float away too. He sighed and draped an arm over his eyes. Why couldn't he go back to sleep and let this all be a dream?

The scent of brewing coffee tickled his senses, clearing the fog from his mind. This was it. The first day of the rest of his life. The last day he'd have a chance at love. He checked his phone for messages. Maybe Macey had returned one of his calls or texts.

Nothing.

Time had run out. What the hell was he supposed to do now? He sat up and chunked the phone across the room, slamming it into the back of a padded chair. It bounced off the seat and slipped onto the carpeted floor. The phone remained in one piece, which was more than he could say for his heart.

"Everything okay in here?" His mom paused in the doorway, a cup of coffee in one hand, a tuxedo draped over her other arm.

A goddamn tuxedo.

"You almost broke your phone." She laid the suit on a chair and offered him the coffee. He only grunted in reply, so she set the cup and the phone on his nightstand. "It's a big day today. My little boy, becoming alpha. I'm so proud of you." She sat on the edge of his bed and patted his leg.

He sucked in a deep breath and blew it out hard. He was acting like a child. His mom deserved better. "Thanks."

She gazed at him, her eyes full of sympathy, as she rubbed circles on his knee. "Your tuxedo is pressed and ready to go. Make sure you do something about that bedhead before you get to the ballroom." She mussed his hair with her hand. Thankfully, she didn't mention the other thing that was happening at the ceremony…before he could become alpha. He still didn't know who they'd chosen as his mate. He didn't care.

"What time is the ceremony again?" he asked.

"Seven. But the meeting starts at six. Then dinner at eight."

"Right."

She stood and traced a finger over the suit. "You've got

plenty of time if there's anything you need to do this after-noon. Any last minute business you need to take care of."

"I just have to show up, right? Or was I supposed to take care of the catering too?" He forced a half-hearted grin and winked at his mom.

A sad smile curved her lips. "I'll see you tonight, sweetheart. Don't forget about Great-Grand Ma Ma's ring." She blew him a kiss and shuffled out the door.

He lay there until he heard the front door open and close, her key turning in the lock. Then he swung his legs over the side of the bed and opened the nightstand drawer. There, in a burgundy leather box, sat his great-grandmother's wedding ring. He opened the lid and gazed at the stone.

A one-and-a-half carat round diamond sat atop an intricate platinum art deco setting. Three smaller diamonds accented the large one on each side, trailing down to a detailed, tiny rose molded into the metal. His great-grandfather had given this ring to her in 1933, two years before he became alpha.

A small slip of yellowing paper sat folded in the lid. Luke pulled it out, carefully unfolding the brittle note. The letters wobbled from a shaky hand. His great-grand-mother must have been eighty when she'd written it.

For Luke.
May his true love bring him as much happiness as Arthur
brought me.

He folded the note and placed it back in the lid, and then took the ring from the box. The diamond glinted in the sunlight, and he laid the ring on the table next to the box. There was only one person who could wear that ring.

But she wouldn't answer his calls.

If he couldn't reach her by phone, she'd have to talk to him in person. He couldn't go through with the ceremony tonight unless he'd done everything he could to win Macey back. He jumped out of bed and got dressed. Leaving the coffee on the table, he grabbed his phone and slipped the ring into his pocket before darting out the door.

He tried Macey's house first, banging on the door until Thor jumped into the window sill and rubbed his side against the glass. She wasn't home. Where else could she be? He sat on her steps and pulled the ring out of his pocket. Great-Grand Ma Ma's words rang in his ears. *May his true love bring him as much happiness as Arthur brought me.* Macey would make him the happiest man alive if she'd give him a chance. He fished his phone from his other pocket and dialed Alexis. Surely her sister would know where to find her. The call connected.

"Where's Macey?"

"Well, hello to you, too, Luke."

"Cut the crap, Alexis. I've got six hours to find Macey and convince her to marry me. Do you know where she is?"

She hesitated, her voice lowering in concern. "I think she's at her parents' house in Metairie."

"I know where that is. Thanks." He pocketed his phone and raced to his truck. His palms were so slick with sweat he could barely grip the steering wheel on the twenty-minute drive. Last time he was there, he'd approached through the trees, watching Macey and Roberta deal with the damn demon spirit. He had no trouble finding the one-story home from the street, and he barreled into the driveway, stopping just short of a row of hedges.

He jumped out of the truck and jogged up the front steps. Tendrils of ivy climbed a lattice behind a white, wooden porch swing. The red inner door hung open, a glass storm door separating the summer from the chilled air inside. The sounds of a pre-season football game drifted out from the living room, and he could see the back of a man's head through the door. Luke rapped on the glass.

The man was tall, with receding brown hair and glasses, and he paused when he saw Luke through the door. This must have been Macey's father. He rested his hand on the handle, but didn't open the door. "Can I help you?"

"Mr. Carpenter?"

"Yes." He drew out the word skeptically.

"I'm Luke Mason. Is Macey here? I need to talk to her."

An amused grin lit his face, and he opened the door. "It's nice to meet you, Luke. Come on in."

He stepped through the doorway into the small foyer. A bright yellow kitchen sat off to the left, and a hallway ran down to the right.

Mr. Carpenter straightened to his full height. "You've caused my little girl all kinds of heartache."

"I don't mean to, sir. I'd like to make things right."

He chuckled. "Macey, you've got company."

She padded down the hallway in denim shorts and

bare feet. A white tank top clung to her curves, and her hair spilled around her shoulders like spun gold. His chest tightened, his arms aching to hold her. He wanted to run to her. To take her in his arms and never let her go. It was all he could do to keep his feet planted on the floor.

She stopped midstride when she saw him, her face taking on a range of so many emotions, he couldn't count them all. Her disapproving gaze flicked to her father before settling on Luke. "What are you doing here?"

"I need to talk to you."

She rubbed one arm. "I have nothing to say."

"Then listen. Please."

Her dad took her by the arm and led her toward him. "Give the boy a chance. He drove all this way."

She let out her breath in a slow hiss. Her teeth clenched, the muscles in her jaw flexing taut. "Fine." She threw the storm door open and stomped onto the porch.

Luke followed. "You didn't return my calls."

She spun around to face him. His expression must have been pained because all the anger drained from her face as she sank onto the swing. "I didn't know what to say. I…still don't."

"All you have to do is listen. If you're not convinced when I'm done, I'll leave and never bother you again." He sat down, his leg brushing hers. She scooted away, and a stinging pain shot through his heart. Resting his hand on his leg, he could feel the ring burning a hole through his jeans. It belonged on Macey's finger, and he ached to put it there.

"I love you, Macey."

"Luke, please don't…"

"Just hear me out, okay?"

She nodded.

"I've loved you from the moment you walked into my dad's bar in that tank top and flip flops. Hell, maybe I even loved you before then, but that's the moment I knew. I'd been watching you since the whole demon ordeal started and you took on the case. It was my job to get rid of the evidence and keep you from finding out the truth. And I told myself that's all I was doing when I hung around watching you clear the scenes. But it was so much more than that. I was enamored."

He turned in his seat to face her. "Then you came into the bar and shook my hand, and I knew you had magic in you. I spent the next week trying to find out exactly what you were, to see if there was any chance we could be together. My folks were in Paris, and I called them and begged my old man to let your magic be enough."

She stared at the ground. "I guess he said 'no?'"

"'Werewolves only.' That's what he said. Then I found out you *are* a werewolf. And, yeah, I said those things Alexis told you. But I said them before I knew what you were. There was enough tension in the pack with the demons and Stephen trying to step in. I couldn't let them know I was in love with a human, but you know what I figured out?"

She glanced at him, her eyes tight with worry or confusion, before returning her gaze to the ground.

"It didn't matter what you were. I was in love with *who* you were. Who you are. You could be a human, a witch, or even a vampire. I would love you regardless. But it doesn't matter anymore because you are a werewolf. We *can* be…we were *meant* to be together. You are the only one I'll ever love. You're my fate-bound, Macey. My soul mate. So, please. I'm begging you." He sank to his knees in front of her and took her hands in his. "Take me back."

Her lips parted, and she sucked in a breath as her gaze lingered on their entwined hands. Tears shimmered in her eyes, dampening her lashes when she blinked. He held his breath, a glimmer of hope sparking in his chest as she raised her gaze to meet his. She licked her lips and leaned toward him.

"Luke…"

The whisper of his name on her lips nearly crumbled him. He reached for her, taking her cheek in his hand, sliding his fingers into her hair as she nuzzled into his touch. "Please, Macey."

She shot to her feet, yanking from his grasp. With her arms crossed, she held herself, shaking her head. "I can't."

She had to. He couldn't let it end this way. Not after everything they'd been through. She was his world. His destiny. Screw the laws. Screw the pack. He couldn't live without this woman. Pressure built in the back of his eyes as he rose from the ground. "Then I'll step down. I'll let someone else take over, and you can have all the time you want. We can take it slow, whatever you need."

"Don't say that. You can't let Stephen take your place; you can't do that to your pack. You're supposed to be alpha."

"I'm supposed to be with you. It's fate, Macey, and I know you feel it too."

She dug her nails into her arms. "No. You were born to lead the pack. I'm just a distraction."

"Macey, please. What do you want me to do?" He'd do anything—*be* anything—for her. Life would be meaningless without her by his side. Why couldn't she see that?

She sucked in a deep breath and looked into his eyes.

"I want you to leave. Go back to your pack and become the alpha. Forget about me."

Her words severed his heart from his chest. With his hands in his pockets, he toyed with the ring. No matter her answer, it belonged to Macey. So did his heart. "If you change your mind, the ceremony is at seven. Once I become alpha, it will be too late."

She opened the glass door and looked at him with sad eyes. "I'm sorry. Goodbye, Luke."

Macey closed the inner door and watched through the blinds as Luke drove away, the hole in her chest where her heart used to be growing wider as his truck disappeared into the horizon. She stepped away from the window and followed the smell of coffee into the kitchen.

Her mom poured two mugs and set them on the table. "Do you want to talk about it?"

Macey picked up the cup and inhaled the comforting aroma. "Not really."

"What did he say?"

She shrugged and traced the swirling pattern on the tablecloth. "He said he loves me."

Her mom reached across the table and stilled her hand. "Do you love him?"

"No...maybe...I...I don't know." She sighed. "Yes. Yes, I do." She loved him fiercely, and she couldn't imagine spending the rest of her life with anyone but him.

"Then what's the problem?"

"What if he leaves me?"

"What if he stays?"

Macey folded her hands in her lap. "You don't understand. Everyone I've ever depended on has abandoned me. I can't take that chance again."

Her mom raised an eyebrow and sat up straight. "Everyone?"

She rested her face in her hands and took a deep breath. "Okay, not *everyone*. You and Dad never left."

"So, three people then? Your biological parents and your sister. That's not even close to everyone."

Her mom had a point. Put that way, her abandonment issues sounded petty. Almost ridiculous. But they had been the three people she'd needed the most. That counted for something. "I'm scared. I've never been in love before. I need more time."

"Why?"

Because he's a werewolf who thinks he can't date me after he becomes the alpha. But she couldn't tell her mother that. "It's scary."

"You don't think he's scared too?"

"No." Luke wasn't scared of anything. He was confident. Charismatic. Everything he did, he did with gusto, as if failure never crossed his mind. He was kind and sexy, and those piercing eyes were…and his body…Oh! She had to stop thinking about him.

Her mom folded her hands on the table. "You've rejected him, hon. What are you going to do when he moves on?"

Moves on? Thoughts of him finding someone else had never crossed her mind. She sipped her coffee to warm the chill that crept through her veins. "I don't… It's complicated."

"It's not complicated at all. He loves you. You love him. You're happy when you're with him and miserable without him. Love won't always be easy, but it's worth the risk."

Was it though? She'd sabotaged every relationship she'd had before anyone could get close enough to hurt her. It was easier that way. Safer. She could easily spend the rest of her life alone, guarding her heart. But what kind of life would that be?

CHAPTER THIRTY-FOUR

LUKE SLOUCHED IN A CHAIR IN THE MEETING ROOM and watched his mom fiddle with her hair in the mirror for the fifteenth time since they'd arrived at the hotel. All two-hundred pack members would fill the ballroom soon, and his mom had spent the entire afternoon running around, making sure everything was perfect for the ceremony. Seven members of the werewolf congress would attend to ensure they performed the rituals to code, making Luke's succession official.

The meeting would come first—a sort of state-of-the-pack address from the current alpha. They'd discuss the business of the year, and people could express any concerns they might have. Then the ceremony would begin. A new family, who'd recently moved to New Orleans, had applied to join the pack. Their admission would come first, followed by the announcement of Luke's mate.

His stomach turned. Could he spend the rest of his life with someone he didn't love? He'd have to figure out a way. He looked at his old man. "Why Jackie?"

"We interviewed several candidates," his dad said. "When I researched their lineage, hers was the strongest. No dilution in the bloodline."

He ran his hand over his forehead, trying to rub away the pounding in his head. "Have you told her yet?"

His mom settled into a chair next to him. "No. We wanted to give you a chance to...to make sure we made the right choice for you."

"It doesn't matter."

Concern filled his mother's eyes. "Do you have the ring?"

His hand instinctively went to his pocket, his finger tracing the outline of the cold metal. "I'm not giving it to her. It was meant for someone else. Someone I love."

He gripped the arms of his chair. He'd been on a rollercoaster of emotions all afternoon, from the slow build of anger to the sharp drop of fear and finally settling into the steady ride of resignation. Now the anger was back in full force like a tornado ripping through his chest.

"It isn't fair." He slammed his fist down on the table. "I'm the only one this damn archaic law applies to. Why can't I have more time?"

His dad steepled his hands under his chin. "You know why, son. It's to guarantee the lineage—"

"Yeah, I know. But I can guarantee Macey would come around if I had more time."

"Well, you don't," Marcus said. "It's the law, so there's no sense in whining about it."

"Our laws have changed before. Werewolves are evolving, and I think it's time this law changed too. Half the congress is here. If I appeal to them—"

His dad leaned forward, lowering his voice into a

commanding growl. "You've made your choices and missed your chance. The ceremony will go as planned."

Luke reined in his anger, calming the burning flames down to a slow simmer. His father was right. He'd tried to win Macey, but she'd made her decision. There was nothing he could do about it, except go on with his life and become the best damn alpha New Orleans ever had. Still, it wouldn't hurt to check his messages one more time. He pulled his phone from his pocket and tapped the screen.

Nothing.

He tossed it on the table.

His old man grabbed it and slipped it into his jacket pocket. "I'll hold on to this. You don't need any more distractions."

He started to protest, but what the hell? If she hadn't called by now, she wasn't going to. "Did the congress approve Chase as my second?"

"Paperwork came in this morning. It's a done deal."

Since Stephen had attacked Luke's intended mate, he'd be spending the next six months in the pit. The council stripped his cousin of his rank, and since he'd been incapacitated in the challenge, he didn't have the strength to contest it. Chase would step in as Luke's second in command until a child of the first family bloodline was old enough to take over. Hopefully Luke's first-born son.

The son he wouldn't be having with Macey. He closed his eyes and imagined her swollen belly. Her golden hair cascading around her shoulders. The warm smile dancing on her pink lips as he rested his hand on her stomach to feel the baby kick.

He shook his head to rid his mind of the heart-breaking image. "I need to get some air."

"The meeting starts in fifteen minutes," his mom said. "I'll be there."

A crowd had gathered in the corridor, so Luke straightened his spine and held his head high. He had to appear confident and strong, even though he was falling apart inside. People gathered in small groups to chat before the meeting while others filed into the ballroom to take their seats.

"Congratulations, Luke." John, a man around his father's age, clapped him on the shoulder. "Who's the lucky lady?"

Luke forced a smile. "It's a surprise."

He needed some privacy. Five minutes to compose himself, so he could go into his new life with a clear head. He wouldn't get any peace out here.

"Hi, Luke." Jackie approached him, prancing across the hall, her lavender gown swishing around her ankles. "I'm curious. Does your mate already know if she's been chosen? I don't want to get my hopes up if…" She ran her hand over his arm and grinned shyly.

He instinctively jerked away, the thought of enduring someone other than Macey's touch making his stomach turn.

Jackie shrank in on herself, and Luke patted her shoulder. *What an ass.* He needed to start acting like an alpha rather than a scorned teenager. Forcing a reassuring smile, he muttered, "It'll be a surprise to everyone. Excuse me."

He walked with purpose now, eyes straight ahead, his mouth pressed into a line. His pulse thrummed in his ears. He couldn't breathe. He had to get out of this crowd before he exploded. Skirting the wall, he checked the door handles, finding each one locked. There had to be another meeting room, or even a supply closet open. Just five minutes. That's all he needed. Five minutes to breathe.

The corridor made a T at the end, and he jutted right around the corner. The next door opened, and he rushed inside, slamming it behind him. The hotel's second ballroom sat silent. Empty like his chest. A massive chandelier hung in the center of the rectangular room, its dripping crystals glinting in the sunlight that poured in through the window.

Three wooden steps led up to a set of French doors that opened onto a balcony. He threw open the doors and stepped onto the terrace overlooking Bourbon Street. The sounds of jazz mixed with hip hop and pop floated through the air as the sun sank closer to the horizon. The revelers below went about their partying, oblivious to the events about to unfold.

Life went on. His would too.

"Luke?"

He turned around to find Alexis standing on the steps. Her emerald dress matched her eyes. It would've matched Macey's eyes too. "I didn't hear you come in."

She lowered her head sheepishly. "Sorry. I…followed you."

He stepped back inside and closed the balcony doors, bringing peaceful silence back to the ballroom. "It's okay. I needed a few minutes to compose myself."

"So, I guess Macey…"

"No."

Alexis shook her head. "I really thought she'd change her mind."

"I hoped she would." He sat on the top step and ran a hand through his hair. "I hurt her too much."

Alexis sank down next to him, resting her forearms on

her knees and wringing her hands. "I'm the one who hurt her. The whole reason she's acting this way is because I ran away. Now I've screwed up her life and yours."

"You were a kid. I won't hold it against you."

"She does. And worse than that...she's holding it against you. I can't believe she'd step aside and let you take another mate when she's obviously in love with you."

He cleared his throat.

Alexis narrowed her gaze. "She does know you're taking another mate."

"I didn't tell her that part."

"What?" She jumped to her feet. "She doesn't know?"

He stood and crossed his arms. He didn't owe her an explanation, but he gave her one anyway. "She already felt enough pressure knowing there was a deadline. I didn't want to add to it."

Alexis crossed her arms to mirror his posture. "So you didn't tell her. She probably thinks she still has a chance with you."

"No. I told her she had to commit before I became alpha."

"But you didn't tell her why."

"It doesn't matter. She made it very clear she didn't want anything to do with me."

She blinked at him, her expression incredulous, before turning on her heel and marching away.

"Where are you going?"

"You may make a great alpha, Luke, but you're a stupid man." She stormed out the door.

He tried for a witty reply, but words escaped him. Time had run out anyway. The meeting was about to start.

Thankfully the corridor was clear as he made his way to the ballroom. Everyone would be taking their seats by now. Two guards stood outside the entrance, ensuring the pack's privacy. His mom had reserved the room under the pretense of an engagement party, with strict orders for the hotel staff not to enter until the ceremony had ended.

He nodded to the guards, gripped the door handle that would lead him to his fate, and closed his eyes. With one last deep breath, he pushed through and entered the ballroom. Twenty-five circular banquet tables drenched in white linen sat atop lush green carpet that stretched from wall to wall. A similar chandelier hung in the center of the room, but this one was lit and sparkled like a million diamonds. He pressed his hand against the ring in his pocket.

The entire pack had gathered for this momentous event, dressed in their best formal clothes. So much pomp and circumstance for such a heart-wrenching day. He scanned the crowd for Alexis. She'd been dressed for the party, but he couldn't find her. Apparently his stupidity was too much for her. He did spot Stephen's mate sitting at a table in the back, a sullen expression occupying her face. Luke had spared her mate's life, but she refused to make eye contact with him.

Luke's parents sat at a long, rectangular table at the front of the room. Behind them, on a raised platform, sat the seven congressmen. Luke straightened his spine and nodded to the men before striding to the table to join his parents.

At precisely six o'clock, Marcus commenced the meeting. Luke sat rigid, his face turned toward his father. He nodded occasionally, hoping to give the illusion he was listening intently, while his mind drifted a thousand miles away. He didn't hear a word his old man said.

"Son?" Marcus put a hand on Luke's shoulder, snapping him back to coherence. "Your report?"

"Right." He cleared his throat and stepped to the microphone. As he brought the pack up to speed on how they resolved the demon infestation, his heart clenched each time he mentioned Macey's name. Surely this would get easier with time. He sat down and slipped his hand in his pocket to feel the ring. As soon as he got home, it would go back in the drawer and stay there.

"If no one has any more comments, this will conclude our annual meeting," his father said into the microphone. The crowd remained silent. Marcus nodded. "We'll begin the ceremony with the pack pledge, followed by our new member initiation."

Luke stood and recited the words he'd known by heart since he was a child. His pulse raced out of control as his father conducted the initiation. The new family knelt before him as he went through the formalities, officially approving their membership.

It was happening too fast. He wasn't ready.

"As you all know, I'll be retiring." His dad glanced at his watch and grinned. "By the end of the hour." Some of the audience chuckled. "I'll be passing the torch on to my son, who I know will do a better job running this pack than I ever did. But before he can become alpha, there's the matter of selecting a mate."

His stomach roiled. Sweat beaded on his forehead.

"Since he's not married, Luke has decided to trust his mother and I to select a mate for him. We've thoroughly reviewed each applicant and chosen the woman we think will compliment him best. Son, would you like to make the announcement?"

No. The room tilted on its side as he rose from his

chair. He caught himself on the edge of the table and let out a half-hearted chuckle to put the pack at ease. No matter how torn up he was on the inside, he had to give the illusion of control. Of dominance.

He stepped to the microphone and scanned the crowd one last time. She wasn't there. The tiny sliver of hope—that maybe Macey would show up and say she'd changed her mind—died away. He pressed his hand against the ring in his pocket, took a deep breath, and prepared to utter the words he'd never be able to take back.

CHAPTER THIRTY-FIVE

MACEY IGNORED THE POUNDING ON THE DOOR AND buried her head deeper into the pillow. She'd come to her parents' house because she didn't want to be alone. Now she wished she'd stayed home.

"Macey, you have another visitor," her dad called.

She groaned and rolled out of bed, glancing at the clock. Six-fifteen. Luke would be at his ceremony, so it couldn't be him. A small part of her wished it was. If he came back now, she might not be able to say no. Would that be such a bad thing?

She pushed the thought aside and padded down the hallway into the living room. Alexis stood near the door while her mom and dad sat on the couch looking at her expectantly.

"Is this *the* Alexis?" Her mom's eyes darted back and forth between them.

"Yeah, Mom. This is my sister."

"We need to talk. Now," Alexis said.

Macey turned to her mom. "It's a long story. I'll tell

you later." She motioned for Alexis to follow her. "Come on. We can talk in my room."

"We don't have much time," Alexis said as Macey closed the bedroom door.

"Time for what?"

"To get you back to Luke and stop the ceremony."

Macey let out a huff and plopped onto the bed. She picked up a fluffy pink pillow and hugged it to her chest. "I'm not going to stop him from becoming alpha."

"No, but he needs you to be his mate."

Mate. There was that word again. Luke had called her his soul mate, and the idea sounded too good to be true. They were meant to be together, though; she could feel it in her bones. But for something so huge…so monumental…she needed time to wrap her mind around it. Her entire world had changed in a matter of weeks, and she was still trying to absorb it all. She waved her hand dismissively. "He just thinks he needs me right now. I'll call him next week after things settle down, and we'll talk again. I don't want to rush into anything."

Alexis put her hands on her hips. "You don't have a choice."

"There's always a choice."

"Not if you want Luke. Do you love him?"

"Yes." She narrowed her eyes at her sister. Why was Alexis so wound up about this? Why wouldn't she have a choice?

"You're losing him. Every second that you sit there holding that stupid pillow, he's slipping further away."

Macey tossed the pillow aside. "Come on. You're being dramatic. I'm being cautious. It's not my fault I have abandonment issues."

Anger flashed in her sister's eyes. "How long are you going to play the victim, Macey?"

"I'm not—"

"You've changed. You used to be a fighter. Tough. Resilient. Now look at you. So scared to get your poor little heart broken, you're walking away from the best thing that's ever happened to you."

Macey clenched her hands into fists. How dare her sister talk to her that way? "You want to talk about walking away? You've been gone for twenty years, and suddenly you come back thinking you know what's best for me? You don't. I am strong. I am a fighter."

Alexis took a deep breath and exhaled slowly. "This isn't about me, Macey." Her voice was quiet. Calm. "This is about you and Luke. He's not going to be available next week. Or ever again if you don't get your ass to that ceremony right now and stop it."

Her breath caught. "What are you talking about?"

"He has to have a mate to become alpha." She glanced at her watch. "He's about to select one now."

Her heart stuttered, her veins running cold with ice. Did she hear that right? "He's…getting married?"

Alexis shook her head. "He's taking a mate. It's more like a business deal to ensure the alpha has children. He won't marry her, but he also won't be able to marry anyone else. Werewolves mate for life."

Her head spun. Or was it the room? Either way, her stomach lurched, and she ground her teeth to stop her lunch from making a reappearance. No wonder he was relentless in trying to talk to her. "Why didn't he tell me?"

"Because he's a man. He thought he'd pressured you enough. Said he wanted you to love him on your own."

"I do love him." She couldn't let him take someone else as his mate. *She* was his soul mate, his…what did he call her? His fate-bound. Yes, they were bound by fate, but in her idiocy, she'd torn them apart. She had to repair their bond.

Alexis tugged her to her feet. "Then get dressed and let's go. The ceremony is formal, and it's a twenty-minute drive to New Orleans."

She couldn't make herself move. What if she was too late? Would he really go through with it? Her throat tightened, and she could barely force out the words, "I don't have any clothes here."

"Trade with me then." Alexis unzipped her dress and tossed it to her sister.

Macey stared at the emerald fabric in her hands, the shock of the ordeal making her limbs heavy like lead. "What about you?"

"This isn't about me. Hurry up."

Her movements finally caught up with the urgency, and she stripped, giving her clothes to Alexis. Her sister's dress was made for someone taller, and the straps slipped off her shoulders.

"Safety pins?" Alexis said.

"In the drawer."

Alexis folded the straps and pinned them to the inside of the dress. The sparkling gown hugged Macey's torso, flaring slightly at the hips to cascade down to her knees in the front. The back brushed the floor. "There. Now it's perfect. Shoes?"

Macey stepped into the pair of black flats next to her bed. "These are all I have here."

"They'll do." Alexis grabbed her by the arm and dragged her into the living room.

"Where are you going?" her mother asked as they rushed out the front door.

"To get Luke back," Macey called over her shoulder.

"Have fun."

Macey climbed into the passenger seat, and Alexis peeled out of the driveway. She tore through the neighborhood and merged onto the highway like a professional Indy Car driver. Macey clutched the door and closed her eyes. "How much time do we have?"

"Thirty minutes. Plenty of time if there's no traffic."

"Who is he going to choose if we don't make it in time?" Pain pierced her heart at the thought of him in another woman's arms.

"I don't know. He let his parents pick for him, and they haven't told anyone." She squeezed Macey's hand. "Don't worry. We'll make it."

Alexis zipped in and out of traffic, bouncing between lanes and cursing at the slower cars. Macey dared to peek at the speedometer. They were pushing one hundred. She said a silent prayer that they'd make it there alive. She'd only *thought* her partner was a scary driver. Alexis was a maniac.

As they climbed an overpass, a sea of red brake lights stretched out before them, disappearing into the horizon. Traffic slowed to a crawl as they descended the bridge and inched their way forward at an excruciating speed.

"Oh, no. No, no, no." Alexis blasted the horn. "Can't you wave your badge around and get these people out of the way?"

"Where would they go? It looks like an accident up ahead." She pulled out her phone and unlocked the screen. Six unread voicemail messages from Luke waited to be heard. Her fingers trembled as she opened the map app and typed in the hotel address. The phone slipped from her sweaty palm and bounced under the seat. "Damn it."

She reached beneath the seat and found the phone. "If you can get off at the next exit, we can take back roads to the Quarter."

Alexis gripped the steering wheel and checked her review mirror. "Screw the exit. I can run faster than this." She slammed on the gas and cut across the grassy median onto the frontage road. "Which way?"

"Take the next right."

She fishtailed around the corner and floored it. "Seriously, though. If it were dark out, I'd shift and run you there. It'd be faster than this."

Macey crinkled her nose. "Then I'd smell like dog."

"We *all* smell like dog."

"Good point. Turn left."

Alexis turned and rolled to a slow crawl behind a city bus. The damn thing stopped every fifteen feet to pick up more passengers.

Macey's head pounded. At this speed they'd never make it in time...and not making it was *not* an option. "Can't you pass it?"

Alexis leaned her head out the window. "There's too much traffic." She eyed something to the right and raised her eyebrows at Macey. "You can get me out of a ticket, right?"

"Probably," she said warily.

"Hold on." She cut the wheel right and lurched onto the sidewalk. Pedestrians scattered as she barreled toward the bus stop and made a hard right turn to skirt behind it. They barely fit. Bushes scraped down the side of the car like claws on a windowpane. She jerked the wheel left, and they bumped over the curb, back onto the road.

If I survive this, I will never complain about Bryce's driving again. "It's a straight shot from here to the Quarter. What time is it?"

"We've got ten minutes."

Her heart jack hammered in her chest. She dialed his number. Straight to voicemail. "He's not answering his phone."

"Text him."

I'm on my way. Please don't choose a mate. She pressed send and counted to fifty. No response. Tears stung her eyes. "We're too late."

"No, we're not."

"What if they started early?"

"They didn't."

"How do you know?"

"We're going to make it."

Finally, they crossed Rampart and entered the French Quarter. They raced up Bienville as fast as the bumpy, narrow road would allow and stopped just before Bourbon.

"You've got to be kidding me," Alexis said. "A parade? On a Thursday?"

"New Orleanians will find any excuse they can to have a parade. Try to find a place to park."

She pulled the car into an alley, and they jumped out. A man on a balcony yelled down to them. "Hey! You can't park there. I'll call the cops."

"I am a cop." Macey kept running. She plowed through the mass of spectators on Bourbon, shoving her way down the street, Alexis on her heels.

"It's there." Her sister pointed to a hotel across the street.

Macey leaped over a metal barricade and darted across

the parade line, weaving her way through a sea of women in elaborate headdresses and sparkling masks, and narrowly missing a mounted patrol. She stumbled, caught herself with her hands before she fell, and looked up at the officer.

"Detective Carpenter?" The look on the man's face was incredulous. "Do you need backup?"

"No. No worries." She turned on her heel and dashed across the street.

"I'm right behind you," Alexis called as Macey paused to look for her. "Go! Go!"

She pushed through the door and skidded to a stop in the lobby. "Where's the ballroom?" she called to the hotel clerk.

"What?"

"The ballroom."

"Down there." He pointed. "But you can't—"

Macey sprinted down the hall.

Two burly men stood guard outside a set of double doors. This had to be the place. As she approached, they crossed their arms, widening their stances and blocking the entrance. She adjusted the straps on her dress and smoothed the gown down her torso. "Sorry, I'm a little late for the ceremony. If you'll excuse me." She reached for the door handle, and a guard grabbed her wrist.

"This is a private event." His grip was firm, his voice gravelly with warning.

"But I really need to talk to Luke." She considered playing the cop card, but these guys didn't seem like the type to back down, regardless of the law.

He released her arm and straightened his spine, crossing his thick arms over his chest. "Not today."

"Macey!" Alexis sprinted toward her.

"They won't let me in."

"Out of the way, guys," Alexis said. "This is official pack business."

The other guard looked down his nose at her. "I don't take orders from rogues."

Alexis gave her sister a meaningful look, a tiny nod of her head letting Macey know they were about to do something they couldn't take back. Then she launched herself at a guard. The surprise of her impact made him stumble far enough away from the door for Macey to get close. She threw herself at the entrance and screamed, "Luke!" Her fist slammed into the metal door with a *thud*, shooting tingling shards of pain up her arm. The guard grabbed her around the waist and pulled her back.

"Luke!" She flailed in his arms. "Luke, stop! Don't do it!" This couldn't' be happening. She *had* to get through that door. She didn't finally come to her senses and race across town to get to him, only to be stopped at the entrance.

She wiggled, twisting and turning, but the guard tightened his grip. Alexis climbed on the other guard's back, doing everything she could to keep him away from the door. The entrance stood unguarded. If Macey could just wiggle free and get to the door before the guard, she'd be in. But he held her around the waist, her arms pinned at her sides. She wiggled some more and managed to shimmy down far enough for her mouth the reach his arm. Her teeth sank into his flesh. The guard yelped, loosening his grip enough for Macey to break free.

"Luke!" Macey screamed again. Flinging herself at the door, she pounded it with her fist. Her trembling hands reached for the handle, and she pressed it down. The door opened a crack before the guard snatched her up again, yanking her away. The handle slipped from her grasp. The door clicked shut.

"Luke, please!"

"Luke!" Alexis's voice was hoarse. Her guard pinned her to the ground and slapped a hand over her mouth.

"Give it up, rogues," Macey's guard said. "You're not getting in that room."

"But I was supposed to be his mate." Macey stopped struggling. By now, he'd probably already chosen another. And it was her fault. She'd been so afraid of letting him get close enough to hurt her, she'd driven him into someone else's arms. She was too late.

Her body went slack in the guard's arms, the will to fight—to do anything—draining away like flood water after a rain. He let her sink to the ground and released her as she crumpled to her knees and buried her face in her hands. A deep sob hitched in her throat. She'd been so stupid. Her sister was right; she'd been playing the victim for so long she didn't know how else to act. Yes, she'd been abandoned. And, yes, it had hurt. But the events from her past didn't have to control her future. She knew that now.

Now that it was too late.

"Macey?" Luke's voice danced in her ears. She looked up to find him standing in the doorway, confusion furrowing his brow. He looked at the other guard. "Let her go."

Alexis scrambled to her feet and pulled Macey up by the arm. "Go," she whispered in her ear.

She took two tentative steps toward him. "Luke, I…"

He tilted his head and blinked. His left hand went to his pocket. "Macey."

She ran. Throwing her arms around his neck, she

buried her face in his chest. He stiffened. His heartbeat slammed against her cheek, but he hesitated to hold her.

"I'm so sorry, Luke. I was stupid, and immature, and…"

He patted her back awkwardly.

"Oh, no." She covered her mouth with her hand as she stepped back to see his face. "I'm too late, aren't I? Have you already chosen a mate?"

His gaze lingered on her eyes before traveling down her body and back up again, the intensity of his stare piercing her soul. Why wouldn't he speak? "Say something. Please."

He swallowed. "I have chosen."

"No." Her body trembled, her heart wrenching as if being ripped from her chest. Tears welled in her eyes, and she dropped her gaze to the floor to hide them.

She'd lost him.

"Macey, look at me." He hooked a finger under her chin, raising her gaze to meet his. "I chose you. It's always been you." He took her in his arms, hugging her tight.

"So you haven't…"

"I told them they'd have to take me single or not at all."

She melted into his warmth, sweet relief flooding her body as the tension drained away.

"Son?" An older man stepped through the doorway. "You can't drop a bomb like that and walk away from the pack. You need to fix this."

"Just a minute, Dad." He gripped Macey's shoulders and stared intently into her eyes. "You need to know what you're getting yourself into. When we step into that ballroom, we'll take an oath. A pledge to the pack to be mates.

Once you're in, there's no way out. Werewolves mate for life."

Life was exactly what she wanted. She slid her hands up his chest to cup his face. "Do you promise?"

A sly grin pulled up one corner of his mouth. "Yes, ma'am."

"I'll hold you to it." She rose onto her toes to place a soft kiss on his lips. "I'm yours."

Luke's dad cleared his throat. "We need to finish the ceremony." He motioned for them to enter the ballroom, his voice rough with warning. "The pack's waiting."

Luke nodded to his father and stepped toward Alexis, holding out his hand to shake. "Thank you for bringing her back to me."

She hugged him. "Be good to my sister."

"Always."

His dad clutched the door handle. "If you don't get your ass back in there, there's going to be a riot."

Macey took her sister's hand. "Come on."

Alexis shook her head. "Go in there? Dressed like this?" She motioned to Macey's shorts and tank top she now wore. "No way. I've got some unfinished business to take care of outside of town, anyway."

"You're leaving? I just got you back." Macey smiled at her sister. She could tell from the look in her eyes this wasn't goodbye.

"Not permanently. I need to tie up some loose ends. I promise I'll be back in time for the wedding." She nodded toward Luke.

Macey turned to find him standing in front of her, toying with a ring in his hands.

"I'll see you later, sister." Alexis kissed her on the cheek and shoved Macey toward him.

"This ring has been burning a hole in my pocket all day," he said.

"It's beautiful."

"It belonged to my great-grandmother. She left it to me when she died, with a note that she hoped my true love would make me as happy as my great-granddad made her. I wanted to give it to you this morning, but…" He held up the ring and examined it. The diamond glinted in the light, and he let out a nervous chuckle. "I'm going to try this again." He knelt on one knee and took her hand in his. The familiar electric tingle shot up her arm, making her breath catch.

"Macey, no one can make me happier than you can. If I spend every day with you for the rest of my life, it still won't be enough. I need more from you than a mate. I need you to be my wife. Will you marry me?"

"Yes. Yes!" Her hand trembled as he slid the ring on her finger and pulled her into his arms. "I love you, Luke."

"You have no idea how badly I've wanted to hear those words from you. I love you too."

CHAPTER THIRTY-SIX

"IF YOU TWO LOVEBIRDS ARE DONE MAKING UP, WE'VE got a ceremony to finish, a riot to stop, and a panel of hungry congressmen to feed." Luke's dad held out his hand for Macey to shake. "By the way, I'm Marcus. It's nice to finally meet the woman my son's been so worked up about."

Macey shook his hand, and the tingle of werewolf magic shimmied up her arm. The sensation was different than when she touched Luke, though. Duller. She might have missed it if she didn't know what to look for. It appeared only Luke's energy could make her heart skip a beat, and that's the way she liked it.

She slipped into the ballroom, and Luke held her tight to his side. From the noise and commotion, what he'd said to the pack must have meant mutiny because every person in the room looked either livid or terrified. Some grumbled. Others yelled, their fists clenched tightly at their sides. All because of her.

She gripped his bicep, her throat tightening. He did

this for her. Even when she'd rejected him, he hadn't given up on their love.

A group of seven men standing on a raised platform turned toward them. "This is unacceptable," one of them boomed.

"It's taken care of." Luke pressed his hand into the small of her back and led her onto the stage. A hushed murmur befell the crowd as he stepped to the microphone and raised a hand to silence them. "There's been a change of plans." He pulled her into his side and wrapped his arm around her. "I'd like to introduce my fiancée, Macey."

Silence ensued as the pack seemed to hold a collective breath. Then Chase stood, and the remaining pack members joined him in a standing ovation.

"We'll take that oath now, Dad," Luke said.

Marcus read from an antique, leather-bound book, and Macey repeated the words required of her. She made promises to uphold the pack values and follow their laws. The entire oath sounded more like a business deal than a union, until she got to the part where they had to promise to have children together. Luke smiled and squeezed her hand as she agreed to everything.

As Marcus read the final words, making the union official, Luke leaned in and whispered in her ear, "I promise the wedding will be much more romantic."

The rest of the evening went by in a blur. She joined Luke's mother at the table as he and his father went through the ceremony of changing leadership. Luke accepted the role of alpha, and the pack cheered. The weariness in Marcus's eyes lifted, and a smile played on his lips as he and his wife stepped off the platform and joined the pack.

The sun dipped behind the horizon as they finished dinner, and the pack members slowly filed out the door. Luke stayed by her side, his arm around her possessively as they said their goodbyes. She leaned into his warmth, allowing him to lead her, to take care of her. For the first time in years, she opened herself to need, admitting—at least to herself—that it was possible to depend on someone and still be independent at the same time. She needed him in so many ways, and the smoldering look in his eyes told her he felt the same.

As the last guest left the ballroom, he wrapped his arms around her and caught her mouth with his. "Your place or mine?"

"I think my house is closer." She couldn't wait to get him home.

"Let's go."

Macey's hands were steady as she slid the key into the lock and opened the door. Luke couldn't keep his hands off her. As soon as they stepped through the threshold, he pulled her close, cupping her butt in his hands. His cock swelled, pressing against his zipper, and it took every ounce of self-control he could muster to stop himself from taking her right there in the living room. He'd come so close to losing her, but now she was his. A vise of possessiveness gripped his heart, and he held her tighter.

"I love you, Luke." Her breath tickled his ear.

"I love you too. And I can't wait to call you Mrs. Mason."

She stepped away, a playful smile dancing across her lips. "Macey Mason? What have I gotten myself into?"

"I don't know." He ran his fingers along her skin,

sliding her dress straps over her shoulders. "But I know what I'd like to get *myself* into."

She bit her bottom lip and laced her fingers through his. "Well then, Mr. Mason, you should come with me." She led him to her bedroom, and Thor jumped off the bed to wind between his ankles. He let out a soft mew and rubbed his head against Luke's shin.

Macey picked up the cat and set him outside the door. "Thor says, 'Welcome home.'"

"I like the sound of that." He chuckled. "I'm going to be the only alpha in history with a pet cat."

"He's a good cat."

"He is."

Tugging on her bottom lip, she furrowed her brow. "Did you know I was coming? Is that why you said that to the pack? You caused quite an uproar."

He traced his fingers along her shoulders, marveling in the softness of her skin. "I've never been one to let an archaic law hold me back. I told them to give me a year." He shrugged. "I figured I could win you back by then."

"What if they didn't agree to your demands?"

"Then they would have had to find a new alpha. Good thing you showed up when you did."

Snuggling into his chest, she slid her arms around his waist. "Thank you for not giving up on me."

"I knew you'd come around." He glided his hand up the back of her dress and pulled the zipper down. The emerald fabric cascaded to the floor, revealing her porcelain skin wrapped in lacey pink lingerie. Soft moonlight filtering through the curtains gave her an ethereal glow. He watched as she undid the buttons on his shirt, memorizing every detail of the way she moved. The way her hair spilled over her shoulders. The fire in her eyes as she popped the button on his pants and tugged the zipper down.

She grinned wickedly as she unhooked her bra and slipped her panties off. All he could do was stare at the image of perfection before him. His hungry gaze traveled up and down her body, his cock aching to fill her, his heart pounding with the need to possess her.

Her fingers danced across his chest, trailing down to his stomach. "Now that you have me, what are you going to do with me?"

He grinned, scooping her in his arms. "I'm going to love you for as long as you'll let me." He laid her on the bed and climbed on top of her, pressing himself between her legs. Her breath caught as he filled her, and she gazed at him with eyes full of love. "And I believe you promised me forever."

"I did." She smiled and wrapped her legs around his waist, holding him tight. "Werewolves mate for life."

ALSO BY CARRIE PULKINEN

Fire Witches of Salem Series

Chaos and Ash

Commanding Chaos

Claiming Chaos

New Orleans Nocturnes Series

License to Bite

Shift Happens

Life's a Witch

Santa Got Run Over by a Vampire

Finders Reapers

Swipe Right to Bite

Batshift Crazy

Collection One: Books 1-3

Collection Two: Books 4 - 7

Stand Alone Books

Flipping the Bird

Sign Steal Deliver

Azrael

Lilith

The Rest of Forever

Soul Catchers

Bewitching the Vampire

ABOUT THE AUTHOR

Carrie Pulkinen is a paranormal romance author who has always been fascinated with things that go bump in the night. Of course, when you grow up next door to a cemetery, the dead (and the undead) are hard to ignore. Pair that with her passion for writing and her love of a good happily-ever-after, and becoming a paranormal romance author seems like the only logical career choice.

Before she decided to turn her love of the written word into a career, Carrie spent the first part of her professional life as a high school journalism and yearbook teacher. She loves good chocolate and bad puns, and in her free time, she likes to read, drink wine, and travel with her family.

Connect with Carrie online:
www.CarriePulkinen.com